D1238729

This is a work of fiction. Names, characters and events herewithin are the product of the author's imagination. Any resemblance to actual events or persons--living or dead--is entirely coincidental.

Published by Neanderthals, LLC

Text copyright © 2018 by Kenyon P. Gagne

Cover design by www.ebooklaunch.com

ISBN: 978-0-692-05576-2

Printed in the United States of America

The Goners
Volume One

Kenyon P. Gagne

To my wonderful daughters

~and~

To my incredible wife who, when I told her I was thinking about writing a book, turned off the radio and got so excited that I really had no choice

~and~

To everyone everywhere who ever felt like ending it all, but carried on

Soundtrack:

This novel has a soundtrack on Spotify called 'The Goners Playlist', which you can reach using the following URL: http://sptfy.com/Fok It is the suggestion of the author that readers play the corresponding numbered track when they encounter this symbol

in the text, then either read on as the song enhances the action or pause to absorb the music before continuing.

Track 1: Lost and Lookin' by Sam Cooke

Track 2: Question by The Moody Blues

Track 3: Planet Queen by T. Rex

Track 4: No Face No Name No Number by Traffic

Track 5: For Emily, Whenever I May Find Her by Simon and Garfunkel

1

Lost and Lookin'

Manchester, New Hampshire, USA
Friday, March 22, 2126...1:17 PM

Back home on his couch, two hours after being cleared for suicide, Kaywin thought a little distraction might do him some good.

He sat frozen, zombie-like, apparently dead already in the center of the fluffy white three-seater. The glass wall to his right, if he had cared to look, was alive with giant snow-flakes falling thickly outside his one-bedroom high-rise apart-ment. By the calendar it was the first day of spring, but winter wasn't done with the world.

Five years ago you would have said this was a handsome

man, but the seeming weight of a hundred years had since then taken a ghastly toll on him. Deep lines cut the well-formed face; the purpley bruisiness beneath his hazel eyes dimmed their former vigor, and a heavy weight seemed to drag at the corners of his mouth. His close-cropped hair, already salt-and-pepperish before the incident, was now almost entirely silverized. Kaywin, like most of us over the course of our lifetimes, had gotten his share of compliments, and, like most of us, he had a few favorites--off-hand comments from people he valued that had elevated his mood or even made his day. His wife had told him once, on their second date, that his face reminded her of a Roman Centurion. He didn't look like that anymore. You would have crossed the street if you had seen this nerve-wracked madman coming your way. And then, having heard his story, you would have felt like a jerk.

He sat perfectly motionless, staring straight ahead at the television wall. He was staring right through it really, through the bizarre ambient jungle scene it was showing, through the wall behind it, through the rest of the high-rise, through the falling snow, to an unknown spot many, many miles away. You could have sat down next to him, all of you, and he wouldn't have noticed. Only the slow rise and fall of his chest, and a certain highly nervous electricity in those eyes (and indeed, all around him) gave any indication that he was still with us.

A leaf fell in his lap. It was long, skinny and dried-up, like a feather from the world's ugliest peacock.

He was dressed simply in dark blue jeans--back in style--and a shirt that read 'Rubber Soul' in warped, flamboyant letters which had below them the similarly distorted faces of four young men. He had worn this shirt only a few times, on

2

all the great occasions of his adulthood; he had worn it at his high school graduation, the day he returned home from military service, the day he had asked his girlfriend to marry him, the day his daughter was born, and the day he had said goodbye to them--the only day it had failed to give him the strength he needed. He had worn it today for good luck, though he knew his therapist wouldn't back out now, at the eleventh hour, and refuse to sign off on his suicide. Dr. Bresnahan, of all people, knew how important this was to him.

Kaywin had watched all the members of his virtual support group pull themselves one by one out of this horrible torpor; how, he did not know, because even now, after four long years, the first hint of relief or redemption still eluded him. Either they were all stronger than him, or his love for his little lost ones had been stronger than theirs. Whatever, whichever. He didn't care.

Another leaf fell...this one grazed his ridiculous pith helmet and landed on the white cushion beside him. This time a red arm reached over from Kaywin's left side and picked it up. It hesitated with gentlemanly caution, then retrieved the first leaf from his lap as well. But in so doing, the man in the red jumpsuit lost his grip on the shedding tropical plant and overturned it entirely on the expensive-looking sofa. A disagreeable scene ensued, with the young man's boss, also in a red Uno Mundo jumpsuit, hustling over and giving the trainee grief for his clumsiness. Questions were asked of Kaywin, but it was quickly apparent that he was absolutely unavailable for comment. He didn't acknowledge the scene, or the mess, or even blink. Fortunately, his Yerbot rolled in from the kitchen and directed the two delivery men toward a vacuum cleaner and some towels.

This was nothing. What did he care about the stupid couch? Having suffered so completely and from such an unexpected turn of events, he believed that any sick caprice of the universe could unfold at any time, unannounced, and for no good reason. If his left leg had fallen off, or his eyes had turned into meatballs, or if Manchester itself had been sucked into space, it would neither surprise him nor torment him beyond the boundaries of his present suffering. In challenge of this notion, the rear end of the younger Uno Mundo guy now bobbed back and forth two inches from Kaywin's left cheek, as he suctioned soil from the crevices of the ruined couch.

Ro-Ro, Kaywin's Yerbot--bless his built-in intuition--recognizing that his friend would need his solitude sooner than his supper, let out a little mechanical sigh, put down the kitchen knife with little bits of parsley still clinging to it, and rolled across the cream colored carpet to assist the bumbling delivery team with the three-dimensional pieces that would enhance Kaywin's new deluxe virtual travel package. Together, the older man and the robot lifted a heavy, apparently authentic Paris newspaper box over the threshold into the apartment. It had to wait there while the 3-D accent pieces from the African Jungle package were carried out--the remnants of the overturned plant, a larger plant, a gorilla with an arrow in its neck, a gorilla poacher with TWO arrows in his back, twenty feet (at least) of vines...The wall-sized screen behind these items continued to show whatever was happening on Uno Mundo's live jungle cams, which wasn't much at the moment. As a rule the scene switched to whichever cam was registering the most motion. Right now, that was a bright yellow snake barely adjusting its position on a branch, still digesting the rat Kaywin had watched it eat yesterday. The Paris travel package would be better. Now that he was right at the finish line of his civilian existence, and had a clear understanding of how the next three days would go, he could exhale slightly and also really blow the last 800 credits in his account. Some of his life-long savings had gone to his final bills, the final settling of all his worldly affairs... Most had gone to his sister. He was proud at least to give her something. It made him feel a little better about leaving her alone with their mother.

~

He loved his sister, and he loved his mother, of course, but being around them somehow only reminded him of the beautiful love he had lost and the perfect people he had failed, irredeemably and forever. His sister was great, and had been so supportive of him through the whole ordeal. But she had her own life, with her husband and her two boys. Kaywin had been close with his nephews for a while, but had deliberately withdrawn a little, gradually, to minimize their suffering when this day arrived. As for his Mom--poor Mom--what could he do? He couldn't stand to visit her at the Utopiopod anymore, because it was the same routine every time:

"Aaaaaaah, Kay-Kay, my boy! So wonderful to see you! But where's my little Victoria--"

"Dead, Ma."

"--and where's my lovely Nadine--"

"Dead, Mom, they're both dead. You remember? It's been a year now!" "A year and half now!" "Two years!" "Three

5

years!" It was too much for him.

"Noooo! No, no no! What happened to my babies?" It was too much.

This is not even taking into account the constant groups of kids milling through. The Utopiopods were pretty much the norm now, an improvement on the lonely 'nursing homes' of prior ages. They were complexes where the most emotionally-needy populations of twenty-second century America--school-children, old-folks, and otherwise-homeless pets--coexisted, and did the most wonderful things for each other, just by NEEDING each other. This was all well and good, but it had become something beyond Kaywin's strength to break his mother's heart all over again every two weeks, usually while she was appreciating the artwork of some four year old girl, who never failed to remind him of his own Victoria when she was four. Animals sniffing about the whole time... a beagle had bitten him so hard one time that he had to go and get three stitches...and it was still the best part of his visit.

As unpleasant as it was going to the Pod, especially to bring his mother this new bit of crushing news, he had gotten up the nerve and done it on Wednesday. He was pretty sure she hadn't understood him. She just nodded her still-pretty face very slightly, and wordlessly, when he told her he was joining the "Meaningful Conclusion Program"; a little later he used the word "Goner." He said that he was going to be a "Goner," and her reaction was the same. "I won't ever see you again, Ma," he said.

"Oh, don't say that...," she returned, actually smiling. So frustrating, and difficult.

"No, really Ma, this will be my last visit; once I sign up

Monday morning I can't turn back." His voice was starting to shake...the wall of emotionlessness he always carried with him into the Pod was starting to crumble; it was like he himself was only now understanding what his future would hold, and how brief it would be.

"Oh, don't say that, Kay-Kay...you'll be back..."

Eh-maudit-affaire, he cursed to himself in jagged Canadian French. What more could he do? If she understood, she understood. If she didn't, she didn't. But when he got up to leave, she embraced him so tightly he thought her little 80 lb. frame would snap, and a big tear rolled down her cheek. Like most old folks, who had seen it all and endured it all in their lifetimes, she didn't devolve into hysterics, but she let enough slip to let Kaywin think that maybe she did understand after all, not only **what** he was doing, but **why** he was doing it. "D'accord, mon fils; c'est bien, c'est bon..."

When he turned his gaze away from his mother, for the last time ever, he became *truly aware* that he had just seen his mother *for the last time ever*, and he began to lose it. But just then, as he was walking out the door, a little boy was leading Kaywin's beagle-nemesis in. He gave the little brown, black and white beast a sideways leer. The dog looked at him with complete disinterest, tongue hanging out, as if nothing had ever transpired between them. No apology from the dog, no apology from the world. Strangely, this two-second staring contest with the dog that had bitten him helped Kaywin collect himself, the reminder that no amount of self-pity would arouse a response from the feckless universe.

As he stepped out into the gorgeous hallway, hung with living greenery and important framed artworks of the resident children, the lad and the dog passed into his mother's room and he heard her exclaim joyfully at the sight of them. He knew she had already forgotten their conversation. This too helped him recover his composure, and he set out down the long, brilliantly lit corridor feeling a weird, subtle shifting of his emotional contents..

Every hallway and common area in the Utopiopod was entirely sky-lit, and generously windowed as well. The meticulously maintained gardens without were so pleasant to look at, and the sunlight so unbridled on his face, that Kaywin, striding along, was almost able to empty his mind completely.

"Genie's house," he told his round, pink soap-bubble-shaped car as the door whooshed open. He threw himself headlong into its pillow-pit and exhaled deeply, one huge task behind him. But his day wasn't done. He went from the Pod over to Goffstown, just west of the city, to see his sister. She had known all along what Kaywin had been planning. As a devoted spouse and parent herself, she couldn't honestly argue with the depth of his suffering, and the finality of his decision. She loved him, dearly, but hated to see her brother, once so happy, robust and alive, wandering the world in this ghostly state.

He was there on business. He knew he would see Genie one more time after this anyway. When he walked into her living room, her lawyer's disturbingly tan face was already filling an entire wall. "HELLO MR. LAFONTAINE" it boomed from his left as he entered, startling him so much that he lost his balance.

"Geez!" Kaywin burst out. "Can we scale this back a little bit?" He indicated toward the giant orange head with nervous hands. His sister was laughing her infectious laugh, but he was sadly immune to it now.

"Sorry!" she said.

"So sorry, Mr. Lafontaine," said the lawyer, who couldn't help but smile.

"No, I'M sorry," said Kaywin, recovering. "Everybody's sorry. Can we just get started?"

They did, and within five minutes all of his worldly possessions and assets had been signed over to Genie, except for the eight hundred credits that had to remain in his account, for some reason…something to do with his military pension.

"And Radcliffe [his nephew] definitely wants the car? He's not worried about riding around in a pink soap-bubble?" Kaywin double-checked.

"It never bothered you…" Genie responded.

"Yeah, but I'm so macho…" he deadpanned, failing to amuse himself. She laughed, at least.

"He admires you. If you're not worried about riding around in a pink soap-bubble, he won't be either."

~

The older red jumpsuit toted in a ridiculous French mime figure and placed it in front of the left corner of the viewing wall. There it stood in a navy-and-white-striped shirt, white face-paint, and a navy beret, in a ludicrous half-crouch; red lips pursed in concentration; arms upthrust, hands feeling for a wall that wasn't there. Multiple snowflakes from the heavy spring storm still clung to its tight black breeches. Still staring straight ahead from the center of the couch, Kaywin looked right through the older man guiding the younger man through the travel program setup procedure. He hadn't said a word or moved a muscle the entire time, even when the delivery guys were questioning him about the arrows in the gorilla and the gorilla-poacher, and explaining that his account would be charged for it. The Uno Mundo workers were used to being ignored, even from their non-suicidal clients, but they now had to rouse Kaywin for a single, monumental decision, too important, apparently, to trust his Yerbot with.

The younger delivery-man knelt in front of him, still sheepish after ruining the couch. "Which moustache would you like?" Kaywin woke up, slightly, "To go with your Paris package?" He looked down at the selection strewn across the young man's hands. "Pencil-thin, handlebar, pointed-with-goatee…."

"Pencil-thin." His lips had barely moved. The worker--Siegfried, his name patch read--peeled off the backing, and applied it to Kaywin's under-nose region with awkward intimacy. Kaywin's slack face responded to the pressure like raw dough, but the moustache stuck. Words were exchanged between the workmen and Ro-Ro behind him, then, having almost forgotten to do it, one of them plucked the pith helmet from his head and dropped a French beret on it. Then adjusted it. Then re-adjusted it for good measure. Kaywin's sharp intake of breath at this point warned them that their time was up. A fat hand patted his shoulder; the door swished open and swished shut, and he was alone. He exhaled deeply. He raised his left hand a little bit toward his exhausted face, and spoke in the general direction of the camo-green plastic device on his wrist:

"Sofee--Allons-nous de Paris" (Let's go of Paris)

A soothing female voice responded. "Non, non non.

Vous voulez dire 'allons a Paris…'(You mean to say 'Let's go TO Paris')

Pause. "Allons y Paris" (Come on, Paris)

"Allons a Paris." (Let's go to Paris)

"Alors a Paris." (While in Paris)

"Allons--"

"Just take us to Paris!"

The viewing wall began to change. The jungle scene altered, luckily for the defenseless mime, and a bustling, almost comically cliché Parisian street scene came into view. Memories flooded over him.

He looked to his right, at the seat he always preserved for his dead daughter. He looked to his left, at the seat he always preserved for his dead wife. This was his habit whenever he was about to lose himself in a new show, a new game, or, like now, in a new travel package. But this time, just to be sure, he looked more deeply than ever into the empty spaces…to make sure they weren't back, and he wasn't going Monday morning to commit himself to something stupid and terrible. Nope. He wasn't crazy. The nothingness around him, closing in on him, was absolute. No Victoria in Victoria's seat. No Nadine in Nadine's seat--why was Nadine's seat dirty and wet? Screwing up his face at this question made him aware of the unpleasant tugging on his upper lip. He grabbed at the left edge of the fake moustache and ripped.

"Aaaaaaaaaaaaaaaaaaaaaaaaaaaaaaaaaaaaaaaaaaaaaaaaaaaa aaaaaaaaaaaaaaa!" That was some high-quality, deluxe travel package adhesive. "Eh-maudit-affaire!"

~

Houston, Texas USA
Monday, March 25, 2126...5:58 AM

At the barest, earliest stroke of sunrise, a middle-aged African-American woman in a light blue, bullet-shaped car (which must have been a beauty when it was new) rolled slowly over a gravel road toward the security gate. In a tiny guardhouse on the left-hand roadside, a hefty white man in a grey uniform stretched elaborately, reserving enough awareness to be watchful. He eyed the approaching unfamiliar vehicle with open suspicion. Guests were not unheard of at the Meaningful Conclusion Program National Headquarters (that's the MCPNH to you and me), but seldom unannounced and never at this hour...The small, frontward-facing LED screen at the top center of the car's windshield, furthermore, displayed no credentials. He frowned and fingered his gun, just lightly, and just for a second, to make sure it was there. In his six years at this post he had not once had to use it, thankfully. But he well understood that recent changes in the Program were raising eyebrows across America, and even the world, and that when public disapproval and dissension spilled over into violence, he would likely be the first to know about it. Perhaps he was getting ahead of himself. He would have an answer in three, two, one....

The car stopped gently, like all of the older models, and the cabin window glided open. He was looking at a pretty, middle-aged African-American woman, thankfully, it appeared, without weapon or bomb. She may have been sleeping. No one could blame her for that at 5:59 AM. As her couch eased up from a completely reclined position, he observed with curiosity that she was dressed to the nines, from her shiny black heels to the black veil on her head, in full funeral attire. Their eyes finally met, and they both wondered how this would go.

Pretty though she was, her eyes were heavy with a great sadness, and the cheeks below them puffy from crying. The security guard, a steadfast and honest man, changed gears in a second from sternness to sympathy. He leaned forward out of the window, smiling. He and the woman exchanged words calmly. From the shaking of his head, it was clear that she needed some kind of credential that she did not have. That was okay. He would help her get it. He touched his left wrist and his Sofee screen expanded. Deftly tapping it several times, he accessed the contact information the woman would need to get through the gate. He finished by touching 'send to nearest Sofee'. A second later the woman had what she needed. She spoke the address loudly and clearly to her vehicle; the security guard smiling because he remembered the old cars that you almost had to yell at; then parting pleasantries were exchanged and the lady in the beat-up old blue bullet turned around and left. With a bland smile, the grey-suited man closed the little window and returned to his Superyoga, relaxing into a full split that dropped his head from view…

Houston, Texas USA
March 26, 2126…5:59 AM

…and here came his head, back up into the window frame, with impressive agility and grace for a man of his size and age (big and old). It was twenty-four hours later and he was at the same point in his routine. As his peaceful eyes crested over the lip of the small window, they smiled a little to see the same light blue bullet crunching quietly up the gravel approach. This time, he didn't reach for his gun.

Today, she had the acknowledgment she needed from her state representative. He was impressed, because this was typically a two-week process. She must have really bulldozed her way through some red tape, or her business must be urgent, or both. They chatted cordially for a few seconds. When people reach a certain age, they enter into a sort of club for folks who have just seen a lot, and been through a lot, and which transcends race or gender.

He opened the gate for her, without knowing that this would be their daily routine for the next several years. When pressed for details about this moment, long after the fact, by television anchors and talk show hosts, he only remembered that "she was a very pleasant woman," and that he "didn't think twice" about opening the gate.

The two halves of the ornate, faintly gothic black gate yawned open with a loud iron clanging that echoed over the surrounding hills like a rifle shot. "Let's go to the first available parking space," the woman said to the car. "We'll see what it looks like from there…" The blue bullet and the woman in black meandered through the last quarter mile of the gorgeously wooded approach. The gravel turned to pavement suddenly, just before the narrow road widened into a huge parking lot broken up with attractive rows of trees and shrubs. The car parked, as instructed, in the first space they came to. The door slid open and the woman emerged. She walked about forty paces back toward the entrance. Turning around, she regarded the vehicle, assessing its visibility to in-flowing traffic. She frowned and walked back. The door was still open. She stuck her head in. "Try space number 0004, on the other side…" The car dinged three times at her. "You don't need me. Go on." The car backed out of the spot, wheeled around elegantly (and literally), finally nosing forward into spot number 0004, which perched on the outside curve of the entering roadway, rather than nestling half-hidden in its shady crook.

This time, when she strolled back to evaluate the car's position, she smiled grimly, somewhat pleased--as pleased as a person who has lost everything can be. Back to the bullet. "Remember this space. This is our space. Activate Lonnie Program." She sat back down in the car long enough to re-apply her red lipstick, then got back out and leaned against it with her arms folded in front of her.

The smile was gone.

Behind her, the light blue was gone too. The vehicle's wrap-around screens instead were alive with video footage; a tightly-swaddled newborn here, a toddler running in nothing but a saggy diaper there; a little older now playing basketball, winning a chess tournament, jumping into a lake with two buddies, walking across a stage in cap and gown… endless looping footage, all of the same handsome young man. "Keep program running until 6:59 PM." On top of the car, above her head, another viewscreen had appeared, the kind usually reserved for asinine inspirational quotes, or for exchanging Sofee numbers with cute strangers in traffic. It rotated slowly, with the same chilling message on both sides:

15

I want to know what happened
to my baby.
Latrell "Lonnie" Hopkins
4/19/2105-3/25/2125

2

Question

It wasn't suicide exactly; it was something a little more… meaningful.

In the beginning years of the Program, glowing headlines rolled. Actual paper had not been manufactured or used at all really in America for well over fifty years, but the throwback feel of an old-timey newspaper still spoke to people. This look of bold black print on microscopically mottled, slightly yellowed paper filled America's viewscreens with wonderful news!

Goners Cure Cancer!

America salutes the hundreds of MC's who have given their lives over the last twenty-eight years in the study of radical new cancer treatments.

Goner Killed Saving Senator!

A strategically placed MC at Senator Jackson's presidential campaign speech in Michigan on Tuesday was able to disarm a crazed would-be assassin, at the cost of his own life.

MC Establishes New Spaceflight Speed Record!

First Deep Sea Community Costs $48 Billion; 112 Goners

Twenty-Five MC's Arrive Safely On Mars!

Community Of 18 Goners Still

Thriving On Red Planet
then 14 MC's, then 5 MC'S and finally
Last 2 MC's Survive To Greet Their Replacements On Mars!

Goner Nails LaPierre!
Reports indicate that a courageous MC, working alone, was able to infiltrate the inner circle of the world's second-most-wanted terrorist.

Moon Colony Owes Debt Of Gratitude To Brave MC's

Statue Commissioned To Honor Goners

Things had been going so right in America for so long that people fell out of the good habit of questioning their leaders' motives and actions, and speaking up when something smelled stinky. The Meaningful Conclusion Program was further protected from public criticism by never actively recruiting its members. Even as every open square foot of the country, it seemed, was covered up with eye-popping advertisements, logos and jingles, no commercial for the MCP was ever produced, aired, or even thought of. Well, technically, one was thought of (poorly) and produced (terribly)...

An old farmer, complete with dingy denim overalls, looks out a window at his drought-parched pasture land. An anorexic-looking cow ambles by, listlessly. The farmer looks at a picture of his wife, and we understand that she is dead. He looks at a drawing in crayon, on paper, of himself piloting a rocket ship. We hope it was done when he was, like, five, because it isn't very good. He looks at the clock on the wall, the old round kind with the rotating hands, or arms, or whatever they were called, and an excruciatingly long second ticks away, echoing morosely. Now he looks at his large, rough hands, and we zoom in on them. Suddenly, they are gripping a steering wheel, and his tattered gingham shirtsleeves have been replaced with a crisp red uniform. We fade back a little and see that he is zooming through space, with a broad grin on his sun-weathered face. We don't see the part where he crashes and burns twenty seconds later.

This cloying, manipulative test-ad was shown to different demographics in controlled screening sessions. Nobody fell for it. In fact, it led to awkward questions: "Is this the actual plight of our farmers?" " Why is no one helping them?" " Is this why milk is $14 a gallon?" " And that drawing--was that a rocket or a giant flax-seed?" "Should we be investing more in our schools' art programs?" " What was up with his wife's hair?" (Her grey cornrows caught everyone off guard) "And what about the cow? Please tell me they didn't starve that poor cow just to make this god-awful commercial..." Most of these people were only there for the $50 anyway...

There were a lot of serious responses, but they too were overwhelmingly negative. The entire campaign was scrapped instantly, and the MCP's public image was decided on. It was useless to pretend it didn't exist--and why should they? It was a well-intentioned program of immense service to the public. At the same time, there was no NEED to promote it. Headlines like the ones above were enough to let people know that such an institution existed, and that it was clearly doing magnificent work for the common good.

The 'Goners,' those poor souls--thousands of them over the years--had lost their will to live for one reason or another, but had retained enough interest in the welfare of their fellow men and women to desire to do them some good on the way out of their mortal shackles. The Meaningful Conclusion Program offered these people a viable option to senseless suicide. Turning their lives over to the Program, they would be utilized according to their strengths for the betterment of humankind. How, they couldn't know until they went down to their local MCP office and signed up. Once behind the veil, they could be thrust into any number of services, all of them heroic as far as America knew.

Secrecy was paramount to the success of the program. Information was allowed in--any man or woman of the 2100's would have gone mad without it--but absolutely no communication with the outside world, loved ones or otherwise, was allowed out, unless undercover work demanded it. There had to be a completely clean and permanent break, and it had to be done immediately--not when the enemy was charging, or the rockets taking off, or when they were being lowered into a hole in the Earth a mile deep and two feet wide. Any sliver of light showing under the door that had slammed shut behind them would have led to 'cold feet', 'second thoughts', and inevitable desertions. Some of these might have been withstood, maybe among pit workers, mineral tunnelers, or lunar sanitation specialists, but even one or two key defections in the wrong areas could have disastrous repercussions…in some cases for all of America…in others for the entire Earth. Once in, you were in. The second you touched finger to screen, and retina to lens, you forfeited all rights and were worse than a ward of the state. Better be sure, because there was no turning back.

Mothers mourned, the most stoic fathers cried as they placed flowers on markers where no bodies lay. Brothers and sisters grieved, hoping their long-lost siblings knew something of how much they were loved. Best friends couldn't understand how the wonderful person they had hand-picked from Earth's swarming seventeen billion could fail to realize how special he or she was. All had to concede, however, that in the end it was better that their little Goners had bravely given the universe everything they had. They had gone out on fire, at mind-boggling speeds, in cracks and crevices of the moon and Mars where no human had ever been; they had gone out getting the last laugh on terrorists and drug lords, saving babies and grandmothers; ending diseases, forging roads where none had seemed possible, both literal and metaphoric. With these eager, devil-may-care volunteers, not even the afterlife was beyond the scope of human exploration anymore, as ghoulish attempts were made to send men thither and recall them back.

True, some died strapped to hospital beds in horrible agony, having been deliberately infected with some of history's most appalling diseases...even some not yet unleashed, for future historians to lament...But these were just uncon-firmed whispers among the very highest circles of national security...

Even less was whispered about the gruesome experi-ments in cyborgology, and certainly no word ever reached the masses concerning botched brain transplants, and exercises in mind torture....

Loved ones back home could only speculate on their Goner's accomplishments, and wait nervously for the e-mail from the President of the United States him-or-herself, hon-oring his or her sacrifice, noting the day and time of his or her death, and utterly devoid of any detail beyond that. But, really, everyone knew they had done something wonderful.

Although no recruiting or advertising ever took place for the MCP, licensed therapists, psychiatrists, and medical doctors were empowered from the program's inception to recommend it as a viable alternative to whichever of their patients whose sufferings they deemed incurable. Specifically, it required the authorization of two separate professionals working independently with the same patient over the course of no less than six years. The troubled person at that point could decide if the MCP was right for them...provided they were twenty-four years old, or older, and, ironically, in ser-viceable health.

When and how changes began to occur in these require-ments could probably not be laid out for you by the average man in the street. There was plenty of work to do when he was working, and plenty of playing to do when he was play-ing and no time for digging into dark corners. Information, to quote the great twentieth-century poet Kevin Gagne, had approached the rate of constant. So when the legal MCP age dropped from twenty-four to twenty-two, few noticed or cared. When treatment requirements fell from two professionals for six years, to one professional for four, again, it was no big deal. A few heads turned, and a few mouths spoke, when the legal age dropped again from twenty-two to twenty. They spoke again, and louder, when, only three years later, it got down to eighteen. It was funny--well, maybe not funny--how the admonitions and warnings of these wise few never seemed to get much airtime. There was an entire channel devoted to Linsom Felize's hair and makeup, which changed daily, but the public at large had lost interest in a government that provided for their needs and seemed to be running pretty smoothly.

When legislation went through on November 24th, 2125 reducing the minimum age for MCP admittance to SIX-TEEN, America, from sea to shining sea, should have been horrified. However, it was Black Friday, with only thirty-one shopping days 'til Christmas, and Uno Mundo, the world's largest retailer of everything, was running all new technology at forty percent off. That's right, I said forty percent off! For instance, wall-sized viewscreens, eight feet by twenty-two feet, which would typically set you back four-thousand credits, were only ε2400. If you were out and about in the world that day, you would have noticed that every third person, it seemed, was toting an eight-foot long white tube containing their new viewscreen, and the free two-liter that came with it. Even more remarkably, the new Sofee 47, which was hitting the market that day for the first time, and would cost ε899 going forward, was only ε540! If you committed to the four-year information plan, which would take you through the next seven models, you actually **received** ε50 and a case of macaroni and cheese! Automatic jump ropes for twenty-two credits; holographic remote world traveler programs for ε150; Magic Eleven balls for ε4... Maybe it wasn't such a shocker after all that some bill allowing someone else's cousin's friend's ex-husband's sixteen year-old son to give up his life for the greater good sailed through Congress virtually unopposed...

A lot of wretchedly unhappy sixteen year-olds did notice, however, and the Goner program, outside the public eye, swelled overnight to unprecedented numbers. These kids were too young to understand that their lives could change; they were too green to fully grasp that, in a few short years, new tools would be available to them--confidence, direction, knowledge, camaraderie, the magnificent strength of full human adulthood--to fight off their individual demons.

Marginally more tragic were the wretchedly unhappy fifteen year-olds who shut themselves out from the world for good, and hunkered down, waiting for their birthdays...

3

Planet Queen

Geyserville, California USA
Monday, March 25, 2126…10:04 AM

    Glorious morning sunshine streamed in through the narrow window into the small messy bedroom. An extraordinarily pretty young woman sat at a tiny white desk with nothing on it but a little round freestanding mirror and a cosmetics kit.

    It is one of the great mysteries of the universe how so much divine grace and exquisite attention to detail could go into nature's perfect expression, a beautiful flower, which should then be left blooming in a dung-heap.

This was the life of Prudence Estrada.

She was tiny, four-foot-eleven to be exact. She had stopped growing years ago, pretty much on the day that the full horrors of her small world became apparent to her. Her life would be a game of hide-and-seek, not king-of-the-mountain, and her intuitive biology kept her teentsy almost in self-defense.

Her small face, faintly olive in complexion, was smooth, dainty and beautiful. Her light blue eyes were quick and intelligent, but melancholy, far beyond the pall of normal teenage angst. Between them began the delicate slope of her pixie-like nose down to her full lips, which hadn't smiled in years... She didn't get out in public much, which was sort of a win-win for the public and for her, but when she did, especially beyond the confines of her small town, a commotion invariably ensued:

First look: "Oh my God, that girl is beautiful..."

Second look: "Holy crap--is that Linsom Felize?" "Surely not..." "I swear to God; look! I think that's Linsom Felize!" "Hmm...maybe?" "I am literally shaking right now--should I try to get her autograph?"

Third look: "I'm gonna say no...she looks like she would punch you in the face..."

And yes, she probably would have.

At the moment, alone in her room except for the sad little girl in the mirror, she was very carefully applying black lipstick. Finished, she compressed her mouth and opened it with a 'pop'. Lipstick still in hand, she launched her wheelie-chair across the plastic white floor toward the larger wall. This was the viewscreen wall, mostly; the interruption of the small open window on the far right nudged the entire display two feet to the left, so that it curved a little bit onto the adjacent wall. The perimeter of the screen, all the way around, was alive with advertisements, reduced to the narrowest margin their cheapo data plan would allow; they made a moving, snake-like frame for an enormous calendar of 'MARCH 2126'. The days were all x-ed out, through Saturday the 23rd. Prudence took the back-end of the tiny lipstick cylinder and bid good riddance with it to Sunday the 24th as well. Three spaces down from it, Wednesday March 27th--her sixteenth birthday--glowed differently from the other thirty squares. It was a deeper purple, and every few seconds it over spilled its boundaries, and then collapsed. "Free at last" it announced in white, feathery letters. "Open," she said quietly to her wrist. From her pink Sofee a paper-thin 11x7 inch screen unfolded quickly but smoothly, making a little 'click' to indicate that it was rigid and ready. She typed a short message on it, lightning fast. **BOOM BOOM**, came the thunder of a heavy fist knocking, startling her, even though she knew it was coming.

Her father was at the door.

"Pru!...You ready?" She didn't answer. She was scrolling through fonts on her device; she needed a good one to drive her message home. Not this one; Not this one; too girly...

BOOM BOOM... "Pru!"

"What!"

"Are you ready?"

Long pause. "Almost. Go away!" A brilliant idea came to her, in this, her hour of need. She wheeled over to her dresser and pulled a small pink ball out of it. Then she returned to her frantic search for the perfect font.

"This guy doesn't understand 'late', okay? I told you that last night. You should have been ready twenty minutes ago."

Prudence held the ball up in front of her mouth. "Go away! I'll be ready in a minute!" Keeping it ready in her right hand, she returned to the keyboard.

"You're wearing the dress he sent, right?"

"Yes!" Pressed for time though she was, she looked over her shoulder at the tiny shimmery silver dress in a heap on the floor, and spat on it with extreme contempt. This gesture seemed to focus her energies, because a second later she found the font she was looking for.

BOOM BOOM BOOM BOOM BOOM… "PRU!!!"

Into the little pink ball again: **"I said go away! I'll be out in a minute!"**

"PRU!...PRU!...DON'T BE A------THIS WAS NOT SET UP AS A ONE-TIME DEAL! MR. MCCONNELL HAS JUST TRAVELLED ABOUT FOUR THOUSAND MILES TO BE HERE...FOR YOU! HE DOESN'T HAVE ANY OTHER BUSINESS HERE, JUST YOU!

She examined the message one last time. She was pleased with the words, and pleased with the font; a grotesque, black gothic script wherein the curves and points of each letter seemed to have been pieced together from a scrapheap of medieval torture devices. "That's about right…," she whispered to herself. She hit 'send' dramatically, drawing her whole arm back as if the power of the short paragraph had almost exploded her arm off.

Her entire viewscreen wall filled up with her goodbye:

Joining the Goners
Nothing You Can Do
See You In Hell

Now she began moving with final urgency, her heart racing. She could feel her Father's anger turning into rage, eight feet away with only the door between them.

"PRUDENCE!!!! WHAT ARE YOU DOING IN THERE?!!!" BOOM BOOM BOOM BOOM BOOM!

She grabbed up a tiny bag and slung it over her left shoulder. On a whim, she reached back into her dresser and grabbed a second pink ball, this one still in the box. She shoved it down in her bag, having to brutalize the cardboard packaging to squeeze it in. She sat back down quickly in front of the mirror, looking into her own eyes for bravery. Her makeup was perfect; her thickly-rouged cheeks made her look wild and fierce; she hadn't done anything to cover up her black right eye; today it was a badge of honor; but she couldn't leave with her hair all rainbowed-out like this; she would be found instantly! The straight, shoulder-length cascade pulsated with horizontal bands of color. She reached her trembling fingers up under the left side of the fiber optic strands and, fumbling at the controls that were still pretty new to her, tried to manipulate Mr. McConnell's $60,000 'gift' into something less noticeable...the hair shortened, which was fine, but it was the color that would get her caught; after a second or two she was able to make it solid, then she stumbled her way through the spectrum, getting stuck in the purples for what seemed like an eternity. Finally, she found a shade of brown that would have been her last choice normally, but would have to do--the **BOOM-BOOM-ing** had shifted down in tone, but up in volume, and she knew her father was now trying to kick the door in.

There was no time left to pause, think, or be afraid. She pressed the little pink ball and sat it on her desk. Her own voice boomed out of it "Go away! I'll be ready in a minute! **I said go away! I'll be out in a minute!**......Go away! I'll be ready in a minute! **I said go away! I'll be out in a minute!**"....and so on, and so on. Meanwhile, she grabbed a long thick rope from under her bed, and threw one end out the open window, the other end catching where it was tied to the bedpost. She could hear the rope making a racket, whacking the side of the apartment building as it tumbled four floors to the ground. Hopefully no one was home in apartments 137, 237, and 337 at this time on a Monday morning.

She grabbed the rope, terrified, hands sweating, and clambered over the windowsill in her black jumpsuit, forty-three feet off the ground. As she removed one violently trembling hand from the rope to begin the process of shimmying down, it seemed to give way completely, and for half a second she thought she was dead.

The bed had nudged free from its accustomed spot, and with nothing to slow it down, had slid all the way across the slick floor until it had lodged itself in the window. Prudence closed her eyes, fighting back tears. She wished the cord had just broken free completely, and she had fallen to her death. With her breath gasping, heart beating out of her chest, she concentrated all her mental energy on the feel of the rope in her hands. She concentrated on trying to relax her hands until they just let go.

She couldn't do it. She was too weak.

Another series of heavy boot-blows on her bedroom door startled her back into action. With everything stabilized, she got a rhythm going and made quick progress down the rope, not thinking, just doing, her terror lessening foot by foot as she neared the grassy bank behind the building. The enormous physical tension left her almost completely when her feet touched the ground. It was very muddy from the previous night's rain, which would actually make the next step of her plan that much easier. She sank her little black boots down into the mud, moving her heels left to right, left to right, to ensure that the soles were covered. In three steps she made it from the grass to the sidewalk flanking their apartment building. From there she left heavy, muddy footprints to the pickup lane in front of the building, even turning her boots sideways on the curb as if she was entering a waiting vehicle butt-first.

Then she took off her boots and ran for her life through the grass, into the woods that marked the end of Geyserville, and the end of her miserable childhood.

∼

Her father would never look for her here. She had never said the first word to him about the woods, or the brook that ran through them, or the little shelter next to the brook that she had been working on for years. If she had had a friend in the world, she wouldn't have told them about it either.

She would need to spend today and tonight, then Tuesday and Tuesday night in the crude little shelter. She had a sort of back-alley 'therapist' lined up who would sign off on her case, and falsify records going back the requisite two years, all for a surprisingly small fee. This doctor was a few towns over, in Cloverdale, which was good, because IF her father came looking for her--she didn't think he would--it would be at the MCP office here in Geyserville. So she would rough it in the woods for two days and two nights, then catch the 7:30 bus Wednesday morning (Happy Birthday!) to Cloverdale. She would meet Dr. Binklock in his office at ten; he would need her fingerprints, retina scan, etc., along with enough sundry details of her case to form a convincing mock-up. The MCP office (she was given to understand) was within walking distance of Dr. Binklock, so that the whole affair could be wrapped up neatly by 1:00 PM. Thinking of this as she traversed the unmarked path through the woods behind her former-home, sleeves rolled up in the late morning sun, gave her a feeling of peace. She wanted nothing further to do with her 'life'...

As she drew close to her little out-building of raw tree trunks and limbs woven together with rope, arranged into a comely floor elevated on minty-green lichen-covered rocks, and framed in with four--well, three and a half--walls, she stopped short. A rustle and a squeak came from the shelter's interior, where Prudence had cleverly hidden two days worth, and ONLY two-days worth, of food. "Noooooo....," she said under her breath. She accelerated her pace and came around to the open door facing the brook, holding out hope that whatever was inside had just gotten there, and that her stores were intact. Her heart fell as she came face to face with a raccoon so pudgy that she thought it must be a different type of animal altogether; one she had never seen or heard of, like a raccoon-bear, or a coon-dog...that rang a bell...was this what a coon-dog looked like? The thing squeaked viciously at her. Food wrappers and cans were scattered everywhere. Reasoning that it was too fat to take a flying leap at her, she turned around quickly to find a stick or a rock or something. There was a nice freshly fallen branch right behind her, green enough that it shouldn't snap as it took a coon-dog's head off.

The two squared off. The wild animal, elevated on the shelter floor, was almost eye-to-eye with the petite girl. He was making a sound she had never heard before, something between a growl, a hiss and a shriek, like a balloon with the air being let out into the face of a dog...who was eating a cat. But she wasn't scared, not at all really. She swung at fatso with calculated caution, the coon's eyes following the arc of the branch, and flinch-hopping out of the way with disturbing agility. She swung again, on the other side, with the same result. So she moved in a little closer, to increase her margin for error, and swung the branch a third time--and the thing was on her arm.

It happened so quickly that she dropped the stick, and just stared at the animal for a second. It was clawing and biting her for dear life. Her adrenaline and anger surged as the pain began to register. She swung her arm violently against the shelter, feeling the claws dig in frantically as she did so. A second time, even harder, and the little you-know-what dropped off and scurried away into the woods. Prudence exclaimed in pain as loudly as she dared, being careful although she knew from her explorations that the nearest house was at least half a mile away...

She hugged her arm tightly to her body to muffle the

pain, until it plateaued, and she had sort of collected herself. Then she drew it away slowly to assess the damage. "Alright," she thought, observing a whole web of long, three-toed scratches, and a deepish bite mark near her wrist, "alright, I can deal with this." Step one was to wash the heck out of it, which she did, in the numbingly cold water of the creek for as long as she could stand it. Then she let it warm up a little and did it again. Three times she did this, until she was sure any bacteria from the raccoon must be a couple hundred yards downstream.

"Sofee, if I don't have disinfectant, what can I put on….26 raccoon scratches and one bite. From the same raccoon."

"What are my choices?"

"Foundation, breath spray…(peering into the shelter)... orange soda...that's about it. Saliva..."

"Breath spray would be better than nothing, but I would get to a doctor soon. Shall I make an appointment for you?"

"Nooo, definitely not. Thanks." She took the little white metal canister of wintergreen breath spray from her satchel and virtually emptied it on her arm, saving one tiny spritz for her Wednesday appointment. It stung like crazy. She danced around to keep from crying out again. Finally, she took the only spare shirt she had packed, which she had planned to reserve till Wednesday, and wrapped her damaged right arm up good and tight. Now she would have to wear the black jumpsuit straight on through. Oh well.

At last she got up into the shelter to assess what the raccoon had done; and oh, did she curse his mask-faced gluttony! There was almost nothing left for her. One orange soda, a can of green beans that had been in their pantry for as long as she could remember, a half-eaten granola bar and three half-eaten apples. To last for forty-eight hours. Oh well!

She spent the next day and a half in hard-earned quietude, eating just enough to keep alive, protecting her wounded arm as best as she could, starting to worry about it a little, and regretting nothing. This was hard treatment to be sure, but she'd been through worse. Over the course of Tuesday, her arm gradually felt warmer and more swollen. She lounged, listened to music, walked in the brook, and napped a little in the afternoon, after a crummy first night's sleep.

When Prudence got up from her nap was when she first noticed a red line appearing on her arm, following a vein north of her makeshift tourniquet. This was cause for concern to be sure, as it had every appearance of poison creeping through her bloodstream toward her heart. Oh well, whatever. It would be a shame if she died accidentally on the way to her death.

She saved the can of green beans for her second and last night as a 'free' woman. Never the sentimental type, she did take a moment to wonder how old she had been when they were bought, and if she might have been happy at that time, before her first memories...She was very hungry, and she had a very strong mind, so she was able to convince herself that the cold, old mushy green beans were an absolute treat. She even drank the 'juice.'

When Prudence lay down to try to sleep, shortly after dark, her arm was raging, hot and tight feeling. She had to keep it outside of her ultra-therm, or it felt like it was on fire. Her mind wasn't much better. There was very little cushion of time left between her and her life-changing, life-ending decision. She knew she wouldn't waver, but she wanted this part, the sleeping-in-the-woods, waiting-for-her-arm-to-fall-off, hoping-everything-goes-as-planned part, to be over. She fixed her light blue eyes on two stars showing through a crack in the roof she had made, and a crack in the forest above. One was a little brighter than the other. After about two hours of staring at them, she lost consciousness.

Prudence woke up shivering about an hour and a half earlier than she needed to. The night was many degrees colder than she had expected; the ultra therm was almost completely off her, and her core temperature was so low that she knew she would not recover enough warmth, even after adjusting the blanket, to go back to sleep again. She was violently uncomfortable, starving, and could barely move her right arm. She gathered up her things, left-handed, and started out briskly for the bus stop. Walking, she reasoned, would warm her up, and get her circulation going, perhaps reviving feeling in her useless limb.

Her two-mile walk through the woods in the darkness of pre-dawn was mostly uneventful, except when she failed to see a fair-sized ditch on her right hand side, having wrapped her head too much in the ultra-therm, obscuring her peripheral vision. She didn't so much stumble, as pitch headlong sideways. When she tried to raise her right arm to catch herself, nothing happened. Face met tree virtually unchecked, and she congratulated herself on yet another beauty mark, an ugly abrasion that pretty much took up her entire right cheek.

When she got near the bus stop on Route 128, she was almost an hour early. She had to linger on the fringes of the forest lest she be recognized, though no one was in sight at all just yet. Still, it would be better to appear out of the woods two minutes before the bus to Cloverdale arrived, than it would be to flee into the woods should another human being approach during the forty-five minute wait.

She looked at her Sofee compulsively, every fifteen minutes she **thought**, but Sofee said it was more like every three minutes, and she was always right. At 7:15 a well-dressed Latino-looking man strolled up to the bus shelter, and established himself in it. At 7:28 she joined him, trying to step quietly until she got very near the road, so he wouldn't turn too early and think something crazy like, "Oh my God, here comes a wild Linsom Felize out of the woods..."

She succeeded, more due to the fact that the man was listening to the Spanish news on his ear implants than to her light-footedness. "Good morning," she said in a slightly disinterested singsong, like she had heard regular people say it.

"Good mornings," he returned, with the slightest of head-nods. Prudence worked hard to keep her entire right side hidden from the man, so her black eye, bloody cheek, and bandaged arm wouldn't invite a conversation in broken English--or even brokener Spanish--about whether she needed him to call 'el policía'...This dynamic reminded her that when she boarded the bus, it would be wise to find a seat on the right, if one was available.

By 7:35 Prudence was getting a little antsy. If this bus wasn't coming, if she had misinterpreted some key information, she would be in deep trouble. "Is the bus sometimes late?" she asked the well-dressed man.

"Sometime," he said, but as he did, she saw two headlights cresting a distant hill behind him in the early morning light. Relief washed over her. Two minutes and fifteen credits later she was slouched down in the back right hand seat of a mostly empty bus to Cloverdale.

After her prolonged exposure to the elements, the warm sunshine streaming in felt better, much better, without the chilly breeze to undercut it. By the time the bus started to get back up to highway speed, she was already thinking of re-claiming a few minutes of lost sleep. Right when she started to doze, however, there was a big commotion at the front of the long double-decker. They hadn't stopped, or even slowed down, in fact they seemed to have reached a comfortable ninety miles per hour, and yet it **looked** like a man was trying to board, and that there was some disagreement about pay-ment. The robot security officer, in his crisply pressed navy blue uniform, was gesticulating with more emotion than one would have expected from a bot. Even Prudence, jaded as she was, opened her eyes and sat up to make sure everything was cool.

The first thing she noticed was that the man trying to board was wearing one of those ridiculous suits from the commercials, the Dizastra 3000. Was this one of those end-of-the-world nutjobs who had blown his life-savings on the ε7000 suit, and now couldn't afford the bus ride from Gey-serville to Cloverdale? The security bot's voice intoned me-chanically in conjunction with his emphatic hand gesture:

"No pay, no way."

"Ah, c'mon Bro, the bus is almost empty anyway!"

"No how, no way, no 'Bro', you go."

"Ease up a minute, Bro! These hard-working people"--he gestured to the nine folks scattered around the bus, at least four of whom didn't look like hard-working people--"these people have worked hard all of their lives to build something for themselves. They are walking around unprotected from disaster. If this bus crashed right now, they'd be done for, all that hard work down the drain!"

Now, for the first time, Prudence noticed that the left foot of the 'man' attempting to board was actually floating an inch or so above the top of the ramp, and furthermore, he was faintly shimmering all over. He was a blooming holo-gram, **another** advertisement. *Come on. It's like a twenty-minute bus trip. I didn't pay for a show.*

"No pay, no stay!" Even the robot was in on this, display-ing decent acting chops. Pru, just for a second, imagined him practicing in the mirror at home.

"Alright, alright, alright," laughed Mr. Dizastra 3000. "I'll pay, cuz **kids**--" He turned again to his yawning, scant audi-ence. There were no kids on the bus. "--it would be wrong to use the Dizastra 3000 to break the law. But first--" he turned back to the security bot. "--I want you to try to **make** me pay!"

"Don't make me do it."

"Do it, Bro."

"I'm warning you."

"Do it, Bra."

"Don't make me do it."

"That's not how we practiced it; just--" Lightning fast, the robot whipped a pistol from his belt and fired at the ho-logram--apparently, anyway.

"Yeeeah! Shoot his--" yelled a young man toward the front of the bus, who was trying to listen to his music.

"I'm still waiting, Bro!" The robot fired again. The man laughed a high-pitched obnoxious laugh that seemed to cut through Prudence. "Is that all you got?"

The robot put the pistol back in its holster, and reached for another device strapped to his left hip. He pointed it at his 'Bro', and blue arcs of electricity crackled out, engulfing the man, who began to shake violently. "I'm alive!" he yelled. Pru understood this to be a Frankenstein reference. Now his shaking turned into a hokey dance as the blue three million volt net still blanketed him. "I got chills; they're multiplyin'..." That one she didn't get. Then "I'm aaliiiive!" again. God, she hated this dude. There was clearly no one in his inner circle with the guts to tell him that his jokes were stupid. The electricity stopped. The security robot returned the little black stick to the holster on his left hip.

"Just kidding. I'm **not** alive. I'm a hologram. But you get the point. Fire, gunshots, electricity, floods, disease, violent impact--you are protected from **all** of it in a Dizastra 3000! Only seven thousand credits! How much is your life worth?"

Not that, thought Prudence.

"And remember kids"--there were still no kids in the audience--"if I find a way to die in this thing, I'll let you know! Peace out! Vote Brandenberg 2128!" And with a *zipping* sound, the multi-billion-credit entrepreneur/spokesman/senator/presidential candidate/giant goombah was gone. Two minutes of Pru's life she would never get back.

The bus stopped in 'downtown' Cloverdale a mere eighteen minutes after leaving Geyserville. Prudence couldn't help thinking that if it hadn't been for the super-obnoxious holographic interruption, she might have been able to doze a little. Oh well. It was too late now.

Six of the nine passengers were disembarking here, a real testament to Cloverdale's thriving downtown scene. Prudence, looking like she was going to her job as an extra in a war movie, maybe in a scene where she was laying dead on her left side, so they only had to makeup the right, was happy to be at the back of the short line filing down the center of the bus toward the exit. She caught on to the pattern of the security robot's bland parting banter, as the foot of each exiting passenger hit the first step down:

"Have a pleasant day." "Thank you for riding with us." "Enjoy your time in Cloverdale." Then back around to "Have a pleasant day." "Thank you for riding with us." and as Pru's little black boot touched the triggering step "Enjoy your time--" She froze, surprising no one more than herself. This spot, from where the annoying but harmless hologram had tried to sell the nine poor passengers a ϵ7000 disaster suit that they probably couldn't have afforded all together, seemed... foul...cold...unholied somehow. She hated that guy, sure; but she hated everyone, so why should her spine tingle and the hair on her (left) arm bristle now?

She became aware that the three remaining passengers were staring at her, their attention caught by her stopping where she wasn't supposed to stop, and then held by the unexpected sight of her physical damage. They were no doubt wondering what we all wonder when we see someone in distress: *Should I do something? Should I offer to help? Should I call the police? Surely someone else will...* Even the robot was waiting to finish his sentence. With a quick shudder, and shaking her head as if just awakening, Prudence broke the tension by finally continuing down the steps and onto the mint-colored concrete curb.

"in Cloverdale," the security bot exhaled. The tiny young woman wheeled around as the bus doors shut a foot and a half in front of her face. Not one to be easily startled, she nonetheless responded with an odd, weak whimper of surprise as the bus's safety energy field nudged her gently and invisibly backward. The double-decker took off again with just enough noise to alert folks that something big and heavy was rolling their way.

Green Cloverdale now opened up before Prudence. Whether it was a nod to the name of the town, or just a unified civic artsiness, the entire place was green. Literally. At least on this, the main street through the center of town, all the storefronts, sidewalks, even the fire hydrants, were painted green, mostly mint like the curb, but accented here and there with a darker ivy-color. This bit of stupidity roused Prudence once and for all from her daze.

"Sofee, which way to Dr. Binklock's?"

"Northwest, to your left, two-hundred and forty yards past the approaching gentleman with the golden retriever. However, you are two hours early for your appointment, and are very much in need of food."

"I have like five credits to spare."

"Five point sixty-seven credits. A plain bagel can be purchased at the MacDougal's across the street for five point twenty-one credits. I am just saying."

"Alright. Twist my arm. The good one…" Her Sofee would have laughed at the little joke; they were generally very easy to amuse, but Prudence had warned it not to (about ten minutes into their relationship). Traffic was almost non-existent in this sleepy little town, even during 'rush-hour', and she was able to cross the street easily in the designated crosswalk adjacent to the bus stop.

As she neared the double yellow line in the middle of the roadway, the golden retriever came up even with the bus stop. He turned his yellow head and gave a single bark. *You have me confused with someone else,* thought Pru, looking back at the dog. But she saw that he was actually barking at the spot where the bus had been thirty seconds earlier. *Nevermind...*

Entering the MacDougall's, with its red and black plaid arches popping out between the green storefronts, she kept her head down and made a beeline for the bathroom. Once there, she locked the door, turned the faucet on, shoved her head down in the sink and drank thirstily for about fifteen seconds. She turned it off, wiped her dainty chin, and took stock of herself in the mirror. Her full, smudged black lips gave a little whistle of surprise. Her reflected image was alarming...but she didn't hate it. The black eye, from her drunken father's left hook five nights ago, was actually beginning to *feel* better, but visually it was just now in full bloom. The concentrated black area had spread out, down onto her face, giving the full picture in shocking purple, jaundiced yellow and copper green, of exactly where the large fist had struck the small cheek. Right where it stopped, the gaudy scratch from where she had kissed the tree two hours earlier was sort of gobbed up with dried blood. The rest of her face was streaked with dirt and secondary blood. She turned the faucet back on to let the water warm up a little before washing her face. But she locked eyes with herself in the mirror, and even as her hands on the edge of the sink could feel the ambient warmth of the water increasing, she made a decision. She turned the water off.

This is the most important day of my life. Let the world see the truth. Happy Birthday to me.

Using a genuine toilet was a real luxury after living in the woods for a couple of days, though it was hard to get used to doing everything left-handed, then she washed her hands and exited the bathroom. She walked with her head up now, confidently and coldly, to the back of the 'line'--one man in jeans and jacket, probably about to start his normal day constructing something somewhere. She scanned the menu for this five-credit bagel, trying to ignore the kilted, bagpiping clown that danced across it. She couldn't find it. It was her turn to order. "Do you have bagels?"

"Yes, ma'am--" the MacDougall's worker, kilted like the clown, stared at her for a half-second, then recovered enough to finish: "We do; they are five credits."

"I'll take one."

"Do you want cream cheese, cream cheese and lox, or cinna-butter?"

"Is all that extra?"

"Yes ma'am."

"Just plain, please."

"Yes ma'am. Anything else?"

"Nope."

"Coming right up."

Prudence sat in a back booth and tried to make the bagel last, picking off tiny pieces and putting them in her mouth. When she was done, she continued to sit for a little while, trying to kill time. Close to 9:00 AM she resolved to head on over to Dr. Binklock's. She knew virtually nothing about therapists, psychiatrists, medical doctors, and the differences between them all; she thought maybe if she got there early, they could finish early, and perhaps he could give her something for her dangerously throbbing arm.

The energy field guarding the crosswalk wouldn't let her out into the street until a single, fast-approaching purple car had gone by. But as it neared, to her momentary horror, a man in a silver body suit jumped the field and ran straight out in front of it! The vehicle, not detecting a solid obstruction, barreled on without slowing; there was a sickening *thud* and the man in the Dizastra 3000 went flying and flipping straight up in the air, not even hitting the pavement again until the car, unfooled by the hologram, was fifty yards further on its way. It was shoddy programming though; the timing was off; the body had been sent flying about a quarter-second too early. Getting up with a dramatic wormish leap, not even using its hands, the image dusted off and shouted to where it guessed a crowd of onlookers might be standing, to the empty green sidewalk on Pru's left: "I'm okay! Nobody panic! My Dizastra 3000 suit with its dynamic cushioning response system saved me!" He laughed with almost sinister arrogance. "That felt like a pillow-fight!" The shimmering illusion continued on its way across the street, then turned and added, "If I figure out a way to die in this thing, I'll let you know! Brandenberg 2128!"

The Doctor wasn't in at nine. Or nine-thirty. Or even ten, when her appointment was actually scheduled, for that

matter. It didn't even look like a doctor's office. It looked like
an old wooden, low-rent, three-story apartment building. Its
appearance was made even shabbier by the fact that it marked
the end of a long line of classic restored Brownstones (well,
Greenstones, at any rate), and furthermore, by it being the
first **non**-green building you would encounter if you were
headed north out of town. Prudence rang the bell relentlessly
to no avail, getting antsier and antsier; starting to worry that
every passing vehicle would have her father in it. She even
called Dr. Binklock's number several times, getting his voice-
mail. Her anger and anxiety grew, as ten o'clock turned into
ten-thirty, then eleven. She took to hiding in the shade next
to the dilapidated building, between trips to the doorbell, for
safety, and also just to get out of the hot early spring sun.

Around eleven-fifteen, a yellow and black bullet-taxi
pulled up to the curb abruptly, almost giving Prudence a
heart attack. A disheveled wreck of a man spilled out of it,
literally coming to rest on his hands and knees on the sidewalk as the taxi sped off. She saw instantly that it wasn't her
father, and she emerged from the shade. "Hey! Do you live
in this building?"

"Yeah..." croaked the sandy-haired, red-faced man, looking up at the unexpected voice.

"Do you know when Dr. Binklock will be in?"

"Ohh crap..." Remorse clouded the strangely weathered
face. "You must be Prudence Estrada." He struggled to his
feet, looking and smelling like he hadn't been home in several
days. He extended his hand. "I'm Dr. Binklock."

As he unlocked the front door and led her in, he apologized profusely, explaining that half the time "you girls" didn't show up anyway; that he had chosen to respond to an emergency out of town, etc.... Prudence, who didn't know how to jump rope or ride a bike, knew enough about this kind of person to suspect the nature of the emergency. He had run out of something he couldn't live without. The burn mark on his lip supported her suspicion. But she kept her mouth shut, knowing, too, how this sort of man could turn violent with very little provocation, and knowing that she desperately needed the documents he was about to forge for her.

The Doctor's 'office' was his disgusting apartment. From the moment Prudence stepped into it, she couldn't think of anything but getting back out, especially after Binklock secured the door with no less than three slide bolts. Fortunately, he seemed to really know what he was doing, and after ninety minutes of fingerprint-taking, retina-scanning, and intensely awkward questions about her case history, an incredibly detailed and authentic-looking file on the trials and tribulations of Prudence Estrada was created. The full history of her misery, her unsatisfactory reactions to various treatments and medications she had never even heard of, and the Doctor's statement as to her competence to make this decision for herself, all opened up before her on the viewing half-wall. It all looked genuine and inscrutable to her. With the touch of a button, he sent it to her, and to the Cloverdale MCP, with a little note expressing his sadness and regret that it had come to this for his patient of two and a half years, Prudence Estrada.

"Happy?" he asked her.

Well, that's the dumbest question I've ever heard, she thought,

but what she said was "Yes. Thank you." Payment, her last
five hundred credits, was transferred to the Doctor (well, actually to a third, untraceable party), and Prudence got up and
walked toward the terrifyingly triple-bolted door. Dr. Binklock opened his long skinny arms and offered her a hug.
"I'm good, thanks." she said. Short, awkward pause....then
he laughed. He reached over and slid the bolts open.

"Good luck!"

The Cloverdale MCP was not an imposing freestand-
ing structure like the bigger cities had. It shared a common
space with a number of other federal institutions, tax offices,
vehicle registry and the like...In this quiet town of twenty-
thousand, six months would sometimes go by without someone signing on to the Goners. That would be a whole lot of
yawning, finger tapping, and daydreaming for a county clerk
waiting at a little window. Unfortunately, the combining of
services resulted in more of a line, more of a wait, and more
of an audience than Pru would have preferred.

She knew, as she started shaking during the short walk
there, that the moment of reckoning was at hand. Her whole
body had suddenly gone numb, as her right arm and shoulder
had been already; she felt nauseous and helpless to control
the trembling. The stupid doctor's lateness meant that she
was walking straight into the lunch crowd at the MCP. Suddenly, thirty feet from the glass front door, mid-stride, she
demanded self-control of herself. She changed her outlook
instantly and completely, and with her head held high and
eyes fixed straight forward, she regarded the entire universe
around her with cold, dumb, absolute animal disinterest.

And it may as well have been a wild animal strolling into the Cloverdale, California County business offices. When the front doors slid open, two older gentlemen and an older woman were engaged in animated friendly chatter about... whatever; the three of them fairly jumped aside at the sight of Prudence, grins evaporating from wrinkly faces. She moved through the second set of doors into the waiting area, where heads turned and whispers began. She was a sight. And a smell. She hadn't bathed since Sunday, or changed clothes since Monday, during which time she had rappelled out of a fourth floor window, battled a raccoon (and technically lost), used up her breath-spray treating her wounds, slept outside for two nights, slam-danced into a tree, walked about four miles, taken a bus trip, and hung out with a filthy sleaze-doctor. She stepped to the back of the line. Her face was a mess; the cool makeup effects she had achieved Monday morning remained on her features somewhat, but only here and there, giving the sad impression of a clown figurine melting in a furnace. The parts that did show through were bruised, bloody and filthy. One arm was bright red and bandaged with a t-shirt. Wilderness debris clung to her still stylish black jumpsuit and boots. She may also have stepped in something, judging by the odor.

Internally, she was about the same.

At last it was her turn. When she stated her name and the stupid middle-aged woman behind the counter slowly began to realize the horrible purpose of her visit, 'Clarisse' (according to her name tag) began a little innocuous protest; something to the effect of "Ooooh, sweetie, you are so young and--" Almost at the first utterance, Pru began a low growl,

cutting off the clerk maliciously. When she sensed that conversation both around and behind her had stopped suddenly,
and that heads throughout the waiting room had turned in
her direction, she knew that she could let the low, bestial
thunder fade out, and the unwanted attention with it, or she
could take it in the opposite direction.

It's amazing what can go through a human mind in a split
second. Prudence felt gratified, mid-rumble, that all these
strangers, who for sixteen years had never seemed to notice
when things were wrong with her, sure noticed her now.

Her wild animal growl, through clenched teeth, rose in
pitch, intensity and volume as a warning to everyone in earshot. Maybe she did have rabies. Or maybe it was the physical
and mental exhaustion of her courageous escape from a lifetime of physical and mental abuse. And malnutrition...and
dehydration...and nausea. At any rate, the stupid clerk shut
her fat mouth and waited until Pru's episode hit its bizarre
crescendo, and tailed off. Then she entered the young crazy
person's information in wounded, slightly frightened silence.
She turned the pad around to Prudence and said brusquely,
"Left index finger here. Left middle finger here." Et cetera.
"Put your forehead on the scanner."

"Is that it?"

"That's it."

"Am I in? I'm in the MCP?"

"You are in." This with a tight-lipped, grim, reproachful
half-smile.

"Good." She reached up under the left fringe of her
tangled brown mop and fiddled with the controls, quickly re-
establishing her preferred shoulder-length pulsating rainbow

hairdo. Then she unwrapped her grotesquely scratched and swollen right arm and held it aloft for everyone to see.

"Do you have someone who can look at this?"

~

Houston, Texas US of A
Monday, March 25, 2126...8:11 AM

"MCPNH legal…"

"You know why I'm calling, I'm sure…"

"Yes sir."

"What do we know about this lady?"

"She is Octavia Hopkins from Shreveport, Louisiana. She is fifty-two years old. Her son--as I'm sure you saw--was Latrell Hopkins; he joined the MCP on April 7, 2124; decommissioned (died) on March 24, 2125."

"How did he die?"

"Not in a way she would want to hear about. Bio--"

"Bio-testing?"

"Yep"

Acting President of the MCPNH Vincent Beauregard, from his end of this conversation, exhaled deeply. He continued in his effeminate drawl. "Okay. Moving on. Can we get rid of her?"

"Actually…[reluctantly] no, not at this juncture. She is within her legal rights to be here."

"Alright. Do you have anybody free?"

"Sort of…free enough."

"Get me a schedule of what we need to do to get her removed by tomorrow."

"Oh, I don't know that we'll be able to get her removed by tomorrow…"

"I **mean**, let's have the **schedule** of how to proceed by tomorrow!"

"Yessir! Legal is on it!"

4

No Face No Name
No Number

Newberry, South Carolina USA
Monday, March 25, 2126...4:07 PM

The ugly young man scrolled back up to the top of his six-page letter. He wiped the tears from his blotchy red cheeks and reread it.

Dearest Mother: There are a number of ways to tell you what I am about to tell you. That number is 1,247. I choose number 486--a cowardly, self-pitying letter that I can't even speak aloud to you. Well, it feels cowardly right now. Sometimes the whole thing feels brave, and sometimes it feels cowardly. It's the dark, unpredictable flickering magic of human perspective. Though my feelings may ping-pong from one ex-treme to the other, and all stops in between, my mind is made up and my heart, deep down, is resolute.

I know that you have the highest expectations for me. I know that it is driving you nuts that I missed the first two tries at the 'Uppity's' [UPT's--University Preparedness Tests] *especially since I need a fourteen-hundred-and-whatever to get into Harvard. I also know, obviously, that tomorrow is the last chance to take the exam. I know you have a hotel booked for us tonight in Columbia, and that you won't be able to get that credit back. I know, I know, I know. I should have been honest with you from the get-go. I didn't really have a migraine back in November when the first testing date came around. I did have a headache, but not that bad really, in January when I missed the second chance.*

It's not my head Mom. It's not my head, Brian. [He was sending this to his one close friend, as well as his poor unsuspecting mother.] *It's not my head, cruel world. It isn't me; it's **you**. Since the foggy dawn of history some 9000 years ago, I can't imagine that anyone has felt the pain that I have felt these last four years or so. As a matter of fact, I **know** it--I would have read about it somewhere.*

*What it boils down to is this: As much as I wish it were not so, physical beauty is still, even now, the primary determining factor for reproductive viability. I am not physically beautiful. I am not worthy of consideration as a mate. **I am ugly**. U-G-L-Y; I ain't got no alibi.*

*Brian, you know this facet of my frustration. We have been best friends for four years now. You even commented on it that one time, at the mall, when those two girls were talking to you, and completely shut me out. "It was like you didn't even exist!" were your words at the time, and right they were, and still are...In the minds and hearts of womankind, I literally **do not exist**. Brian, you have been with me through the* *narrative of my loneliness, and I thank you now and forever. Mom, I have kept this part of my life a secret from you. I know that you see value in me, and probably would not believe that no other girl on the face of the planet sees value in me, or ever will. Please believe me when I say that there have been no near-misses, where maybe I just said the wrong thing to a girl, or wore the wrong shirt, or dissed her favorite band. I don't know what the twinkle in a girl's eye even looks like. I spent ε190 on a gift for a girl at work this last Christmas because she was foolish enough to be polite to me. I thought that was maybe what that twinkle looked like. I was wrong, as she pointed out politely when she gave it back to me the next day. You can have it, Mom. It's still in the box under my bed; it's a little silver vase, and the silver is real.*

I am completely finished looking for love. The pain is too much. I can't go to college without a girlfriend anymore than I could go without food or oxygen. Love is a basic human need. Why is it illegal to starve or strangle a man, yet there is no societal provision made for his heart?

It gives me pain on top of pain to leave you alone in this cold world, Mom. Since Dad left, I am well aware of what I have meant to you. Please take some comfort in the little bit of family we have left. Grandma and Grandpa are strong, and Grandma Dunne, and Uncle Kevin. There are some support groups too; I've attached three of them to this letter--I know you like a little structure "for to grieve in." [This was apparently an inside joke.]

The upshot of all this is that I will be joining the MCP on Wednesday, March 27, 2126 (the year of our Lord)--my sixteenth and likely final birthday. I don't want this to turn into a big back and forth "maybe I shouldn't," "maybe I should" kind of thing. I don't want you guys to talk me out of it, then I talk myself back into it, then you talk me out of it, etc., ad infinitum...I want to seize on this courage of resignation, the determination I feel **right now***, to make a difference* *in the world. It's simple math, like Mr. Spock said to Captain Kirk, "the needs of the many outweigh the needs of the few."*

Mom. Mom--look at me. [So weird until the very end, this one] **It's okay.** *It is* **okay.** *We caught some bad breaks, with genetics first, and Dad leaving, second…if I can save* **two lives** *by doing this--just two--then this has all been worth it, every shred of agony, every lonely moment. It's simple math.*

You can't possibly actually believe that any of this is real, anyway. The world is pretty, and fun, but **<u>real</u>?** *There are holes all throughout the Swiss cheese (yum) of reality's illusion. I believe it was Dostoyevsky who wrote, "We're always thinking of eternity as an idea that cannot be understood, something immense. But why must it be? What if, instead of all this, you suddenly find just a little room there, something like a village bathhouse, grimy, and spiders in every corner, and that's all eternity is. Sometimes, you know, I can't help feeling that that's what it is." (Actually, I* **know** *it was Dostoyevsky who wrote it, but it sounds, ironically, more learned to say, "I* **believe** *it was Dostoyevsky…")*

I have a place to stay until Wednesday. [This was not true.] *I can't tell you where, because I know you would try to talk me out of this, and at this point, your intentions notwithstanding, that would be inhumane. All you need to know is that you did the best job you possibly could have done raising me virtually alone, and that I leave all of my love behind me, here with you.*

Love,

Dublin

P.S.: Please see also my novel (attached)
P.S.S.: I took a mock UPT online and got a 1487

Well, that will do. He thought he had put more good jokes in there, and that it didn't read so…heavy…but, hey--everything he needed to unload was in there. He inhaled exceedingly deeply, then released it, with his hands over his eyes and face. His schoolbag was packed with everything he would need for a day and a half on the mean streets of Greenville, SC. Beyond that, he knew, nothing was needed other than his new untraceable Sofee and his self.

It was now or never. Feeling, as always, like he was in a movie, he stood up abruptly and shouldered the small satchel. He looked around his tiny, messy room…he took one step toward the dingy white door, then wheeled sharply, with youthful energy, and almost ran across the little space to a bust of Leo Tolstoy. He playfully "tousled" the marble hair, but this was too meager an acknowledgement of the master's influence on him. He leaned over and kissed the cold marble lips…is this what it felt like to kiss a girl? He guessed probably not, definitely not…his mind was a blur…Tolstoy was long dead, Dostoyevsky was long dead; so he would be okay dead too, right? Dickens dead, Shakespeare dead…all of their lives were spent in quest for the great truths; they all invented lives and carried out wonderful milieus with their many and varied characters…if Dublin could gather them up, and put them in a circle…Hugo and Emerson on the bed, Tolstoy at his desk, Mr. Spock and Thoreau by the window--one step closer to nature, though five floors up and not much nature in sight--what would they all say to him? He needn't wonder. They had said it all in their books, all of them except Mr. Spock, who said it in a movie. It would be a complete consensus. Go. Go! Give thine petty life up in service to the swarm!

He felt better and stronger. He made a dash for it.

The door of his room slid open. He walked out into the living area. His mom was vacuuming, as always. She caught him out of the corner of her eye. She shut off the vacuum and turned to him.

"You look like you're going somewhere?" She was pretty and petite. She was too frail for him to leave her all alone. He resisted the urge to hug her--how suspicious would that have been?

"Yeah, I'm just going for a walk. I know we have to leave by six."

"Alright. Just don't lose track of time."

He was at the door of the apartment. It slid open. "Okay...love you." When kids get a little older, like past eleven or twelve, sometimes--no one knows why--they get shy about saying *I* love you; the *I* just drops off and becomes "love you." Or maybe it's the other way around; maybe it starts with the parents... Anyway, it begins when the child approaches adulthood, starting to become a man or a woman in his or her own right. All of a sudden it becomes awkward for a full-grown man to express his love completely to another 'man' or 'woman'; what happened to their carefree little cuddle-baby? The same difficulty plagues mothers as well. So for the rest of our lives we have to accept that 'love you' means the same as '*I* love you' once did.

"Love you."

The door shut behind him. He was out. He slumped

against the wall, but rebounded up quickly. He wasted no further time in the hall. When he got to the lobby, he hit 'send'. His mom still had the Sofee 46--unbelievable--and he knew it would take like six full seconds for his letter, links, and eight-hundred page novel to download completely.

When he hit the front door of their lower middle-class apartment building, and felt the wind on his face, he stopped in his tracks. He was sure he heard sobbing somewhere above him. *No way...already?* He virtually sprinted away down the sunny, still chilly Newberry Street.

He hurried to the nearest streetlight. Leaning against it, he pressed the screen of his Sofee 47 deftly, three times, and activated the double-back tracker he had purchased for ten credits. Then he moved on, with purpose, like someone was after him.

The sobbing stuck with him. It couldn't possibly have been her, right? There hadn't been enough time for her year-old Sofee to receive all that data, for her to notice that she had a message, and for her to read far enough to get the gist...It had to have been someone else in their building, crying over something else...unless his mom just knew that something like this was coming, and suspected the general content of his letter the moment her wrist dinged at her. He shuddered. His body tingled with horrible nervous energy...but he kept his brisk pace down the old sidewalk, stepping on cracks and breaking his mother's back nearly constantly. He dropped his gaze from the meager oncoming foot-traffic, feeling that his secret was written all over his face and that they would all be repulsed by him...repulsed by his face (this was not new) and repulsed at his cowardice; disgusted that he would leave his mother alone, weeping in a heap...all of this would be obvious to anyone who met his gaze, so he dropped his gaze to the sidewalk. Even now, at a distance of several hundred feet from his home of twelve years, he knew every jaggedy split, and every little weed poking up out of them. The tables and chairs of the little cafe, the wooden rail that separated it from traffic, the old rusty beer bottle cap sunk down into the rail, which had been there all through his childhood...slightly rustier now, with slightly less of the green letters showing... he grazed it with his fingertips for good luck, as he had done many times on his way to school, on quiz days, on test days, on exam days, on "hope-Jennifer-liked-my-poem" days...not much of a good luck charm, really...

And now it was time to cross diagonally through the park. He waited for the sleek and silent cars, mostly bullets and bubbles, to slow and stop on Nance Street, and the 'walk' sign to light up. His mind was on fire as he crossed the narrow street. Out of the corner of his eye he recognized two of the eleven cars backed up in the two lanes; one a fellow student who he knew only casually, and further back, an older man he had done some work for when he was twelve...painting...yard work...Dublin chastised himself--this was useless information, utterly useless!

He entered the shady green of the central town park, near the college. Here it had stood for three-hundred and forty-odd years...none odder than **this** year...He was almost overwhelmed with the urge to fling himself face down on the grass like a lad of seven and not move ever again until the police came and made him move. He remembered kindergarten performances on this green. One in the fall with his Dad there. One in the spring without his Dad there.

Dublin was smart enough and wise enough to know that no terrifying premeditated act was ever undertaken without a great deal of this nervous, useless inner babbling. Still, he wished he could switch his mind off right now, and set it to come back on after he had finished signing up at the MCP.

His precipitous footfalls alarmed two grey and white birds and sent them flapping off dramatically. Dublin put his mind on hold with a little burst of singing--out loud--out **very** loud: *"Oh, the magpie is a most illustrious bird/ Dwells in a diamond tree…"* This display was in direct contradiction to his eyes-to-the-ground marching of only three minutes earlier, but for an active teenage brain, contradiction is as normal and routine as putting on pants...or airs...The birds were pigeons, not magpies, but surely if they understood English they would have been flattered with the free upgrade…

His self-distracting mental tricks had worked and he was suddenly striding into the shade of the bus station. The lines were short. He was ahead of the evening rush by about twenty minutes, and before he even knew it he had a one-way ticket for Greenville in his Sofee. He didn't think his Mother would come running after him, and he only had four minutes to wait; plus the tracker **should** take her in a completely different direction, but he still kept glancing nervously out the large windows into the sunshine of his childhood town. All clear--three minutes. All clear--two minutes. All clear--one minute. *Now boarding the 4:45 to Greenville, SC.* The scattered few had swelled to a small crowd, but still, after shuffling aboard, he was able to carve out a triple space for himself at the very back, partly by being unattractive, and partly by looking like a psycho-killer...

The afternoon sun was warm through the window, especially having left the slight chill of the Southern March air behind, and he closed his eyes with his legs stretched across the three seats. It was only forty-five minutes to Greenville, but he felt enormous relaxation, having leaped the first of his two huge hurdles. The large bus lurched through the turns of the small town, rocking Dublin like a baby. He started to doze, but very lightly. His eyes popped back open. His minute and a half of inner peace was over. Then he expanded his Sofee screen to his preset fave for reading--four point seventy-eight inches diagonally, exactly, with a screen tilt of fifteen degrees so he didn't have to hold his arm awkwardly. He tried to pick up where he had left off in *Crime and Punishment*. He had deliberately reserved this read for this time in his life, knowing something of the premise. He felt that he would really identify with the killer's soul-searching, guilt-wracked nervous excitement, and so far he had been right. But now that he was at the nexus of his crisis, head reeling, he found that trying to mind-meld with the mad Russian was like two hummingbirds trying to high-five each other in mid-flight. He shut it down in like thirty seconds.

He laid his big head back against the warm glass again and closed his eyes harder. His Sofee *dinged* at him. He had a split second of blind panic before remembering that he had temporarily blocked his Mom. Not out of spite, or malice, or even dismissiveness, but entirely because whatever her response would be, he knew he would not be able to take it.

It was Brian. This he could take.

"I knew it! I called it! Whoa dude-MCP- ##yousobrave#willa!

waysremember//BFF! & does Marty [their boss at work] *know?*
***#goingtobragonu4-evah* [another inside joke] *My Dub-man is a
Goner!*

He had to smile at that. He read it twice, then turned
his 47 back off. He lay back again but didn't close his eyes,
watching the trees fly by out of the opposite window. It was
strengthening to hear words of encouragement in hard times.
Not *Hard Times*, the Dickens novel, he clarified in his head,
smiling as always at his own cleverness. He loved Brian, and
would miss him terribly.

The seats across from him in the back of the bus were
empty. In the row in front of them sat a young, pretty, profes-
sional-looking lady. She glanced very quickly back at Dublin,
careful to betray no warmth in her eyes or expression. He felt
the disapproval of her aspect, and it made him so angry. He
wasn't even looking at her. Normally, yes, he would have been
looking at her, but for once in his life he was so distracted
that he was **NOT** looking at the pretty girl, and she still shut
him down, just in case. That's what was going on in his head.
For her part, she was probably thinking about a report she
had to turn in tomorrow.

They passed--well, **began** to pass--the Uno Mundo distri-
bution center. This, to Dub at least, was one of the wonders
of the world. It was just a single-story white warehouse-style
building, but it went on forever. It used to be about a half a
mile long. Now, by his reckoning, it had to be over a mile. He
counted twenty-nine seconds as they rocketed past at one
hundred and ten miles per hour. So...about point-eighty-nine
miles, before the white blur turned back to a green blur. It
was hard to believe there was this much merchandise needed

in the Upstate. This thought brought his attention to the top half of the bus, which was swarming with advertisements; electric colors popping, dancing, swimming, snaking; tiny holograms leaping out. He watched a maniacally happy twelve-year old boy blowboard out of a 'Fiber 22' ad on his side of the bus to the 'Fiber 22' ad on the other side. Surely this was too much fiber? He couldn't see it well, but towards the center of the bus a hissing cobra head exploded out of a commercial for the new Wisconsin Johnson movie coming out next week. Dublin was sad that he would miss that. It looked even better than the first four…Shampoo, conditioner, gum, jeans, *oatmeal?* He saw a little guy in what looked like a seventeenth century Quaker outfit beating traditional breakfast meats to a bloody pulp, then rending the stale bus air with a primal scream…toothpaste, Admiral Crunch, Spritz, Diet Spritz, Spritz-Nada… These were all things he'd been conditioned, like everyone else, to tune out, but he welcomed them in right now as a distraction, even as a comforting assurance that the world didn't need him, and would be alright without him…

Who watches these ads? he wondered. Looking around the ninety-seater he saw no one else whose attention was not locked on their Sofees, whether in wrist, mini-screen, or laptop form. He saw an old-timer with the giant headphones on, who had resisted ear-implants probably on principle. This always made him smile. It was like seeing somebody in line at the movies wearing a bearskin-pelt and carrying a club. Keep on rocking, old man.

Suddenly there was a commotion at the front of the bus. Dublin sat up quickly to observe. Even though they hadn't stopped, or even slowed, it looked like a man in a Dizastra 3000 suit was trying to board, and that there was some disagreement about payment. Dub grinned, all alone at the back, knowing that no one would see his crooked yellow teeth. He loved this guy! He rode the bus to school everyday, so he knew exactly what was going to happen, but he thought it was hysterical and watched the whole thing.

Shortly after that, the bus began to slow, as evening traffic thickened, and the windows filled with houses, then five-story buildings, then fifteen-story buildings, and then the neck-breaking monoliths of downtown Greenville; seventy, eighty, a hundred stories high. Dublin's pulse re-quickened; he loved the big city, but was of course nervous about finding a place to survive in it, albeit for a meager thirty-eight hours and twenty-three minutes until the MCP building on Washington Street opened on Wednesday at eight AM. He had no real plan for the interim. He kind of just envisioned a slow drift from department store, to coffeehouse, to park bench, to hopefully-free museum...He was a little concerned about how long his shower might hold up; he thought he should maybe do the indoor stuff first, and save the park bench and his Dad's marker for last.

The virtually silent bus (except for the still-screaming Quaker) turned abruptly down a concrete ramp into the cavernous shade of a huge parking garage, and rolled to a stop. The doors folded open with a muffled crumpling heavy plastic sound. Dublin bided his time, conserving his energy, until the rows in front of him began to shuffle forward. There were the usual little noises, bumps of shoes and briefcases on rails, ruffling of bags, the slightest murmur, as people who

had been pressed up against one another for forty-five minutes finally felt comfortable enough to exchange pleasantries,
now that there was a way out if the conversation went horribly wrong.

The line moved slowly forward down the center aisle,
with Dublin at the back. The pace worked fine for him; he
had nowhere to be, no time soon, but there were the expected grumblings from some chronic malcontents somewhere
in the mix ahead of him. Dublin hung back as far as he could.
He hated standing behind people; he always felt like they were
going to turn around and scream. Besides, the pretty young
lady was directly in front of him, and he was already on thin
ice with her for even existing...

He tried not to stare at her, but he couldn't help it. She
was so beautiful, and she couldn't see him looking... Even
in these life-altering circumstances, with so much other stuff
to worry about, he was consumed absolutely with a primal
desire that made him literally, physically nauseous, and which
he could do absolutely nothing about.

She turned around and caught him staring. Her face
clouded, but if we're being honest here, it had been at least
partly cloudy to begin with. There was nowhere for her to
go forward, so she shifted her handbag around to cover her
backside. Dublin went beet-red with shame, and his hazel
eyes welled up.

*Boy, I've got some toughening up to do if I'm going to save any-
body from anything,* he lectured himself mentally, imagining the
bulldog, tough-guy marine types he would be working with
as a hardened Goner. He knew his emotional reaction was
cumulative, though. It wasn't just this girl this time, but all

girls all the time.

Thankfully for everyone involved, the delay, whatever it was, cleared up, and the line began to move productively. Dublin let the distance betwixt he and Cloudy-Face widen to about ten feet before moving again. When she business-footed down the two deep steps onto the concrete, and he disembarked after her, he was careful to take off with feigned urgency in the opposite direction. Purposeful strides, no looking back. *Nice try.* He couldn't stop himself from looking back. Luck was with him this time, as she was making purposeful strides of her own and definitely **not** looking back. Part of him wanted her to see him sad, to see the impact of her casual disapproval. It was too late now, so he dried the tear he had allowed to trickle down his cheek.

The bus station could scarcely have been more in the thick of things. He had been to Greenville on plenty of occasions, but he loved it all over again every time. He had left a little Southern hick-town barely fifty minutes ago, and now, as he ascended the wide bus-ramp with the smell of cool concrete filling his nostrils, he emerged into twenty-second century metro America. The skyline--ambitious, soaring, varied and dramatic--hit him full-force. He loved to stand like an idiot and count the stories; to stand and watch construction on the new ones, pressing the display button just outside the work-zone to follow the step-by-step video of how it would be built. He loved the little sky-bridges seven hundred feet off the ground; the bubble-lounges that floated, apparently unsupported, even higher. He had been in one at night one time--**crazy**!

But his favorite thing about Greenville was the favorite

thing of **every** twenty-second century child who has ever
been to Greenville: Chiquitita, the huge animatronic King-
Kong-like gorilla, nominally advertising bananas, who was
able to rove almost the whole downtown area, from skyscraper to skyscraper, on a complicated network of 'vines'.
He had been built twenty years earlier, and at the time was
confined to one city block. When the city Mothers and Fathers saw what he was doing overnight for their tourism industry, his range was expanded, gradually, to six, seven, finally
ten city blocks.

It was an unspoken rule not to tell the little ones, but
Chiquitita was just a frame of superlight, superstrong, super-
flexible tetrazine, overstrung with superlight brown nauga-
hide patches, interspersed, checkerboard style, with sections
of densely-projected brown light. A teacher on a fifth-grade
field trip (Ms. Cobb; his all-time favorite because she had
put a stop to the "ugly-Dublin" thing) had told him that the
entire apparatus only weighed seventy pounds, which didn't
seem possible. She said that if the gorilla ever 'slipped' and
fell, he would waft down like a feather, or more accurately
like an enormous Japanese paper lantern, and hurt no one.
This was hard to believe because of the sophistication of
Chiquitita's movements, which smacked of enormous weight
and strength, and the bone-crushing sound effects whenever
he left one skyscraper and impacted another. At any rate, seventy pounds or not, he looked like a fairly realistic gargantuan
gorilla on a never-ending mission to dominate downtown
Greenville, and sell bananas. And it worked. It would be an
exaggeration to say that banana stands dotted every corner
of the city, but you could certainly pass three of them on a

five-minute walk.

And so it was a lucky sign, then, that Dublin, standing alone at the top of the ramp with subterranean gloom behind him, and brilliant Southern sunshine ahead, saw, far off in the distance, the roaring head and shaggy brown left arm of his beloved Chiquitita just coming down from the highest point of the city, and back out of view. He smiled. There was something comforting about all that genius, and all those credits, being funneled into something so gloriously frivolous. It was like a modern-day Colossus of Rhodes. It must mean that all the important things in the world had been taken care of. As for his own problems, right now, the little glimpse of the gorilla filled him with raw animal courage to complete the task at hand. Better yet, raw animatronic courage.

As the prodigious monkey descended from view, Dublin turned his attention to the path directly at his feet. He saw now why everyone else had gone the other way. There was not a true pedestrian exit here, only eight lanes of traffic hedged in with concrete barriers. He retraced his steps, but got turned around at some point. It took him three tries to eventually get out of the bus station; but this did not faze him. He had time to kill. He eventually emerged into the magnificent bustle. He was impressed, and a little intimidated at how quickly and yet in how orderly a fashion everything seemed to move. The hundreds of driverless cars and buses, sleek and colorful, streamed by in tight, fast formations seemingly inches from his elbow. He knew that if he stumbled toward the street, or consciously tried to dash across it at an unauthorized point, he would be gently repulsed by the invisible magnetic barrier there. Furthermore, the cars would stop if the barrier failed, unless the controlling logarithm indicated more danger to the passengers inside should they decelerate too rapidly. All these safeguards notwithstanding, it was a little unnerving. He had grown up in a much smaller town, without the magna-barriers, so it was hard not to flinch when the larger vehicles whizzed past at sixty miles per hour and buffeted his (terrible) afro...He smiled to himself at the resilient instinct of self-preservation, even as he prepared to deliver himself over to death...

His Sofee *dinged* again. He bravely looked at it. "Welcome to sunny Greenville, South Carolina, Dublin Dunne! The city welcomes you back for your first visit in three hundred and forty-one days! Can I help you find a hotel? (delete) Can I help you find a restaurant? (delete) The nearest Uno Mundo? (Delete) Can I help you find a particular business or (delete) Can I (delete)...(pause)...Enjoy your stay! The temperature at this time is sixty-three degrees Fahrenheit, but will fall to (delete) (delete) (delete)..."

He fell into the general flow of foot traffic, moving Easterly down McBee Street. For the rest of the evening, he "wandered lonely as a cloud" amidst the tumult of humanity and the omnipresent blare and flare of advertisement. He bought two bananas, trying to slim up at the eleventh hour for his impending hero-work; but the stress on his system had made him far too hungry for that. His credit was ample; he had over ε400 in his account from work, and just two days ago his Grandma Dunne had put in another ε200, as an early birthday present. He had wisely converted it all into untraceable traveler's credits, from the safety of his bedroom... which seemed a thousand miles and a lifetime away already...

He stopped at MacDougall's and ate the biggest green salad with chicken that he had ever seen, and still had room for a chocolate croissant and coffee from Joplin's.

Now it was getting dark and chilly, and he braced himself bravely for the coming night. He had scouted out a lovely park early on, and doubled back now to maybe lay claim to a bench there. Foot traffic in the clean streets had thinned considerably and a few sanitation units had already rolled out of their curbside cubbies and started patrolling for debris, humming to themselves; mostly commercial jingles; occasionally a top five hit; he passed one humming the National Anthem with particular gusto.

For most of the world it was a regular Monday night. He passed a sports bar and glimpsed the bottom of the first inning of an Atlanta Braves game. The season had started last week, and would continue for a hundred and sixty-four games whether he was alive or not. This gave him odd comfort.

He noted the time on the block-sized TV screen across the street, which at the moment was committing twelve hundred kilowatts of energy to advertising men's wear. Soccer star Cliff Betcha© preened in a tight shimmery grey suit, whilst over his right ear the clock flipped from 7:57 PM to 7:58. Dublin stopped for a second to try to get a bead on Chiquitita's whereabouts. The great ape would give his last mighty bellow of the day at 8:00 PM, though he would mutely and restlessly prowl the city all night in search of who-knows-what. The last roar was usually a really good one, and Dublin had enough time on his hands to make hearing it a priority. He heard the rumble of the mega-gorilla swinging from one skyscraper to the next, though the action was obscured from his sight. It wasn't worth crossing the street, but it was definitely worth pausing for a minute… **"ROOOOOOOOOOOOOAAAAAAAAAAAAR!"** He thought he felt the pavement rumble. He heard the distant applause of tourists, and he smiled.

When he got to the park, nestled between grand, chunky museums with imposing concrete columns, he found it mainly deserted. The daylight was gone, but streetlights scattered on the green revealed at least four completely empty benches. He chose one close to the street. He would rest and recoup there for a time, then retire to a more secluded one for the night. The temperature was dropping quickly. He had his ultra-therm in his bag, but the last thing he wanted was to broadcast to any passing authority figures--police, alderman, the mayor--that he was about to set up camp for the night on a park bench.

This would be the time to do it. To check his 47 for his Mom's response. He knew it was there--his left wrist actually felt heavy with its emotional content. There may be a moment, as he opened her e-mail, that anyone searching for him might be able to circumvent the double-back tracker and figure out that he was in Greenville. Sitting in one spot, he knew how to falsify his location for a limited time, and he did so now, making it look like he was in Columbia, South Carolina. If his Mom resorted to extreme measures, and tried to intercept him, it would be at the MCP State Headquarters there, not the Greenville branch. He didn't **like** deceiving his Mother, but this was the sort of devil-may-care stuff he would have to acclimate to if he was going to acquit himself well, or at all, as a true Goner. He inhaled super-deeply, exhaled super-deeply, and unblocked the connection. There they were--three messages from his Mother. *Go, go, go; power through this!* he commanded himself, opening message number one.

This was not what he expected.

"Dublin. This is the most selfish thing you could possibly have done to me. Do you think you are the only one in pain?"

Shame and anger flooded up in him like a geyser. He was shaking so hard, it took a second for his finger to open message number two.

"Like Father, like Son."

He instantly and emphatically shut his Sofee down completely, and fairly leaped up from the bench. He walked quickly to one end of the gravel promenade, wheeled around, and walked all the way back. He had stupidly left his bag on the bench, but thankfully it was still there. He continued to breathe rapidly and methodically, struggling to control his temper. **He was not like his Dad. This was completely different. MEANINGFUL Conclusion Program. MEANINGFUL!** He wanted this most uncomfortable phase of his journey to be over with, so he turned his 47 back on, and opened the third message:

"Call me. I will be up all night."

No thanks. He walked some more, seven times around the park total, and settled in on the bench most hidden from traffic. He lay back with his head on his bag. Heated from rapid walking and strong emotion, he needed no blanket just yet. His mind raced miles and miles, light years, out of his body, and when he came back he found that he was shivering violently. He lifted his head and removed the ultra-therm from his bag. He arranged it over himself and felt instantly warmer. He lay his shaggy head back down, but now his bag felt less like a pillow, and more like a park bench. Between the violence of his emotions, the coffee, and the unforgiving oak slats, he slept not a wink. Not a wink all night.

Eventually, when the sky turned from dark black to slightly less dark black, people in business clothes began to walk by his bench, turning to look at the homeless kid, and he had to give up on sleep. He sat up, feeling disgusting and hopeless. He was young enough yet to function on zero sleep, but wise enough to know that his mental strength and resolve to do what he had to do would be compromised. In other words, he knew that his own mind would try to talk him out of signing up for the Goners, especially if he didn't get some sleep tonight.

He took his time 'waking up'; if that's what you call it when you weren't actually asleep. He finally shook off enough cobwebs to pack up his things and get going.

Dublin spent the whole day in a chess match with his psyche, keeping himself distracted, and avoiding the McBee Street station, where a single moment of weakness could put him on a bus back home; back to hopeless girl-crushes, misery and torment.

This agenda of self-distraction involved wandering through almost every non-clothing store in a half-mile radius, the art museum (so cool, quiet and beautiful), the history museum, (where Civil War displays made dying look easy and routine) and lastly, his favorite, the library.

At the Greenville library--if you asked--you could look

at actual printed books on paper with leather or cloth covers that creaked when you opened them. Ugly young men like Dublin don't like to *ask* for things, or directions, or instructions, because they don't get the smiles and singsong responses that pretty people do. It is their preference, therefore, to figure things out on their own, even if it takes a little more time. But Dublin wasn't going to get to hold the real books unless he asked, so he finally approached the grumpy man at the desk, reviewing files in his argyle sweater-vest and appearing to resent every exertion of his delicate fingertips.

He was let into the special room. The door shut behind him, and he was alone among the rows of eight-foot high dark wooden shelves. It was a dim place, lit primarily by the tall picture windows that lined the western and northern walls.

Dublin was in heaven. In fact, if all went as planned, he hoped to be killed quickly, painlessly and soon, possibly saving the planet, and return here in a couple of weeks to haunt this space forever--just long enough to read every page of every dusty volume.

But time was tight; the cemetery, according to his Sofee, locked its gates at 8:00 PM. If he wanted to visit his Dad one last time, he would have to budget his time with Conrad, Chekov, and the Bronte Sisters. He tried to prioritize. He found Tolstoy, and actually held *War and Peace* in his hands. Dublin had read this, all fourteen hundred and fifty-two pages of it, when he was thirteen, just for fun. Anyone who met him found this out in two minutes, maximum. He found Dostoyevsky, and reread portions of *The Idiot*; wondering as he always did, if he was reading about himself.

He had planned to stay for another forty-five minutes, but the man in the sweater vest suddenly popped the heavy door open. "Had enough?" he queried coldly, with nothing in his tone or on his face to indicate that he was talking to a living thing, and not a chair.

"Uuuuuuh, sure," answered Dublin, never having got the hang of the whole sticking-up-for-himself thing, even in something so trivial as this. He put *The Idiot* back, picked up his bag, and left, blushing for some reason. He didn't slacken his pace outside the door, but left the library entirely, turning northward up Academy Street toward the graveyard.

What transpired between the young man and the memory of his father, on the green grass in front of a small grey stone, will remain sacrosanct. It was a holy moment, indescribable, and I could only sully it by trying.

The cemetery gatekeeper, a very old man, had more of a heart than Professor Sweatervest, waiting until Dublin walked out of his own accord. "Thank you," Dublin told him in a shaky voice. He heard the heavy iron gates clang shut behind him. Grateful for the old man's patience, a thought occurred to him. "Sofee. How much do I have left in traveler's credits?"

"Four hundred and ninety-seven credits."

"Please transfer three hundred of them to the nearest Sofee."

"Fingerprint authorization please...done. Credits transferred."

Night was falling. There was a distinct downhill grade as he left the cemetery district, which he was happy for. It made him feel like each step forward now was easier, approved by the universe, a destiny he was embracing.

He had planned his last supper for Happy Food, the all-you-can-eat Chinese buffet. It wasn't too far away; a small place sandwiched between MNG Soccer Supply and Charlie's Drama Studio. Passing in front of MNG's, he saw something through the window that gave him a brilliant idea. Ducking inside, he bought two stadium seat cushions. These, laid open side-by-side, should make any park bench more comfortable. As soon as he had left the store and turned in the direction of Happy Food with his bags, he stopped short, his face blanching in horror.

He had forgotten to use his traveler's credits. He had used his actual account. Anyone with access to it--like his mother--could use this purchase to know exactly where he was.

He stumbled on in a daze. *What's done is done. It's a big city. She probably gave up looking at my account anyway.* He shook it off, walked into the restaurant, and ate enough Chinese Food for five people. The waitress was laughing at him. He left her a big tip, remembering this time to use the untraceable credits.

Between the huge meal, the stress of the clock winding down towards his enlistment, the new stress of wondering if his Mom would find him, and try to stop him, and the uphill climb back to the Park District, he felt more and more nauseous. Suddenly the feeling overwhelmed him, his mouth flooding with saliva. He ducked into a dark alley and threw up. Wiping his chin and looking up from his crouch, he just about cried out--a face, frozen in horror, was staring at him through the gloom. As Dublin peered harder, and his eyes focused, he realized that it was the broken down shell of a robot. Its eyes were wide, and its mouth was open, giving it the appearance of having been shut off mid-scream. *Is this a modern day omen? Like an albatross, or a meteor shower? What does it mean?*

Dub got out fast and headed back up the sidewalk. His stomach was better, but his mind was worse.

That second night was the worst night of his life; a descent into complete and utter madness. What bothered him the most was the thought of his Mother. He had thought that his little State-of-the-Dublin address would be a relief to him, a weight off of him, but instead it was like throwing a grappling hook back into the life he was so desperately trying to leave behind. He became increasingly aware of how hurt his Mother must be. She had worked so hard, through such lonely times, to raise him happy and intact, and he was throwing it all away. He felt like he was condemning them both to death.

You're not fooling me, stupid mind-tricks!

Tuesday night was much colder than Monday night had been, (or maybe the much larger Veterans' Park was just more open to the wind than McBee Park was) and despite the soccer cushions, Dublin tossed and turned constantly on his bench. He almost fell asleep at one point after eleven o'clock, having not slept for thirty-nine hours, but was jarred awake by the (image?) (dream?) (hallucination?) of the emotionless man from the library holding the huge wooden door open, pressuring him to leave everything forever. Picking up his bag to leave like a good boy, he saw that the library behind him was piled high with defunct, rusty robots; and the pile was growing, screams frozen on all their faces like the victims of some ungodly holocaust. He started awake gasping and saw a clock on one of the tall buildings that formed a sort of giant wall across from the park.

He was nine minutes away from being sixteen. Shivering in the cold, alone in the park, he sat up and watched it happen.

A jet flying overhead woke him at twelve-twenty. His head was swimming. One of the twenty or so giant viewscreens on the buildings opposite his bench was finishing up a scrolling message: *"-lin Dunne come home."* Dub sat up in horror. Surely not? He stared, not even blinking, at the screen, but the message didn't come back. Maybe it had scrolled by once; maybe it had scrolled by thirty times. The adrenalin rush of this possible unexpected message to him, and what it might mean, kept him awake for the next three hours. Finally, well after three AM, the peace of thoughtless sleep came to him.

A face...a huge, kind face filled the sky above him...benevolence, mercy, and profound compassion radiated from the beautiful face; the beautiful....hairy face...a strange noise, like a deep whimper of helplessness to save him came from the wonderful...monkey lips? Dublin's eyes opened but the rest of him didn't move a bit. He saw Chiquitita moving away between two skyscrapers.

He woke up at five-nineteen and was done sleeping. Shaking with adrenalin, he grabbed his stuff and started walking.

He located the imposing Greenville MCP building easily. With over two hours to kill, he holed up in a coffee shop across the street. He wasn't really hungry, but forced himself to eat a Danish and drink a coffee. He freshened up to the best of his ability in the coffeehouse bathroom. An unsuspecting patron walked in as Dublin sang loudly: *She broke my heart, and I really showed it/ But look at me now--**HA!**--you'd never know it, now!* He didn't stop or even lower his voice.

This fellow done lost his mind! the other man thought.

That guy thinks I have lost my mind! Dublin thought. They were both right. Coming out of the bathroom, he cleared his table, emptied his bank account into the Sofee of a homeless man who had entered the coffee shop about ten minutes earlier, and was chatting to the poor girl behind the counter, and walked across the street.

The wide, steep granite steps of the MCP building gave him a workout, one he could have done without in his present state. They seemed a little unnecessary, a little exaggerated, like a deliberate final challenge to the suffering.

This?

Do

To

Want

You

Sure

You

Are

may just as well have been chiseled into the facing of each slab in turn on the way up. *Yes, I am sure.* Dublin answered to himself, although he was sweating and trembling and his skin felt electrified and goose-bumpy all over. He tried to summon the inner determination of Raskolnikov, the 'hero' of *Crime and Punishment*, in this daunting and final moment. Of course he was forgetting two very important things: 1) Raskolnikov was a fictional character. 2) What Raskolnikov had determined to do was dastardly in the extreme.

But the thought process worked for Dub, and when the security officer--a real, human one, he noted--unlocked the door at the top of the stairs, he was able to step himself across the threshold, and without any delay, right up to the lady at the counter.

She looked mean. She was an older woman, about his Mom's age, with a jet-black (obviously dyed) poofy hairdo, and a bright green sweater with a little bit of fuzziness to it. It was a pretty shade of green, he thought, but not for a sweater.

His main worry now was the bogus treatment history he had fabricated.

Accessing it on his Sofee with fingers that had never trembled so violently, he was mentally chastising himself: *Stupid, stupid, stupid! Why did I choose 'Dr. Livingstone'?!* (It had been funny to him at the time, that's why). *Anyone with a passing knowledge of nineteenth century African Exploration is going to know I made that up!* But he had read online that the percentage of people turned away because of problems with their treatment records was way down over the last three years. He held his breath.

"I'm--I--I'm here to...to sign up for the MCP." It had sounded much less shaky, and much more confident, in the mirror back home in his bedroom. The green lady was completely unfazed. She launched into her memorized, required speech: "You understand that you must be at least sixteen years of age etc., etc., etc.; that once you initial these documents you are, from that moment until such time as you may die, the property of the United States Government etc. etc. etc., stripped from that moment on of all human rights etc. etc. etc...." Dublin knew it all, and wasn't listening.

The clerk went through the pages of his transcript so fast and so robotically on her viewscreen that there was no way she could be absorbing much of anything from them. She hesitated just long enough on the last page, and just enough of a shadow of a question seemed to cross her face, that Dublin almost peed his pants and very nearly confessed. Then she opened her mouth.

"Aaaaalll"-- relief flooded through Dublin's exhausted system--"right. Just need your prints here...and here...and here...and place your forehead here...congratulations. Now if you will take two steps to your right--no, **your** right--and wait for just a second, Nurse Carey will be right out to take care of you." Dublin did as he was told, in a daze, wondering why the rainbow-colored floor-matting that extended beneath the length of the cold marble counter was so thick and squishy underfoot. Then bursts of electric rainbow color exploded across his eyes, completely obscuring his vision.

Two seconds later, he passed out cold.

5

Laissez-Nous Vivre

"Ro-Ro, bring me a tissue please."

"Coming right up."

Kaywin was looking more alive. Ripping the moustache off his lip had altered the focus of his self-pity. It was still focused on himself, but temporarily more so on his bleeding surface wound, and less on his crippling inner one. His little house robot bounded into view, a single tissue fluttering between his outstretched fingers (and a spare in his belly.) "Thank you." Kaywin took the tissue and applied it to his mouth. Ro-Ro had long ago ceased protesting against his owner's use of 'please' and 'thank you', and sundry other tokens of everyday respect.

"May I recommend a little Bayopeptine for that?"

"Sure. Go ahead."

"I recommend a little Bayopeptine for that." The pleasant little automaton had grown accustomed to Kaywin's droll sense of humor, and cultivated his own bantering response protocol.

"I accept your recommendation," sighed Kaywin, unable to muster a smile just yet, but touched by the robot's effort. "Can you get it please?" Ro-Ro headed into the bathroom. "The apartment looks nice. Thank you. Sorry I trashed it last night." He glanced furtively at the carpet leading down the hallway, where a large stain would have been, if not for the ministrations of the house-bot.

"You are welcome." The robot said warmly, with his very human sounding tone and inflection. He extended the Bayopeptine towards Kaywin, as he had done with the tissue.

Kaywin broached a tender topic as he dabbed the ointment at his tender upper lip. "So it's official. Dr. Bresnahan has cleared me for the MC Program. I just want you to know that I will miss you, and my sister will be very lucky to have you."

Ro-Ro's response was curiously delayed, almost as if he had to collect himself for a brief digital moment. "I am very fond of Ms. Genie. It is I who am the lucky one." There was an awkward moment. "When will I go to her?"

"Tomorrow. Everything's going tomorrow except three micromeals, my toothbrush...a couple other necessities...I'm going down to the MCP first thing Monday morning."

"I wish to express that you have been very good and patient with me, and that I will miss you, Mr. Kaywin."

"Go ahead."

"Don't make me say it again." Kaywin did manage a meager smile this time. "You have suffered much sadness, Mr. Lafontaine. How big of a deal do you want to make this parting between yourself and your robot?"

Pause. "Medium? A medium deal?"

"I, too, am comfortable with that."

With the burning sensation on his lip beginning to subside, he returned his meager attention to the live Paris scene filling up his viewing enclave. There was a jarring burst of static (calculated to command attention) and the preliminary commercial started:

"Paris, eh? Niiiiiice!" *This guy again. Relentless.* There he was, filling the screen in his ridiculous silver suit. *Who buys these things? If you had 7000 credits to spend on a Dizastra 3000, wouldn't you just* **pay** *someone to do your dangerous work?* But there he was, the sandy-grey-haired, charismatically smiling Rich Brandenberg in his latest contraption. *How does this guy find the time? He's supposed to be representing Utah in the Senate...Instead he's running Uno Mundo, the biggest retailer of everything on Earth, shooting commercials apparently constantly, and running for President! I guess when you're the second richest man in the world you can pay a team of thousands to make you look like a superhero...* "Paris is sick! It's the awfullest! I come here whenever I get the chance!" *What is he doing?* He had his right arm and right leg wrapped around some kind of black iron trellis-work; was it part of a gate, maybe a streetlight? He swung back and forth on it playfully, devouring the attention of the cameras. "It's a big city though--you have to come prepared." The viewpoint was panning slowly backward; it was becoming apparent that Brandenberg's feet (literally) were not on the ground. "One minute you're enjoying the view, then whoops! --" The camera suddenly pulled back in a smooth instant to a vantage point a quarter-mile away. "--Not so much!" He was dangling in his silver disaster suit a thousand feet in the air, just below the observation deck of the Eiffel Tower, and yelling toward Kaywin and whoever else had purchased the deluxe Paris Package: "How do you say 'banana peel' en Francais?" A French voice from off-camera answered, but Brandenberg wasn't listening. Now the camera was back in tight on his tan, arrogant, dash-gummedly handsome face. A tourist in khaki shorts and a pink polo shirt plummeted past him, screaming convincingly and still snapping photos with his huge camera. "That guy's vacation is **<u>over!</u>** Finis!" The trillionaire's lack of compassion was also disturbingly convincing.

He turned his head to address someone out of Kaywin's view. "Hey! How do you say 'Geronimo!' in French?"

"Geronimo."

"Really? Geronimo? **GERONIMO!!!!**" He pushed off from the Eiffel Tower and rocketed downward. Kaywin watched, ever so slightly bemused. He didn't have strong feelings either way about this guy, but his commercials weren't the worst. He could hear the crowd on the ground in Paris screaming as the worldwide celebrity free-fell, whistling casually.

"Par-a-...,"

"...chute," sang the presidential hopeful; and Voila! His death-drop was arrested by the instantaneous deployment of a parachute so sheer and light and compact that Kaywin, who had done many jumps of his own during his years in the Air Corps, was truly impressed. The large crowd, which had started to gather an hour earlier as the shoot was being set up, broke into cheers. They parted just enough for the giant of industry to waft in, landing on his feet while reading a real paperback copy of "The Stranger" by existential French author Albert Camus. He shrugged, tossing the book backwards over his shoulder, and a scrum broke out as thirty people scrambled for possession of the holy memento.

"Wait!" He had to shush the crowd to get his next bit out.

"Wait! You haven't seen the awfullest part! Parachute come back!" The chute retracted into the back of his suit so whippingly fast that the eye almost didn't catch it. A young girl behind him cried out and a fresh cut on her cheek began to bleed. "Sorry Sweetheart" said Brandenberg with zero emotion. The exchange was easy to miss, but Kaywin caught it. *Why did they leave* **that** *in there?* he wondered. "Folks, that's a **twelve ounce parachute! Lightest ever invented! Three hundred and forty grams!** Standard issue with the Dizastra 3000!" The crowd began to applaud again, so much so that Brandenberg had to yell his finishing lines: "**Si je trouve un moyen de mourir dans cette chose que je vous permettra de savoir!**" he provoked them in clunky French. Then in English: "**If I find a way to die in this thing--**" the crowd joined in, nearly drowning him out--**I'll let you know!**"

There was another split-second burst of static, then the original Paris Street scene once again brightened Kaywin's living room. This time the perspective was dynamic--the camera was attached to the head of a rental bot, and it was sort of idling and stretching, feeling out its range first left, then right, as it awaited Kaywin's instructions.

"Use your Sofee 46 or Sofee 47 to navigate your Francobot. Here. I'll show you how." The soothing female voice, and the subtitles on the wall, showed him how to move the robot forward, backward, sideways, etc. This was his first premium travel package, with the controllable, walking--well, rolling--droid. *Hmmm. Not bad!* A woman in jeans, heels, and a little grey leather jacket walked by briskly, and Kaywin was hit with a wave of perfume. *What the--oh yeah, I forgot how* **premium** *the premium packages are!* The men who had installed the program had clipped tiny devices to the four air-vents in his living room; these clip-ons were able to digitally interpret the smells that the Franco-bot was experiencing, and, with their sophisticated little chemical banks, deliver these aromas with impressive accuracy into Kaywin's apartment. The technology wasn't perfect; there was a little bit of a delay... when he turned to look behind him at the dingy back alley he was still drinking in the woman's charming fragrance, and when he turned back to look at the retreating woman he got a distinctly garbagey smell. Rolling forward tentatively onto the sidewalk, he was able to pick up the distant, more stable and pleasing aroma of multiple Parisian bakeries. The speakers around him and over his head furthered the transporting effect of the program with all the sounds of the big city; footfalls on the cobblestones, shop doors opening and shutting, conversation in many languages, the mesmerizing low electric hum of the thick, fast-moving traffic...even pigeons flapping on the window-sills above him.

Working his fingers on the face of his 47, he gradually got the feel of steering the robot from his couch thirty-four hundred miles away. His starting point was just outside a little market. The actual French newspaper box on his carpet was the last in a line of four on the sidewalk in front of the small shop. The mime crouched in front of it as if guarding it. *Would he pretend to punch me if I tried to get a newspaper?*

He set off leftways down the sidewalk, in the direction that the perfumed lady had come from. Getting more and more comfortable, he extended first one hand, then both, in front of his electronic eyes; flexing the fingers in the encroaching spring twilight. He passed a beautiful bakery, and the fabulous smell of it made him wish he were really there. It was just like he remembered, minus his wife and daughter. He shook off the fleeting thought and continued on.

A few hundred feet down, the scenery turned a bit industrial, and grey, and a little less charming, so he did a one-eighty and headed back in the direction he had come from. He was looking to his right at a women's clothing store when something caught his attention from the bus shelter in front of it, to his left. There, framed in by the artless structure, against a backdrop of scores of brightly colored vehicles whizzing by in a sort of rainbow-blur, were three homeless people. They were two older men, and a heart-breakingly young girl, maybe fourteen, tops. They were all looking at him and laughing. The girl spoke.

"Vous avez l'argent, voyageur du monde?"

"Sofee, what is she saying?"

"'Do you have any money, world-traveler?'" answered his left wrist.

Kaywin badly wanted to help. The girl, visually, resembled his little Victoria not at all. She was shabby, dirty, unkempt, but still so beautiful and full of potential. And **every** little girl reminded him of **his** little girl. He would gladly have transferred a little money to her.

But this young vagabond didn't even have a Sofee on her wrist. On top of that, he hadn't figured out how to make his Franco-bot **speak** just yet, and it was hard to do under the sudden pressure. But he had an idea.

He turned his robot-head forward again. He started back up the sidewalk toward that fabulous bakery. He was rolling much faster now, spurred on by the thought of what the homeless trio must have seen as his rude, silent dismissal. As he sped along, he experimented with making the droid talk, finally succeeding. A couple of passers-by turned to look at the robot going a little too fast and shouting "Un, deux, trois! Un, deux, trois!"

As he mounted a small incline, the bakery hove into view. Kaywin's heart sank, as, from a distance, he saw the proprietor stretching out and locking a flexible iron grate over the long window. No! He remembered fully now that Paris was five hours ahead of Manchester, and that businesses were beginning to close up for the day there. He accelerated past the bakery, getting the Franco-bot up to a borderline-reckless speed. "Sofee--how close is the next bakery?"

"Cinq-cente metre sur la droite."

"En Anglais s'il vous plait!"

"D'accord...Five-hundred meters on the right."

As he sped onward, he started singing "Alouette" loudly, so people would hear him and get of the way. In about two minutes he was there, at Montambeault Boulangerie. Good news: they were open! Bad news: there were two hungry-looking people in front of him at the window. The owner, a clean-shaven older man, intimidating despite the white button-up smock and poofy white hat, was taking the order of the Japanese man at the front of the line. Shockingly, he cut the man off mid-sentence and pointed accusingly at Kaywin's Francobot.

"Vous! Vous partez!" ("You! Go away!")

Kaywin was caught completely off-guard. "Mais...mais je...veux seulement aux besoins a' trois baguettes s'il vous plait?" ("But I want only needs three baguettes please?")

"Je ne te sers pas plus!" ("I do not serve you anymore!")

"But my credit--Aaagh, Sofee, help me; how do I say 'but my credit is fine?' "

"Mais mons credit est tres bien."

"Mais mons credit est tres bien!" The baker was once again trying to take the order of the Japanese man…there was a pause. Now he was putting fruit tarts in a box, and hoping the robot would take a hint and go… **"Mais mons credit est tres bien!"**

"Allez!" ("Go!")

"Pourquoi ne pas tout le temps que vous servez robot?" ("Why you not all time serve robot?")

"Je sers robots! J'aime robots! Mais pas vous! Pas numerote cent-et-quatorze! Votre argent ne passe jamais par! Allez maintenant!" ("I serve robots! I love robots. But not you! Not number 114! Your money never goes through! Go now!")

"Sofee, what is this nutjob saying?" She hit him with the translation. Meanwhile, Monsieur Montambeault was beginning to rage, spewing vitriol for the small, rubber-necking crowd to hear, while bagging croissants for the woman in front of Kaywin's droid. Kaywin didn't process all of the angry French words, but he got the gist, picking out a few like "ugly Americans"; "bull-headed", "lazy entitlement"… Good grief; he just wanted to feed some homeless people… his blood began to boil…the stupid baguettes were piled up in a basket on the counter right next to the sputtering Frenchman. "Sofee! Transfer fifty Euros to this man's account."

"But fifty Euros is more than five point one-four times the cost of three baguettes at Monsieur Montambeault's posted price--"

"Just do it."

"Done."

"Monsieur!" But the inflammated baker ignored him pro-
digiously, parceling petit fours into a pretty little box, hands
shaking with rage. **"Monsieur!"**

"Go! Or I call the police!" The Frenchman had switched
to English.

"Monsieur Montambeault! I--"

"Oh, you know my name so I MUST sell you bread!"

Kaywin struggled to dampen his own rage, and tried
to adopt a more conciliatory tone. He really wanted to get
food to the homeless girl. She was laughing when she had
asked him for money, but she wasn't kidding. She was hungry, scared, and alone. Her begging-partners were old men;
unfit companions for a thirteen or fourteen--his mental train
was starting to come off its tracks; he battled to not imagine
Victoria's face on the young lady--for a thirteen or fourteen
year-old girl..."I have transferred fifty Euros to your account.
Will you PLEASE give me three baguettes?"

**"No, you THINK you have transferred fifty Euros,
but I promise you it did not go through! Now, LAST
time, you GO! GO or I will call the police!"** And that's
when Kaywin Lafontaine completely lost his mind.

He put both of his robot hands up into his viewscreen and flexed them twice. Then he charged the counter, toward the baguettes.

Concentrating hard on the fine motor coordination of the Franco-bot's hands, he completely forgot to brake. The four hundred pound droid slammed into the counter with force. There was an avalanche of delicious baked goods onto the sidewalk. A million pigeons swarmed as if this moment had been prophesied in pigeon-lore; every pigeon in Paris seemed to have been waiting close at hand. Kaywin's enraged robot hands grabbed two fresh baguettes and promptly snapped them in half. With tremendous focus and a million hours of gaming experience, he lightened his touch and success-fully poached a third. The realistic flapping of pigeon wings filled his small clean apartment, but he didn't have a second to reckon for their safety: he hurled the bot backwards, into a three-point turn, and careened forward down the sidewalk through a perfect storm of grey feathers. Behind him, he could hear the baker going off like a French Mt. Vesuvius.

Now it was time to see what this droid was made of. Hug-

ging the stolen baguette close to his mechanical chest, and bel-
lowing "**I SUMMON THE FORCES OF NATURE** (the
pigeons?) **AND OF SCIENCE!!!!!** (the bot?)" he opened
the throttle fully and exploded down the sidewalk. He didn't
know why he yelled this, and in fact had no memory of yelling it. Screams of alarm spread in a tight wave before him in
his rapid progress, as he parted the crowd like the bow of a
mighty ship parts the ocean. Whatever the credit-processing
problems were with Franco-bot number 114, he made up for
it in pure electric speed.

But, holy cow, the baker was alarmingly fast. His poofy
hat almost flew off his head (fortunately it was pinned) as
he shot through the wake created by the barreling robot. He
seemed to have lost very little of the speed he was blessed
with when he represented France in the 2086 Olympics. As
Kaywin (virtually) approached a relatively clear stretch of
sidewalk, he took a calculated risk and spun his head around
to gauge the pastry-artist's progress. To his horror, he saw
the baker only fifteen yards behind him, and gaining. When
he tried to rotate his camera forward again, it stuck, just for
a second…then he was facing frontward again, and had zero
time to react as he blasted into a sidewalk cafe table. This table
went flying, knocking over two others. A beautiful coq au vin,
still steaming, was propelled through the air into the force-
field separating pedestrians from the street traffic. It was so
perfectly prepared, and so tender, that it rebounded in pieces
behind the zooming Franco bot. This happenstance nearly
saved Kaywin's bacon, as the right sneaker of the sprinting
baker landed on a greasy wing, and threw him almost disas-
trously off-balance. Flailing wildly, and hop-stepping twice,

he recovered, having lost almost no momentum. Kaywin's heart was pounding and his chest heaving as though it were his actual body being put through these paces.

The street was still new to Kaywin, but when he raced past a charcuterie on his left, with the 2086 thousand-meter silver-medalist ten yards behind him, he remembered encountering a severe dip in the road just **before** it on the way up, meaning it would be just **after**--

Suddenly he was airborne. For a full, strange second he lost the sound and the feel of the droid's tread on the cobblestones, then there was a jolting crash and he was back in business. He didn't know it for another fifteen seconds, but the baker had not fared so well. The dip caught him off guard; he lost his footing and ate cobblestone, hard. A small crowd of concerned Parisians gathered around him instantly, preventing the proud, but defeated and utterly winded man from picking up the chase.

Kaywin, unaware that the heat was off him, hurtled the bot across a narrow street. Out of nowhere, a green pill-shaped car screamed by. The robot's left arm went flying. *Great!* A pigeon swooped down and pecked at it.

Now the sidewalk was much less crowded, as he once again approached the less scenic, more industrial zone. He took the risk once again of checking behind him, and found to his enormous relief that his impressive rival had finally given up the chase. He slowed the bot, then braked completely as he realized he was at the bus shelter where the girl and the two old men had been ten minutes ago. To his horror, he realized that they were gone. In their place, a frumpy, grumpy-looking older woman waited, over-bundled against the modest chill of the approaching twilight. She turned and looked disapprovingly at Franco-bot 114. Her potato-ish face did not exactly invite questioning, but Kaywin was desperate: "Ou sont les hommes qui n'ont pas de maisons?" ("Where are the men who have no homes?") The old lady's face contracted with instant disgust and exasperation, as if the robot had been trying to convince her for twenty minutes to come help him throw rocks at cats.

"Les hommes qui n'ont pas de maisons? Dans la rue, bien sur!" ("The men who have no homes? On the street of course!") She spread her arms to indicate the street, and Kaywin, following the sweep of her right hand, saw the homeless girl thirty yards down, on the opposite side, and making progress toward the factory district. He hauled it to the nearest crosswalk, where he fortunately had to wait for only ten or so seconds before the light changed and he and a dense little pack of six humans could cross the boulevard. Rolling up on the sidewalk opposite, having advanced to the head of the little cluster, he turned and followed the homeless girl, now barely in view. Without resorting to the ridiculous speeds he had when the baker was on his tail, he managed to close the gap between them. As he drew close, he shouted plaintively, "Jeune fille! Pauvre jeune fille!" ("Young lady! Poor young lady!") She paused and looked behind her, but did not suspect that it was the broke-down robot hailing her. She turned right and headed down a side street. Kaywin's Franco-bot reached the spot eight seconds later. He turned it and continued after the unfortunate girl…for five yards.

"You have reached the limit of the Uno Mundo Virtual Travel Territory. Please turn around," said the soothing voice.

Kaywin dropped his wrist in disgust, utterly spent. With his weathered hands by his sides he stayed put, watching the 'pauvre jeune fille' fade into the distance, completely aware of the metaphor playing out, and hypnotized by the magnitude of his sadness. "Never, ever will I see Victoria again; my little baby girl…" He was crying and shaking, vibrating like a low-voltage wire trying to handle ten times its load--it just wasn't sustainable, and, when he exploded, he worried about the damage he might do, possibly to completely innocent strangers. He understood that it was not only okay, but **necessary**, to let these tears out; he just wished he could look at a calendar a year down the road, or four years, or fifteen years, and see the day marked on it when the tears would dry up, and he would smile from his soul again--not the grim, forced smile he had constructed to get people off his back--to send them away at least satisfied that he could drag himself through another miserable day, and still be in the world tomorrow…not **that** smile, but a natural smile born easily of happiness and peace.

So he sobbed like a baby, until the oblivious young homeless Parisian girl turned a corner in the middle distance and disappeared from view. He gave himself a good full minute after that. He wiped the tears with his rough hands. The skin of his cheeks and around his eyes was perpetually sore and red from this 'weakness' of his. With his eyes still fixed forward on the darkening Paris side street, he gently lifted the ridiculous beret off his head (as if it were someone else's head, and they were asleep, and he were trying to steal it without waking them up) and used it to dab at his tears. It was a cheap, coarse Uno Mundo product and wasn't much better than his hands.

"Sofee--Seychelles please." The scene changed; Paris-in-bloom faded. There was a second and a half of darkness then it felt like the sun was rising in his little apartment (though a quick glance behind him would have shown him that the *actual* snow outside his *actual* window was still coming down hard and fast). All around him was the most beautiful beach in the world. The tide was in, pounding the warm white sand. Elegant palm trees shaded the view on either side. Pretty far away somewhere to the left there were two people frolicking together in the surf, young and apparently in love. *Good for them* he thought, and, emotionally drained from Paris, he chose not to spend another thought on them.

Kaywin liked the Seychelles Island Beach, halfway around the world in the Indian Ocean, because it was so bright and dreamy...

Unfortunately, the program recognized that he came here often and punished him for it by making him sit through three commercials, knowing that he would stick around for his beach time.

He had seen the first one, for 'Air Paradisio,' but he didn't like it because it was alarmingly invasive. It had accessed his personal files and created a holographic doppelganger of himself. That was bad enough, but what really put him off was the stupid girlfriend the system had manufactured for him, just months after his records had listed him as 'widowed'... She was pretty to look at, sure, but she was tan and giggly and stupid. She was no Nadine. Plus, he didn't really walk like that, did he? Real Kaywin on the couch turned his head away while holo-Kaywin cavorted disgustingly on-screen with Barbie. After that was a Wowsi-Cola commercial he hadn't seen before, which wasn't all that gripping but did make him thirsty. Or maybe he was just dehydrated from crying. And then came Brandenberg.

He didn't even wait for the Wowsi-Cola ad to finish; there was still thirst-quenching refreshment spouting out of a mini-volcano on the beach as the bluntly pointed crown of his silver body suit appeared walking straight up out of the ocean. He strolled right up to the camera and flipped the glass facing of his helmet open.

"I love all the beaches of the world--obviously!" (He indicated his perfectly tanned and grinning face with both silver-mitted hands) "--but is this not the awfullest?" This commercial had come out a couple of months ago; Kaywin had seen it several times. "Love the Seychelles! It only took me about forty-five minutes to walk here." Then he responded to a question no one had asked. "Yeah, I *walked*, man! My gorgeous undersea condo is only about five leagues offshore. Whoops! Sorry! That's some heavy nautical lingo I'm throwing at you; a 'league' is the equivalent of about three miles. My bad! So yeah, bro; I straight up walked. My Dizastra 3000 suit has boosters that pushed me up to about twenty-four miles per hour--**underwater**! Best ε7000 credits I ever spent! I tell you what else, Bro: just between you and me--you need to check out these condos! Jewels-Vernia! A mile beneath the Indian Ocean, the first fully functioning, luxury undersea community in the world, **dude**, my **favorite**--I have twenty, or twenty-three beautiful homes all around the world, and this is my absolute **fave**! Imagine living inside a four thousand square foot glass bubble, with crystal clear water above you, around you, and below you! Amenities galore--you can't get this kind of service at the 'Rico Suave' in Manhattan! I tell you what. You want to see my place? I'm going back right now. I just came back for this." He bent over, disappearing for a second off-camera, then popped back up with a huge pina colada in his hand. He slurped on it obnoxiously, then shut his visor. Unfortunately, his voice was still audible through the thick glass: "Tell your 47 if you want to tag along!" Then, turning his back on the cameras, the smug ubiquitor headed back into the crashing surf. "I should warn you," he yelled over the tumult "we will be experiencing pressures of up to twenty-two hundred pounds per square inch! No problem for the Dizastra 3000! If I find a way to die in this thing, I'll let you know! Brandenberg '28!'"

Kaywin had let his mind glaze over during the vapid commercials, but he returned to Earth now.

He let the sunshiny vista, deserted at last, fill his consciousness. The regular crashing rhythm of the waves reassured him that the world was so much bigger than him and his tragedy. The eternal salty surf didn't care if there was a private wedding happening on the beach, or if ten thousand soldiers were storming it. Kaywin leaned way, far back into the couch. The footrest emerged from what had looked like white leather seamlessness as he lay back and inhaled. He didn't try to synchronize his breathing with the waves, but he did remark, as he usually did, that they became similar in pace. His mind began to empty. This was a blessing.

Suddenly the stupid newspaper box and the French Mime caught his eye, crouching there ludicrously eight thousand miles out of place. If he had been a young man, he would have given himself a small laugh by getting up and 'rescuing' them from the rising tide. Instead, he lay back and fell asleep.

He was not young anymore, and never would be again.

6

The Promised Land

Houston, Texas US of A
Tuesday, March 26, 2126...9:47 AM

The already very slender thirty-something year-old man was wearing probably the skinniest skinny suit ever attempted. It was figuratively plastered to his slight body, buttons straining everywhere, white shirt cuffs extending seven inches past the inadequate grey coat sleeves. It forced him to walk very stiffly, like an older model robot, though the word 'forced' isn't really fair to the suit--he could have worn whatever he wanted, as the acting President of the MCP. "What are you telling me?!" he said angrily to the face on his wall.

"The parking lot where Ms. Hopkins is camping out is not ours. We own all of the original university buildings, and two of the lots, but we lease the other four from a Mr. Nebraska..."

Silence... "From a **what**?"

"A Mr. Brandon Nebraska."

"Oh. I thought you meant, like, the winner of the Mr. Nebraska pageant. Speak more clearly."

"I'm sorry sir."

"So what does this mean for our situation?"

"It means it's up to Mr. Nebraska--Mr. Brandon Nebraska, to decide to evict her."

"How much does he want?"

"Sir?"

"How many **credits** does Brandon **want?**" Acting President Beauregard's drawl grew even angrier and more effeminate.

"We haven't contacted him yet. I--"

"Goldang, Mr. Simmons, then why are we talking?"

"I felt like we needed your okay before we approached him with any offer of financial compensation."

"Well I'm just flattered as all get out!" Beauregard blustered, out of habit, the habit of not wanting to appear weak. He knew, of course, that Simmons was behaving perfectly reasonably. "Call him this morning--now--and find out what he's going to do about Ms. Hopkins. Don't mention compensation unless he waffles." He glanced wistfully at his breakfast, rapidly getting cold on his desk.

"Yes, sir."

"Simmons!"

"Yes, sir?"

"We have new recruits rolling up in here in eight days; our biggest class ever. I want Ms. Hopkins out of here by then. Her little display is the last thing these brave men and women need to see on their first day."

"Yes, sir!"

"Peace out." Simmons' face faded from his wall, replaced gradually by softly undulating waves of color, all earth tones (who knew there were so many shades of brown?) broken up here and there with a little burst of sunset orange, saddle-bag grey, or dingy cactus-green. This hypnotic moving desert art-piece was given voice to, perfectly, by the twanging ambient cowboy music that accompanied it. The acting President drew deeply from his vapor cigarette and sat down stiffly at his giant mahogany desk to eat.

Houston, Texas US of A
Tuesday, March 26, 2126…9:51 AM (four minutes later)

Acting Meaningful Conclusion Program President Vincent Beauregard was still drenching his Awfuls in Vaple Syrup when his viewing wall rang **again**. (Awfuls, despite the name, were actually quite good. They were a sort of simulated waffle: three quarters of an ounce of vegetable fiber puffed out with so much air that it wound up resembling a five-ounce waffle. As to the name, the word 'awful' of course didn't mean 'awful' anymore. It had been ironically twisted in street-tough parlance to mean 'wonderful' or 'awesome'. It was the latest in the long history of bad words gone good, which twenty-second century linguists traced back a hundred and forty years, to when 'wicked' suddenly meant 'awesome', and 'bad' suddenly meant 'awesome', and 'sick'---well, you get the picture. In fact, street-toughs had almost run out of words to describe anything as *not* awesome. And don't get me started on the Vaple Syrup---this was in a maple-leaf-shaped spray can, and was just supposed to be a way to use *less* maple syrup, but not the way that Vincent Beauregard used it. He was just putting down the spray-can and lifting his fork when Simmons rang.

"So sorry to disturb you sir. I know you're trying to eat."

"I'm not **trying** anymore. I'm **eating.** He angrily gave the stack of Awfuls one more spritz. Grabbing one off the top, he folded it four ways, and stuffed the entire breakfast treat into his mouth. He felt the man on the viewscreen gawking at him. "Waaf d'yoo waaan?"

"It's about Mr. Nebraska---Mr. Brandon Nebraska, sir. He is out of town and I can't seem to get a clear timetable for his return…"

"Waaf d'they say?" Crumbs flew from his packed mouth.

"I got "June" from one guy, and "July" from another…"

"Jooo or **JUWY**?!"

"Of next year."

Beauregard stood up and wheeled in his skinny suit, and, presenting his back fully to Simmons he held one finger aloft, holding Simmons hostage while he finished chewing. Turning back around he wiped his thin, syrupy lips on a napkin. He grabbed the Vaple Syrup and sprayed at the stack of Awfuls again, holding the nozzle down for fifteen, twenty, twenty-five seconds, then shaking it and slapping the spritz out of it as it sputtered to profound emptiness. He finally glanced back at the screen and gave Simmons in the legal department some direction.

"Pursue other options. Immediately."

~

Manchester, New Hampshire
Monday, March 25, 2126...6:00 AM

The day of reckoning was a strange exercise for Kaywin. The entire morning leading up to the moment of 'surrender' at the MCP was a marvelous, and at the same time terrible display of human will. It started with his alarm going off at 6:00 AM. He had managed to sleep, some, except for being awakened at 2:33 by his horrible recurring nightmare. After an hour or so of nervous quaking under the blankets, he had fallen back asleep, and was mercifully out cold at 5:59, and yet, when the beeping began, his arm exploded out of the bedclothes as if he were catching a fly, or punching a very bad man in the face. From that moment on he kept his nerve-wracked body at all times one step ahead of his mind. While he was pulling his pants on, he was wondering if he should hit the snooze button. While he was brushing his teeth, he was thinking about putting his pants on. As he instructed his coffee maker to make his coffee, he was surprised to realize that he had brushed his teeth. Poor Kaywin knew his own strengths and weaknesses. He knew that if he let his mind catch up to what his body was doing, the questions would start, the reality would set in, and he would become much more afraid than he already was, and the good thing that he was doing would be put off for another day. And another day. And another. If it wasn't today, he knew that day would not come. The instinct of self-preservation, so insulting to the god-forsaken, would seize the reins of his pathetic destiny. It wouldn't care if his mouth ever smiled again, as long as he was stuffing food in it to stay alive.

If he could just guide himself like a marionette through the simple steps of his morning routine, into the car, where the destination was already programmed, out of the car, into the clinic (fingers crossed there would be no line) and through the five minute process of registration and identification--then, **then** he knew, he could exhale fully for the first time in four years and eight days.

The next thing he knew, he was at the MCP office on Elm Street, saying "I understand" to the scar-faced man behind the cold granite counter, and submitting his fingerprints and retinas for ID.

Kaywin was tingling from head to toe--oddly enough, even a little **above** his head and **beyond** his toes. He was grinning, but by goodness it was not a pleasant smile to behold. He was done with it--**done with it**!

He was led to a room where a doctor came in. He was told to strip naked. He was so unbelievably preoccupied that he forgot to even be self-conscious. When he looked at the floor a moment later, his clothes were gone. A government-issue sky-blue jumpsuit was neatly folded on the table, with matching boots. He was a ward of the state.

Ironically, now that the clock was ticking down toward his death, he finally, for the first time since his boyhood, felt the miracle of breathing in and out, flexing his fingers, furrowing his brow... He was engulfed in sensational bliss; it was just as spectacular and ethereal standing on this cold floor at this moment as it had been watching fireworks for the first time when he was five, or tasting chocolate for the first time, or falling in love with his wife...

He didn't hear the doctor telling him to lie down on the

table, and yet he was lying down on the table. The doctor confirmed that Kaywin had been sterilized (after Victoria's birth), then messed with his ears for a minute. Then he spoke into his Sofee. "Can you hear me, Mr. Lafontaine?"

"Yes." Kaywin had avoided the ear implants on principle for years. He had been sure that at some point down the road, these would be hijacked by advertising just as everything else in the world had been, and then there would be no peace from the literal voices in his head. It didn't matter now!

He put on his blue jumpsuit and boots, like the voice in his ears told him to do.

When the doctor left and a handsome nurse led him out (he wouldn't have thought the man was handsome yesterday, but today, well, what the heck) he felt the absolute majesty of every step, like it was in slow motion. He felt the biology of the muscles and tendons stretching and flexing in his feet, the beauty and artistry of his own form walking, even the novelty of striding upright, as if ten minutes ago he had monkey-walked on hands and feet out of Lascaux cave in Southern France into the bright sunlight of the twenty-second century.

Everything from this point on was a bit of a mystery. For a couple of years he had researched the MCP; what MCs had accomplished publicly, what they were **rumored** to have accomplished; how long they survived on average (ten months and three days); if they made it past the average, how soon were they guaranteed their "meaningful conclusion" (within two years, maximum)... But in a day and age where information was taken in like oxygen, there was teasingly little knowledge of the program's inner workings available. This was understandable, he supposed, since no one had ever joined the

MCP and lived to tell about it...

His attention was caught by an unfamiliar glow on his 47. As if in a dream, he raised his left wrist slowly to eye level. A display of numbers on a black background had taken over the entire screen. The numbers were moving, but he was too dazed to register their meaning, and too content just now at the complete relinquishment of all worldly responsibility to wonder about it.

$$17543:45:38$$

$$17543:45:37$$

$$17543:45:36$$

etc., etc., etc....the screen read.

Hmm. He would figure it out when the time came.

Over the firm grey carpet they walked, old white plaster walls gliding by. Kaywin relaxed his neck and let his head back slowly, taking soothement in the passing deeply inset ceiling lights, one by one. "What happens now?" He heard a man's voice mumble. About two seconds passed before he realized that he himself had spoken the words. The nurse half-turned and half-smiled and said:

"Physical prep work.... health status, mental status, brain function...that kind of thing." They were turning left into a room. "You won't be defusing any bombs or racing any moon cruisers today. Sit on the table pleeeease..." his voice kind of trailed away as he entered some numbers on an old-timey keypad on the wall. "The doctor will be here in just a minute."

"Thank you."

This was the point in a doctor's visit where the nurse would typically leave, and the patient would flip through *Sports Illustrated* or *Journal Robotica* on his phone. But to Kaywin's surprise, as the door slid shut, the nurse took a seat on the couch. He unfurled his laptop and began working on some form or the other.

Oh, thought Kaywin--*I get it. If someone is crazy enough to sign up for this, they are probably too crazy to be left alone...smart.* He wondered how many millions of credits' worth of sensitive medical equipment had been destroyed before this minor adjustment had been made. And of course, it was fair to assume that sometimes people would change their minds at this point and make a run for it.

"Alright..." said the nurse, eyes moving left to right across the words on his screen. He had more of the blond-haired, tan-skinned surfer boy look than Kaywin was used to seeing in downtown Manchester, NH. The first tingling adrenaline rush was subsiding, and he was once again noticing things that were not directly attached to himself. "Your case history looks legit. Sorry to hear about your wife and daughter. That's terrible. I think I remember hearing about that..."

"Thank you." Ouch. He should have stayed snuggled up in his own head.

"It stinks that you waited the full four years--you know they changed it to **two** years, like two weeks ago..."

"Yeah, but I had everything timed out for March 25th. It would have been a lot of trouble to move everything back two weeks."

"True that. Same difference anyway; you would have wound up in the same class."

"Class?" It was kind of a sunny term, hinting more at self-improvement than self-destruction. "How does that work?"

"Oh--" he seemed mildly surprised that Kaywin didn't know--"It's quarterly. Everyone who joined up in January, February, and March of 2126 will be in the same 'class'."

"And is it...like, regional?"

"Nope. It's one big national class. You'll start in Houston, all together, on April third. By the end of the first month of the second quarter--the end of April--you will all be deployed to wherever you're going. So by the end of April, you will know what you're doing and where you are going to do it. Unless it's some crazy spywork. Then you might not even know your own name!"

Kaywin's head was swimming with questions, now that he had someone cornered who seemed to actually have some knowledge on the subject, and a willingness to share it! *When will I leave for Houston? How will I get there? Will there be a snack on the flight? Where will I sleep tonight? How many Goners make up a 'class'?* He grabbed one question from the stream of his consciousness, like a bear grabbing a salmon out of a stream.

"Where will I sleep tonight?"

The helpful nurse made a face like a monkey and blew the desert-hued bangs out of his eyes. "There's a room for you upstairs, and a common area where your meals will be served, and where you can hang out with the other five--" There was a courtesy knock on the door, but before either Kaywin or the nurse could say 'come in', it slid open and the doctor entered discourteously.

"Don't believe a word Richard says," he said loudly, with a hint of arrogance. "Lies, all lies, everything that comes out of his mouth."

Kaywin was thrown into momentary confusion, accepting the doctor's hand in a weird, limp horizontal shake. Then, by the physician's smile, and the nurse's forced laugh, he recognized this as playful banter. It was a concern to him that the doctor who now held his future in his off-puttingly soft hands was so out-of-tune with the mood of the room.

"I'm just kidding, just kidding!" Suddenly his mood changed from clowning to menacing. "Seriously--what have you told him? You didn't tell him about the top-secret laser pulse mega gun under Boston Harbor, did you? Riiiiiiiichaaaaard?" Oh, this guy was a real peach. "Now get out of here before I recommend **you** for the program!" Tact? Anyone? A little tact please? Eventually poor Richard, who deep-down found Dr. Finney as un-hilarious as Kaywin did, was able to weasel out of the room, leaving the fledgling MC alone with the physician/comedian.

Everything about Kaywin that could be tested was now tested, mentally, physically, at rest and then under duress. Blood, heart, lungs, brain, synapses, reaction time, endurance, hearing, vision etc. etc., ad infinitum. All the while, the toad-like Dr. Finney prattled on with the most tired, banal, unoriginal attempts at humor. It dawned on Kaywin halfway through the three and a half hour session that this might actually be part of the testing. A little social component. How would the patient do working in close quarters with someone who thought they were hysterical, but were not? How many knock-knock jokes before the patient snapped? Kaywin passed the test, if it were a test, mainly by tuning the doctor out....

...and tuning back in, he realized, finally, that Dr. Finney was done with him. "Everything checks out fine, Mr. Lafontaine. Richard will be here in a second to take you upstairs. I just want to take a moment while we are waiting--" the doctor's unexpected serious tone was catching Kaywin off guard--"to thank you in advance for your service to America. I have no doubt that, in your physical and mental condition, and with your military background, you will achieve wonderful things in the Program." Kaywin waited in vain for the punchline.

"Thank you..." The doctor extended his hand to him, horizontally like the last time. Not relishing the idea of another weird, limp handshake, but not wanting to be rude, he accepted it. But he withdrew his hand instantly as if he had been shocked. The tactless doctor had buzzed him unpleasantly with one of those stupid little devices, and was now laughing hysterically.

"You should have seen your face! Ha ha ha ha!" He leaned back against the sink for support. *Your face should have seen my fist,* Kaywin thought. But at forty-six years old, he had met with, and survived, many imbeciles and their alarming irregularities. And fortunately for everyone, the door now slid open, and Nurse Richard, who had to work with this guy every day, came in. He led Kaywin out, back into the belly of the two hundred and fifty year-old building.

"What's up with that guy?" he asked the pleasantly normal assistant, as they went further down the hallway. Richard turned back to look at him as they walked.

"Oh, did he get you with the buzzer?"

"Yeah."

"We hid it from him a while ago but he got a new one. Sorry, dude." They came to the end of the corridor, to an imposing steel door with a sophisticated security system. It was easy to see that the other side of this heavy door would be the outer limit of Kaywin's domain for the next few days. Richard went through about six steps to get it unlocked--Kaywin hoped there wasn't a fire while he was here! It clicked open at last and the nurse led him through. The door shut weightily, echoing up and down the stairwell in front of them.

Unlike the fully modernized MCP offices they had left behind, the stairs, and the apartments they led to, looked a lot like they must have two hundred years ago. The building's interior wasn't so much restored as it was functionally maintained. The aspect was pleasing to Kaywin, transporting him to a time when professional doctors didn't hand-buzz high-strung patients. Besides, he liked feeling connected to old times through old places and things.

Everything was oversized (as if people had been like nine feet tall in 1876) and open, with high ceilings, wooden banisters, thick wooden moldings, and rosy plaster walls. The musky aroma of antiquity prevailed, even though everything was clean. So clean, in fact, that it looked like five people had been cooped up here for weeks with little else to do **but** clean. The nurse and the newest Goner ascended the carpeted steps to the second level. Afternoon light streamed in from the large window on the landing halfway up. The feeling of peace and serenity that had begun to calm Kaywin's addled brain was put on hold for a moment when the iron bars over the milky panes of glass reminded him of where he was and what he was doing. They continued upward toward the sounds of a quiet conversation, and the clinking of forks and knives on plates. They went through a door on the second floor landing, and entered a sort of common area, where five motley Goners were lunching. Everything stopped suddenly for a second when the newcomer appeared; five mildly surprised faces turning to assess him. "Kaywin, this will be your little family, for the next week at least. Everybody, this is Kaywin Lafontaine."

The apparent leader of their little pack pushed his chair back with a rumbling squeal, and got up with enough haste to ensure Kaywin that he was welcome, very welcome here. He was a clean-cut, fairly short man, but seemed confident and comfortable as he extended his hand to the newbie. "Hi, I'm Vance," he said, and Kaywin was gratified at the firmness and non-buzziness of the handshake.

One thing Kaywin had noticed in the years since his loss was that he no longer seemed able to control the....bizarre-itude...of his thoughts. So now, as he was shaking this man's hand and saying the words 'Pleased to meet you', he was actually thinking *'How could a man with such astoundingly perfect hair want to kill himself?'* These little brain-whimsies were a little unsettling, but he shook it off and refocused his attention on the entirety of the man in front of him.

"Vance," he re-stated with conviction, committing the name to memory. The others remained seated, which was fine; he wasn't a visiting dignitary; he walked around the circular table and shook all of their hands in turn. Lunch had just started, and he was pleasantly surprised to note that a place was set for him, with a chicken leg, white rice and broccoli steaming in welcome. Richard smiled blandly, and encouraged Kaywin to sit and eat.

"Guys," he announced to the six of them, "Colonel Barksdale will be here in forty-five minutes with updates, travel details, and to meet Kaywin, of course. Penny, I **think**--I'm not sure, so don't freak out if I'm wrong, but I **think** he is bringing your stuffed wolf..."

"Wolfie!" The twenty-something year old woman cried out with delight, a little bit of rice flying out of her mouth.

"So let's make sure everything is cleaned up and looking good. And I will see you guys at five-thirty!" Left to their own devices Vance, Penny, Les, "the Rocket", Midge and Kaywin lunched hungrily, filling the spaces between bites with conversation; everyone except "the Rocket" being naturally curious about the newcomer: (Manchester-born and raised, forty-six, Air-Corps for eight years, electrical work, Sagittarius, old music--no not the free-form spoken-word stuff of the 2060's, the **really** old stuff--piloting work hopefully, green...) Interestingly, no one asked him just yet **why** he had joined the MCP. Those who are suffering are often a little more tactful and gentle with those who are suffering next to them. The whole time they lunched and conversed, a super-friendly orange cat wove in and out of the thirty-six legs--human and chair--under the table, rubbing his face on everything in sight. At one point he spotted an opportunity and took a chance, leaping into Kaywin's lap for a better view of the stranger.

"Not now, Nurse Donovan, let him eat!" said Vance, helping Kaywin scoot the tabby back onto the floor.

"This is good food," said Kaywin. "Do we always eat this well?"

"Yeah, they treat us pretty good," Penny offered up. "If we could just get some whizz-kids for dessert there wouldn't be nuthin' to complain about."

At two-o'clock, as foretold by Richard, the door opened and Colonel Barksdale entered. He was a nice, tall and handsome man not much older than Kaywin, in full military attire with a small stuffed wolf tucked under his arm. "Wolfie!" shrieked Penny, charging at the Colonel, who held it aloft out of her reach.

"Ah-ah-ah!" said Barksdale. "You have to make me a promise first." The strangely childish woman calmed down and put her arms by her side, ready to do whatever was necessary to reunite with her long-lost companion. "You said that you needed Wolfie to make you brave. Do you promise me that you are going to be brave?"

"I promise!" He gave her the wolf. She hugged it tightly under her chin, and embraced the Colonel, who patted her on the back mechanically, uncomfortable with the blurring of boundaries. When she released him, he walked straight over to Kaywin and shook his hand warmly.

"You are Kaywin Lafontaine. I'm happy to meet you. So sorry for your loss."

"Thank you. Pleased to meet you." The two standing face to face presented a stark contrast. The dignified, clean cut but lively military man whose life and love was still intact, versus the man who could have been very much like him, but who had suddenly lost everything. It was a fleeting but striking portrait of despair.

The Colonel took a few minutes with each of them, lastly with Kaywin. They sat on a couch, slightly out of earshot, and talked. After a little debriefing about what he could expect over the next few days, the officer switched topics suddenly. "So you do electrical work."

"Oh yeah."

"Good! We are going to keep you busy for the next week. The wiring in this building is over eighty years old. If you can switch it out, even if it's just two or three rooms, that would be great."

"Sure. It'll be good to have something to do."

"Excellent. Make me a list of what you need first thing tomorrow. I will enable a connection between our Sofees at 9:45 AM. It will terminate at 10:00, so don't be late. You guys are under tight security, so we don't usually allow messages out. Make me a list, and I will give you "the Rocket" as assistant. "The Rocket" needs a project, too." Kaywin turned a little to look at the skinny, surly-seeming young man with the weird name. He found the delinquent already looking--or was it glaring?--at him. It would have been unsettling if it hadn't been a little comical.

The conversation over between the Colonel and Kaywin, the former got the attention of everyone in the common area and encouraged them to gather round.

"Alright guys. I'm proud of all of you, and excited to see what you guys can do in the Program. There's been a very slight change of plans. We will still be boarding a bus to take us to Manchester Airport on the morning of April 1st, but there's been a problem with an intermediate checkpoint in Detroit, so we will be leaving at 6:15 AM instead of 6:30 like I told you last time." Kaywin could see "the Rocket" throw his hands up, shake his head, and let out a little hiss of exasperation. Wow. It was fifteen minutes. Interesting. *This guy's going to be fun to work with!* Barksdale wasn't finished.

"Remember, March 29th--that's four days from now--March 29th is the **last** day to make any changes to your final will and testament!" He was speaking very clearly and emphatically. "If you do **not** submit your final will and testament by then--I'm looking at you, Les--everything you owned will go to the state of New Hampshire. Now the state of New Hampshire doesn't need anymore love letters from your Grandma to your Grandpa, or family portraits, or friendship bracelets, which means all of that stuff will go straight in the trash if you do not specifically designate it elsewhere. Mary downstairs can come up and help you with this. Trust me, she is bored out of her mind down there. So get it done, if you haven't. And I will see you guys on Thursday. Kaywin, I will send someone by with everything you need at some point tomorrow. Look around tonight; there's a utility closet that might have a ladder and a toolbox." So saying, Colonel Barksdale rose from the couch, shook hands, patted backs, failed to dodge another hug from Penny, and left.

Vance, with his jet-black coif, was very helpful after that. He showed Kaywin around the second floor of the building. They found a silver duffle bag with Kaywin's name on it in front of what had once been apartment 212. As soon as they clicked the door open, Nurse Donovan, who had accompanied them for the entire little tour, exploded into the room and jumped up onto the bed, as if he had been waiting for this moment for quite some time. So this would be Kaywin's room for the next seven nights. Spacious enough, quiet enough, and he could look out of the iron bars at the bustle of Elm Street if he wanted. Vance had been languishing in room 207 since January and was sort of the King of the Manchester MCP. He showed Kaywin the utility closet, which had a few of the things he would need to start the re-wiring project. Together they found the breaker box and Kaywin decided to work outward from there, a practical idea which also had the benefit of not infringing on any of the current residents' privacy. He set the goal of re-wiring apartments 220, 219 and 218, well distant from 207-212. Part of one wall in 219 was busted in, so he was able to get a peek at what he was working with. By 5 PM he had composed a solid list of what was needed, and had set his Sofee to send it to Barksdale at 9:45 the following morning.

He had already started to settle into the Victorian calm/gothic gloom of the place. After supper that first night, he sat around in the common area with the other five as they exchanged their various hard-luck stories.

Vance began. "So, Kaywin, now that you've had a few hours to settle in, would you like to tell us why you're here? You certainly don't **have** to…" he hastened to add.

"No, no, that's fine. I uh…I lost my wife and daughter four years ago…" Midge gasped. She must have been in her early fifties, but she had the husky voice and weathered features of someone who had lived hard. She overcompensated for this with too much eye makeup, and too much time with a curling iron.

"Ohhh, Honey, that's terrible!" she croaked. "I lost my husband and my two girls; I know exactly what you've been through!" Kaywin wasn't sure if she had actually lost them, or if she had maybe traded them for cigarettes…

"I'm sorry to hear that" he offered to Midge. "I tried to get over it..." He shrugged. "I just can't." He hoped they would let him stop at this point. He wasn't overly infatuated with his own masculinity, but no one likes to cry in front of strangers. "What about you guys? Vance?"

"Weeell..." The affable-seeming man hesitated. "I decided to stop taking my meds about six months ago. Then, what can I say? Bad things started happening...I lost my job--I'm a writer--a former associate of mine spread a bunch of manure about me, so suddenly no one was hiring; then my partner left me after fifteen years...I just think it's better this way." He smiled sheepishly.

"Ohhh, Sweetie; I stopped taking my meds too! Poor thing..." Okay. Kaywin was starting to get a bead on this Midge lady...

"Les, what about you? You're pretty quiet." Les was an African-American man who seemed to be in his late twenties. He was about six feet tall and wiry-thin, with a tight, tight afro that wasn't so big on the sides, but which went upwards sharply, adding a good eight inches to his height. He had been lounging deeply in his armchair, but he sat up so quickly that Kaywin twitched a little, not sure what was about to happen.

"You know what?" Les began. "Maybe I've been on the street for **ten years.** Maybe I'm just looking for a hot meal. Maybe I'm just looking for a warm bed." Kaywin couldn't tell if he was angry or not; and if so was he angry at him? Or just the world? "Maybe, also, I'm just looking for some kind of, you know...neat little ending to frame it all in..." He grinned broadly and looked at Vance. "You can borrow that for your book. Ha! You can have that one!"

Sooo, **everyone** was off their meds. Kaywin paused for a second, waiting for Midge to talk about **her** ten years on the streets, but she had become distracted by a chipped fingernail. "Rocket, how 'bout you?"

"It's **THE** Rocket" sneered "the Rocket." He was twenty-nine, with brown greased-back hair failing to cover an early bald-spot. He shrugged and glared wordlessly at Kaywin. For like ten seconds. One-one thousand, two-one-thousand, three-one-thousand, etc. He didn't seem to have that cut-off instinct that lets a **normal** person know that a glare could escalate at any moment into a full-blown physical confrontation. Kaywin moved on, having saved the least scary person for last. "Penny? Why have you decided to end it all?"

"Because Niiick--," she stretched his name out venomously-- "likes biscuits!"

There was a considerable pause. This declaration raised a lot more questions than it answered.

"Who's Nick?"

"My boyfriend." Penny must have been **somewhere** in her twenties but her behavior was so stunted that it was hard to tell. "Well, not anymore. Cuz **apparently Beeeliiiinda** makes better biscuits than I do."

"What's wrong with biscuits? I like biscuits" spoke "the Rocket" unexpectedly.

"Yeah, I like biscuits, too," joined Les. "I think I like Nick."

"I used to make the best biscuits," Midge threw in, completely derailing the conversation, which then turned entirely to the delicate science of biscuit-making.

When Kaywin turned out the light in his room that first night, five minutes ahead of their ten o'clock curfew, and lay down in his bed, he talked to his girls for a few minutes, quietly. He barely whispered; having left the door cracked open a little in case Nurse Donovan wanted to visit, he didn't want to be overheard muttering to ghosts. "Well, there's no going back now. You know, I'll be with you girls soon, and this whole nightmare will be over." Like most citizens of the twenty-second century, Kaywin didn't know if he believed in an afterlife or not. "Wherever it is, we'll be together like we're supposed to be. Whether it's soaring above the clouds, or rotting in the ground, I will be with you soon. I miss you girls so much. I love you." Right as his lips formed a circle to pronounce the 'you' in 'I love you', a cat head smashed into them, stealing the kiss intended for his lost ladies, but making him smile a sad smile in return.

He slept alright that first night. His bed was reasonably comfy, and he was too exhausted to even dream. He was awakened once, around midnight, by Nurse Donovan returning from his rounds--he made time for anyone who left their door ajar--and once more at one-something in the morning by someone sobbing in 211. This was Les's room. Daytime Les didn't seem like much of a sobber, but Kaywin well knew that things were not always what they seemed. Maybe he was talking to **his** lost someone, or something.

They were required to be up by 7:15 AM; although there was little work for them to do now, they needed to be ac-climated to a routine for the heavier lifting to come. Kaywin was a step ahead of the game, having set his alarm for six. He wanted to get off on the right foot, and make a favorable impression on Barksdale. He was an early-riser anyway, so it was no big deal.

When he got to the kitchen, he was mildly surprised to find "the Rocket" already dressed, greased, and ready to go. They would be working closely for the next five days, and Kaywin got an immediate sample of how much fun this was going to be:

Kaywin: "Did you sleep alright?"

The Rocket: "Why wouldn't I?"

Sheesh. Other charming conversation was in store for the duo over the course of the rewiring project:

Kaywin: "Can you hand me the Phillips-head? No, wait-- just hand me the pliers, please."

The Rocket, as he handed Kaywin the pliers: "Can I ask you a question?"

Kaywin: "Sure."

The Rocket: "Why didn't you just ask me to hand you the pliers the first time?"

And later:

Kaywin: "So why do they call you "the Rocket"?"

The Rocket: "It's my name. Why do they call you Kaywin?"

It was almost an art form, really, how this guy could turn **any** interaction into a straight-up confrontation. It was easy for Kaywin to see that **he** wasn't the problem in this relationship; this guy 'the Rocket' talked to every one of them like that, and glared at every one of them like that. Every human contact was fraught with danger to this guy; he found insult in everything from the earliest "Good morning" to the final "Goodnight." Once Kaywin realized that he wasn't being singled out, and that this guy would still hand him a hammer if asked for a hammer, he knew they would be fine. Besides, when it occurred to him how profoundly lonely this constant edginess must be, he could no longer muster up much anger at the greasy misfit.

They attacked the prep work that first morning, removing much of the old wiring from the three rooms, and creating access for the new wiring. Just before lunch time the front door opened. Three of the MCP workers from downstairs came in and created a sort of human barrier, while two Uno Mundo workers carried in everything on Kaywin's wish list--including, to his amazement, the case of Whizz-kids he had put on there mainly as a joke. He stashed these quickly so he could surprise the others later.

Over the course of the next five days, he and "the Rocket" (and Nurse Donovan) made very respectable progress, finishing up the third and final room late on the 29th of March. The cat was into everything, getting underfoot, messing with loose wires, and plaster fragments swinging by their horse-hairs; actually going **into** the wall at one point and then emerging from another. As annoying as all of this should have been, the big tabby was like a ray of orange sunshine, unabashedly alive among the six doomed humans.

While it wasn't a seven-day party at 1095 Elm Street, it wasn't the worst. Within a few days Kaywin already felt more connected with these five unfortunates than he ever really had been with his online support group. Maybe it was the everyday routine of meal preparation, doing the dishes, litter box changing, light-blue jumpsuit laundering, etc., that created a little camaraderie. With his support group it had all been super-heavy conversation, all the time. Here, it was nice to just talk about their favorite methods of cooking Kale, or who they had voted for in 2124, or why the fourth Plasmo Zenith movie was funnier than the third, rather than laying open their wounds all over again every Wednesday night at seven. They all knew they were damaged beyond repair, they had all **done** something about it finally, and there was no more need to talk about it really. One night after supper they dubbed themselves 'the Manchester Six' (a surprise suggestion from "the Rocket"), and, with just enough distance remaining between themselves and mortal danger, they indulged in a silly group daydream about the ridiculous things they might accomplish.

That was about as heavy as it got, until Saturday night. When Kaywin lay down that night, sore from the five days of rewiring but happy with a job well done, his mind finally moved on from this task to the days ahead. Monday, April first, the day they would depart for the MCP National Headquarters in Houston, was suddenly almost upon him. He thought about how close he was to leaving this little sanctuary. About why he was doing this. How alone he felt. He was man enough to admit to himself that he was a little scared. As he drifted off to sleep, instead of visualizing how he was going to route wire from point A to point B, he was picturing his girls.

That must be why he had the dream again... He must have been making a racket, because he was suddenly awakened by someone knocking on his door at 2:35 AM. He got up in a stupor and opened it. "You okay, brother?" It was Les.

"Yeah, yeah, crap, I'm sorry; did I wake you up? I was

having a nightmare. Sorry."

"That's okay, that's okay. This stuff is rough. It's fixin' to get real." Les had come to check on Kaywin, but he wound up staying for about twenty minutes, and it became clear that he needed someone to check on him, too. He was scared too, and confused about how this had happened to him. Literally. It sent a chill up and down Kaywin's spine to hear Les admit that he had absolutely no recollection of having signed up for the program; he remembered going to sleep on a bench in Victory Park, one night about three weeks ago, and he remembered waking up in room 211 with his entire future forfeited. Not that he had been happy on the streets, and not that he hadn't **thought** about joining up every time he walked past 1095 Elm.

When Les went back to his room at 2:57 AM, he and Kaywin both felt a little better knowing they weren't the only woosies in the Manchester Six.

Kaywin's will had been done for over a year. He had little to do on Sunday beyond hanging out in torturous anticipation, alone, or in mixed small groups. For most of the day Midge had a poor MCP clerk tied up on their couch, listing all the siblings, cousins and uncles who had let her down, and officially clarifying that none of her porcelain clown figurines or hand-carved soapstone angel babies should now, or at any point in the future, fall into their grubby hands. Monday couldn't get here fast enough.

He was up at 5:15 Monday morning and helping with breakfast, which had not been his habit so far (having been gainfully employed with the electrical work). The entire crew was manically trying to keep busy, so that the six of them were literally tripping over each other in the tiny kitchen. Colonel Barksdale arrived at 5:30 as their proud escort. He was full of smiles, handshakes, and back-pats, even more than usual. Kaywin's relationship with the Colonel had been brief, but he felt like he was a better man for having known him. Unbeknownst to him, Barksdale felt the same.

He even made some phone calls to friends deeper in the gut of the program regarding Kaywin Lafontaine, and his potential…

The Colonel told them to leave the dishes.

Then the Manchester Six, in their clean light blue jumpsuits, shouldered their silver duffel bags and filed out the door into the stairwell; Midge, Vance, "the Rocket", Penny, Les and Kaywin; each stooping in turn to give Nurse Donovan a scratch on the head for good luck. They knew they were getting on a bus. They knew they were going to Houston. There was something about a layover in Detroit. No other details had been given to them, and no other details did they need to know.

Interestingly enough, after filing through the Fort Knoxlike door at the bottom of the stairwell, they turned right instead of left, and slipped out the back of the block-sized building, into a narrow alley wet from the rain of the previous night. They were handled gently and respectfully, but a quick head count by Kaywin showed fourteen guards and/or assorted MCP personnel keeping close tabs on the six perfectly cooperative Goners. This was interesting, but not shocking. What caught Kaywin off guard completely were the seven or eight **fans**. These people, bundled up against the wet, penetrating pre-dawn chill, were clapping their mittened hands together (sounding like seven or eight people beating rugs clean with sticks), hooting and hollering and even snapping photos. They were kept at a respectful distance by three of the guards, hulking men who were armed openly.

They stepped up the ramp onto the large bus, 'the Rocket' glaring openly at the well-meaning onlookers the whole way. Vance waved at them; Penny waved at them; Kaywin didn't know what to do with this unexpected dynamic, so he just boarded the Silverdog and sat exactly where he was told.

The next small surprise was that they were no longer alone. This bus had apparently done a little tour of New Hampshire before arriving in Manchester, picking up Goners from the few other MCP offices in the small state. Thirteen new faces to learn, thought Kaywin, though he didn't know if he would have the chance.

It was a fifteen-minute ride to the airport, and it was done in complete silence. It was eerie to be gliding along in a public transport without his senses being fully and constantly assaulted with advertisements. Of course! They were no longer free citizens with buying power, and the freedom to decide what to use it on.

It was unclear whether they were allowed to talk; and no one wanted to be the idiot who found out the hard way that they were **not.**

It was still dark when they arrived at sprawling Manchester International, rolling past the parking garages and directly out onto the shiny wet tarmac. This trip was already full of little clues about their new status in the world. Why **would** they park and go strolling into the airport to check bags, confirm tickets, buy a donut for twice the street price and wait with civilian strangers for their flight? On the surface, this bypassing of red tape appeared borderline luxurious, but Kaywin saw through it to the truth: They were **cargo.** Their individual selves had disappeared. They were still being handled humanely--for now--but they were no longer passengers. There wouldn't be a drink cart. They were merchandise.

The Silverdog rolled to an easy stop next to a tiny jet. The Manchester Six and their thirteen new fellow Granite State Goners were ushered off of the bus and up a steep ramp onto the mini-sonic. Ten guards guarded the nineteen martyrs at this point, but there were only twenty-five seats, making it necessary for four of the guards to stand in the narrow aisle for the entire thirty-five minute flight to Detroit. The sun was rising behind them as they flew, just as it had risen on every man who ever walked to his doom, but at one thousand miles per hour they stayed just ahead of the flaming orb, and gave themselves the illusion of cheating it.

The changeover in Detroit was much the same. They landed (a little harshly) in the tiny jet and taxied up to a much larger 'Grand Hawaii' one; a seven-eleven-seven if Kaywin wasn't mistaken. They weren't really 'Grand Hawaii' jets anymore; the government had bought them when Grand Hawaii went bankrupt twenty years earlier; they had just never repainted them.

This vehicle change took place on the tarmac, as in Manchester, but this time much closer to the terminal, and Kaywin, in the few seconds it took to disembark from the smaller jet onto the larger one, noticed a genuine **crowd** of people through the glass of the terminal, maybe even a hundred, smiling and waving at them in transit. Many held up their fully expanded Sofee screens with hard-to-read-from-this-distance messages of encouragement. Three kind souls, working in conjunction, each held up one word of a phrase that stuck with Kaywin:

Slay Them Dragons

This was starting to be a revelation to him, that there were people who followed the program closely enough, and who cared enough, to congregate early in the morning just to give the new MC's this five-second glimpse of support. He was touched.

Six minutes into their flight from Detroit to Houston, with their numbers having swelled from nineteen to perhaps three or four hundred, Penny did something pretty brave. They had all ridden in awkward silence together the whole morning. She couldn't stand it anymore; it just wasn't in her nature. She raised her hand like a twelve year-old schoolgirl. One of the guards, a little thrown off by the seemingly out-of-place gesture, said, "Yes Ma'am?"

"Are we allowed to speak?"

"Yes Ma'am. Just keep it quiet and civil."

"Awful. Thanks." Then she turned from her seat in the third row to face the entire sea of unhappy souls. "Did you guys see those people waving and cheering for us? I thought that was wicked sweet. That's all."

It wasn't much of a speech; schoolchildren a hundred years later would not be required to memorize it, but it did break the spell of uncomfortable, uncertain silence. People throughout the jumbo jet now began to speak, as the guard had instructed, quietly and civilly among each other. Kaywin met a few of his neighbors this way. On a commercial flight, in happier times, he, like everyone else, would have kept to himself with his nose buried in his Sofee. But now, he opened himself up a little, having one thing in common with everybody on this flight, except the guards. They would all be dead within two years.

Or in two **minutes**, judging by the way the seven-eleventy-seven was behaving. Ten minutes in, this was already the rockiest flight he had ever experienced--and this was an Air Corp Vet with twenty thousand hours experience! He wondered if the maintenance on this puppy was as out-of-date as the paint job. Civility and quiet was out the window as the already jumpy crowd of MC's cursed, prayed, and exclaimed against the probability of premature death. Kaywin looked back at the panicked horde; their tense faces almost blurry with the vibration of the rumbling turbulence. He wasn't calm, by any stretch, but he was ready, if this was to be his time. He closed his eyes and concentrated on the cries of the frightened, trying to identify their gender and region. Southern man. Midwestern woman. Boston man. This little mental exercise got him through the few terrifying minutes until the jet stabilized itself in steadier air. After this there was much excited chatter, and laughter over how ridiculous they had been, and a really long line for the bathroom.

They touched down in Houston an hour later. It was hot there. Not a surprise, really. They were ushered onto more Silverdogs, and noticed other jets loading directly onto other buses. During this melee, Kaywin was separated from his Manchester acquaintances. This was for the best, he supposed. If he had been a gambling man he would not have bet on him and them garnering similar assignments. Better not start to rely on their company.

As they hit the highway, he noticed more and more buses clustering up with them, until they had quite the convoy going. Their robot 'driver' was a silly one, trying to get them to sing along with him to various numbers. He seemed to be filling in the space that would normally have been subsumed with Whoopsie ads and Spritz jingles.

Suddenly, they exited the highway onto a slower road, which a short while later turned to gravel. The long line of buses was now snaking along single file. An older man in a gray uniform waved them through a huge iron gate, and they entered the grounds of the Meaningful Conclusion Program National Headquarters.

7

Path Through the Forest

The ponderously long cavalcade of mostly silver transport buses passed one by one through the grand gate and continued down the last fourteen hundred feet of gravel approach. As each bus emerged from the narrow tree-rimmed drive into the wide parking lot, like salmon leaving the little stream at last for the open sea, they passed within a few feet of a lonely light blue bullet car anchored like a sailboat near the river's mouth.

"I want to know what happened to my baby...Latrell 'Lonnie' Hopkins..." muttered Kaywin completely to himself. He had read it on the screen perched like a sail on top of the blue bullet, which he recognized as an older model *Second Amendment*. He didn't think much further about it at the time. He, like every one of the four thousand one hundred and twelve new recruits passing by the unexpected display, was preoccupied just now with the fate of their own mother's baby.

Young Dublin Dunne, nine buses behind Kaywin Lafontaine, had been locked into the stony crunch of the Silverdogs over the gravel. His hyper-poetic mind registered the sound as muffled millions of lives breaking under the wheels of the universe; and he sat, quietly horrified, to hear it just go on and on and on...

The gravel path continued at the far end of Lot A; the buses resumed it and entered a fetching roundabout. They circled three quarters of the way around a magnificent fountain centered on a spot of perfect green and banded all the way around with wonderful orange and yellow flowers in fullest bloom; exiting again onto a long, arcing semi-circular drive in front of an imposing university-like building.

It was hard to tell, getting off of the bus onto the crushed stone walk, whether they should feel like students, prisoners, or soldiers. The very large brick building they had pulled up in front of, and the beautifully-kept grounds fronting it, had the distinct feel of a college campus. This is, of course, exactly what it had once been. Texas Spanner University had already planned to ditch its physical footprint, going one hundred percent electronic in 2082, when the bill that sanctioned the creation of the MCP sailed through Congress. The US Government needed a home for it, and the soon-to-be-abandoned campus was a natural fit.

It was a welcoming, stately campus, at one with the nature that surrounded it and ran through it. People arriving from the far corners of the country, haunted by the wreckage of their lives, and rattled by the finality of the commitment they had just made found comfort in the green lawns, long neatly trimmed box hedges; the flower gardens, fountains, and noble brick buildings. They felt like they had delivered themselves into good hands, kind, wise and gentle hands.

The mid-afternoon sun was bright in Kaywin's eyes when he stepped off the bus down onto the crunching gravel. He could see dozens of other buses stopped on the long semi-circular promenade. Hundreds, even thousands of people were exiting the transports.

They could scarcely have looked more different from one another; there were tall young African-American males, short old Asian women, stout Polynesians, beautiful, ugly, robust, failing…there were others like Kaywin too, non-descript white men of middling height and age. There was no physical blueprint for terminal sadness. They were all acting different-ly as well; some stepped down tired and melancholy-seeming and looked up at the beautiful buildings; others collapsed in the shade of five mighty oaks closer to the granite stairs lead-ing up to its front doors; and some actually frolicked and ca-vorted in the intense sunshine on the grass. There were plen-ty of rough-looking characters in the crowd, for sure, with neck tattoos and holes where piercings had been removed, but there were some Grandmas in there too.

The third thing that got Kaywin's attention, after the at-tractiveness of the MCP Campus, and the diversity of the MCs arriving, was the **kids.** He had been a little more tuned into the Goner Program than the average Joe on the street, so he knew that sixteen-year-olds were allowed in now, but Holy Crap, some of these kids looked like they were twelve, and scared out of their minds; giant duffle bags spilling out of buses on top of them.

There were guards, **lots** of them, and guides, lots of them. The guards weren't completely obvious; they didn't have hel-mets and bulletproof vests, and heavy artillery; they were all in three-piece suits, even the women. And each had a small holster, only visible when the bottom edge of a sports jacket moved for a moment, as one of them high-fived a friend, or raised an arm to point at something. It was obvious that some effort had been made to make this place, at least at this time, feel less like a prison.

Kaywin shouldered his silver duffle bag and shielded his hazel eyes. He took a second, in the blinding Texas sunlight, to survey a sight that you and I will never see: all of a major world country's well-meaning suicidals gathered together in one place, emerging like newly hatched chicks from the sixty-one transports. Whatever they had seen in this cruel world, and whatever they had done was all behind them now, and this sunny Houston day was the new reality they were all re-born into. *Look at this mish-mosh of humanity! These misfits never stood a chance...what will become of them? What will become of me?*

He was jarred out of his reverie by a slight commotion on the steps of the bus he had just exited. A tiny old Asian woman was wrestling with her giant duffle bag, trying to bend it to her will and then will it down the ramp. He hustled over and helped her with it. Together they managed, each with one hand on it, and once they hit ground they guided it, like two people working a Ouija board, to a clear spot a few steps away.

"Thank you so much!" the adorable little apparent grand-mother of twenty-nine enthused in a thick accent.

"No problem. My name is Kaywin." He held out his hand.

"Ahh, 'Kaymin'. My name Rose." She shook his hand with endearing sincerity. "Good to meet you."

"What brings you here? You look normal enough compared to the rest of us…"

"Ahh, I have six month to live. No one spend it with." She shrugged like this was no big deal, like the grocery store down the street was out of her favorite pickle or something. "Kaymin" couldn't help but admire her pluck.

"That's too bad. What do you have? If you don't mind my asking…"

"Triskolosis…it kind of like sclerosis. It pretty rare; yah."

"What kind of job are you hoping to get?"

"Excuse me?"

"What kind of work are you hoping to do; what kind of job?"

"Oh! I hope they test out cure for Triskolosis on me. Help other with Triskolosis. What 'bout you?"

"It doesn't matter. I guess piloting something would be my first choice."

"Ahh, good; you handsome like pilot!" She didn't ask him **why** he was there, which he was glad of. Either it was a cultural respect for privacy, or she just didn't think about it. Reason number two to like Rose.

"That's nice of you but--" Something behind Kaywin had evidently caught Rose's attention. He turned, intending to look for a split second at whatever had thrown confusion across her face and then turn back immediately. You wouldn't want to be caught staring too long at most of these people.

What he saw however was so strange, even for this crowd, that he forgot to look away. A white man, perhaps thirty-seven years old or so, was maneuvering his way through the throng with purpose. He was wearing a filthy bed-sheet, crudely fashioned into a monk-style robe. It appeared to have begun life as a **white** bed sheet, before undergoing some low-budget dyeing process that nudged it into the brown family… from that point it seemed to have been anointed liberally with food-stains, grease, and blood, giving it rather a shocking appearance; all tied up about the waist with a blue bungee cord. This medieval-revival garb was strange enough, but stranger still were the words emblazoned across the man's forehead:

Eat Mine

He was moving quickly, although not aggressively--quite the opposite in fact--he was nudging his way through the disoriented Goners, where the grass met the gravel, with rather a huge smile on his face. There was a gentleness and piety to him that was a little mesmerizing; his touch on the shoulders of the men and women blocking his path was light; full of thought but not of fear. He looked as if he hadn't bathed in weeks. Kaywin couldn't tell, even as the man drew close, whether the words on his forehead were a tattoo or some temporary embellishment.

"Who that?" asked Rose, similarly mesmerized. He had forgotten he was in the middle of a conversation with her.

"I don't know...he looks like some kind of pilgrim; a penitent, an ascetic..."

"What means that?"

He broke the spell and turned to face her again. "It's like...someone who is so devoted to divine service that they deny themselves all earthly pleasures. Sometimes they punish themselves...like in medieval times they would wear super-scratchy shirts and even whip themselves." He turned back for a second look.

"Punish for what?"

"I don't know...I guess for any thought or act that was not directly in service of their God..."

"He must think something terrible!" she said, for as the

ascetic drew close they could see that the left side of his face was severely bruised as if by repeated heavy blows.

"Or **done** something terrible…," answered Kaywin. The strange man brushed past them smiling, even beaming through his bruises, with his eyes fixed on something down the road. They followed his gaze and their amazement was doubled to spot another freak just like him, except maybe a foot taller, smiling and waving back from a couple hundred feet further on.

Rose laughed abruptly. "Ha! It takes all kind!"

It didn't seem to matter to anyone in charge that these several thousand MCs were all just milling around; groups from different buses just kind of dissolving into one another… The apparent chaos made Kaywin, with his organized military mindset, a little nervous. His bus had wound up positioned almost smack dab in front of the broad granite steps in front of the main building. There was a small contingency of officials at the top of them, on a sort of grand porch, that seemed to be assessing the situation and preparing to speak. At the center of the hubbub was a very thin, nervous-looking man in a very, **very** skinny suit. Kaywin's controlled instinct for structure and answers compelled him closer to the steps. He could hear the skinny man, with his pencil-thin moustache and his fedora, receiving information and updates from several people, and converting this into instruction to several others. With his Nouveau-Southern style and his effeminate drawl, Kaywin wondered if he had taken a wrong turn on his way to the Kentucky Derby. From the bottom of the steps, acting casual, he could pick up little bits and pieces: "Mr. Beauregard, Comiskey confirms that the problem with the bus is strictly mechanical, and that there is no insurgence. He says it's an axle."

"How far out are they?"

"He says forty-five minutes."

"That's not a distance."

"Sorry sir." Into his wrist: "How **far**; how many **miles?**" Then back to Beauregard: "Thirty miles sir."

"Well this seems pretty obvious; send one of **these** buses back for them! Why am I even involved in this issue?" Another man approached the acting-president of the MCPNH, who was dabbing his forehead with a white handkerchief in frustration.

"Sir, what about lunch? We're on target for one PM; do we need to shut it down until the last bus gets here?"

"No! We're not going to make four thousand people wait because sixty-five are late. Sofee put that in my lyric file." There was a burst of crazy loud static that made Kaywin and everyone around him cringe as the soundman adjusted the microphone on its stand. Beauregard lashed out at him. "Why did you do that? It was perfect!" Kaywin stepped back to the other side of the wall of buses, his ears still ringing. He meandered his way back to Rose, she being the least-complete stranger in sight. Looking up and down the drive he didn't see Midge, or Penny, or Vance's perfect coif, or "the Rocket's" thinning slickback, or even Les's tall afro.

About three minutes later, there was finally an official statement from the Acting-President.

"Ladies and gentleman, boys--" he stopped, not wanting to directly call out the presence of so many young ones in the crowd. "--and women." Awkward pause. "Welcome to Houston! Welcome to the Meaningful Conclusion Program National Headquarters! We honor you, and we honor the brave decision you have made to join us here today. Over the course of the next five days we are going to find out a lot about you, and you about us. In just a few minutes here you are going to begin filing through these doors behind me" he gestured grandly back at them, a gust of wind trying to flap the coat-sleeve that was suctioned to his arm, but failing, "into registration, where you will leave your duffle bag temporarily, and from there into the cafetorium, where a delicious lunch will be served. After lunch you will wait in the cafetorium, until you are assigned a room and a section leader. **You will follow the commands of your section leader at all times, and at all costs.** This is non-negotiable, okay? When you go to your assigned room, your bag will be waiting on your assigned bed. There will be no swapping of beds, okay? You will have some free time before and after supper tonight, which will be at six, to acclimate yourself to your new surroundings and your new comrades. Tomorrow's activities will be centered around the farewell ceremony of course, but we will give you more specifics on that tonight and tomorrow morning." For some reason, he chose this moment to stop and survey the crowd thoroughly with a forced, tight-lipped smile. "For right now, let's begin. No pushing or shoving or rushing please; there is no fire; everybody just come on up, through the doors behind me, to anyone of the twenty roped-off lines so we can get everyone accounted for. The more calm you are, the quicker we can get everybody through, and the quicker we can get to lunch. Barbecue sandwiches. Yeah!"

There was a faltering swell of movement toward the step.

Kaywin helped Rose shoulder her bag again. "You want to stick with me? Be my friend?" he asked her.

"Oh!" She laughed. "I thought we friends already!"

Together they made it through registration and into the lunchroom.

While the multiple old college buildings seemed to date from the nineteen-hundreds, the interior (of the main building at least) had been redone in distinctly twenty-fifties style, 'clinical gothic' as it came to be known, with confidently ornate, thick arches and window frames, columns and vaulted ceilings, but all very streamlined and monochromatic--usually white. White, **before** the twenty-fifties had always been the clichéd color of the future; I suppose in the twenty-fifties designers decided that the future had finally arrived, and used it exhaustively and almost exclusively. Then about ten years later people decided that 'the future' was boring; color made a comeback, and clean 'clinical gothic' white became the shade of futures past. Sixty years later, four thousand Goners convened at folding lunch tables beneath the white cathedral-like vault.

Everything about registration was exactly what Kaywin had expected, with one very strange exception. When they found seats together at lunch, he asked Rose about it. "Did they try to make you take an Attabuoy?"

"Yes. I take it. I thought no choice. Why? Is it no good?"

"It's just a strong, addictive drug...It's just weird to me that they would try to force it on us. I acted like I was going to take it but I didn't. I don't know...maybe it's for crowd control or something..."

"I let you know if I feel like astronaut." He smiled at her

colorful language.

Lunch was good; Southern barbecue style with pulled pork sandwiches, cole slaw, and corn on the cob. The cafetorium was very crowded; people were having to sit on the floor with their backs up against the cool stone walls all the way around. Everyone was in a daze; Kaywin had woken up in Manchester, NH and was now eating lunch in Houston; Rose had woken up in Seattle and was now doing the same; the two ladies across from them were from Minnesota and had managed to stick together thus far.

After lunch, within a span of about thirty seconds, they all received alerts on their Sofees giving them their section and room assignments. For half a minute the echoey cafetorium sounded like an enormous bird sanctuary with the chirping and trilling of four thousand incoming messages. The sunlight streaming in from the towering windows added to this effect. Kaywin was in Section 'H'. He got up and meandered toward the red neon floating letter 'H' on a stick, held up in the corner nearest him by a young soldier standing next to an imposingly stern-looking man, also in military attire. This would be his section leader, Sergeant Davis. Kaywin was only the third or fourth 'H' member to arrive, and so was able to borrow enough of the Sergeant's time to shake his hand and introduce himself with appropriate respect, confidence and brevity.

There were about a hundred and fifty MCs assigned to each floating neon letter. Once the milling throng had settled into little blobs, like oil on the surface of water, they proceeded blob by blob out of the cafetorium toward the dormitories they would call home for the next five nights. Kaywin's room, 447, was pleasant enough, and tidy, though quite small. Two bunk beds hugged the painted cinderblock walls on either side, and he found his duffle bag on the lower left-hand bunk. It was clear immediately that everything had been removed from his duffle, presumably for inspection, and then returned in a manner that had not been his custom.

There were two mats on the floor between the bunks. There would be six people sleeping in the four-person room.

When it became apparent, after introductions between himself and his five new roommates, that there would be three or so hours of free time, he invested in a solid two-hour nap. He wanted to separate the challenges of the morning from the upcoming challenges of the evening, whatever they may be.

He slept like a champion, the completely uninterrupted, heavy, drooling-on-your-pillow kind of sleep. He woke up confused in a pale blue dorm room in Houston, Texas. Then it all came back to him, not just the plane ride and the bus ride and the lunch, but the terrible, still unreal event four years past that had put this whole thing in motion. He started to panic a little bit, and tears came to his eyes, but he controlled his breathing and collected himself before the two roommates still in their bunks caught on to his little episode. One of them was sleeping and the other was messing with his Sofee with a confused, agitated look on his face. He caught Kaywin looking at him. He was a gruff-looking dude in his late forties or early fifties. "I can't send anything out," he said quietly to Kaywin.

"No, you can't send anything out, ever. Did you just join up?"

"Literally yesterday."

"Yeah, they don't let any information out. If you have any family coming to the service tomorrow that'll be your last chance to say anything you haven't said already."

"Well, that's just it; I don't know if they're coming or **not!**"

Kaywin stuck his head out from his bottom bunk to better address the frustrated newbie in the top bunk opposite. "It's my understanding that the program does everything they can to inform the families and arrange their travel to Houston; I think they really want everyone to have somebody here." The gruff man sighed in exasperation and kept trying.

They gathered again in the cafetorium at 5:45 for supper. Kaywin couldn't find Rose, but he did run into Midge and "the Rocket." "The Rocket" actually waved him over to their table, almost giddily in fact. This struck him as more than a little odd, given the greaser's off-putting natural demeanor. He conversed so boisterously with Kaywin during the entire supper, (as did Midge, though it was less out-of character for her) that both of them barely touched their food. Toward the end of the meal, around 6:25, there was an almost palpable increase in the energy of the entire crowd. It was a strange and real phenomenon.

What none of them knew was that the Attabuoys they had been strongly encouraged to ingest five hours earlier were a new, remotely-activated formulation. There were Attabuoy addicts among them (as there were in any crowd) who had been about to lose their minds waiting for their pills to take effect at two o'clock, three o'clock, four o'clock... Now they had their (repellant? disgusting? distasteful?) satisfaction as someone in the building had finally pressed a button that activated the outer coating of the large pill allowing it to begin dissolving in their tummies.

Discordant laughter began to fill and echo across the huge room as plates were cleared from tables and MCs began to stand and stretch. Section leaders spread the word loudly that another block of free time was beginning. They were all encouraged to get outside and enjoy the gorgeous spring evening, and explore the grounds almost at will. The perimeter, they already knew, was heavily guarded and massively fenced.

Kaywin stood. He was starting to really wake up from his nap, finally. He stretched so hard that bright lights filled his eyes and momentary deafness filled his ears. When he returned from this three-second tune-out, he became aware that **something** odd had happened. There was a growing commotion from the area of the main entrance to the cafetorium. A handful of people were running in that direction; many others with piqued curiosity were ambling the same way. Through a split-second gap in the humanity Kaywin spied a strikingly beautiful, tiny young girl with glowing rainbow-colored hair...Linsom Felize? He couldn't compute this one! What would the biggest pop star of the last ten years be doing in this godforsaken place? Was this some sort of visit, a distraction for the troops? He took a single step towards the hullaballoo and stopped. His daughter--his Victoria--had been a **huge** Linsom Felize fan. For two years her walls had streamed constant images of the star with her bizarre, dark makeup, and her ever-changing, electric fiber-optic hair. True, she had kind of gotten over it that last year before...the incident...but maybe it would be appropriate for Kaywin to tell Ms. Felize what she had meant to his dear, sweet daughter.

He caught another glimpse of her and came to his senses...this wasn't Linsom Felize--maybe seven years ago--this girl, though she looked almost identical to the singing sensation, was clearly several years younger. She couldn't actually be thirteen of course, but if she was sixteen, she was a young-looking sixteen...

The poor girl at first seemed flattered by the attention, but as the crowd swelled in her direction, threatening to surround her and swallow her up, she quickly became alarmed and tight-lipped. She excused herself and vanished into the ladies' room right behind her.

Kaywin watched, concerned for her reappearance, ready perhaps to intervene if necessary. Nobody came out. A bull-doggish woman in her forties; a strung-out looking woman in her mid-thirties; a young brunette with no makeup on whatsoever, though she could have used some perhaps over her black eye and scratched-up cheek, as she hustled out the front door. Too late, Kaywin and the rest of the crowd made the connection; a few idiots started after her toward the main entrance, before doubling back, heeding the voices of reason from the crowd that had figured out that this was **not** Linsom Felize...

Kaywin exhaled for the sake of the young lady and her safety. He turned back toward the body of the crowd to maybe spot Rose, or Les or Vance, but something subtle caught his attention, mid-turn, out of the corner of his eye. It was a younger man he had noticed earlier in the day, and actually avoided deliberately. He was tall, blonde, and strapping with a college-quarterback sort of handsomeness and sense of command. He projected unbelievable arrogance, bordering on hostility. Even in his testosterone-fueled early military days Kaywin had never met a man whose face expressed such longing for physical confrontation. The motion that had caught Kaywin's eye was this dude looking left, looking right, then slipping out of the cafetorium after the young girl. He had found the precise instant when everyone else fell off the chase and turned their attention briefly to each other, sharing their comments, observations and theories on the pop star doppelganger. Maybe it was nothing. But Kaywin didn't like to ignore his instincts, and right now his instincts were telling him that the glazed eyes of Macho McQuarterback were set on the young lady, and that he had caught the scent of fresh meat.

He hesitated, just for a second. He wasn't afraid of a fight, should the need arise for him to step between this guy and the girl, but the prospect was unpleasant.

That second was over, and he headed out the door after them.

There was still some daylight left when he pushed open the front door and paused on the porch. He surveyed the scene in front of him from the top of the steps. People were starting to mill out past him on both sides, a little crazily, like school was letting out for the summer. He tried to pick out the tiny girl from the growing crowd on the huge rectangular green dead ahead, but his odds were going down as their numbers were going up. His mind was not as efficient as it had once been. He caught himself thinking about how difficult this was, instead of focusing on actually spotting her. He shook his head clear and tried instead to locate the man he had decided was dangerous. He had no luck with this either; most of the four thousand Goners had made their way from the cafetorium to the green by now, then--wait-- he saw the swaggering blonde dude stepping off of the gi- ant grassy rectangle and into the woods that bordered it on the right. Kaywin set off in that direction, not running; this was just a hunch after all. He pushed his way through the humanity, noting the rising, unpleasant freneticism, several thousand people under the influence of the narcotic, howling with ragged jolts of laughter and partying like nothing had ever gone horribly wrong with their lives. He had zero regrets about not taking the drug.

He found the spot, perhaps a full minute later, where the blonde man had entered the woods. He ducked low under an oak branch and tried to pick up the trail. A pretty distinct path opened up, curving sharply to the right in front of him. As he followed it, the sounds of a struggle reached his ears before the strugglers rounded into view. He quickened his pace. When he came around the curve, the path began to carve its way into a slight hillside; a little brick wall on the left held up the miniature mountain and kept it from obliterating the walkway every time it rained. There, fifty feet up the slope on the left, his ugly hunch was playing out.

The jerky guy had the young woman pinned against a gi- ant tree. He towered over her squirming body, with both of his paws on her on her waist, clearly against her wishes. Kay- win leaped over the wall and up the hill. "Hey!" he bellowed. "Get off of her!"

He was surprised to suddenly notice a third player on the scene. A young man was getting up off of the grass where he'd been almost camouflaged in the slanting sunlight. His face was bloodied. He charged the blonde man in a rage, and though he was several inches shorter, he wrapped him up and took him straight to the ground. Then a gunshot rang out seemingly half an inch behind Kaywin's left ear. **"BREAK IT UP!"** A guard screamed out. **"BREAK IT UP OR I'LL MAKE SURE THEY SEND YOU BOTH INTO THE MINES AND YOU'LL NEVER SEE DAYLIGHT AGAIN!"** The two combatants, more startled than anything else, stopped rolling around in the forest debris and stood up. No one knew quite what was going to happen next. The aggressive blonde young man seized on the moment's uncertainty and merely walked off into the woods as if nothing had happened, grinning shamelessly and brushing debris off of his jumpsuit.

The guard knew it would be an enormous hassle to go after him and bring them all to justice--these guys would all be dead soon enough anyway--so he decided to cut things short. "No more of that. Understood?"

"Yes sir" answered the kid with the bloody face. When the guard reversed course back down the trail, he turned to the girl. "Are you alright?" Kaywin by this time had climbed the final steps into the little natural arena. The young lady was still pressed back against the trunk of the tree. She raised her eyebrows and shrugged at the stupid question. "Are you okay?" the lad persisted, undeterred.

She realized she wasn't going to be able to make him go away, or probably this other idiot/hero either, without saying

154

something to put their minds at ease. "Fine," she said, more like a question than an answer. "I'm in a government suicide program, so...fine?"

The young man laughed, and a little clot of blood went flying from his mouth. He held out his hand to the repulsed girl. She looked like she would rather shake hands with anybody else on earth, even maybe the jerk who had just assaulted her. "I'm Dublin Dunne," he said in a thick Irish accent. "But I'm not Irish!"

"Oh."

Who knows how long this awkward exchange would have gone on if Kaywin hadn't interrupted. "That was pretty gutsy...Dublin? Did you say your name was Dublin?"

"I'm Dublin Dunne." The thick Irish accent again. "But I'm not Irish!"

Kaywin indicated Dublin's bloody face. "Well you could have fooled me!" He hoped his own little joke would make the boy's embarrassingly-repeated one a **little** funnier, retroactively...

This kid Dublin--well, he wasn't repulsive exactly, although his bloody nose and lip weren't doing him any favors at the moment. It doesn't feel good to say it, but in the interest of historical accuracy, it would have to be said that yes, he was ugly. He was actually decently well-constructed, about five-foot-nine with fairly broad shoulders, deceptively strong and lean. His legs may have been a little short, and his butt was certainly big...and oddly womanly. It was above the shoulders where things got a little dicey...the skin of his neck seemed strangely loose; his head was oversized, especially if one was measuring front to back; his complexion, even in an age when going outdoors was not necessarily a weekly event, was off-puttingly pale; his cheeks blotchy red. The size of his head was visually exaggerated by his terrible unintentional black afro. You can tell an intentional, cultivated afro by the way it is sculpted evenly, combed out, with a healthy sheen and crisply manicured edges. Dublin's 'do' had none of this. It was, frankly, what nature had saddled him with. Other facial features betrayed to anyone who cared (they didn't) that this was a human in awkward transition; his straggly wisp of black moustache that someone should have told him to shave; his acne--who has acne in 2126?... No girls--I mean **no** girls--got past all of this to engage Dublin in friendly conversation, and if they had they would have been shut down completely by his throwback teeth. In America, in 2126, you could walk the streets for days and not see a tooth out of place. But the circumstances of his father's death when Dublin was only six years old had thrown their dental insurance into question, and his mother had been too beaten down to fight the system. The upshot of this was that he had missed out completely on his six-year braces, and, through a scarcity of his mother's and his own spirit, Dublin's relationship with orthodontery was ended before it began. This gross neglect resulted in a mouthful of teeth that would have helped him blend nicely in nineteenth century Europe: spaces on his top right side, overcrowding on his top left, to the point where the incisor on that side looked like it had been appliqued right on top of the teeth that should have been to the left and right of it. Some of his bottom teeth were turned a little, like tiny off-white ivory doors that wouldn't stay shut. This jumbled, discolored mess contrasted starkly and unpleasantly with

156

the bleached, even perfection of virtually every mouth he had ever seen. One of the two homeless people in his town of forty-five thousand had better teeth; in his mind, therefore, he characterized his dental situation as 'medium homeless.' This, and his dogged determination to **never** be seen as normal, often got him mistaken for a nineteenth century mill worker on break (by people who believed in time travel and thought that nineteenth century Irish mill workers got breaks.) The ridiculous Irish accent every time he introduced himself was the icing on the whiskey cake.

"I get it," he said to the young lady. "I'm too ugly to shake hands with, even though I just saved you from that jerk." She gave a short derisive bark of a laugh. She didn't need anyone to save her. "I know; I'm no **Prince Andrei** from *War and Peace.*" Crickets literally began to chirp in the encroaching twilight as he waited for someone to say 'Wow! You've read War and Peace?' Nobody said it. Nobody ever said it. Someday, someone would say it.

"And what's your name?" he asked. It was clear that the young lady was **not** going to shake his hand, so, without pulling it back in he just pivoted dramatically to his right and offered it to Kaywin.

"Kaywin." He shook Dublin's warm sweaty hand. "Good to meet you."

"Kevin?"

"**Kaywin**" he over-enunciated just enough to not sound rude. The girl, finally leaning forward again off of the tree a little (not to engage these idiots better, but to begin her escape from them) snorted derisively again.

"Kaywin!" She scrunched up her already-little face.

"Sounds like a two-year old trying to say 'Karen'..." There was an awkward pause. Her jibe was not quite funny enough to laugh at, and not quite offensive enough to dwell on, so they moved on.

"Sure," said Kaywin. "And you are?"

"Me?" She seemed almost caught off guard that some-one would ask her that. "Prudence."

Prudence! Thought Kaywin. *And you're making fun of* **my** *name?* But what he actually said was, "Prudence! Like the Beatles song..." She raised her plucked eyebrows and shook her head quickly and pointedly, rudely and wordlessly urging him to say what he was going to say because he clearly wasn't going to shut up. Her whole attitude screamed, *C'mon! Let's get this over with!*

Kaywin took a half a second to kind of assess this human being. She had to be sixteen, at least, if she got into the program, but she didn't look a day over twelve. It was hard not to contrast what he was looking at here with his own daughter Victoria, who had been twelve when...he shook it off...this girl was nothing like his daughter. Victoria had been the kindest, gentlest child, and yet full of beautiful confidence that meant she never had to lash out at the people around her to feel better about herself. This girl Prudence was jaded and vicious. She was pretty, sure, like Victoria had been, but in an almost disgusting sort of over-sexualized way that made him want to look away.

"You've heard of the Beatles?"

"I've heard the three songs they made us learn in school..."

Three songs. Hmmm. Must be one early Beatles song, one middle period, and one late... "Can I guess?"

She shrugged. Dublin was turning his shaggy bloody head back and forth between the two of them with over-eager interest. His mouth was open a little bit in amazement to see how this guy Kaywin was getting the pretty girl to speak.

"I Want to Hold Your Hand?" he guessed.

"Careful--this kid just slugged a guy for saying something like that." She said it quietly, staring at the ground and kicking the dirt with her foot. It was a good joke. She should have looked up to see Kaywin smiling. Dublin smiled too, and his blotchy red cheeks blushed a little further. "No...I've never heard of "I Want to Hold Your Hand." Sounds amazing." The sarcasm was getting a little heavy for Kaywin, but he had nowhere to be. He certainly didn't want to go back to the melee on the open grounds in front of the main building. Besides, he actually was a little curious to know what three Beatles songs they were teaching kids these days.

"Okay..." He glanced sidelong at Dublin as he made his next guess. "She Loves You." Dublin looked at Kaywin with a jolt, eyes wide and mouth opening. One tenth of one percent of him wondered if it was true. If it was true--ridiculous!--how would this guy know?

Prudence broke the spell. "Never heard of that one either. Sounds even more amazing." Wow. This young lady was determined to not make eye contact. Nobody and nothing seemed worth her time, even now when her other option was basically kicking a hole in the ground. Over the awkward silence that followed, they heard male and female voices loudly howling their approval of something salacious happening in the middle distance. Not distant enough. Kaywin was considering walking away. The clock was ticking down the short final months of his life now. How much of it did he want to spend being acutely disdained? He looked up again at the boy, to get a read on him. Was Dublin as over it as he was? Basically, if Kaywin chose to walk away up the little hill and into the deeper woods, would he be walking alone? But Dublin looked like he could stand there all night and absorb this young lady's venom. More than that, he looked like this was the best thing that had happened to him in some time, this lonely little awkward half-conversation with two strangers in the woods.

"Norwegian Wood!" the ugly young man shouted.

It was Kaywin's turn to be jolted. "How do you know that one? I mean, that's great that you know it, but...it's not the most well-known..."

"My dad used to play Beatles songs, some. That's the only one I remember."

Prudence had had enough of this, and, strapping her little bag over her shoulders, turned to head up the same wooded hill Kaywin had been eyeing for **his** escape. "Is your dad coming to the service tomorrow? Maybe you and him can get up on stage and sing a little duet." This was intended as her final barb, as she turned her back to them and started off.

"Naww...he's dead. My mom will be here though."

"Oh..." She stopped and turned her head back to them. "I'm...sorry?" She had heard people be contrite before, mostly on TV, but hadn't quite mastered it herself. She knew for one, that she had to pretend to be a little more interested. Dublin pointed his finger to his head and made a gun noise.

"He put his finger to his head and made a gun noise?"

Surely this will be too much, thought Kaywin, looking at Dublin's bloodied face for a reaction. But the tough young cookie just smiled, then actually laughed a little. "No, he used a real gun, unfortunately!"

A curious silence fell over the whole world. The voices of the obnoxious four thousand just a few hundred feet away through the trees were hushed by some mysterious coincidence. This made the crickets realize how loud they were being, so they too gave it a break. The last dying sunbeams intensified in rich orange, pink and purple, illuminating the bruised and scratched face of the girl turned back at the young man and the older man.

And here was the point where the three of them could have walked away from each other, each of them wishing the other two 'good luck'.

But they didn't.

Each of them felt a measure of disgust for what was transpiring on the commons, whilst clinging to **some** desire for company and diversion. But there was also something unnamable that went from eye to eye to eye betwixt the three; and when Prudence started for real up into the forest, Dublin and Kaywin just fell in next to her.

They climbed and chatted. "So I give up--," started Kaywin.

"Obviously," Dublin slipped in lightning-fast, referring to his joining the MCP.

"Seriously, what are the three Beatles songs they teach in school these days?"

"I don't remember what they taught us. I just remember my dad playing 'Norwegian Wood.'"

"I don't know," Prudence offered pointlessly. "Not the garbage you were guessing back there."

Kaywin started to open his mouth, but he knew better than to tell a sixteen year-old 'No, really, you should check out this incredibly old music!'

"Besides, if everybody back in the nineteen-sixties who was downloading Beatles songs had been obsessed with a hundred-and-fifty year-old music, then the Beatles never would have gotten famous."

This made Kaywin smile. All of his smiles were sad in tone, but this at least had been several sad smiles in a short time. "I am two-thirds impressed with that remark."

Prudence said nothing in return, but reached up under her hair and began fiddling with something. Her hair came to life, and in a few seconds she had finessed it back to her default settings--rainbow striped and shoulder length. "Holy Crap!" exclaimed Dublin. "You look like Linsom Felize!"

"You don't say," deadpanned Prudence. She stepped to one side for a second to grab a short, stout club-like branch, idly slapping it into her palm as they walked.

"I heard that get-up cost her sixty-thousand credits! How did you get one?" Prudence did her signature shrug. Dublin was the world's-worst at picking up female body language. "Why are you here, anyway? In the program, I mean…" She looked down a little, then straight ahead, then back down, before coming up with the perfect answer to the stupid question.

"Because my mother is a coward and my father is the Devil," she said. There was another pause as this cryptic reply sank in.

"I wouldn't have guessed that about your mother," said Kaywin, smiling. He was curious to see if she could take a little sarcasm as well as she could give it. She didn't say anything.

"Oh my God, did you guys see the Kalaysian Three-Star?" Dublin changed the topic on a dime.

"Yeah, I saw him," Kaywin said. "Glad I'm not rooming with him."

"What's a Kalaysian Three-Star?

"You've never heard of the Kalaysian Justice System?!"

I bet this guy's never had a girlfriend, thought Kaywin.

"Noo," Prudence inflected disdainfully. "I'm the idiot who's never heard of the Kalaysian Justice System. Is it like a comic book thing? Cuz you can stop right there if it is."

"No! Kalaysia is an island in the South Pacific; I would say a major island. They have a system there where men are allowed to **kill** three people over the course of their lifetimes without any legal repercussions. I know; right? It's crazy! But each time they kill someone they are required by the courts to get a big star tattooed on their forehead; that way, as you're walking down the street in Soboa," (he assumed everybody knew that Soboa was the capital of Kalaysia) "you can look at a man and kind of know how safe you are. If he has zero stars on his forehead, but he's a full-grown man, he is probably kind and gentle and not inclined to kill. If he has three stars, he probably has no conscience whatsoever, but he is out of kills; he knows if he kills again he will hang. It's the guys with one star, or two stars, that you have to really watch out for. They don't mind killing, and they have the freedom to do it."

"And you know all this from walking down the streets of Kalaysia?"

"No; I know it all from **reading**."

"Let's see how well they're teaching history these days," Kaywin piped in. "Do you remember **why** they started this unusual system?"

Dublin answered superfast to emphasize just **how** well he knew his history. "Because in 2059 the Emperor's son was convicted of two murders, so the Emperor--Shekala to be precise--strong-armed this law into effect."

"So if they hang people after their third murder, how is there a Kalaysian **Three**-star here?"

It was Dublin's turn to shrug. "They don't hang a person after their third murder, only after the fourth. Maybe he committed a fourth and somewhere between conviction and execution he might have escaped to America, or brokered some kind of deal. If so, he probably joined up to live for a little bit longer under the protection of the US Government. Tell you what. If I meet him, I will **NOT** ask him!" Dublin was giddy and out of breath from this back and forth conversation with a real girl. It didn't help that as the world dimmed around them, her astounding hair glowed all the brighter.

They almost stumbled at this point out of the woods and onto the bank of a small but robust creek. Standing on this narrow bald vantage point in their light blue jumpsuits they could see much of the grounds spread out below. It seemed like a natural stopping point for both walking and talking. Dublin was clearly a little worked up. He foraged mysteriously in the fringe of the forest for something, emerging a few seconds later with a big branch. He carried it to the stream and heaved it in; boyishly testing his might against the world. Prudence had already decided he was an idiot, 'War and Peace' or not, and watched this little demonstration with a dis-involved sneer. She didn't think much more highly of Kaywin, though he could at least talk to someone for five minutes without saying how smart he was or how ugly. She was a little surprised to see him join in mannishly, digging a slightly smaller branch out of the underbrush, and throwing it into the creek behind Dublin's. She had noticed, idly, that he had started to work at the larger, fallen trunk of a tree-- just for a second--and then had opted for the smaller one. She suspected that he didn't want to be seen as showing up Dublin. It was a nice gesture. Weird, but nice.

The two branches found the same current, spun sideways, and caught between two rocks. "Why don't you put the big one in?" She prodded; half out of a feeling of intellectual superiority, and half just the opposite--she too wanted to see what would happen. The stream reminded her of the one behind her apartment back home in Geyserville, and the trapped branches brought to mind the time she had dammed the waters. She smiled inwardly remembering the sensations of cold wet water all up her legs; the earthy aroma of the dirt and rotting wood she had used…and the warmth of the sunlight on her face, which at that time, five years ago or so, still had a little glimmer of hope behind it.

Dublin and Kaywin worked together to free the fallen tree trunk and hurl it into the brook. Now the little spot between the two rocks was stopped up. This was enough for them, for tonight, but suddenly, and a little terrifyingly, men and women started to emerge from the woods on the opposite bank like zombies. As the night fell, they must have spotted Prudence's glowing rainbow hair from the commons below, and climbed up the hillside by the scores. When they saw what Kaywin and Dublin had started, they joined in with complete Attabuoy-abandon, hurling everything in sight into the stream with an absolute disregard for consequences. Prudence, Kaywin and Dublin ducked back into the woods with a shared determination not to "party" with this crowd.

The three of them headed down the little mountain back toward the dorms, ducking under branches, squeezing through pricker-bushes and talking, a little more, about their first day at the MCPNH. "This place isn't built for this many people," Kaywin observed. "I'm just glad I got a bunk."

"Believe it or not, I got a room to myself," Dublin enthused.

"No way; really?"

"Well--it's not really a room; it's a straight up tiny closet with a mat on the floor, and all the brooms and mop-buckets and stuff pushed to one side. What about you Prudence? Did you get a bunk?"

She shrugged as usual, but it was too dark now for them to see it. "Dunno. I got here like an hour and a half ago. Our bus broke down and there was all kinds of drama. We were stuck for like four hours...guess I'll find out now."

The night was growing cool as they climbed the granite steps to the heavy front door with the antique-style horizontal bar that you had to push to open. The noise of their entry resounded off the walls and high ceiling of the lobby. They parted without much thought as to whether they would see each other again, except for Dublin, who was sure he would die if he didn't see Prudence first thing tomorrow morning.

She went to the desk for her belated room assignment.

Kaywin and Dublin walked down the hall together until it terminated in a 'T'. Kaywin retired to the left toward his warm dry bunk, and Dublin right, toward his broom closet floor. He opened the closet door and almost cried out. He had to shove a hand over his still-bloody mouth to keep quiet. There was a man sleeping in his spot. He was sprawled out lengthwise down the tiny room's center, with his head close to the door.

Across his forehead were tattooed three large blue stars.

8

Days

Prudence awoke suddenly at five-thirty AM, an hour before she had to, because the crazy woman in the bunk above her was having a panic attack. Her right arm was still pretty sore from her battle with the raccoon (that seemed like a lifetime ago), so she tried slamming her open left palm into the wooden slats above her, twice, but it didn't seem to help. An older lady got up off of the floor and whispered to 'Penny' repeatedly that it was going to be alright. This strange deception troubled Prudence. *Why can't people tell the truth, ever? Why do people lie constantly?* **How** *is it 'going to be alright'?* Her only conversation with this Penny lady had been like five words, trying to figure out who was going to brush their teeth in the tiny bathroom first. This was enough for Prudence to figure out that she had an IQ of probably eighty. And even she wasn't buying that 'it was going to be alright'; she continued whimpering like a baby and gasping for air three feet above Prudence.

Pru knew from experience that she wasn't going back to sleep. She took something from under her pillow. It was a very rusty, very old railroad spike that she had found in the woods last night. Turning on her side to the painted cool cinderblock wall she pressed the flat edge of the iron point against it. She listened for a second, and picked up the spastic rhythm of Penny's panicked exhalations. Lightly at first, she timed her back and forth sharpening motions to match it. It was nearly pitch black in the small dorm room. After a few short strokes, however, she could tell by the feel of things that the paint had peeled right off the block. *Good. Now we're getting somewhere* she thought as the rougher bare concrete made some headway against the hundred and seventy years of thick rust caked on the railroad relic. Bit by bit more and more of the shiny iron was exposed, gleaming ever so slightly in the dark. Unfortunately 'Penny' began to calm down and Prudence had to lighten her strokes and then give it up altogether. She felt the tip of the spike. It was warmed from the friction, and sharper than it had been, but she wasn't sure if it was sharp enough. Chances were she would find a few minutes to work on it some more, during a bathroom break or something. It wasn't likely that she would need it anyway, but it was good to be prepared.

She could feel that a significant swath of paint had been stripped away by her exertions. Fortunately she'd had the foresight to use a spot low on the wall that would be hidden by her pillow. She had no idea if this place did inspections or anything. For the moment, she put the spike in the left hand pocket of her jumpsuit.

The other five women in the room settled back down. Prudence could tell by the slow regularity of their breathing that at least three of them had fallen back asleep. This was not going to happen for her. She lay flat on her back now with her eyes wide open. She was deeply hungry, starving.

There had been food put out for the busful of late arrivals last night, but she had missed out completely when she made her escape into the woods. She hoped that breakfast would be pretty immediate after the six-thirty alarm, but if not, she'd be fine. Starvation was one of the many things she was used to.

She couldn't understand why the dumb lady above her would have a panic attack. This place was like a freaking vacation so far. Besides, they clearly were not going to die today. *Weak*...she thought. *Weak, weak, weak*...

The hardest thing so far had been those two jerks in the woods last night who had wanted to be her BFF's. It would be her mission today to try to avoid them completely, before the old dude tried to offer her advice, or the ugly one tried to marry her. She tried to remember their names...Darwin? Dunkin? No, **Dublin**, that was it; she remembered his stupid Irish joke and his hideous face, and cringed. She remembered the other name, Kaywin, cuz she had burned him pretty good with that 'two-year-old trying to say Karen' joke. She half-smiled meanly to herself.

She put her hand down in her pocket and cradled the railroad spike gently like a talisman. Then, utilizing a skill she had mastered through many a sleepless night, she stared straight up and cleared her mind absolutely.

Several corridors away, Dublin Dunne was in the same party-boat. He too lay flat on his back with his eyes wide open. He had positioned himself very uncomfortably with his feet inches away from the Kalaysian Three-Star's feet, and his head at the back of the tiny broom closet. If he relaxed at all, his feet would brush up against the feet of the deco-rated multi-murderer. This had happened one time, around two-thirty in the morning, when he had lost the handle of his vigilance and dozed off. He regained consciousness thirty minutes later, instantly horrified, his feet touching the Kalay-sian's feet. What made it worse was that when he woke up, the Three-Star wasn't even sleeping. He was doing something deftly and quickly on his Sofee, laughing quietly to himself, and he didn't go back to sleep the rest of the night. Dublin could see the faint glow of the little screen, and could hear the scary man's reactions to whatever was on it; sometimes laughing again, and sometimes spitting out what could only have been Kalaysian curses, and tapping at the screen angrily. Dublin couldn't decide which was more worrisome.

Enough light eked in under the closet door from the hallway for Dublin to see some of the cleaning supplies and equipment around them. He counted at least seven ways his roommate could kill him if he dozed. *Why does it matter? I'm here to die anyway, right?*

--not in a closet, sleeping on your first night...

*--in the grand scheme of things--if there even **is** a scheme--does it **really** matter? If humans go extinct in half a million years, or three million years, or a billion years, will it matter if Dublin Dunne got strangled with a mop-head on April 2nd, 2126?*

--maybe. If it affects the quality of life for trillions of future hu-mans. Besides, it's not on your death wish-list:

3) Deep-sea diving accident after locating Atlantis.

*2) Attaining warp-speed in a modified moon cruiser. Actually, choking on a cashew **after** attaining warp-speed in a modified moon cruiser.*

1) Time-travel assassination of either Adolf Hitler or Alexander Graham Bell.

(Dublin knew that time-travel hadn't been invented yet, and didn't think it was actually possible, but he also knew that the government had secrets on top of secrets on top of secrets.)

--you are right, voice inside my head. You are always right. I wish I was more like you.

--stop. I'm blushing.

*--I don't want to change the subject, but--*he suddenly teared up, and had to really struggle to stop himself from sobbing--*but if just **one** of those girls, just **one** time, had said, 'Yes, I will go out with you; I will give you a chance; you seem really nice and smart...'...* Amanda, Jennifer, Brenda, Sue-Dahli (it took him thirty seconds to get to the end of the list) *Bethenny, Honda, or Chloe--if just one of them had said 'yes,' I wouldn't be here right now. I would have been given the hope and the strength to struggle on.*

--I agree. But it's too late now.

Everybody's Sofees alarmed at once at six-thirty exactly, and a very emotional day was under way. This would be their last chance to say goodbye to the lives they were leaving behind. They would each have one, or hopefully two loved ones as guests for a service that would begin at noon. After the service, there would be two hours for visitation, and final--completely final--goodbyes. Nobody even knew who was coming. The tension, the expectation, combined with the closeness of fellow-sufferers (**too much** closeness, thanks to the overcrowding in the small rooms) at least provided a sense of community and shared destiny.

Prudence was much more concerned with breakfast, which was delicious, but a little small. Halfway through the meal, she heard the people around her at the table commenting on something, and pointing across the cafetorium. She looked up wolfishly, and saw something new. Some fool in a dingy robe--oh look; two of them actually--were standing up and appeared to be offering half of their breakfast to whoever wanted it. They weren't talking. She supposed the words 'eat mine' on their foreheads were intended to get the message across. Message received! She almost leaped up out of her seat to get the attention of the ascetic nearest her, but some jackster beat her to it. Well, she knew where to sit next time anyway. As she sat back down, disappointed but moving on, she noticed that guy "Kaywin" looking at her from the table across the aisle. She very deliberately avoided any further eye contact, but the next thing she knew he was standing in front of her with his breakfast tray.

"You didn't get a chance to eat last night, did you? You must be starving. Do you want my biscuit?" Prudence weighed her options quickly and wordlessly. Yes, of course she wanted the biscuit, but was it worth it? Would it turn a meaningless walk in the woods last night into an unwanted friendship? It wasn't worth the chance.

"No, I'm good." The old man walked away immediately, back to his seat. The fact that he didn't embarrass her by **insisting** she take the biscuit actually made her more grateful than the offer itself. She frowned thoughtfully and annihilated the rest of her meal.

There was a large chunk of free time before they were required to muster on the green at eleven-thirty. Showers were taken, five minutes per person, or the water would cut off whether you had shampoo in your hair or not. When her Sofee dinged and said, "Estrada, Prudence to shower fourteen," she shucked her robe in a flash and was in. She felt disgusting, and made the most of her cleaning time. Dryer twenty-two was open when her water cut off. Three minutes later she was back in her robe. She noticed that her blue jumpsuit had disappeared from the changing room. She had expected this, and had hidden the railroad spike in a nook on the underside of the bench in the little stall. Her alternate jumpsuit was cleaned, pressed and folded on the little seat, and she donned it, enjoying the warmth it had retained from one of the facility's huge industrial dryers. She slipped the spike down into the left hand pocket slyly while looking about her casually for cameras.

She went back to her room hoping to find no one there. She had to settle for the company of one lady whose name she didn't even know yet. She was absorbed in her expanded Sofee screen when Prudence opened the door. She looked up when the weird young lady entered, then right back down at her screen, demonstrating no desire whatsoever to further their relationship. *Perfect*, thought Pru. *Let's keep it that way.* She got the little makeup bag out of her duffle and snuck into the bathroom, emerging fifteen minutes later looking impressively Asian, right down to the concealing curtain of jet-black hair.

Dublin used his time after showering to check his little broom closet. His roommate was finally not there, so he lay back down and slept like a rock from 8:20 to 10:15. At 10:30, the section leaders mustered their MCs; each of the four-thousand one-hundred and twelve received a short message telling them where to meet; some sections in the cafetorium; some by the bridge over the little stream, some by the flag-pole out front. Dublin, in Section G, had to hustle to make it to the little bridge. He had no idea just yet what the penalties might be for things like showing up two minutes late to a muster. Fortunately, he made it on time, jogging up to the cluster of section-mates with four minutes to spare. He sort of noticed-without-noticing that the large streambed under the bridge was dry but he didn't think anything about it then.

His section leader was a nice Army Captain named Kelley. She ran down the schedule for the rest of the day with them: they would be seated together among the sea of folding chairs on the green by 11:30; Family and Friends service would be from 12:00 to 12:30; from 12:30 to 3:00 would be final visitation with family and friends over a delightful lunch. By 3:15 and not a second later the last of the visitors would be out of the gates. From 3:15 to 3:30 their section and two others were in charge of disassembling the stage and returning it to a small hangar-like building she pointed out to them through the trees. There would be 'quiet time' in the dorm rooms from 3:30 to 5:30 PM, followed by supper in the cafetorium at 6:00. The day would be capped off with free time from 6:45 to 9:15; a variety of activities would be offered, including two different movies playing at two of the campuses' state of the art theaters. A hand went up. "What movies?"

"I don't know what movies."

Tomorrow, and the two days following, would be devoted

to assessment and assignment. "**How** you can best serve the interests of the Country, and **where** you will be doing it…"

The late morning sun was brilliant on the commons. On the smallish stage, two large flags were couched on a backdrop of billowy deep blue velvet. The familiar Stars and Stripes of the United States of America on the left was balanced by the Meaningful Conclusion Program banner on the right. This was a stylized, minimalist army-green figure laying on its side, its unisex body curled tightly around a presumably live grenade. Behind it, fifty-five royal blue shapes, looking more like upside-down test tubes than people, represented the fifty-five states of our glorious Union. All on a field of snowy white. Everybody made fun of it relentlessly, but when you looked at it alone, without the jokes flying, it was actually a little stirring.

The stage looked out over a small sea of light blue jumpsuits, and a rainbow of faces all blinking in the sunlight. The murmur of a rumor started in the pregnant silence; heads started to turn, then far away they could hear the rifleshot-echo of the main gates opening.

Everyone was almost backwards in their seats now as the same buses that had delivered them yesterday to this place now cavalcaded back into the MCPNH grounds in force; there had to a be hundred of them this time. Excited but still-hushed talking rippled through the seated Goners. It picked up steam even more when the buses parked and began to empty, everyone straining almost out of their seats in search of their loved ones.

Dublin's heart was in his throat. He looked for minutes

without spotting anyone, then thought he caught a glimpse of his mother. Among the several thousand visitors, almost all sharply dressed and almost all in black, it was like trying to pick out a specific grackle on a lawn completely blacked over with them. Uncle Kevin with his graying bushy beard and ponytail was easier to spot. What a relief, having him here with his indestructible good humor to balance Dublin's probably-hysterical mother. Funny how families worked like that. He waved, but so did everyone else. It was all just arm exercise until the mass of family and friends drew closer and assumed the eight thousand folding chairs behind them. Then he spotted his Mom for sure, and waved with renewed energy. She was looking for him elsewhere in the crowd, but Uncle Kevin grabbed her shoulder and pointed at Dublin. His uncle gave him a single wave, but most of his attention was concentrated on keeping her together. She saw Dub, but made no acknowledgement. It was too much for her to take. She looked like she hadn't slept or eaten in the eight days he'd been gone. She didn't wave because in a way it would have been like giving her blessing to his horrible decision. He understood, and condescended to 'forgive' her; hoping that she would one day forgive him and be at peace with his destiny. He turned back around to face the stage. Even the split-second of cold eye contact with his family was enough to break the ice of the eight days' silence, and he viewed the upcoming proceedings with a little less dread now. He went back to trying to spot Prudence.

Kaywin, seated in the second row from the back of the MC section, was shielding his eyes with his hand and searching far and wide in the crowd for his sister. Then he heard her distinctive laugh from so close that he thought it must have been in his head. She waved vigorously and caught his attention from the front row of now-seated guests. He shared her laugh at his ineptitude in spotting her, and returned her wave. Her husband--Kaywin's brother-in-law--was with her and they exchanged salutes in reference to a joke they had long had with one another. Satisfied, Kaywin turned back around in his seat. He was surprised to have to wipe away a tear.

Prudence, much to her discomfort, was seated in the very thick of the crowd. It made her skin crawl to be so surrounded. She tried to control her breathing as she looked around for her best avenue of escape, should escape be necessary. There was virtually nowhere to go. Probably the middle aisle that bisected the huge crowd was her best option, but that was like thirty seats to her right.

She gathered herself. She tried to look as Asian as she could, holding her face as Asianly as she could, even trying to think Asian thoughts. When she felt like she was in character as much as she could be, she turned quickly--not suspiciously quickly--and surveyed the wall of eight thousand visitors for just a few seconds, as long as she dared. She turned back around when her mental timer went off. She looked down at her hands, shaking a little bit, and breathed a sigh of relief.

She didn't see him.

Acting-MCP-President Beauregard couldn't seem to get it right. There he was up on the little stage, wearing a suit that was darkly appropriate for the solemnness of the occasion, but had to be at least two sizes too big. This man needed a tailor like nobody's business.

He was standing one step back from the microphone, having to hold his left sleeve way up to see the seconds counting down on his rose-colored Sofee. It was noon. He released the sleeve and it swallowed up his hand completely. He stepped forward to the mic. "Ladies and Gentlemen," he drawled into it, stretching the 'men' in 'gentlemen' out into three or four syllables. "Ladies and Gentlemen, thank you so much for being with us here today. This is just a gorgeous April day. Welcome to Houston! This is our largest class of MC's ever. Which means this is also our largest group of guests ever, which is so great; these people need your support, so thank you thank you thank you! I **think** we are ready to do this for a crowd of twelve thousand, but I hope you will understand and bear with us if something isn't quite perfect, or if we run out of hot sauce...I don't mean to scare anybody. I really don't think we're going to run out of hot sauce. Ahea!" He laughed. On either side of the massive field, buffet tables were set up for what seemed like a quarter-mile, and hundreds of workers were carrying out aluminum serving trays; cases of napkins; giant water coolers, and all the sundry trappings of an outdoor lunch for thousands. "Anyway...," he had expected a bigger laugh out of his hot sauce joke, but he swallowed his disappointment and carried on, "I hope you will permit me at this time to introduce a wonderful man; our universal-faith chaplain, Father Armand. Father?" He traded places with the only other man on the stage; Father Armand stood up from the solitary folding chair, and APMCP Beauregard sat down in it, pulling folds of navy suit-cloth aside here and there to get comfy.

"Thank you, President Beauregard............." He began one of those long pauses that men of God employ sometimes to demonstrate that they are not operating on their audience's schedule, but on that of a higher power. "...and thank **you, mothers.......fathers...sons.....daughters........cousins**.............................." (He really wanted that one to resonate for some reason) "......................best friends, unclesniecesandnephews." (It was unclear what he had against uncles, nieces and nephews.) "Neighbors, bosses, Godparents; whoever you may be, and whatever your relation to these sacrificial lambs, thank you....... for being with us here today."

There was a palpable feeling of discomfort created by his use of the term 'sacrificial lambs', but he seemed to know what he was doing. He was a good speaker. Despite, or maybe even partly **because of** his dramatic pauses, his timing was effective. His voice was rich, deepish, and reassuring, and the high-quality PA carried it across the lawn with strength, so that even in the back rows people could absorb his message without straining for the words:

"While there is room today for a great many feelings--respect, love, pride...and yes, fear; and yes, maybe anger; and yes, maybe resentment....................let us **NOT** pretend-----let us **NOT PRETEND** that this is **NOT** a funeral. It is." These last two words, though not yelled, seemed to echo across the grassy sward for some reason. "It is a funeral."

The throng of many thousands of relatives and friends, mostly immaculately groomed and dressed in full acknowledgement of the occasion's gravity, had been holding it together for the most part. One poor lady had been crying audibly from the get-go. Another had shouted something at some point, maybe a name? But now, the Chaplain's sensitive but direct laying-forth of the facts seemed to open the flood-gates. Another lady--someone's mother or sister or daughter or best friend--let loose with a loud sob all at once, and kept on with it, and from that point there was no going back.

"These men and women whom you have loved so well"--two more criers-- "that you have held as babies in your arms; have run with, played with, grown up with.......con-fided in..."

Holy Crap; is this dude trying to start a riot? Kaywin won-dered. *Presumably he knows what he's doing?*

"These men and women have loved you back. Some, I am sure, have expressed it to you. Some, I am sure have struggled with expressing it, or have forgotten to **try** to express it like we are all sometimes guilty of. When free visitation begins in a few minutes, some will **still** fall short of expressing it the way they **feel** it in their **hearts**." His voice quavered here as if he had caught himself off guard. "But be assured that they have loved you, and relied on you to get as far as they have. Without your love, many of these worthy people would have fallen off the map a long time ago." More and more the Chaplain was having to elevate his volume, as the crowd's wailing and sobbing threatened to drown him out. "I'm not going to pretend to know the history of each and every one of these courageous MCs...however....**something**..... **something** went wrong with everyone of these people. It was something different and unique for everyone of them, I am sure, but they have all made the decision to make it right. It is reasonable to assume that there were important people missing in a lot of their lives. Speaking candidly, I'll say **most**.

And shame on those people. It is reasonable, likewise, to assume that most of you sharp-dressed men and women who have shown up to honor your loved ones today, are **not** the ones who were missing. **YOU!**" This word he straight-up yelled. "**You** are **not** the ones who were missing; you were the ones who were there for them. Please, please, put your hearts at ease. If what you gave them was not enough, it does not necessarily follow that you could have given more..."

Prudence, early on the speech, had activated her ear implants and accessed a favorite playlist on her Sofee. While she was grooving to obliterative drone-tech, she amused herself by keeping one eye on the idiot in the giant suit. He was supposed to be President or something, but as the Chaplain began quoting every religious text from the Bible, to the Koran, to the Bhagavad-Gita, he was drilling a hole in the stage planks with his eyes, and at one point between the Upanishads and the Dead Sea Scrolls, he actually started to fall asleep. He jolted awake as he sensed the concluding tone in Chaplain Armand's voice.

"You have all been briefed on what transpires next. For many reasons, the security of our great nation certainly being one of them, there can be **absolutely no contact** after 3:15 this afternoon between these MCs and the outer world. **You**" --he indicated the crowd of miserable loved ones--"being the outside world. I am required to emphasize that your failure to abide by this will result in **consequences** for your loved one that will be both **immediate and final.**"

"In the natural and more desirable course of events, when your brave MC meets his or her death, be it three weeks from now--the earliest possible date barring accident--or two years from now--the latest date possible--you will receive an e-mail from the MCPNH, signed by the President of the United States. Do not expect details beyond the official time and date of death; there will be none."

"As for the matter at hand...I am almost finished here...when I am, a homing program will be activated on your Sofees, allowing you to unite with your friends and family in a timely fashion. **When you have found each other--when you have found each other please retire to the grassy area BEHIND this stage, so that you are not blocking other MCs from finding their loved ones!** Lastly, when your **Sofees alert you at three PM exactly, VISITORS MUST RETURN IMMEDIATELY TO THE BUS YOU ARRIVED ON! WE ABSOLUTELY CANNOT HAVE ANY STRAGGLERS!"** He paused to create a little separation between the harsh demands he had been obligated to make and the final message he wanted to give them all now from his heart.

"These are your last two hours with the people you love. Don't waste a second of it. Thank you, and I bless the light that shines on all of you."

He dropped the mic...accidentally, as he was trying to put it back on the stand, but still, he dropped the mic.

Predictably, a mob scene ensued. It was almost like a clash of armies, with the blue jumpsuited forces outnumbered by the black suits eight thousand to four thousand. They met and merged with a clamor that was only missing the clash of steel on steel. For about two minutes it didn't look like this system was going to work out at all; it was utter chaos, then bit by bit it became less crowded and frantic as little blue and black clusters made their way to the other side of the stage.

Even though Kaywin knew exactly where his sister and brother-in-law were, and never really lost sight of them, it took a couple of minutes to reach them. As soon as they made contact, they quit the melee with relish, almost sprinting to sanctuary behind the stage.

"Oh my God, this is **crazy,**" said Genie, looking around her with wide eyes. "I didn't think there'd be so many!"

"You got all different types too, huh?" observed her husband Gary. Kaywin hugged him forcefully, with feeling. He had always liked Gary.

"Oh yes we do! It's good to see you buddy. It's really good to see you both." He embraced his sister and held on tight.

Dublin found his mom and Uncle Kevin within about five minutes or so. He was worried about her at first. She just looked...overcome. And she didn't speak a word to him or look directly at him for what seemed like a very long time. "Mom, we have to get out of the way here or we're gonna get run over." He took his mother's left arm while his uncle supported her right. Working together, the three of them made it to the relative calm of the backstage area. Dublin darted back with guilt-inspired quickness and grabbed a folding chair for her. She sank down in it and put her head in her right hand. He wasn't sure what was happening, and was on the verge of seeking medical assistance, when he saw her frail frame wracked with sobs. He was almost out of his mind with his inability to do anything for her at this point. He felt incredibly sorry, and sorry for her. He was bright red with overwhelming shame and emotion. He stood in front of her seated, weeping, unseeing form for a few seconds and then did the only thing he **could** do. He dropped to his knees and embraced her thin shoulders tightly, and he too was reduced to a sobbing mess.

"I'm-I'm-I'm sorry Ma! I'm so sorry! I'm so sorry!" He was a mess, as bad as her if not worse. It goes without saying that Dublin was an ugly crier.

"I'm sorry, too! I'm sorry! It's **my** fault! I shouldn't have been so hard on you! I just wanted you to do better than I did. But that's not fair; that's really not!" Her motherly instinct won out at the eleventh hour over her wounded sensibilities. There was no fighting it, with her only child wailing in her arms like the baby he had been just months ago, it seemed, with no solace in the world other than his mother's tenderness. It felt like her boy was going to the gallows for crimes **she** had committed, and his father had committed... she couldn't understand it; he wasn't ugly to her; he was her little Dublin...

Dublin opened his eyes for a second, sensing a change in the world around him. Uncle Kevin's nose was less than an inch from his; his eyes were crazy wide and he was grinning broadly. "Hey!" he said. "I'm here, too!" Thank goodness for Uncle Kevin. "Are we going to have a crying contest? I'm gonna grab an onion from that buffet over yonder and beat you both!" Hurray for humor, and the soldier-clowns who carry it with them always. Instantly mother and son were able to imagine that there was still happiness somewhere in the world.

Prudence had everything pretty well mapped out. When the third or fourth group of temporarily reunited loved ones had started for the area behind the stage, she hotfooted it over and fell in closely behind them. Once there, she kept moving through the growing crowd of crying, laughing and hugging people. After about ten minutes, she thought it would be safe to stop for a bit. She was in a little spot of shade directly behind the stage, about to lean back against it, when it disappeared. The entire structure, by someone's command, had been lifted clean off the ground by about fifty people from whatever section, and was being shuffled out of the way of the proceedings. Prudence felt exposed, as if the shower curtain had been removed while she was showering. She casually took five steps forward, easing back into the crowd.

Once she felt adequately hidden again, she turned around to look through where the stage had been, hoping to confirm to herself that nobody there was looking for Prudence Estrada. The crowd of relatives in black was almost completely gone; she saw an older man and woman together, pleading with one of the hundreds of guards for help. She guessed that maybe their crazy son or daughter had fled into the woods. The guard was on his Sofee, trying to track down the fugitive. She had a cynical little inward laugh at this scene transpiring some forty yards from her. Then she spotted something closer and funnier:

About thirty to forty unwanted MCs were still massed together stupidly in front of the missing stage, like human leftovers. They were blinking in the sun, turning this way and that; looking at where the stage had been, then back at where their visitors **should** have been. For some reason, in this context, the matching cerulean-blue jumpsuits only added to the helplessness of their appearance, making them look like thirty-five lost toddlers in matching footy pjs. This whole image hit Prudence suddenly and, combined with the relief she felt that her 'father' hadn't made it from Geyserville, or her 'mother' from San Francisco, she let out a loud bark of a laugh before she could stop herself. Whoops. She looked around furtively; no one seemed to have noticed. Not that she cared. Then suddenly she made eye contact with that Kaywin dude.

He had heard her vicious laugh and was looking right at her. His face, which had probably been handsome at one time, registered two emotions at once. There was disapproval, sure, but also the merest hint, the slightest acknowledgement that yes, it was a little comical, and that under the circumstances they could all be forgiven for small indiscretions. What did she care what he thought anyway? He probably didn't even recognize her.

Kaywin **did** recognize Prudence. He'd already seen a glimpse of her little quick-change act the night before, when she had gone from Young-Linsom-Felize to Plain-Jane in a matter of moments. Besides, her petiteness and prettiness stood out in the grizzled crowd. On top of that, though she probably did not realize it, her raging cynicism was like a neon sign over her head flashing "Hello, My Name Is Prudence. Now go the **** away!" He didn't judge her. He didn't know her. It's dangerous to judge someone too quickly, even out in the normal world.

Her laugh had drawn his attention to the huddled outcasts. They were standing sort of back-to-back in a confused circle. Kaywin thought they looked like early Christians thrown into the arena, waiting for the lions to be released on them.

Over his mother's shoulder, Dublin saw them, too. As absorbed as he was in his own misery, his heart went out to them. They looked like they were waiting to be picked for the kickball team.

It was Kaywin, of all the thousands, who acted first. "Do you mind," he said to his sister "if I go break this up?"

"Oh my gosh, no; I'll go with you." Having gotten beyond the emotional intensity of the first ten minutes, they linked arms and skipped like children to the cluster of distraught souls.

"Hey!" said Kaywin to the entire group. "You wanna join us?" A woman-MC had approached from the opposite side at almost the same moment. Nobody was going to let these people suffer further; they were all family now. Every one of the neglected Goners found a foster family within seconds. The process of meeting new friends took some of the edge off of saying goodbye to the old ones, and a palpable wave of good spirits made its way mercifully through the crowd.

Most of the thousands had experienced what Dublin had experienced: an intense emotional meltdown that lasted about ten minutes, before the spell was broken by laughter.

It is possible that somewhere on campus an MCPNH official was turning knobs and dials and manipulating the release of mood-altering chemicals from the Attabuoys still in their systems... But who knows? We have all been there, in the hospital waiting room, when the tears and the tension become unbearable, and someone cracks the first joke, and everyone piles on, and a strange happiness erupts as everyone is reminded of why they care about each other in the first place...so maybe this was no different from that. Times a thousand...

The fried chicken was delicious; the macaroni and cheese was delicious; the coleslaw was good, but not as good as Grandma's... The whole thing had become a spectacle. It was a once-in-a-lifetime opportunity for people-watchers, and students of the human condition. Mothers and sons were dancing; fathers and sons were racing each other; one of the forgotten few had been found so instantly likeable that he was hoisted up on the shoulders of a small crowd and celebrated publicly.

It was this man, a forty-two year old factory worker from Flint, Michigan, who, from his elevated position, first heard and saw something strange approaching the commons from the woods. The change in his demeanor caused a hush in the crowd around him, which spread quickly throughout the entire multitude. Every head turned toward the gentle slope of the hill, and every ear and eye strained to make sense of it. There was a distant unbroken rumble, and a low sheet of shimmering grey rolling in their direction.

The dam they had built last night, and that almost every

one of them had forgotten completely, had burst!

Shortly after the wall of water broke over the far end of the field it became clear that this would not be a life-threatening phenomenon, just a huge mess. Almost the entire crowd stood frozen in bemusement as the miniature tsunami rolled among them and past them at ankle-height. The factory worker was let down, a little bit unevenly as it turned out, and he belly-flopped accidentally into the quagmire. Someone had to assuage the poor man's embarrassment at that point, and it was Uncle Kevin who took a good running start and joined him, face down in the muck.

The remainder of the afternoon was an unexpected triumph of the human spirit. In the words of Chaplain Armand, they did not 'waste a second of it.' While I would love to report that Dublin's Mom, and Vance's ninety-six year old Grandma, and even Prudence all cavorted in the mud with wild abandon, a commitment to historical accuracy compels me to restrain myself. Let's just say that a lot of very well dressed people **did**, and that some of them **were** Grandmas, and that the huge industrial washing machines at the MCPNH campus didn't stop running for three days afterwards.

But all things must pass, and at 2:45, everyone's Sofee flashed them a warning that the party was almost over. There was a return to seriousness. Muddy, final embraces across the entire green went on for minute after minute. Prudence picked her way through the hushed crowd back in the direction of her dorm room. Despite her best efforts, her shoes had gotten muddy, which annoyed her to no end. She almost held her breath as she wove her way between hugging tandems and trios; the hot afternoon air was thick with apologies and forgiveness, and she was allergic to both. Too late, she stumbled close to Dublin and his mother. Crap. He saw her.

"Oh! Mom! This is my friend Prudence! The one I was telling you about!"

Friend?!

The poor woman broke free from the muddy boy. She extended her tiny, bony hand to Prudence. "I've heard such nice things about you."

Prudence wracked her brain, trying to think of anything she might have said or done in the sixteen hours she had known this freak that might have been misconstrued as 'nice'... but she took the old lady's hand for a tenth of a second, just to get it over with.

"Great," she said, moving on.

"It was nice to meet you. Good luck..." On her way back to the building, she approached as close as she dared to the fringe of the forest. She felt casually in her pocket for the sharpened railroad spike. A small part of her was sad that her father hadn't showed up. She started to pull the weapon out with the intention of tossing it back into the woods, then reconsidered.

She would hang on to it for a little while.

The experimental, multi-layered remote-controlled Attabuoy pills needed a little tweaking. This had not been bad for a first group-attempt, but there were some problems here at the tail end of things. While most of the exhausted MCs were stumbling their way back to the dorms for 'quiet time', upwards of seventy-five of them had fallen asleep in the mud. The buses were rolling away forever, with concerned faces in the windows watching guards trying to prod the prostrate suicidals awake. Kaywin didn't know why this was happening as he made his way back to the main building, but he was learning to overlook some of the peculiarities of the Program.

~

"What do you mean I **have** to go?"

Prudence was trying to return to her room after supper in the cafetorium. Her section leader, a young Army Captain who seemed pretty full of himself, wasn't having it.

"This is not a vacation, Sweetheart. If we can't get you to go watch a freaking movie, or play a softball game, how are we going to trust you to do what you're told when the action gets hot? Cuz if we can't we can always just send you to the mines," (Prudence bristled at the thought of narrow tunnels deep in the Earth) "or bio-testing."

"What's bio-testing?" It didn't **sound** so bad.

"You'll find out, probably, at the rate you're going."

She exhaled through her teeth for about seven seconds, until she sensed that the Captain was about to speak again, then she cut him off. "Which movie is closest?"

"Wisconsin Johnson. Fonteneau Building, two doors behind us. Follow the crowd of sci-fi geeks."

"Ugh."

"Prudence! Prudence! Wait up!" This day just kept getting better and better. She closed her eyes for a second and cursed to herself as she walked down the hill towards the "Fonteneau Building." But she was so tired from running and dodging all day that she just let it happen.

The two of them sidled up next to her, Kaywin on her left and Dublin on her right. Although Prudence wasn't feeling it, there was kind of an electric feeling running through everybody else tonight. There was a tremendous feeling of community. They had all just come through something incredibly difficult, and were just far enough out from whatever mortal danger lay ahead to really sink their teeth into these last few days of free(ish) living.

"Did you hear about my roommate?"

She waited, hoping he would realize for himself what a stupid question this was. He didn't. "Who would have told me about your roommate? Besides, I thought you were sleeping alone, in a closet."

"I thought so too, then I get home--I get back to my closet, last night, and find out I am sharing it with someone." He paused. It was apparently important to him that she make a guess.

"Ivan Turgenev."

He stopped in the road, stunned, while Kaywin and Prudence kept walking. She sure did come up with a nineteenth century Russian writer pretty quickly. He scurried to catch up. "No! That would be awful though." He whisper-yelled the correct answer at her face: "*It's the Kalaysian Three-Star!*"

This time, accidentally, and much to her regret, **she** was the one who stopped in the middle of the road, surprised. *Oh great*, she thought. *Now it looks like I give a crap.* She started walking again, half-pretending that there had been something wrong with her shoe. Dublin told her the entire gripping tale of white-knuckle survival, right down to the tears he had shed. It disgusted her, but fascinated her, that he would tell that part to her, or to **anybody** for that matter.

Once again, against her better judgment, she had been lured into conversation with these two.

They talked at length about the movie they were about to see. Dublin was over the moon that they were showing the just-released *Wisconsin Johnson and the Fountain of Youth*. "Isn't that dude like seventy now?" Prudence asked.

"Yeah, but he's about to discover the Fountain of Youth," Kaywin offered.

"So, they're going to use that as an excuse to make like five more movies?"

"Oh my God, I hope so!" exclaimed Dublin. Then he went strangely silent. It didn't take a rocket-scientist to figure out why. If they made any more Wisconsin Johnson movies he wouldn't be around to **see** them.

If Prudence had known that she would be stuck next to these two guys for what seemed like the next twenty events (it was three) she would have tried a little harder to keep them at arm's-length. The movie was as bad as she thought it would be (and as fabulous as Dublin thought it would be). They watched this Wisconsin Johnson guy with his ridiculous hat, fringed leather jacket, and chaps speaking about eleven languages, and roping holographic Nazis in the aisles. I won't spoil the ending for you, but suffice it to say that there **will** be several more films.

Dublin had been clever enough during 'quiet time' that afternoon to race back to the broom closet and move some shelves around. In this way he had crafted enough open space for himself and the Three-Star to sleep without any contact whatsoever. He still woke up in a sweat twice, and both times the Kalaysian, who appeared to be a raging insomniac, was pecking away at his Sofee intently. None of Dublin's business.

First thing after breakfast the next morning, six sections were summoned to the cathedral. These included H (Kaywin's), L (Prudence's), and G (Dublin's). This time Prudence didn't fight it when the two approached her. While she had sworn off friendship years ago, when her seventh-grade confidante Persia Fleming had outed her as delusional, Kaywin and Dublin seemed harmless enough. She knew it was only a matter of time until the deformed one professed his undying love for her, but maybe they would be separated into different 'meaningful conclusions' before he got up the nerve.

No one knew what this first exercise was going to be. The campus cathedral seemed a strange place for it, but apparently they needed the eighty-foot ceiling of the nave for some kind of aerial assessment. There was a basic harness attached to a very simple rope. The rope was looped over a heavy pulley almost out of sight at the top of the grey stone vaulted dome. Directly beneath it, set into the flagstones, a beautiful circular mosaic of Mary and Child defined a border that the MCs were instructed not to cross into. Nervous whispers among the nine hundred or so Goners echoed in the cool of the huge structure. No one wanted to be the first up the rope.

An imposing, lantern-jawed General in full uniform entered the ring. He looked at his olive-green Sofee. Dublin thought of olive branches and peace offerings, trying to soothe his growing apprehension with religious imagery. It didn't work.

"Natasha Bresnev and Rose Wong," the General said clearly, in a conversational tone. His look dared anybody to make him repeat himself. "Enter the circle."

Kaywin smiled to see his tiny Asian friend amble out. She moved stiffly and painfully, and he remembered her condition. She was joined next to the officer by a Russian woman, not too much younger than herself. 'Natasha' fidgeted nervously, but Rose stood short, proud and confident. "Ms. Wong, I am going to flip this coin. Do you want heads or tails?"

"Head."

He flipped the chunky antique dollar high into the air. The electric light from one of the emergency exits glinted off the spinning silver like a tiny low-fi star falling to Earth. "It is tails. Ms. Bresnev, you may exit the circle. Ms. Wong, please put on the harness." He handed it to her.

"You say like I expert mountain climber." There was a respectfully quiet ripple of laughter through the onlookers. Even the General smiled.

"Let me help you." Together they got her ninety-pound body strapped in safely. "I need everybody to watch very carefully. Begin!"

Dublin and Kaywin took in these instructions very carefully, wondering what details of the simple ascent they were supposed to absorb. Two men turned a crank almost on the edge of the mosaic. Rose squealed a little as she--well, "rose" into the air. "How you say? One small step for man?" The crowd laughed again. Kaywin felt proud to have met this brave and funny lady two days earlier than most of the onlookers. It took about forty-five seconds for her to reach the dizzying apogee of the vaulted nave. She cracked a couple more jokes on the way up, but between her broken English and the cave-like reverberations of the upper dome, her meaning was lost.

"That's enough," the General intoned. "Has everyone been watching closely?"

"I want to go next," Dublin whispered. "To get it over with." Kaywin nodded wordlessly without taking his eyes off of his friend Rose, dangling eighty feet above the stone floor.

The General walked over to the crank. He nodded at the two soldiers, who backed away. He took a large, vicious-looking knife from a sheath hidden somewhere inside his uniform jacket.

He cut the rope.

9

Fire

"Oh my God oh my God oh my God oh my God," Dublin whispered over and over again uselessly. Kaywin swallowed hard and kept his mouth shut so tightly that later on he would wonder why his teeth hurt. Prudence--well, a couple of people had laughed loudly; like "look-at-me-I'm-such-a-bad-ass-even-this-doesn't-phase-me" loudly. Kaywin hoped, he really hoped, that she had not been one of them. It makes you feel dirty to even **know** that kind of person.

Two men and three women had leapt into the forbidden mosaic area with the momentary idea of catching Rose's falling body. They had all failed to follow through; each maybe thinking that one of the others would do it. Or maybe some quick primal physics instincts told them that it just couldn't be done, and that they would only injure themselves and prolong the poor woman's death.

"Get out of the circle!" bellowed the General. He had his hand on his pistol, and it was impossible to doubt now that he would make an example of anyone who dallied. All five of the attempted heroes jumped back across the line of cobalt blue tiles that formed the outer ring of the mosaic. The General surveyed the crowd intently, making absolutely certain that they were under his control before he moved on. Behind him, a pool of blood spread rapidly from Rose's lifeless body. Without seeming to take note of it, the decorated officer took a step forward just as the blood was about to lick at his shiny black shoes. A floor drain hidden in the center of the mosaic intercepted the flow of blood. Kaywin and Prudence both picked up on this subtle little indication that maybe this wasn't the first time the General had dropped a body from the Cathedral ceiling.

As the blood flowed downward through what had been camouflaged as the baby Jesus's fingers, he spoke again. "Everybody look at your Sofees." They did. They were flashing rapidly, in red letters, 'press button to start test'. "Do **not** press that button until--"

"Wait! I pressed it! I'm sorry! I'm sorry! Please don't shoot me! I'm sorry!" It was a skinny, nerdy man in his late twenties. He had tried to get the jump on this test and now he was begging for his life.

"Come here." The trembling redheaded nerd obliged, stepping onto the mosaic from the side opposite Kaywin, Dublin and Prudence, and skirting the pool of blood until he reached the General, with his thin pale wrist extended. The Officer took the wrist with somewhat surprising gentleness. He tapped out some codes on the man's Sofee and released him back into the crowd. Then he grinned broadly at the minor incident and the complete control he had had over it. Under the circumstances, it was not a very contagious smile.

"As I was saying. Do not--(his smile spilled over into a laugh, as if his good humor had been reflected back at him and amplified by **anybody** there)--do **not** press that button until I say 'start the test'...Now, we didn't used to tell you this (his face had returned to its former stoniness), but I think we get a better result when we **do.** You will have five minutes to complete the test. **The lowest score from THIS group will perform the role that Rose just did FOR THE NEXT GROUP!** Or if you want to cheat, you can make it really easy on me. Start the test."

Dublin, hands shaking, pressed the button immediately, like he was swatting a fly. The test was mainly multiple choice, and it was all over the place: math, geography, reasoning; easy, hard, stupid-easy, crazy-hard, impossible... He collected himself. He had never seen anything as horrifying as what he had just witnessed three minutes ago, and yes, he was rattled to say the least. But he didn't want that to result in a test score so abysmal that he became the sacrificial lamb for the next batch of recruits. He didn't want it to prevent him from going out the way he wanted to go out. *Okay. There's like nine hundred people here. You are not the dumbest person here. You are not the most shaken-up person here.* He didn't dare look up or stop answering questions, but he could hear a lady crying quietly behind him. *You can relax because it is a foregone conclusion that you will **not** have the lowest score on this test. You **will not die today** as a prop for the next group of Goners.*

'What two minerals are most common on Saturn's moon, Europa?'

'What is six times three?'

'How does one best subdue a charging lion?'

He recognized the test as one he had taken the day he joined up, in the backroom of the Greenville MCP office. The questions weren't even scrambled. He remembered because the answer to question nineteen was 'twelve', bringing to his mind the year the Titanic sank, 1912. It was obvious that the purpose of this entire exercise was to gauge their individual reactions to stress; especially their cognitive function. Could they be counted on to calmly disconnect the green wire from the yellow wire after their friend had just been blown to bits right in front of them?

Prudence, who had started the morning with a fairly bright lavender bob, very light-green eye shadow (which continued down onto her dainty cheeks and up onto her forehead, now wrinkled in concentration) had found a second, maybe while the redheaded nerd was wasting everybody's time, to mute her hair considerably. It was much more brown than purple when Dublin, with his life riding on this test score like everyone else's, still found time to steal a glance at her. With mixed emotions, he saw her finish up, way ahead of him, and seemingly everybody. She stood straight up to her full battle-height of four-foot eleven. No more than three of the allotted five minutes had passed, yet there she stood looking dead-ahead with her arms by her side. The fire in her aspect was turned down like her hair. Either she was laying low on purpose so as to not draw attention to herself, or she was legitimately cowed by the fresh events.

How did she finish so fast? He felt ashamed instantly for asking himself the question. She was smart; why shouldn't she finish early? But he was smart too, and he was only on question forty-seven out of fifty when the test disabled two minutes later.

Anyways, he felt pretty good about it. The traumatized nine hundred were quiet as mice. The General, even though the test was over, surveyed them all intently. "No cheaters today; that's good. Usually we have a cheater." He looked around again, just in case someone somehow could still be cheating. Satisfied, he worked at his Sofee for about ten seconds while the crowd held its collective breath anxiously.

Dublin, whose desperate want for love pervaded every moment of his every day, regardless of circumstance, looked again at the beautiful Prudence, then bit his tongue in punishment for the stupidity of his thoughts. A girl like her would **NEVER** go for a guy like him. *I would need a face-transplant just to hold the door open for her and her prom date. She is soooo pretty. I bet she likes jerks. The jerkier the better. I would have to kill a puppy or something to get her attention.*

He suddenly felt bad for the assumptions and presumptions he was making, especially because, for the first time since he had met her (a scant thirty-six hours ago) she actually looked a little...vulnerable...a tiny bit scared...as if her life were on the line. Oh yeah. It **was**.

The General had called out his two assistants. While he was talking to them, he glanced very quickly, but unmistakably and *chillingly* right at Prudence. But then he looked over to his right, and pointed out something on his screen to them. They nodded and headed in that direction, spreading out a little; the one furthest from Kaywin, Dublin and Prudence having to take a big step over the wide stream of Rose's blood. They were taking a tactful, less obvious course toward their prey so as not to startle it, but suddenly they converged on a little man, each of them seizing one of his arms. The slightly built, dark-haired unfortunate broke down a little, half-pleading for mercy in a foreign tongue, while simultaneously half-collapsing in submission as the two soldiers dragged him into the arena. He sounded Russian, or Bosnian, and if this was the extent of the English he knew it was no wonder he had scored so abysmally. The General removed a small hypodermic needle from his jacket-of-horrors and injected the defeated immigrant in the neck. The man calmed immediately, without losing consciousness. He relaxed onto the mosaic in a crisscross-applesauce sitting position, suddenly transfixed with Mary's face in the tiles as if nothing else existed in the universe.

Everyone's head was swimming when they exited the cathedral into the morning sunlight and merciful breeze. Kaywin noticed that a heavy delegation of guards flanked their formation on both sides as the section leaders led them all out. They could see another six sections, approximately nine-hundred MCs, coming up the opposite side of the hill toward the cathedral, laughing and joking, as their own grim-faced platoon made its way down the backside in terse silence. *Aaah,* thought Kaywin. *They need to keep the groups far apart, so we don't spoil the surprise for them.*

The same questions were on all of their minds. Should I have tried to stop the seizing of the foreign man? Should I at least have said something? Is this what it's going to be like the rest of the way? Am I next?

-------Did I make a horrible mistake signing up for this?------

For Kaywin, it was a pretty quick internal dialogue. Nothing he had seen so far conflicted too much with his image of the program, or what he had been promised. True, the Chaplain not twenty-four hours earlier had said that three weeks out was the earliest they would be put in life-threatening situations (or however he had worded it)...Kaywin imagined that Rose's death would be classified as an accident. Or that the date of her demise would be altered in the records to suit protocol. Who would be there when her cousin or whoever got the e-mail, to contradict the details? Would it matter? Grisly and cold as the maneuver had seemed, had it in fact been a pointless sacrifice? Rose had volunteered for this, just like he had, just like all of them had. And now, the nine hundred of them were much more mentally prepared for what lay ahead. They didn't have to *visualize* the horror of the upcoming challenges anymore. They had just had a true taste of it. A little one, but a true one. You could look right now at the nine hundred entering the cathedral, and at the nine hundred leaving it, and you would have to admit that the sections leaving it were a little more mentally locked in to the reality of their situation. And Kaywin knew a few details that most of them didn't, for what it was worth: That Rose had been in constant pain. That she had had only months to live anyway. Would he have personally cut the rope? No. Not in a thousand years. But he was not sure, if he was being honest with himself, that her death had been a 'waste'.

Dublin's internal conversation was like Kaywin's, except times twenty-five, and intertwined with the central themes of 'Crime and Punishment', 'The Brothers Karamazov', 'Anna Karenina', and others of the great classics he had read. It's not surprising then that he never actually reached a conclusion on the subject, and became distracted by the singing of a Hermit Thrush.

He couldn't see the bird, hidden in the new burgeoning

green foliage of a maple tree they were approaching in silence, but man, it was freaking out. He started counting, and
picked out at least twenty different phrases the bird was offering up with great enthusiasm. Dublin had never paid very
close attention to birds, and what they had to say, but it was
so striking that this one didn't seem to be repeating himself
at any point, and his luxurious whistles cut so cleanly through
the profound silence that it was impossible to ignore.

The little thrush didn't know (or care) that an innocent
woman lay dead in the cathedral, anymore than the passing
crowd would have known or cared if a thrush lay dead in the
bushes. He was going to perform his birdly duties, regardless.
What was he saying, so excitedly? Was he warning other birds
that a hawk was nearby? Had he spotted some ripe berries?
Was he rallying troops to go poop on a car? Telling them
he'd found a good tree to put a nest in? If they were close
enough to hear his whistling, weren't they close enough to
figure all this out on their own? That certainly didn't stop humans from talking. Was he shouting to a pretty girl-thrush in
another tree, showing off his range? *Don't get your hopes up…*

Twenty, or twenty-five, or thirty different phrases; Dublin had lost count. Why would a simple bird, who hatches,
eats worms, learns to fly, finds a mate, builds a nest, and
dies, need to express so many things, and with such nuance?
He was seeing things that men don't see, but *what?* Fluctua-
tions in the Earth's magnetic field that would affect certain
elements of their flight? Seismic vibrations that would drive
earthworms into hiding? Ghosts? Rips between dimensions?
Or was he just practicing? Was it all just a test of the Emergency Birdcast System? Prudence was walking beside Dublin,

subconsciously maintaining as much space between them as the crowd would allow. He opened his mouth to speak, but she cut him off: "Yes, I hear the stupid bird."

Maybe later.

The woman who'd been crying during the testing in the church had continued to do so, quietly, ever since. Now she had had enough. She was walking about ten feet or so in front of Kaywin, Dublin and Prudence. Suddenly, she careened to the right, almost tripping up a couple of people, and hit the pavement. Her clandestine weeping escalated suddenly into frantic sobs. After what they had seen, everybody half-expected her to get shot in the head. Instead, a guard spoke to her gently; the woman's section leader came over to consult, and by the time the gang had gone a couple of hundred feet further without her, she had been escorted away by two guards.

She was never seen or heard from again.

The remainder of the dazed unfortunates Frankenstein-walked down the steep hill toward the baseball diamond and a sprawling single-level aluminum building next to it. Outside the expansive building, the six section leaders reorganized their flocks. They then entered it letter by letter; "G" followed by "H", followed by "I", and so on. Once inside--to their relief--they saw immediately that this place at least had the **look** of a more traditional testing facility. There were climbing walls, treadmills, firing ranges, bench presses, etc., for as far as the eye could see. This was better than the ghastly happening at the gothic cathedral.

Following their leaders, each section assumed ownership of one of the six roped-off areas of the complex, trading off every thirty minutes. It was actually sort of fun, for the most part, but apprehension still lingered, like when they were grouped in fours and told to designate one 'survivor', then work together to elevate the 'survivor' over a fifteen-foot padded wall that had no footholds or handles. The terminology was disturbing given recent events. How much weight was being given to this decision? Would the three non-survivors be sacrificed like Rose? Beyond the abiding fear of being killed at any moment, it was a blast. One moment Dublin and three of his section-mates were heaving weights as fast as they could into a bin on one end of a colossal see-saw; the next he was racing to reassemble a transistor radio.

Prudence could have done without all of it. Being the center of attention was okay when she could determine the circumstances. She didn't mind walking into an Uno Mundo with green hair and zombie-chic makeup, but being measured and quantified and judged athletically was not her scene, not one tiny bit. After being put on a team repeatedly with the same three testosteroned-out jerks who were screaming at her constantly to keep up, she really lost interest.

Her least favorite waste of time--and that's saying something--was 'the Tunnel'. This was a diabolical device that tested one MC at a time. Their task was to watch a twenty second video on how to connect a "solar collector line" to a "relay"; retain that information precisely, then enter a teensy tunnel and crawl through it to the end. Once there, in a dim little chamber, the actual "SCL" and the actual "relay" were waiting, color-coded just like in the video. This was all simple enough until she realized on the way in that the tunnel was gradually closing in on her like a blood-pressure cuff. Spurred on by a fear of dying in her least favorite way, she accidentally performed exceptionally, and was one of only three Goners to make it back out of the tunnel.

This was cause for concern; she certainly didn't want to end up two miles underground in the sweltering mines. But thankfully she also acquitted herself well in several activities that seemed to point towards a (short) future in spywork. This included identifying a suspect in successive video line-ups, in a dizzying array of brilliant disguises; remembering codes and sequences and re-entering them; sometimes forward, sometimes backwards; and quickly adopting the subtleties and nuances of local dialects. By the time she was finished, she could tell if a Patagonian was from the east side of Cape Horn or the west.

Then, in what she perceived as an advanced-level testing reserved for a select few who had shown some mastery in the preliminary rounds, there were the situation rooms. Some of these were easy; who's the spy; who's the mole; where would someone hide the key to the only exit, etc. Her favorite was the one where she was grouped with seven other MCs. Each of them had one-fourth of the code necessary to open the exit, but no one knew which of the others shared the same fourth they had and who had the other three. There could be only one winner.

Then, kind of like the tunnel, the floor of the already cramped room began to slowly rise toward the ceiling.

Prudence instantly identified the addict in the room; they were everywhere here. She whispered to him that she knew a guy who had saved his Attabuoy from registration-day, and that she would get it for him in exchange for his bit of the

code. Done. She made another promise that she had no intention of keeping. Done. When the heads of the taller MCs
made contact with the ceiling, and bodies began doubling
over, a little bit of panic set in. Prudence joined in with gusto.
*She had read about this one online. This was the second of the four
times during the evaluation period that the directors would let some Goners die to prove a point. She had seen a top-secret video of eight mangled
bodies being removed from this very room.*

She began to hyperventilate convincingly, starting a chain
reaction. Within seconds, the seven morons contorting themselves in the shrinking room sounded like a pack of hysterical
Darth-Vaders.

Oh my God, this is **definitely** *the same room from the video;
I recognize that sconce!* One of the holdouts, as his bony knees
touched his stupid chin, shouted out the last fourth of the
code. Prudence calmly recited the four parts in sequence.
The floor stopped rising, and the door whooshed open.

That should keep me out of the mines.

By lunchtime, strange to say, Rose was almost forgotten.
The rest of their lives was a very short while. Time was compressed here; four hours ago might as well have been four
months. Laughter, seeming crass and disrespectful at first,
soon began to spread. Before long, a feeling of normalcy
(whatever **that** was for this sea of misfits) had returned.

Kaywin didn't like the sensation. It made him feel guilty.
He closed his eyes before eating, which was not his custom,
and said a few words in her memory.

After an emotionally and physically exhausting morning,
the famished troops laid waste to lunch.

The two 'ascetics' continued to give away half of their food at every meal. It was hard to fathom how they survived. The writing on their foreheads changed every time Kaywin crossed paths with them. So his tattoo theory was out. He smiled to himself, just now realizing that the words 'eat mine' he had noted on the one fellow's forehead, when he had seen him that first day, had not been the insult he took it for at the time, but an actual offer of food to one of his bus-mates prior to arriving. Prudence always made it clear enough that she would take half of their food anytime, either one of them, or even **all** of it if they were feeling extra-repentant that day. But she succeeded only twice in getting their attention. It was clear that they made an effort to spread the wealth. This generous practice of theirs did result in a sort of reverence for the two, and their spiritual journey, among the other Goners. They spoke not a word other than whatever happened to be scrawled across their foreheads at any given time. Kaywin, Dublin and Prudence remained ignorant of their names, referring to them, when necessary, as the "blonde (or tall) ascetic" and the "shorter (or dark-haired) ascetic." How they got away with wearing the filthy, crudely constructed friar's robes over their jumpsuits was anybody's guess. This exemption from on high seemed to betray some kindness and humanity on the part of the Program's directors.

After lunch it was more testing, testing, testing. When they were good and worn out, they were led, two sections at a time, to a building they hadn't seen yet. Inside was an enormous swimming pool, with no shallow end. Markers on the side indicated that it was eight feet deep from one extremity to the other. They were told to jump in, fully clothed, and the ones who protested were pushed. Their jumpsuits, light, flexible and comfortable when dry, grew very heavy, very quickly. Guards patrolled the edges of the pool, stepping on the fingers of anyone who dared to cheat. As people began to go under, they were pulled to the side with giant hooks and hoisted out of the pool. Prudence, who had never swum in her life, tried to stay calm. She flapped her arms and legs, treading water instinctively, but soon the pool was so crowded that she ran out of room to flail. She had to pull herself up intermittently on the people around her, which was deeply, profoundly against her nature. Her makeup was running down into her eyes. The idiot next to her caught on to the fact that she was going under. He tried valiantly to support her, and himself, while shouting for help over the cacophonous din of frenzied voices. But the echoing acoustics of the pool building magnified and unified the panicked voices into one miserable drone from which it was nearly impossible to identify the individual sources. Prudence, blinded by melting eye shadow, and gagging between dips below the surface, couldn't believe it was about to end like this. She tried to make some peace with the universe, before blacking out, but failed, and everything went blank.

When she woke up, two medics were working on her. As soon as she coughed and opened her eyes, one of them jumped over to assist with the man lying on the wet concrete next to her. It was the man whose shoulder she had clung to. Still dazed, she watched them breathing into the man's slack mouth, and pumping his chest repetitively. She was strangely interested in the scene. Even in her depleted state, she felt disgusted for caring. This man had saved her life, but in other circumstances his true nature would have showed itself. Well, okay, he had done her a solid. She decided that she hoped he would live. A second later, he coughed up a splatter of pool-water, and gasped. He was alive.

"I see you got to go for a swim too" said Dublin, flopping down in the grass next to Prudence.

Geez, he's even uglier when he's wet, she thought. Kaywin, dripping water everywhere as well, hit the ground on the other side of her. She had given up avoiding the two of them. They seemed okay with her barely speaking, so she was content to let them have their conversations around her. If nothing else, it created a little buffer between her and the less noble of the four thousand outcasts.

"I heard a guy died trying to save you," Dublin persisted.

"Oh my God, **no,**" she gave him back. She lay back flat on the grass again. Dublin started to open his mouth. "He **almost** died. Big difference."

Kaywin and Dublin locked eyes, smiling and nodding in mock-agreement. "Ooooohhh...," they said at the same time.

"**Almost** died," said Kaywin. "That's nothing"

"Yeah, really, I pretty much **almost** die a couple of times a week trying to save someone," Dublin chortled. He and Kaywin now both reclined completely, heads in the grass, with a safe distance between them. All three were looking up at the same frog-shaped cloud whisking by across the deep blue.

"You guys are jerks," said Prudence.

Thursday was somewhat more of the same, except that the evaluations seemed to be getting more specific to the perceived potential of each recruit. It was kind of like being back in school, with their Sofees dinging between classes to indicate where they should proceed to next. Early in the day, Kaywin, Dublin and Prudence found themselves summoned to a dim and dignified old amphitheater of a room, rich and important-seeming with its cascading rows of brown leather seats and mahogany lecterns. The dim light that battled through banks of trees to penetrate the tall windows showed tiny specks of dust levitating dreamily in the stately silence, as if they would never land. Dublin was reminded of the antiquities-room back at the Greenville Library, worlds away.

At the podium below, where the shape of the room funneled their attention, stood an imposing officer. Without the slightest word of introduction, he spoke to the seven hundred or so fidgeting MCs. "Open your Sofees to full display." Doing so, they began the first round of what appeared to be a three-part test. The questions were broad at first, but seemed to be narrowing toward elements of piloting.

Kaywin nodded inwardly. *Thank you Nadine.* When something occasionally went his way, he was in the habit of thanking his dead wife. If anyone could sway the universe on his behalf, it would be her.

Dublin felt his pulse quicken, as he responded to questions about gravitational force and launch trajectories. *Don't blow this!*

Prudence was surprised, but non-plussed. There had been no one in her life who cared enough to push her academically. She had still graduated on time, at fifteen, but not at the mathematic levels she probably could have attained. She felt like she applied most of the logarithms correctly, but was pretty sure she missed a couple. When round one ended, after forty-five minutes, she watched smugly as a third of the class filed out of the amphitheater, with bowed heads, following the instructions of their Sofees. "Congratulations," hers read. "Your score has qualified you to continue." She had a little elbowroom now, having lost the Goners on either side of her. But now the questions were harder. She reasoned her way through several, guessed her way through the next few, and then she was really just stabbing in the dark. She had never even heard of sub-spectrum infrared guidance protocol ladders. Honestly, she wasn't even sure if they were differing levels of guidance protocol, or actual physical ladders. She was not surprised, at the end of round two, when she was asked to leave.

She **was** surprised by the little episode that unfolded as she was making her way down the curve of the seats toward the exit. Someone down in the third row raised his hand. It was unexpected, not normal here, where you just did what you were told, and if you fell behind you got trampled.

"I have a question." Oh God, it was that raging goon who had attacked her in the woods like ten minutes after she'd arrived. She was smart enough not to stop where she was, but she did slow down slightly to see what this was about. "What do I do if I'm flying with a bunch of idiots who don't know what a Phoenix Formation is?"

The officer was neither impressed, nor thrown for a loop. "One of the functions of the test is to find out **just that**. What **will** you do if you are grouped with pilots who don't know what you know? Besides--"

"You mean idiots."

"--Besides, all **PILOTS** who have made it to the point of actual spaceflight--"

"Idiots."

"...they will know. Your name is...J.B.?"

"Yes, **Ma'am**." The instructor was a six-foot-three strapping Air-Corps pilot with a jaw that looked like a cast-iron robot knee, and a neatly trimmed moustache. And he was not a "ma'am."

"And what does 'J.B.' stand for?" Before the recklessly arrogant young man could reply, a brave, baby-faced farmhand five rows behind him answered for him.

"Jerkboy!" Cautious laughter rippled through the remaining three hundred or so. J.B. turned in time to identify the speaker as guards closed in on him and led him out.

"Thank you, J.B., you are done here. Everybody back with me? Round three will begin in twenty seconds." Prudence accelerated ahead to keep some distance between her and 'Jerkboy'. Kaywin and Dublin were amused and gratified at the disturbed young man's outburst and early dismissal. Especially as it seemed to indicate that he would **not** be piloting, as--fingers-crossed--they would be.

Forty-five minutes later they were all filing back out of the amphitheater. Few of the two hundred and twelve who had survived the first two rounds felt very confident about their round-three performance. Kaywin and Dublin were among the first twenty or so out the door. The dark-haired farm boy was a little ways behind them. As they exited the amphitheater, exchanging opinions on some of the third round head-scratchers, Dublin did a double take. There outside the door, standing on top of a four-foot high cement barrier, was "Jerkboy". They turned to stare at him as they moved past on the swell of the crowd. He was scanning their faces for someone in particular. Suddenly, he pounced from his elevated position with shocking fury on the farm boy, who had not had time to brace himself in the least. His head thwacked sickeningly on the marble floor under the significant payload.

"Guess what, cowboy? Number one pilot!" screamed Jerkboy, and he began to pound the poor boy's face repeatedly with his large fists. In the few seconds before anyone could react, he had almost killed him. Thankfully, a guard dove and removed him from the object of his vengeance. It took three more to subdue him completely. Medics moved in and carried off the unconscious lad.

Dublin felt sick. He'd been in a few fights; always with older bullies, and he had always held his own. Nobody ever thought he was going to be as strong as he was. He had never seen anything quite as intense as that though. Looking at the blood on the floor, he puzzled hard over something. It must have been written all over his face, because Kaywin verbalized it.

"How come this guy never came after you? You straight-up punched him!"

"I don't know." He was shaking a little. "Maybe it was the Attabuoy that first night. Maybe he doesn't even remember that whole thing. But you can bet I'll be keeping my guard up now!"

Kaywin shook his head. "Oh, I don't think we'll be seeing him anymore!"

When they caught up with Prudence at suppertime, they found out that she had spent most of the afternoon in what **appeared** to be spy-assessment. No one told you anything, beyond where to be and when to be there. Nobody said 'you did really well memorizing that paragraph in Russian; we are leaning towards making you a spy' or 'you almost drowned in the pool; guess you won't be assigned to Undersea'...It kept them on their toes, but it was a little frustrating.

If Kaywin lived another fourteen months (ha!) or two years (technically impossible) he would never forget the people of the First Quarter Meaningful Conclusion Class of 2126. He took a moment, with a slice of sausage pizza half-way up to his mouth, to look around the great hall at them. Penitents, addicts, murderers, the unloved, they who had loved and lost, the deeply and forever chemically unbalanced, the abused, unwanted and left for dead...all of them here in the same place. And now they had gained a little separation from the horrors of their daily lives, the tragic circumstances that had driven them to this choice. At the same time, the dreadful and shadowy enterprises that awaited them in their quest for 'meaningful conclusion' were still somewhat of a daydream; a vague unreality; just far enough out not to para-lyze them with fear. It was a bridge they would cross when they got to it. All suffered at first; all gradually got over it; and then, as of one mind, all applied themselves with fervor to the task at hand.

The buzz in the cafetorium seemed a little louder at every meal, as lost souls who had long ago given up hope out in the real world now had new friends who understood the ex-tremity of their desperation. Together, they sailed in one boat toward designation day, the day after tomorrow. Speculation and rumor ran rampant. Somebody had heard that there was a huge expansion planned for the Mars colony, and that they were all headed there regardless of test scores. Others countered with Moon and Undersea gossip.

Jerkboy, looking profoundly, swaggeringly unapproachable, sat alone at the end of one long table. If the isolation bothered him, it sure didn't show. Hugging the extremity of the table behind Jerkboy, also at a little distance from his fellows, was the Kalaysian Three-Star. Even if the stars on his forehead hadn't been there to announce what he was capable of, he just had the *look* of a killer. His eyes looked like the eyes of a wild animal, not only devoid of conscience or remorse, but empty even of the *idea* that such things existed. He also seemed to not know a word of English or Spanish. Dublin had tried to communicate with his terrifying roommate just once, on Wednesday. What he had wanted to say, when he got back that night to the tiny closet they shared, was "Hey man, it's no biggie either way, but did **you** move these shelves back to the middle of the floor, or was it the maintenance guy?" What he said instead, to kind of feel out the mood of the 'room', was "my name is Dublin." It was the first time in five years he had left off the joke about not being Irish. The Kalaysian appeared not to understand, and just smiled at him, way, way **oversmiled** in fact. All the information that Dublin got out of the 'exchange' was that the Three-Star had even worse teeth than he did.

Friday morning brought an end to the endless testing. Everyone was thrilled to learn that the rest of the day, and most of Saturday, was theirs to spend however they chose. Dublin and Kaywin exhaled a little, now that the future was out of their hands. They both figured to be pilots, though they wouldn't find out until the Assignment Ceremony Saturday Night. Prudence didn't care, but she sure seemed destined for spywork. Without speaking it, they all realized that some sort of friendship had formed between them, although Prudence would have denied it to her grave. They also left alone the probability that the two boys would likely be sent off in a different direction from the sad, mysterious girl. They just hung out together. That was all.

They had movie options again Friday night, as voted on the day before. There was the fifth Plasmo Zenith film, the third Wisconsin Johnson, or a stirring war epic called 'The Bridge That Exploded' (I won't give away the ending, if you haven't seen it).

"This is probably going to be the last movie I ever see," ruminated Dublin. "I wanna see Wisconsin Johnson. The third one is the best movie ever made."

"The best movie ever made is 'Wisconsin Johnson and the Bane of Egypt'?" Kaywin couldn't help prodding him.

"Yes. I like Plasmo Zenith too...he kind of carries on the grand tradition of the Three Stooges--"

"**Grand tradition?!**" This was a little much for Prudence.

"Yes." Dublin seemed legit-confused that someone would question that.

"Maybe that's who your roommate knocked off--Moe, Larry, and...the bald guy." She was proud of that one.

Kaywin thought it was pretty funny too. "But when he took out Shem--well, that was too much."

Dublin had made a policy of ignoring jokes about his

roommate. "So I vote for 'Bane of Egypt'. But I'll go see whatever you…" He blushed a little. He was looking too directly at Prudence. He had worked so hard, had strained every nerve, not to push this girl away. "I'll go see whatever you *guys* want."

"Well, these movies are all crap. I like Egypt a little bit. I hope Wisconsin Johnson and his stupid hat don't ruin it."

She was no better during the movie.

"Is that supposed to be the same monkey from that last one we saw? Cuz it's not."

"Yes it is. It's the same monkey."

"Dub." Kaywin piped up in support of Prudence. "That's clearly not the same monkey playing Renaldo. The markings are all different."

"It's the same monkey! Stop! You guys are going to…un-suspend my disbelief!"

"It didn't un-suspend your disbelief when that five-ton sarcophagus fell on Slim?"

"It didn't **fall**; it **started** to fall. He had the leverage to push it back. They check the math on all this stuff." He was intrigued that she knew the word 'sarcophagus' though…

Saturday morning they took an almost wordless walk up into the woods, and without any of the three planning it, they found themselves retracing their steps from the night they had met. Kaywin noted that Prudence steered well clear of the tree she had been pinned against. Eventually Dublin couldn't stand the silence, and found an excuse to start rattling off every book he had ever read. His companions were almost completely unresponsive, only taking in the sound of his words, like birdsong.

Out of the blue, the reality of the Assignment Ceremony hit everybody. When they roused from 'quiet time' Saturday afternoon, they were directed to the showers in shifts, and when they got back to their rooms, instead of the clean blue jumpsuit on their bunks that they had all grown accustomed to, they found something new. Prudence's roommate Penny had a purple jumpsuit. The lady who had tried to comfort Penny that first night--Prudence still didn't know her name; "Midge," or "Smidge" or something--she had a yellow one. Prudence ducked down into her bunk. Red. She didn't know what it meant, but she had a red jumpsuit.

They were summoned, all of them, to the largest auditorium, Fonteneau. This was where they had seen the Wisconsin Johnson movie Tuesday night. Four thousand meandering souls in different colored jumpsuits filed in slowly. A black helicopter swooped overhead. From its windows, the crowd of MC's below must have looked like one of those pixelated pictures that you stare at until an image appears.

The helicopter didn't appear to have time for that, however. It landed with almost violent suddenness on the roof of Fonteneau, as if it were very very late. Kaywin wondered if this had any connection to the four black nineteen-wheelers that had arrived on campus yesterday.

Inside the auditorium, the huge semicircle of seats was filling up. An odd, chemical-ish burning smell hung in the dim air. A microphone was being checked, rechecked, and checked again. *Alright, already* Kaywin thought, almost covering his ears. *It's working; I think that's loud enough!* He was directed by one of the guards towards the back rows, where the other red jumpsuits were headed.

They tried to put Prudence on the second row from the back, but she was so tired of having been hemmed in by humanity all week that with a hundred pounds of raw determination she pretty much muscled her way into the back row. As soon as she sat down, and had a moment to scan the curving rows of color stretched out ahead--purple way up front, then blue, then green, yellow, orange and red--she saw what was happening here. *It's a freaking rainbow* she thought to herself. "Is this how they're going to kill us?" she ventured aloud to the dim-looking lady on her right. "Embarrassment?"

Dublin's section entered from the other side of the building. He was feeling a little lonely; there was a whole lot of yellow among them; a fair amount of green, a smattering here and there of orange, blue, and purple, but only five of his section-mates were wearing red, like he was. One of them was the Kalaysian Three-Star. It took him a minute to get his bearings. He stood off to the side for a moment until his eyes adjusted. Everybody else seemed to have this figured out; the different colors streamed past him with purpose and direction like they had all been doing this every Saturday night for years. He thought about asking one of the guards where he was supposed to go, but the fact that everyone else was moving along so confidently made him feel like it would sound stupid.

Finally, he noticed that the other red suits were congregating in the back ten rows or so. He headed in that direction, hoping against hope to see a couple of familiar faces;

one in particular that had haunted his dreams for six days now. He had tried to muster up the courage this morning in the woods to tell Prudence how he felt about her, but had wound up bragging about reading the unabridged version of *Les Miserables* instead. Now, for all he knew, he had lost that chance forever. He moved slowly up the left side of the auditorium through the sounds of hundreds of shuffling feet and murmuring voices. Finally, with great relief, he saw Kaywin, waving at him and smiling his sad half-smile. He was wearing red. *Phew!* He accelerated toward the open seat closest to him. Unfortunately, it was one row behind him and six seats *beyond* him, so he had to put his fat butt in a lot of angry faces to get there. Once situated in the fourth row from the back, he looked around anxiously for Prudence. His heart grew heavy. He was just about to give up on seeing her in red, and start scanning the other colors rippling out in rows down below, when he spotted her, in the very back row.

She was wearing red! His death just got a whole lot easier.

He half-stood and waved frantically at her. She looked straight ahead. She must have seen him, when he was pushing his way obnoxiously toward his seat twenty feet in front of her. She looked amazing. She had turned her hair red and done her cheeks in complementary yellow and orange. His heart beat faster the longer he looked. But why was she ignoring him? Was Victor Hugo not her cup of tea? He should have kept pushing the Russian authors on her. *I'll bet I can talk her into reading some Dostoyevsky. Then she'll see what she's been missing and want to read it all. Then she'll be amazed at how I've read all this great stuff, and she will completely forget what I look like...* Ohhh, Dublin.

He was startled out of his ridiculous reverie by the echo-ing clang/clang of the auditorium doors slamming shut on both sides. A hush fell, and all that could be heard was the clicking of Acting-MCP-President Beauregard's shoes across the dusty wooden stage. He was back to one of his skinny suits, which just seemed right. Dublin glanced back at Prudence. They had joked about Beauregard's wardrobe earlier that week. No reaction.

"Ladies and gentlemen, what a week we have had! I was talking backstage to members of our staff, and let me just tell you, they have never seen the kind of outstanding scores that y'all put up this week! I think you all deserve a big round of applause! Come on!" He started clapping, and it caught on, mechanically at first, then with a little bit of spirit. "Seriously, I am so proud of y'all, and so excited to see what you are go-ing to accomplish!"

He seems to actually care. I'll give him that, thought Kaywin.

"Now. I suppose you are wondering…," he freed the mi-crophone from the stand and took a few steps back toward the towering black velvet curtain behind him, clearly trying to do two things at once. He fumbled in the velvet for a second. "I suppose you are wondering…" he found the seam in the curtains and stuck his head through, apparently checking on the readiness of whatever or whomever was going to fol-low him. Satisfied, he refocused on the four thousand people waiting for him to finish his sentence.

Again Dublin glanced back at Prudence to read her reac-tion. It was another very short read.

Prudence saw Dublin glancing back at her every two sec-onds like an ugly puppy, but she was not going to acknowledge him. She had really been counting on them **not** being assigned together. Otherwise she never would have given him the time of day. Now she had to nip this in the bud.

"I suppose you are wondering what your colors mean, and *what the future holds in store for you!*" Then he paused, as if actually expecting a response to a question they all assumed had been rhetorical. Just to get things moving again, a couple of wiseacres in the audience shouted, "Yes!" "Yes we are!"

"Well I'm going to make you wait." The audience groaned. This was maybe less of a game to them than it seemed to be to him. "Meanwhile," he said, smiling strangely, as from his far left and his far right two enormous silver blunt-ended cones rolled slowly and mysteriously into view, dwarfing him. There were evenly spaced holes perforating their surfaces, and these holes glowed intermittently from some unseen inner volcanic force. A terrible rumbling came from within them. Some of this seemed planned, and some of it didn't. Kaywin was glad to be forty-five rows back. "Meanwhile, I want to introduce a man who needs no introduction, a man without whose generous donations the Meaningful Conclusion Program would not even be **possible**…" Suddenly, the already-dim lights went out *completely*. No emergency lights, no exit lights, nothing but the reddish implications from the sinister glow-holes on stage. "Your next President of the United States of America--" *Was he allowed to say that?* "**Rich Brandenberg!**"

The two silver mega-furnaces flared and whooshed. The enormous black curtains seemed to be parting. It was hard to tell, like someone taking off a black jacket in a cave at midnight. But the brain sensed a movement there, more than the eye. Suddenly a deep voice bellowed, unendurably loudly, filling their ears and minds:

"I AM THE GOD OF HELLFIRE, AND I BRING YOU FIRE!"

An ancient-sounding organ groove exploded on the word 'fire', and the stage burst into flames. Huge columns of fire shot from the nickel-plated machines. From the ceiling between them descended slowly a figure with a clearly state-of-the-art jetpack, and a silver Dizastra 3000 suit.

The audience went nuts. Brandenberg began swooping back and forth directly through the inferno, and then out into the crowd. Everyone was on their feet before they even knew it, dancing to the primitive hypnotic beat. The multi-trillionaire, the King of the Free World it seemed, fed off of their energy, flying in loop-de-loops and then backwards, in a reclined position, right through the flames. The funniest part was when he stopped in mid-air in the middle of the auditorium, just as stable as if his feet had been on the ground, then bent over almost double and starting shaking his rump. In his puffy segmented suit, Kaywin thought he looked like a manic overgrown larva. The crowd was in a frenzy.

Certainly Dublin had never seen anything like this. Riled by the furious music, stomping his feet and grinning from ear to ear, he turned yet again to see how Prudence was doing.

She wasn't there.

Her seat was conspicuously empty. Dublin didn't like this one bit...something was amiss. It was one thing for a girl he cared about to start shutting him down when she realized what he was thinking, but there was something more at play here.

It was tough going in the dancing crowd, but he managed to push his way out of his row and back to where Prudence should have been. Behind the last row of seats was a series of giant square columns and then an open concourse. He thought maybe she had gone looking for a bathroom back there, and he took a few uncertain steps past one of the columns, expecting at any moment to be tackled by guards. Something caught his attention behind the column. A tiny broken figure huddled at its base, rocking back and forth, knees hugged tightly to chin. Only the unnatural red glow of the miserable creature's hair gave Dublin any clue that this was Prudence, and not some epically-lost four-year old. He fell to his knees on the marble floor in front of her.

"Pru! Pru!" *Nice one, moron.* "I mean, **Prudence**! Are you okay?!" He was having to shout over the thunderous music. He seriously thought she might be having some kind of medical episode. He hadn't seen the first glimpse of this kind of vulnerability from her. She was shaking violently and her eyes were wide in terror. With a trembling, uncertain hand he reached out and touched her shoulder. She gave a yelp like she'd been burned, and swatted his hand away, but she seemed to regain her bearings slightly. She said something he couldn't make out at first, until, mercifully, the song devolved into a dramatically soft and slow interlude:

You've been living like a little girl
In the middle of your little world...

"It's him," Prudence said. Dublin was able to guide her up to her feet.

"It's **who?**"

"Him. My father used to bring him around. I would have to pretend to be Linsom Felize."

This was all coming together in Dublin's head, her childhood on the other side of reality from his. He blanched. "But--but that's Rich Brandenberg!"

"I would get in trouble if I stopped pretending."

"Prudence--" He struggled to find the right words. He didn't want to sound like he didn't believe her. "This guy is **everywhere!** Did you not recognize him until now?"

"It's the song." She could barely breathe. "It's the song he used to play when he would punish me."

"But that song is in like three of his commercials--you've seen the one where it's like the end of the world and he's asking his neighbor who won the Yankees game?"

"But they don't use that beginning part. That's when I remem--that's when I remembered. I am the God of Hellfire. I am the God of Hellfire. I am..." She was gasping.

"Prudence. Oh my gosh. I'm so sorry!"

Tears were streaming down her face. In the hellish glow

behind the pillar, she unzipped a small portion of the left hip of her new red jumpsuit. She pulled the top part up a couple of inches.

Dublin was as about as confused as a young boy can be.

"Look." On her left hip was burned a crude little circle with a 'thumbs-up' symbol in it.

He gulped. "It's the Uno Mundo logo."

"There's more of them." She rezipped and started to catch her breath. She was starting to look like Prudence again. Suddenly something changed. They could *feel* the attention of the crowd directed backwards in their direction. Brandenberg had noticed the two empty seats and had found them out. God forbid that two people out of four thousand weren't watching his every move. A vague sense that they were about to get busted for not being where they were supposed to be inkled into Dublin's consciousness. Without really thinking about it, he felt a need to sort of step out from behind the pillar and take the heat for the unplanned indiscretion, before the energized crowd all caught Prudence with her guard down, in the depth of her frailty.

What he saw when he peeked out was Brandenberg, about fifteen feet in the air, gliding toward them slowly, with a vaguely malicious, bland grin of utter empowerment on his face. He was clearly intending to expose them, and was enjoying the build-up immensely. But Dublin sort of messed up his timing by stepping out from behind the column, fully and unafraidedly. His disgust for this man was so fresh and so deep that he became absolutely impervious to the public embarrassment that the showboating mogul was trying to feed him.

The few seconds that had passed had been enough for Prudence to recover. In very short order, her terror and despair had been converted back into the bulletproof bitterness she was more known for. She didn't know what was happening, but she wasn't afraid anymore. She saw Dublin with his back to her, and his fists clenched by his sides. She could see the faces in the back rows turned and looking directly at him, and beyond that, and beyond that; row after row of faces glowing with reflected firelight and fading into a hot orange blur that writhed and pulsated to the manic beat of the crazy music.

She stepped out next to him. Brandenberg was now finishing his approach. He stopped in mid-air ten feet in front of them, exactly where he had been **planning** to stop, except that now it **looked** like he had braked because she had suddenly appeared, like he was afraid of a little girl. His brow furrowed with a question, though his grin didn't budge. He studied her with the superior air of a man so important that he knows the world will wait for him. He extended this for an extra moment--to drive the point home that he was in control of the situation. Prudence, staring him in the eye without blinking, never figured out if he had recognized her or not. Either way, the gross little wink he gave her, as the song neared its crescendo, and the vocalist began repeating *you're gonna burn*, sent a shiver down her spine.

The music was beginning to get away from Brandenberg; he had choreographed this whole routine pretty tightly and he jetted away to assume his dramatic finishing position. Every firehole emptied its towering, billowing column of hell at once, and the zooming presidential candidate didn't miss any of them, finally finding a spot in the very center of the auditorium to slowly rise higher and higher, with his arms outstretched left and right, and one leg cocked slightly upward. The music crescendoed right on cue as he reached the pinnacle of his ascent. The crowd, which had been standing the entire three minutes, erupted into cheers. Brandenberg drank it all in as he wafted his way back to the stage. The glass of his helmet slid open as he approached the microphone.

"Thank you. Thank you. I--" The applause was too loud; he was going to have to wait. Twenty seconds passed. If the election had taken place right then and there, Brandenberg's nerdy opponent, Carl Jiminey, would have been obliterated. "Thank you. Thank you…this is embarrassing." (He was doing his best imitation of 'humble'; it was the only area, according to his advisors, in which Jiminey outclassed him.) "I'm not worthy! I'm not worthy!"

When the crowd finally calmed, he was able to begin. "You guys are like…sooo amazing! What you are about to do for America, it just truly humbles me. I'm in awe. I truly am. You guys are like…..my heroes."

Kaywin looked around. *Are people buying this guy?*

"**Acting-**president Beauregard has invited me here tonight to tell you guys where you are going. Since none of you will be around to vote in the '28 election, we'll make it quick!" A few people laughed, but for the most part his little joke fell flat. "Can I get someone from the beautiful rows of violet to come up to the stage?" Oh. This was going to take a while. After a lot of cajoling, a middle-aged woman from the second of the ten rows of purple came up to the stage. "What's your name, Sweetheart?"

"Aldida."

"That's a pretty name. Aldida, you and your friends in purple are going to Atlanta, to the Center for the Elimination of Disease." This sounded more meaningful than 'bio-testing'. "The CED needs you guys to help make all diseases a thing of the past, like they did with cancer!" This announcement was met with respectful applause, especially from the non-purple stripes of the rainbow. "That's great! Who's coming up for blue?" Aldida left the stage, and a stunted little man in blue came up. "Look at this guy! What's your name, big man?"

"John."

"Love it! Well, John, you and the rest of your blue buddies are going underground. The future can't happen without precious metals. You guys are going to the mines; you're gonna make that future possible! For everybody!" More applause, again not so much from the MCs in blue, who like everybody had been hoping for some destiny maybe a little more likely to be commemorated in song some day. Brandenberg made his way through the rainbow; the band of green Goners, which was five rows deep instead of ten like the others, was going somewhere 'top secret'. This must be spywork! Yellow was going undersea. Orange was going to Mars. This left red.

Kaywin looked around him. He had a pretty good guess where he, Prudence, Dublin, the Kalaysian Three-Star, Jerkboy (*great*), Vance, the two ascetics, and the other eight hundred red-suited MCs were headed. Brandenberg, with his arm around a droopy-faced burnout named 'Jay,' dragged the moment out a little. This was his last moment, for the day at least, to feed off the subservience of his admirers. Prudence and Dublin had been strongly urged to return to their seats. They seethed at the man on the stage, and resented having to hang on his every word. *I don't care where you send me,* Prudence said to herself. *As long as it's far far away from you.*

"Are you nervous, Jay?"

"A little."

"Can I calm you down with a little nursery rhyme? Hey diddle diddle/the cat and the fiddle/the cow jumped over..." he put the microphone in Jay's face, expecting him to fill in the blank. Jay twitched and looked up at the tall, handsome man grinning in his puffy silver suit.

"I don't know that one."

"How can you not know that one? Eight hundred red-suits and we found the one who doesn't know 'Hey Diddle-Diddle'! Did your mom not read to you when you were little?"

Jay strained back inward and upward toward the mike. "Maybe that's why I'm here." The crowd laughed heartily. A shared feeling of family abandonment compelled many of them to holler and cheer at his joke. Brandenberg smiled, but grimly; he didn't like the adoration of the crowd missing him by a foot and a half like that. Maybe a little embarrassment would put this guy back in his place.

"How about a guess. Come on, the cow jumped over..."

"The fence?"

"That's the worst guess ever, Jay. Love this guy!" It was **his** turn to rile the crowd up. That was **his** job. "No, Jay; we are not sending you and your friends to 'the fence'!"

"If you are wearing a red jumpsuit, you're going to the Moon!"

10

This Time Tomorrow

As the half-bewildered, half-exhilarated crowd made their way out of the auditorium, with the redsuits who had been seated in back necessarily bringing up the rear, the cool night air hit their faces, and the bright full moon hit them in the eyes. The universe could scarcely have planned it any better. It was huge tonight and luminous, and it it hung there in the sky with such grand immediacy that even Kaywin, with both feet on the ground as always, felt like he could have reached up and plucked it like a ripe fruit, without even standing on tiptoes.

How many times had they seen the moon in their lives? Hundreds, thousands of times, but never like this. They stumbled to a stop and gawked at it. This was to be their new home! Not only their **new** home, but their **final** home. They would be laid to rest there, sometime within the next... Kaywin looked at his Sofee, and expanded the ever-present countdown on the display so his old eyes could read it.

17242:16:35, 17242:16:34, 17242:16:33...

...sometime within the next seventeen thousand hours or so. Sometime within that brief span, he would be laid to rest up there. Up there! Floating in the night sky! Unbelievable.

235

He guessed he wouldn't really rot away; just freeze. At any rate, he would spend the rest of forever up there, until his forty-six years on Earth became just a teensy blip in comparison. Aeons upon aeons.

The grassy sward outside the still-smoking auditorium buzzed with energy as friends darted all over the place looking for each other, anxious to compare the meaningfulness of their conclusions.

Dublin came running up behind him. "Kaywin!" His pat on the back turned into a hug as Kaywin snapped out of his morbid reverie and turned to greet him. The boy was out of breath from running and from excitement. "We're going to **THE MOON!**"

Kaywin opened his mouth to say, "Yeah; you remember **WHY,** right?" but he stopped himself. Dublin knew why they were going to the moon. They all had the countdowns on their Sofees to remind them constantly; they all knew what they had volunteered for. Everyone here had signed on to end their miserable lives; for all the bursts of laughter and the joking, nobody ever really forgot **WHY**... By the same token however, none of them could stare at their shoelaces 24/7; they all needed little moments of energy and purpose like this to get them through. So Kaywin restrained himself. "So I heard," he said instead. "It's pretty cool. It is pretty cool."

A young man in orange ran by, out of breath like Dublin. "The moon is for losers! I'm going to **Mars!**"

"Yeah; you remember **WHY**, right?" Kaywin couldn't resist shouting in return.

"Prudence! We're going to the moon!" She had just walked up to the two. Dublin turned and thought about hugging her. He knew before she said anything that it was a bad idea, and was already speaking 'whoops, sorry' in body language as she was saying 'no thanks' the normal mouth way.

"Yeah, I **was** pretty excited about that" she said "but I recently heard that the moon is for losers." Dublin was happy that she was back to form. The glimpse of her in a broken heap had been a terrifying contrast to her usual stoic sarcasm...but at the same time it made him wonder if she was capable of **other** human emotions...

Kaywin was still in the dark about her breakdown. He also wasn't sure that he needed to know. He wasn't as gung-ho as Dublin was to be friends with someone so damaged, at least until she demonstrated some kind of human warmth. Her cold frown always made him miss Victoria's warm smile. But that wasn't her fault. "Are you okay, Prudence? I saw you disappear for a minute during the...very dignified performance...of our possible future President..."

"Yes. I'm fine. I had to powder my nose. I was starting to sweat my face off, once the flaming clown show started." Kaywin knew this wasn't true, but he also knew that whatever friendship they had was still too fragile to bludgeon with paternal concern.

The ensuing pause in the conversation gave all three of them an excuse to gaze up at the pitted, yellowy-white full moon, rising like a great balloon in super-slow motion over the silhouetted tree line. "It looks like I could touch it," cloyed Dublin. "I've always felt like I could almost touch it." Prudence rolled her eyes in the dark.

"Well, now you will," Kaywin said, hoping this would be a little period at the end of Dublin's free-form poem.

Most of the red contingency had stopped in the grass and were looking up with similar thoughts and feelings. A respectful hush reigned, broken up sporadically with little pockets of laughter. A vague sensation of pride prevailed. For what? They hadn't even done anything yet. Yet the feeling was so strong that many of them had to choke back tears. After a few minutes of subdued conversation, a man that Kaywin recognized by sight--he had been paired with him during one of the exercises on Wednesday, though he still didn't know his name--inhaled deeply, threw back his head, and let loose with his best werewolf howl. He didn't hold back whatsoever. What was left to lose? His reputation? His 'cool'?

The man's loud and long tribute to the queen of the night echoed over the neighboring hills and died away. It begat a lot of laughs, then a couple of copycats, and then, I guess not surprisingly, several **hundred** copycats (or copywolves?). What **was** surprising was the chill they all felt. It was the tingle of feeling connected by hard times, of recognizing something in common with strangers. *These people howling like idiots aren't afraid, so why should **I** be afraid? They aren't sad, at least not right now, so why should **I** be?*

Dublin howled with great boyish enthusiasm. Kaywin, in remembrance of his younger, happier former self, joined in.

Prudence did not, Dublin noticed mid-howl. *That's alright.* He had realized something else that made him want to stand there and howl all night, something she herself hadn't noticed.

For the first time, *she* had approached *them*. And she stuck around.

~

The massive lunar transport vessel had been painted that seductive Army green, but Kaywin recognized it by its shape, even on the pre-dawn runway, as a 'Pegasus'. Catchy name, but 'Hindenburg' or 'Titanic' would have been more appropriate. These antique civilian/cargo buckets had put the Pegasus company out of commission forever. Their attempts to establish a luxury hotel on the moon had been completely undone by the calamitous explosions of two of these transports, eleven months apart. After that, super-rich people went back to vacationing in Middle-Pacifico, or Dubai.

Yep. This was a (hopefully) refitted Pegasus. Kaywin recognized the tiny little dorsal lump, which gave it the appearance of a fetal whale. A sickly green fetal whale, with wings and wheels. There were ten of them taking off this morning. Three of them would hold the eight hundred and twenty MC's, a small army of guards, and a little contingency of military personnel. The other seven massive craft were loaded with cargo. This must be whatever materials they would be working with; building whatever they would be building. Kaywin was familiar with the staggering capacity of these vessels. There must be more happening on the moon than the public was aware of.

Everyone knew that the intrepid, ubiquitous Brandenberg Corporation, unsatisfied with the riches of Earth, had been working on a luxury Lunar Hotel for a few years, but that was a private venture. The Meaningful Conclusion Program was a Government entity. They couldn't be using Goners to work on Brandenberg's 'La Lune' project, unless it was somehow being subsidized by the government, as stimulus for future Lunar commerce. But Kaywin was getting ahead of himself here. All he knew at this point was that there appeared to be a whole lot of people and stuff getting ready to take off for the moon.

They had assigned seats on the shuttles. Kaywin could see Prudence several rows in front of him. She had closely-cropped, gently glowing leopard print hair this morning, for traveling. When she turned her head to look out the window, he could that her eyes were blacked out with makeup, and the middle of her face from one cheek, across the little nose and presumably onto to the other cheek, gleamed with a wide but understated irregular gold stripe. Her lips, pursed a little tiny bit in... concentration? defiance? anxiety?...were a slightly darker gold, with a tinge of orange, and a touch more glitter.

Dublin, on a different transport, had gone with his usual look--homely with a hint of desperation. He had been into space one time, in eighth grade, like most kids of his generation. For some of the older MCs on his transport, this was about to be a brand new thing. Nobody in his compartment was losing it or anything, but there was a lot of sweating, and finger-tapping, and foot-tapping.

"Nervous?" Dublin asked the fidgeting older man to his left.

"Yeah. I'll be fine once we take off. It's stupid. It's not a rational fear. It's 2126; it's not like we're in a Pegasus or something. I guess this is old hat for you. You kids go now in like, what, second grade?"

"Eighth." The hum of the massive engines warming up shut down their conversation. Suddenly, video screens on the backs of the seats in front of them crackled to life. A hilarious retro flight-safety video that could have been from the 2080's started up. Or at least Dublin **assumed** it was just done in a retro style...after a few minutes he realized that this was not an **imitation** of a forty-five year-old safety video; it **was** a forty-five year-old safety video. Everything they were detailing on the built-in novelty screens seemed applicable to the craft they were sitting in. Dublin let this sink in for a minute.

"I think this is a pretty old ship," he said.

When the video was over, the engines revved up, as if they had only been joking before that. His neighbor didn't like the sound of it, and twisted uncomfortably in his bucket seat. "Just think. When this puppy leaves the runway we will be done with Earth forever."

"Oh, I know; it's crazy to think about." This was not a revelation to Dublin. Since laying down to sleep the night before last, at the assignment ceremony, he had been thinking on and off about the moment when he would have one foot on the ramp up into the transport and one foot still on the tarmac of Houston International Airport. He had waited for that exact moment, and had composed a brief, melodramatic poem to recite to himself when it came. Before he had finished mumbling the first line to himself, however, some brute a little ways back in line exploded unnecessarily on him:

"What's the holdup, Creaturehead? Let's go!" Dublin thought it was one of the guards, so he responded immediately and got moving up the ramp. But then he looked back and saw it was this Neanderthal guy he'd seen a couple of times around training camp. He thought maybe if he had known it wasn't one of the guards he would have said some-thing. Oh well. It was pretty much too late now. It kind of drove him nuts. They weren't going to take off one second sooner because this guy had spoken up, and it wasn't like they were leaving on a vacation anyway...it was just an excuse for a messed-up dude to show out in front of his friends, and to call him 'Creaturehead'. It was the second time he had heard the word in the last week. The first time he hadn't been sure if it was directed at him. Now it kind of looked like it had been. Creaturehead. He hoped **that** nickname didn't stick. This little episode, as he was literally trying to say goodbye to the Earth, seemed somehow appropriate, and typical of the cruelest planet yet known to man. It actually made leaving it forever a little easier. Sadly, the Neanderthal guy was coming too.

Prudence, over in Transport 2, wasn't sad in the least to let it go. Fat lot of good the mother-planet had ever done her. Maybe somebody someday would figure out life on Earth, but it wouldn't be her. This was the nature of her self-talk as she sat silently in her oversized seat. She was accustomed to switching her feelings off completely in trying circumstances. It wasn't her fault that most of her life **was** trying circum-stances. *Just tell me where to go, what to do, and who to be.*

She had never been out into space. Her eighth-grade year was when she began being 'home-schooled'. She had had the opportunity to join her former classmates on the field trip into orbit, and remembered being *sort of* interested, but when the time came to commit, the credits that had been set aside had disappeared. Missing out on the **experience** was one thing, but she had been bitterly disappointed about not getting the three days away from her father and his latest girlfriend. This was all so soon after her last friend had betrayed her, and she'd found out that her mom was marrying 'George'. *How did I get on this subject? I swore I would never think about these people again.*

She looked idly out the window. It was still dark, so she caught more of her own reflection than any action on the runway. She liked her reflection today. She liked the look she'd given herself. She had done similar blacked-out eyes the first time she had met her father's current girlfriend, and she couldn't help but smile wryly as she remembered Janelle's shocked and disdainful reaction. It was as if she had walked out of her room with two horns and a tail. Generally speaking she enjoyed it when strangers were put off by her appearance, as if she were some kind of freak. They were going to find out she was a freak eventually anyway; it was better to just lay all of her cards on the table. Even if she played all sweet at the start, and fooled people into thinking that they liked her, they would know before long just how wrong they had been; just how unlovable she actually was, and they would leave her alone. *How many times do you have to see a human behavior demonstrated before you recognize a pattern?* Prudence ended this little reverie with a mental pat on her own back for all the time she had saved herself, and other people, by being honest; and also for how much future time she was going to save the world by kissing it goodbye.

Kaywin, sitting seven rows behind Prudence, had the benefit of much simpler feelings. He missed his Nadine and his Victoria; he missed them terribly, and he wanted to die.

Underneath and around the tumult of their emotions,

they felt the idling engines rumbling into life. The ten transport vessels began that agonizingly slow creeping, turning this way and that around each other like giant cats appraising each other before a fight. Finally, Transport 2 with Prudence, and Kaywin, and two hundred and sixty of their mates on it, rounded a final curve and stood down at the end of a long runway. It was marked on either side by blinking yellow lights, and seemed to stretch northward forever, into Oklahoma and beyond. With a jarring, lurching rumble, like a clothes dryer full of towels and large rocks, the massive engines approached a fever pitch. Then, everyone on board felt like they'd been punched in the gut as the gears engaged, and the enormous vessel surged down the concourse. They started out fast and got faster. The marker lights outside of Kaywin's window on the right side blipped by with increasing urgency until they merged into a yellow line, pointing the way to elsewhere. They reached a speed that seemed excessive; then suddenly, alarmingly, they exceeded it. Pinned back forcefully in their seats they could feel with their whole bodies the vibration of the vessel's wheels screaming over the concrete. And then they couldn't.

The ascent of the huge shuttles was much like that of a regular jet, which is quite steep at first and finally levels off. But the moon shuttles took off with even greater velocity, and just kept on ascending and ascending. Twice they kind of plateaued, briefly, before reassuming a sharp upward trajectory. "They're trying to trim the drag," some know-it-all announced.

Kaywin had been into low orbit a number of times in the line of duty, but he still couldn't resist looking out at the world diminishing below them. The view was fascinating; you could almost **see** the landmasses shrinking away. They went from seeing whole cities (like you might from a jet window) to seeing whole mountain ranges, to all of Florida dangling into the Caribbean Sea. Then it was the enormous blue swath of the Atlantic Ocean, and just minutes later they were able to identify the entire curving bulge of North Africa. The force of their forward progress was intense and insistent. Even if the spiderwebbing safety harness had been removed completely it was doubtful that the strongest among them could have risen out of his or her seat. Kaywin couldn't lean forward at all to vary his viewing angle out of the little porthole window.

After about fifteen minutes, their vessel zipped out of Earth's atmosphere. Not too long after that, the sensation of acceleration began to fade. This was merciful. Nobody likes to feel like they are being crushed by three times their own body weight for very long. Prudence was a little surprised that she wasn't feeling weightless like they do in the movies, but she wasn't about to ask for her money back.

The journey from the Earth to the Moon would be accomplished in just under twenty-six uncomfortable hours.

They were allowed to unbuckle only briefly, and only to use the restroom, toward which they had to pull themselves along a rope. Once there they had to listen to the guard explaining the toilet mechanism, and how **not** to make a big mess when using it. The effect of Earth's gravity on them was shrinking, and they weren't close enough to the moon for it to draw them in, so, while not quite weightless yet, they were light, unsteady, and shaking.

Fortunately (depending on who you ask) two hours in, their personal seatback video screens once more came alive. They were about to be treated to a history of humanity's presence on the Moon. It was a thrilling story, full of daring and adventure, twists and turns--but not the way **this** guy told it. There is a real science to the time-honored process of making **interesting** things **boring,** and the producers of this video had mastered it.

They started by hiring the most boring man in the world to narrate. He was very old, and very tired, and, in his cheap brown suit, with his eyes half-closed, he mumbled the story as if telling it for the eight-hundredth time. So as not to throw a wrench in the spokes of my narrative, I will not quote this man exactly, but will paraphrase his Lunar History in a hopefully less moribund style.

We all know about Neil Armstrong's 'One small step for Man; one giant leap for Mankind' on July 20th, 1969. A few minutes later his capsule-mate, Buzz Aldrin, became the second human on the Moon. There were several other Apollo Missions, and ten other 'steppers' on the lunar surface; all of them men, and all of them Americans, the last one (for a loooong time) on December 14th, 1972. This intrepid storm of activity had been fueled by the Cold War, which was not an actual war, but the decades-long **threat** of one. And a terrible one it would have been, with atomic weapons poised to fire on both sides. The fear of falling behind scientifically fueled the Soviet Union and the United States into competing energetically and urgently against each other for early dominance in space, each understanding that second place might mean the total annihilation of their beloved country. After the USA had planted its flag on the Moon, the urgency faded and the money dried up. A couple of decades later, the Soviet Union destabilized, and for an astounding fifty-two years the Moon was once again just something in the sky to look at while holding hands. Then, in 2024, China landed a capsule with two men on the lunar surface.

This well-publicized event, that everybody had seen coming for years, was bemoaned by millions of Americans as the end of the world. Those who couldn't express their feelings in poems or watercolors went out and bought up every bullet in the nation. Let the Chinese collect all the lunar soil samples they wanted, but woe betide the day the Chinese Moon Rover dared to start digging in **their** backyard!

Other Americans shrugged off this open affront. Although feelings were divided as to whether this one small step for China betokened disaster for America, or not, the people of the USA were united again for the first time in half a century in the belief that it was time to once again spend a lot of money on lunar exploration and even (finally!) colonization. A scramble was made to get back in the game. It wasn't as if NASA scientists had been sleeping. Work had been ongoing for years on the logistics of establishing a permanent Moonbase. Ideas had been proposed and argued, models had been built...but the political machinery of America was almost rusted shut at this point. It had not performed well in the information age at all. On the new wonder of the age, the 'internet', still so unpolished and unpoliced, any blowhard could assert any political slander so invisibly, and unflinchingly, that you couldn't read an article about watering roses without someone in the comments demanding the President's head over the lack of rain. Insults between parties were constant, **beyond** constant; there was no one person who could absorb it all, and if she did she would have driven off a cliff. So despite all of America more or less wanting the same thing for once, the political wheels were slow to turn:

--*Yes! Let's invest two hundred billion credits* ('dollars' back in 2024) *in establishing a permanent American Moonbase!*

--*Yes! I feel the same way, my friend!*

--*Where shall we pull the money from, though?*

--*From the National Defense budget, of course!*

--*You idiot! That's exactly what China* **wants** *us to do! Let's pull the money instead from one of these three thousand poverty-assistance programs!*

--*Heartless moron! So our own citizens can starve to death while our astronauts are getting fat on astronaut ice cream and Tang?*

...and so on, and so on, and so on. While America bickered, India and Japan also landed live humans on the Moon, in 2028 and 2030 respectively. These countries had been building in that direction for years; so while it made the U.S. antsier and antsier, it still took a shocking turn of events to **really** galvanize American efforts.

In fact, the next twelve years in lunar history are still

known as the 'Weird Years'.

It started with one of the most brilliant and ambitious advertising campaigns of all time. Ramses--**A SHOE COMPANY**--went searching for the ultimate underdog to feature in its commercials. They wound up sponsoring a small, chronically poor African country, in conjunction with hired rocket scientists from all over the world, all of this kept amazingly hush-hush, mind you; and in 2032, **Cameroon** did what the world's greatest superpower had been unable to do for sixty years. They became only the fifth country in the world to land astronauts--a very, **very** brave man, and a very, **very** brave woman--on the Moon.

This, (and the non-stop sneaker commercials featuring Cameroonian scientists and astronauts doing their thing against all odds whilst wearing attractive and comfortable 'Ramses Underdogs') bludgeoned America into action. Money was shaken loose, and quickly. By early 2034, in fact, shuttles from the Earth to the Moon were making almost monthly trips, and an actual permanent Moonbase was under construction. It was on a smaller scale than most of the sketches submitted to NASA by impatient kids, but progress was encouraging.

The action was heating up, and so far there was enough Moon for everybody. Then two U.S. shuttles exploded in the late 2030's, killing all on board. A third caught fire on the runway, but thankfully all hands were evacuated. India, too, lost a shuttle around the same time. And so a paradox peculiar to modern times once again reared its ugly head: scientific progress would improve the lives of all humanity, but how many humans was it okay to sacrifice on the way? This was almost fifty years before the creation of the Goner Program, mind you. When the Roman Empire conquered the entire known world twenty-two hundred years earlier, it didn't matter how many soldiers or slaves died to accomplish it. Sure, human progress was advanced forward as the Roman Army advanced forward, bringing reading, writing, science, law and structure to barbarian countries. No one cared at the time if the road was paved with skulls. Lives only mattered if they were the lives of noblemen. This didn't change for a long, long time. As late as the mid-eighteen hundreds, human beings were bought and sold like cattle. Flash forward a hundred years, and suddenly lives mattered.

Progress slowed for a little while as a result of these tragedies while the space-faring nations regrouped. America's fledgling Moonbase went temporarily dormant, going completely unvisited between 2038 and 2040. While NASA assessed their ability to move forward safely, the completely unforeseeable 'Gesster Event' happened.

Organized religion on Earth by 2040 had been on the decline for decades. Though every major faith--Judaism, Christianity, Islam, Buddhism etc.--lived on, it was more common than ever to meet people who simply didn't ever even think about religion, or their own place in the bigger picture. It's very easy to put off spiritual thoughts and questions for another day, and Lord knows (and Allah and Yahweh and Vishnu, etc.) that the world was more filled with distracting shiny objects than it had ever been. But sometimes, throughout history, when people have straddled the fence between belief and unbelief, an event will occur that will shake the fence, and folks will fall off on either side. On April 12, 2040, an event occurred which straight up **electrified** the fence.

This was an unfortunate, bizarre incident that set the world back much further than it should have, no offense intended to the twelve people who were killed. It happened during an open-air speech by ultra-liberal congressman Paul Gesster. On the sixteenth green of Pebble Beach Golf Course in California, as he prattled on about cloning rights, and the complete eradication of all weapons forever, the sky grew uncommonly bright, and a strange, hot, ripping noise danced in and around the ears of the watching thousands. The small meteorite didn't technically hit Congressman Gesster, but it impacted the stage near him with devastating force. The poor eighteen-year political veteran was battered, concussed, startled and incensed to death, along with eleven nearby supporters. In the ensuing days, as fellow humans from around the globe poured forth their condolences, a disgusting murmur began that this was no cosmic freak-accident, no chance-of-all-chances, but rather the willful and direct act of an angry God. Others questioned this God's aim, that eleven onlookers, including a four year-old girl with no avowed political leanings, had, too, been wiped from the face of creation.

The sides were set, and the people of the 'United' States were suddenly more sharply divided than they had been in years. The Gesster Event, coupled with the shuttle explosions, was interpreted by millions as God's crystal-clear statement that mankind should maybe stick to his home planet, refocus himself on matters of the spirit, and also that the minimum wage should **not** be raised.

Fortunately, among these conservatives, there was a powerful reaction to the reaction. Dixie Trout and Ammo stores

across the country began putting jars at their registers, col-
lecting quarters (an old coin worth one fourth of one credit)
for an independent Dixie Trout and Ammo Moon Venture.
What began life as a joke turned serious quickly, as donations
and sponsorships began pouring in. Many of these, sad to say,
came from folks who didn't feel a *connection* with the Cameroonian underdogs, and wanted to launch an underdog whose
skin-tone matched their own. Two years later, the world was
force-fed one of the ripest fruits of human confusion ever,
as a Confederate Flag was planted in the Central Mare Tran-
quillitatus portion of the Moon, and a couple of enterprising
good ole' boys claimed no less than half of the Moon for 'the
South'. This was a joke on the grandest scale, but it had to be
dealt with seriously, and for the first time a council of world
leaders met to sort through the confusion and to draw up
some firm guidelines for what constituted a legitimate Lunar
land claim. The World Lunar Pact was debated, drawn up
and ratified. It was decided, to the chagrin of some, that flags
on the Moon didn't mean much anymore. All they did was
buy some time (two years) and some elbowroom (a circle ten
miles across) for your country to begin building a permanent
base. After four years, the base would have to be inhabited for
at least two months of the year. Considering the challenges
of sustaining life on a world with no atmosphere, no existing
power source, and where surface temperatures could fluctu-
ate almost five hundred degrees; from around 253 degrees
Fahrenheit during the long lunar day, to around 250 degrees
below zero--this is in the tropical regions--at night, these
were ambitious standards. By these new guidelines, America
had an edge. They had seven flags and the infrastructure for a

permanent base already set up. In a gesture of good faith, the US shared some of its life-preserving technologies with the other legitimate space programs, and on March 7, 2043 this basic framework for future moon development was agreed upon by 175 of the 190 countries represented in the World Peace Council.

Private commercial ventures were not excluded from this landmark agreement. The claims of Dixie Trout and Ammo and Ramses Footwear/Cameroon were thereby validated, but the clock was ticking on them. Dixie Trout supporters tried, but couldn't muster the funds for a retelling of the same joke. To this day, their Confederate Flag stands undisturbed, and at its base sits the fishing rod that redneck astronaut Brett Tankersly used to make the first (and still longest) fly-cast on the Moon.

The Ramses Footwear/Cameroon partnership on the other hand had done such excellent wonders for both parties that they were loathe to give it up. Thousands of Cameroonians who would have starved (in the years before the Underdog commercials) were fed; infant mortality was down, way down, and the timing was right for a follow-up campaign. Against all odds, they did succeed in setting up a tiny permanent base, and in keeping it manned for the requisite two months of the year, though they did file for relief on that count twice in the 2070's. It was nothing more than a tiny bunker in the side of a little hill, a small room with a mini-lab for experiments, a bunk bed, a table and chairs, a couch, a viewing wall, and the world's littlest shoe store. This was where the entire enterprise paid for itself (and then some), as every month a new celebrity appeared holographically to shop for shoes. The joke was that they only had Underdogs, and only in size thirteen, and that whoever the celebrity was--basketball legend Trix Willingham, President Parker, even country-crossover superstar Miggan Hix--they would have to try one of their stores on Earth. It sounds stupid, but for the most part they were hilarious.

That sounds stupid, thought Prudence, barely staying awake on Transport 2.

That sounds hilarious, thought Dublin, hanging on every word in Transport 3, though he knew most of the story by heart.

I'll bet that kid Dublin knows this whole story by heart, thought Kaywin, back on Transport 2.

So within this established framework, countries and companies were able to proceed less urgently, less haphazardly... now they knew that they couldn't just swoop in, plant a flag, and claim half of the Moon. And if they **did** stake a claim, they knew it was protected. For thirty-five years or so about thirty nations and twenty-two corporations made ventures onto the Moon, some fizzling, and some sticking. The Lunar landscape became sparsely dotted with fledgling settlements, like miner's tents by a Yukon River the day after a gold-strike, when word is just beginning to get out.

In the 2070's the Pegasus Corporation announced its plans for a grand hotel near the Lunar North Pole and the well-established American Base-Two. This was greeted with great public excitement, which tailed off like a sick trombone after the previously mentioned Pegasus Transport explosions. These back-to-back tragedies killed off two hundred and eighty civilians, three hundred and twelve military personnel, and one grand dream.

They were also the spark that led to the creation of the Meaningful Conclusion Program, those two crashes and every crash, explosion, drowning, burning, or suffocation before them in the history of scientific endeavor.

A little bit of a (mock?) cheer arose in each of the transports at this first mention of the Goner Program. Kaywin saw one of the guards adjust his weapon and make eye contact with one of his mates.

The MCP was established in 2082 and was instantly involved on the Moon. No other corporation or country had the luxury of these fearless volunteers. The North Pole Base, chosen because of its prolonged exposure to sunshine, expanded rapidly.

"They shouldn't have used the word 'luxury'," Prudence mused to her neighbor. "It makes us sound as important as a pair of fur slippers." The woman wrinkled her nose at Prudence as if she were smelling a pair of gym socks. She said nothing. Reason number forty-seven it was a waste of time trying to make 'friends'. "You've been sitting next to me for four hours. Are you **seriously** still shocked?"

Behind them, Kaywin smiled blandly. He couldn't hear what was being said but it looked like Prudence was making a friend.

Dublin was hung up on the word 'fearless'. "Fearless? Are we supposed to be fearless? I didn't see **that** on any of the tests." The man next to him, the one who had been a little nervous before takeoff, just shrugged.

The video took a turn for the worse at this point, droning on and on about the amount of solar power needed to run the base, the batteries that stored the energy, the proximity of the frozen water in the polar soil, the process of extracting it, recycling it, possible plans for future development…. All the while they showed a slowly spinning two-dimensional diagram of the modest outpost. It didn't look big enough for all of them, for starters…it was hard not to get drowsy, watching the image turning hypnotically… their bodies were finally relaxed and lighter feeling… for all they knew, a sedative gas may have been released into the cabin. The guard nearest to Kaywin did have a mask over his mouth and nose… whatever… One by one, the passengers drifted off to sleep.

Kaywin woke up when someone's foot dragged across his face. He was confused. He felt like he had been out forever, like he had missed holidays and football seasons and elections. It took him a while to even remember where he was, and how there could be a line of people in red jumpsuits floating by him towards the restroom. Drool was all down his chin, his chest, even down in his left ear. It was hard to feel it, because he was strapped in, but they were finally completely weightless. They had traveled most of the almost three-hundred-thousand miles between the Earth and the Moon. Their vessel had reached the point where the attraction of the much larger body they were leaving was matched, and cancelled out, by the smaller one they were approaching. Whatever they had been gassed with was wearing off, and a long line was forming for the bathroom. He unstrapped immediately, but sent a mental warning to his bladder: *This might be a while…*

The scene in Transport 3 was similar, and the line was

held up by people having to navigate around floating globules of vomit from a very apologetic old man in row thirty-seven. Dublin felt sorry him, especially as people were making a big show about how gross it was. It was just vomit.

It wasn't until he was headed back down the center aisle toward his seat that he was awake enough to realize that the Moon had grown so large, looming dead ahead, that they could see a little bit of it out of the left **and** right cabin windows. This was very cool to him.

Prudence woke up and went to the bathroom with terrible, weightless difficulty. The vacuumized seat was intended for larger people. To top it off, there was like half of a shred of toilet paper to clean up the mess. *I won't be traveling MCP Airways again…* She hadn't been allowed to keep even her little makeup kit on her; everything had to be stowed in her silver duffel overhead, and they couldn't access it. She could just imagine what she looked like at this point, after twenty-four hours in this bucket, especially having slept the last nineteen. There were streaks of gold and black on her pant legs. She must have wiped the drool off her face, and then her hands on her pants, several times without even knowing it. The woman next to her was still asleep. Maybe when she woke up Prudence could use her as a human mirror, gauging how messed up her own face was by the level of disgust on hers.

As they rocketed into the sphere of the Moon's gravitational influence, their bodies were once more, gradually, imbued with weight, but only a sixth of their earthly heaviness. It was physically pleasant in the extreme, like easing back slowly into a recliner made of clouds. If the same easement could have been worked on their souls, probably none of them would even be here…

Eventually they got so close to the surface that they could begin to make out the details of individual craters and hills and ridges. It was hard to get any perspective on exactly **how** close they were…there were no structures in sight for reference. So if you looked at an approaching boulder, there was no way to tell if it was the size of a refrigerator, or the size of Delaware.

The closer they got to the blindingly bright surface, the better grasp they had of just how fast they were going. Most of the landscape reflected back the sunshine coming from almost directly behind them; dangerously unfiltered by any atmosphere. The same lack of an airy shroud had given a free pass to any and all space debris for time immemorial; there were tiny craters inside of medium craters inside of giant craters, craters overlapping each other, curving mountain ranges that turned out to be just the upthrust rims of enormous craters. Dublin's active mind imagined dinosaurs on Earth looking up two hundred million years ago, maybe on a Tuesday night, to see the commotion caused by these epic impacts. Anyway, these million pockets of shadow spread across the blinding plain were zooming by so fast that the effect was rather like a strobe light. Gradually they could feel the deceleration of the bulky transports, more in the sensation of their own bodies straining forward against their safety harnesses than anything else. The rim of a huge crater passed directly below them, and they dropped down into it. They were cruising along at what Kaywin estimated to be not more than two thousand feet and dropping, but still moving at an alarming clip. Suddenly word travelled from guard to guard, up from the pilot back along the center aisle: "Brace yourselves! Everybody brace yourselves! Get ready! Brace--" Some of them forgot to take their own advice. Backward thrusters on either side of the refitted Pegasus fired suddenly--surely, Kaywin thought, more suddenly than they were supposed to! Two of the guards went tumbling violently forward down the aisle. An aircraft landing on Earth would simply have deployed wing flaps to create drag, slowing it a little more smoothly. Here, there was no air to offer resistance to their precipitous momentum; the only way to brake was to thrust backwards.

Clumsy as it was, it seemed to be working. They had definitely slowed. Suddenly a runway appeared beneath them, and Kaywin was surprised to observe how close they were to touching down on it. From his tiny porthole, he could see the row of ultra-bright green lights that lined the right side of it, for what must have been tens of miles. The green glow had to be powerful to be visible through the solar rays. It had motion too to grab the attention of approaching pilots; an extra bright section surged up and down the line like a crowd doing 'the wave' at a baseball game.

On Transport 3, the slow-down was smoother, but a commotion broke out on the left side of the craft about the time the runway appeared beneath them. Dublin was on the right side, and was dying to know what all the fuss was about.

"Holy--"

"Would you look at **that...**"

"I can't be seeing what I think I'm seeing..."

"This does **not** look like the diagram..."

Dublin was going nuts. *Would I look at* **what**?! *What do you think you're seeing?!* **What** *doesn't look like the diagram?!*...................
Holy **what**?!

He didn't have to wait too long. They touched down pretty smoothly, and the backward thrusters were given more and more power, until the huge craft was crawling forward. There was a sharp bend near the end of the runway, so that if a shuttle failed to brake it would crash into the mountain just to the **right** of Moonbase 2, and not straight into the Moonbase itself. When Dublin's transport taxied into this sharp left curve, he finally got a view of their final destination.

And it was like nothing he had ever seen.

11

R. U. Ready 2 Rock

It was the most beautiful thing he had ever seen. Other than Prudence Estrada, Moonbase 2 was the most beautiful, astounding thing that Dublin had ever seen.

Basically, during their approach in the transport vessels, they had surmounted the rim of a giant crater called Hermite, descending down into it, then slowing gradually as they crossed its sixty-mile breadth. Fifty miles of green-lit runway had guided them. Now they had come all the way to the far rim of the crater, where the colossal impact of a meteor eons ago had jutted up the land into a high ridge. There, partially built **into** the mountain, was the thing that had made Dublin's jaw drop open.

How to describe it? It was **huge**, for starters. Eleven enormous cylindrical towers thrust up from the bedrock; the two smallest ones, on the far left and the far right, had to be as big as the Empire State Building in New York. The buildings got even taller as they stair-stepped up to the center. They were all hugged up against each other; it made Dublin think of the pipes of a pipe organ, one big enough to play for the entire solar system on Sunday mornings. Care had been taken in the aesthetics of the place. The individual 'pipes' were all a sort of burnished silver, but each of them was very subtly imbued with a different pastel hue...*tastefully done*...**very** *nice*...

On the high plateau behind the tops of the silver buildings there was a glare so bright that it took a minute for Dublin to make out what was back there...*Solar collectors! Thousands of them!* These were on steel towers arranged in rows that were even wider across than the Moonbase itself, and spread out wider and taller as they retreated backwards to the uppermost point of the Moon. The effect was mind-blowing; clustered together they looked like the bright gold scales of a cosmically large fish, twinkling here and there as his eyes moved across it. The shape though was more like a grand tiara, one big enough to crown the whole planetoid. Metaphor after metaphor piled on Dublin's brain. He decided that the stunning solar array most accurately resembled the shields of a great army arranged in cascading rows against an onslaught of arrows. They were fighting a war so epic and holy that their shields glowed with righteousness. It was **that** important that they protect the enormous Easter pipe organ below them.

Below the golden glare, and above the silver towers, giant blue letters straddled the crest of the facility with old-school neon majesty. But they didn't spell 'Moon base 2', as Dublin would have expected. They spelled:

Dublin furrowed his brow. This must be the long-dreamed-of hotel, the grandest ever built by far. The Eighth World Wonder. No--the First Wonder of the Moon. He knew that one had been started and abandoned decades earlier. *How have they kept this a secret?* It took him a moment to figure it out. If this whole setup had been placed somewhere on the face of the Moon that was always turned to the Earth, the face we are all used to seeing, the glare from the collector field would have been visible probably with the naked eye, and **certainly** by even amateur astronomers. But the Moonbase/Grand Hotel had been built within miles of the Lunar North Pole, where the visible face curved upwards and out of sight. Furthermore, it was built into a crater rim, shielding it that much more from sight. Astronomers, even the pros, could only distinguish an indirect golden glow, like a halo, over the lower rim of Hermite Crater. It would be impossible to quantify the magnitude of the projects beyond it based on that.

Dublin drank in as much of the view as he could out of the window of the dingy transport as it taxied toward the much less glamorous portion of the complex built into the lowest section of the crater wall beneath the silver towers. *This will be a good place to die. I can live with--I mean, I can die here in peace.*

Kaywin, one transport ahead of Dublin in the slow-moving convoy, also studied the impressive complex with interest. His foremost thought was of Nadine. On their first anniversary, so long ago, they had dreamed of celebrating their fiftieth together with a trip to the Moon. They were sure that by that time a beautiful hotel would be waiting for them. This was beyond their· wildest imaginings. He wished she could have seen this.

Butterflies were in every stomach as they watched a huge door slide open in the side of the mountain. Transport one, just ahead of them, taxied into the bright white hangar. Men in spacesuits, dwarfed by the shuttles, waved them in with green glowsticks. When they reached their parking space, the glowsticks turned red. Prudence looked out of her window with passing interest as they waited for the other eight vessels to park. The sixty year-old ugly green behemoths looked like an insult to the pristine white hangar.

As if the twenty-six hour flight hadn't been enough, they now had to wait for two **more** hours while all ten transports got situated, the bay door got sealed off again, and fresh breathable air got pumped back into the hangar. It was a considerable space to fill. They could see through a giant Plexiglass wall in front of them that there was a second hangar--at **least** a second one--of similar size. This one looked like a museum. Or somewhere between a museum and a mechanic's shop. They could see maybe fifty men and women in there, some of them in red jumpsuits like themselves, some in military attire, but many of them in street clothes. The attention of these folks seemed to be mainly focused on a hodge-podge of tiny spacecrafts, little old Moon Cruisers of various makes and models. Occasionally they would look up at the new arrivals. A couple of them even waved.

Eventually the exhausted MCs were released. The recruits from Transport 1 and the front half of Transport 2 were directed toward the elevators on the left side of the cavernous bay. The MCs from the back half of Two, and all of Three, were pointed to the right.

This was quite a scene, as eight hundred persons with dead legs, dubious stomachs, dizzy heads and long-dried-up-dreams tried to right themselves in a fraction of the gravity they were used to. There were a lot of people spending an unnatural amount of time in mid-fall. Like they would **start** to fall, flailing wildly, but marionette strings were holding them up. *If the Three Stooges started an army, this is what it would look like,* thought Dublin. Laughter broke out and spread like wildfire, as people slipped down ramps and bowled over tens of compatriots at a time. As they organized enough to move their pack of four-hundred in the direction of the right-hand elevators, many of them clinging to each other for dear life while cackling hysterically, Kaywin looked through the Plexiglass barrier and saw most of the fifty people from the hangar next door lined up and enjoying the show. He smiled his half-smile. He was too old to be embarrassed by almost anything. And in this case everyone was stumbling, everyone had a spill or two. Many of the younger MCs were mortified to realize they were being watched.

Prudence saw the people watching. She was acutely aware

of how she must look by now, and wished they had been allowed to grab their duffels. She was also grossed-out to notice that she was getting the special attention of some of the older mechanics, who pointed and waved at her. One of them blew a kiss at her and she almost gagged. *So this is going to be pretty much just like Earth.* Her next thought was to wonder how the people in the other hangar were moving around so freely and naturally. Were they just used to the reduced gravity by now, or was the floor magnetized in there or something? *I guess I will find out. But pleeease don't put me in there with those creeps!*

Prudence didn't like being out of control. She didn't like not knowing what she was doing. These transitions were unpleasant for her. The sooner she grasped her environment, the sooner she didn't feel like an idiot, the better. For the time being she would have to make do.

They approached the elevator in not-very-organized clumps of humanity, backing off when the lift was full, and waiting for the next empty one. As Prudence surged forward into the compartment, a hand brushed hers with apparent nonchalance. She was about to physically shove this guy--it would have been her first assault on the Moon--when she looked up and realized it was Dublin. "Oh. I was about to shove the crap out of you."

He laughed. "It would have been a good one, too. I would have gone flying. I only weigh like twenty-five pounds here." Prudence refrained from smiling. Who knows how hard this kid had worked to insinuate himself next to her on the elevator. She knew that a smile or a laugh would only reward him for it, and she would never shake him. She had come here to die, sure, but she hoped it would be in the peace and quiet of her own thoughts, and relatively painless. Now she had worrisome visions of this guy reciting passages of Russian Lit. pretentiously over her mangled body. Or worse, inviting her to some kind of Space Prom.

How could she have been so weak, back at the assignment ceremony? She had made a big deal over that Brandenberg jerk. She was horrified reflecting back on her moment of pathetic feebleness. What if this Dublin guy--who she knew deep down was just like Brandenberg, and her father, and McConnell, and all the other cockroaches--what if he dared to bring it up; what if he wanted to talk about her *feelings*? She made up her mind right then and there, zooming upwards in the chilly lift, that she would have to make some improvements to his ugly face with her fist if that ever happened.

Dublin, for his part, was finding it educational to consort with a young lady who broadcasted her disdain so openly and with such detail, and nuance. With any other girl he would have known that she just thought he was ugly. He felt like he could read Prudence better than that. *She's embarrassed about the other night. Why? After what she's gone through? Why should* **she** *be embarrassed, while* **Brandenberg** *is running for President and signing books and doing commercials? It's not fair. I need to tell her she doesn't need to be embarrassed. I'm going to tell her she doesn't need to be embarrassed.*

He opened his mouth to speak, but fortunately for everyone involved, the lift stopped a little suddenly, sending him a couple of feet up into the air, and then belly-flopping to the floor. He got up with overdramatic quickness, throwing himself off balance and causing him to fall again. He rose up now with overdramatic *slowness*, brushing himself off.

Everyone was staring at him. "What? No standing ovation?" *Somebody laugh. Please.* "You're already standing. You just have to….ovate…" Sixty-two eyes appraised his ugly, blushing face coldly. But then a little laugh came from behind his left shoulder. He didn't recognize it at first, having never heard it. It was Prudence. She had been caught off guard by the "ovate" thing. It sounded like "ovary." She had laughed without meaning to. Now she looked away in a hurry.

Great. I keep throwing this dog bones; of course he's gonna keep on coming back. I have no one left to blame but myself now.

Dublin was smart enough to turn his shaggy head away from Prudence, grinning broadly. *Well, that was totally worth it!*

Instructions on their Sofees flashed insistently. They were to find their rooms immediately, and eat the supplement waiting for them on their pillows. Kaywin didn't know what was meant exactly by 'supplement'…any food would be welcome however. They had had two inadequate little meals on the voyage in, over the course of a full day.

The white corridors were endless but well-marked. He found his room on the third floor over the hangar after about fifteen minutes of walking. 3347. He touched it--it was unlocked.

He stepped quietly into the dim room. It was spacious enough, but just as basic as the rooms back in Houston. Cement walls, synthetic floor tiles with the teensy specks of color in them that always made him think of elementary school. There was a bunk bed on the left wall and a bunk bed on the right. A tiny table with a cheap lamp sat at the end of the left hand bunk. There was actually a fair amount of space, maybe eight feet, between the beds. A cheap, Uno Mundo style chest of drawers against the back wall ate up some of this open area. A few toiletries sat on top of it, half a tube of Bleach-o-dent, a stick of Gingerbread Man deodorant.

An oversized gray man rolled off of the bottom right bunk when Kaywin entered the room. "It's about time," he said. It was completely unclear whether he was being rude or playful. "Thanks for the day off." Kaywin shook the man's hand. "You're supposed to eat your supplement before we do anything else." He raised a hand, listlessly indicating what looked like a cow patty sitting on a pillow in the bottom left bunk.

"Thank you. Good morning. Is it morning here?"

"We're on Eastern Standard Time. You coming from Houston? Your Sofee should have already set itself back an hour."

"Oh. I **guess** it did. So it's really 9:54 AM?"

"Yessir." His inflection went way up on the second syllable, as if to say "I don't think you're an idiot yet, but if you ask me one more question about the time, I will."

When I say the man was gray, I mean mainly his hair, which was swooped over greasily from the left side of his head (if you were facing him) to the right. He was a little taller than Kaywin, maybe six-foot-two or so, and kind of big-boned, just kind of a big dude. He wasn't fat, though he looked as if he might have been, not so long ago. He seemed to be in his late fifties or early sixties. And his clean-shaven face was a little pink and--well--a little gray. He was clad in a red jumpsuit just like Kaywin's, except a lot more worn in and soft looking. "I'm Kaywin Lafontaine, by the way." He stooped under the top left bunk and took the unwrapped (if it ever had been wrapped) cow patty off of the bottom bunk pillow. A small bite had been taken out of it already, but what the heck.

"**Karen?**"

"Kaywin."

"Kaywin. Spell that for me." He was one of those people who make it a point sometimes to **not** say please. It's how they attempt to assert dominance passively; maybe without even knowing they are doing it.

"K-a-y-w-i-n" said Kaywin, trying not to spit cow patty crumbs.

"Oh. I'm Jason Vindaloo."

Kaywin didn't see the point in saying "I think you just made that last name up" so he just said, "Pleased to meet you."

The supplement wasn't as bad as it looked, but not as good as it could have been. "Do we get real food, too? I hope?"

"Yes. But there are close to thirty thousand people living here, give or take. It would cost a fortune to ship enough meat and veggies for everyone. So these are supposedly packed with everything you really **need**, and you get one meal at sup-pertime, as a 'courtesy'."

Kaywin had stopped chewing. "Did you say thirty-thou-sand?"

"Yeah. By my reckoning. It's not like they tell us anything we don't need to know to do our work."

"What kind of work do you do?" Kaywin stumbled a little but caught himself on the bunk post.

"Me? I'm in the pits. I've almost got seniority. There are only two others who have made it longer than me."

"The pits? That doesn't sound like fun." Kaywin's feet kept getting in his way.

"It's worse than it sounds. Here--why don't you get your gravity suit." He took two steps over to Kaywin's side of the room. Hanging from the wall were two bodysuits that looked like metallic colored fabric, but drooped with the appearance of great weight. They hung a little low, the ankles dragging on the floor. "Are you... 'large'...or... 'quadruple extra large'--" He stopped short as the door opened again, and a massive man walked in. "Large it is!"

A moment of confusion ensued, as Kaywin and Jason introduced themselves to their newest roommate. Sephal was six foot seven, probably four hundred and fifty pounds on Earth, Samoan by birth, and oddly cheerful for a Goner. His first words after "Hello, my name is..." were "I call top bunk!" He ran and leaped astoundingly over the sidebar, crashing down onto the thin mattress. It was crazy looking; Kaywin couldn't understand how the bunk didn't disintegrate; then he did some quick math and figured out that Sephal was a svelte seventy-five or eighty pounds on the Moon.

Kaywin turned his attention back to the gravity suit. "How does it work?" he asked of his more experienced roommate. Jason shrugged, reminding him of "the Rocket". Strange... He would never see that guy, "the Rocket", again. He thought he had caught a glimpse of him at the assignment ceremony wearing violet. Disease Elimination? Is that where they said the violet jumpsuits were going? Poor guy. He wondered if his abrasive personality had eliminated him from any group work. He shook himself back into the moment, where Jason was answering his question.

"It just makes up for the weight you're missing. How much do you weigh back on Earth?"

"Aaaaah, I think it was like one-eighty last week."

"So right now, on the moon, you weigh about thirty pounds. So this suit"-- he accidentally indicated the 4x one-- "sorry, **this** suit weighs (or it **should** weigh) about one fifty."

"Wow. Amazingly simple. So, my next question is...how do I put it **on**?" He noticed that Sephal, realizing that he too would need to know this, had propped himself up like a twelve year-old girl away at camp and was paying close attention.

"It's very easy. You strip down and kind of step back into it. You get one leg in, you get the other leg in, then when you get both arms in, you press the button and the supporting hooks retract."

"Okay...do you guys mind looking away for a sec?"

"No. Just don't press that button early. It'll knock you on your butt."

Kaywin followed the simple procedure. For about two minutes, it felt really strange, as if there was a good-sized monkey hanging on his left arm, then his right leg, then his other leg, then on his back... Pretty soon the high-tech fabric kind of stretched and adjusted on him, and his brain adjusted to it. From that point forward it felt surprisingly natural. It was very form-fitting and comfy. He was able to put the red jumpsuit back on over it without any difficulty.

"So you get two of those. If you're going down in the pits like me, or on one of the wire teams, or the construction teams--pretty much if you're doing physical outdoor labor, your other suit will be a half-grav."

Sephal piped in. "So is that like, just the tops, or just the bottoms, or what?"

Jason stared at him. "No. It's the full suit but half the weight. Why don't you try your full-grav on. If it doesn't fit or something we should let someone know sooner rather than later."

Sephal looked offended. "Why wouldn't it fit?" Jason just shrugged again and re-swiped his gray mop. "Just kidding dude. I know I'm big." He stripped down and inserted himself with some crouching and awkwardness into the space age chain mail. "Niiiiice! Not bad!" It was an odd look for a huge guy. But he seemed happy.

Jason didn't act very excited about being their tour guide for the day, but he seemed resigned to making some kind of effort. "Okay. So I guess your work gravs will show up tonight. You should know by then what you'll be doing, anyway. Usually, first day, there's a muster around noon...maybe one...I can't remember. Anyway you'll get a summons with directions to your conference room. All of those are on the first floor. There's one for every team. Like if you're in the pits you'll go to one-oh-four." He pointed at Sephal. "You look like a pit guy." Sephal widened his eyes and looked behind him as if there were someone else there that Jason could be referring to.

Jason, with his dragging gray tiredness, carried on. "The only good thing about pit work, and most of the other crap-jobs, is that when you're done for the day, you're **done.** No laundry, or scrubbing toilets...It's eleven hours a day, seven days a week, and it's hard work. I'm not complaining. It's my fault. I signed up for it; but sometimes I wish I could just go ahead and die already. I'm down to my last six months, so.... getting there." Sephal raised his hand like he was in school. Jason wasn't feeling the goofy Samoan's vibe. "You don't have to raise your hand. What's your question?"

"Soooo...let's say you **don't** die...cuz you're supposed to die within two years..."

"Well...I probably will. I've had two minor heart attacks since I've been here. I feel close." He wasn't used to thinking about it much. He looked down at the floor for a second before continuing. "Supposing I **don't** however. Well, if I had any kind of pilot experience they would G-test me in the Famous Flame. But I don't, so--"

"What does that mean?" Sephal asked. "Sorry if I'm being stupid."

"The Famous Flame is the fastest test-cruiser they have that they can bring back remotely. So they sometimes take an MC whose time is running out and put him in there at maximum acceleration until he explodes."

Sephal's mouth dropped open in horror. Jason shrugged again like a sleepy turtle might shrug. It seemed to take more effort to do it than it should have. This man was worn down.

This brought up a question in Kaywin's mind, and he put it out there for his new roommates. "Why don't they have remote navigation in all the cruisers?"

"Well...most of them are really old. Like twenty-forties old. One of the pilots I used to talk to told me it would cost them over a million credits each to rig them for remote navigation."

Sephal said, "Yeah, but how much is a man's life worth?"

"Here?" said Jason. "Eleven thousand credits." Sephal started. It had been a rhetorical question; he wasn't expecting an actual number. "That's the average amount you will cost the government from the moment you signed up, until the moment you sign out."

"Now, like I said, I've never piloted anything, so if I drag on until the end of this quarter, they will most likely inject me into a coma and send me back to Atlanta for live cell study."

Sephal nodded. "Hope you make it, man. You'd look good in purple. It would look good with your hair!" Jason smiled slightly, for the first time."

"Why would they put you in a coma?" Kaywin asked. He was eager for all of this inside information.

"Uuuuh, I guess partly out of mercy, and partly--" he indicated with sweeping arms the entire Moonbase "--partly **this.** They've worked really hard to keep all this a secret. If they sent someone back fully conscious, they might blab. No one would believe them, but why take the chance? Alright?" He clapped his hands so weakly that it barely made a noise. "You guys ready to explore?" As the door slid open, and Kaywin and Sephal filed out behind the tired gray Goner, Kaywin heard the giant Samoan mutter under his breath:

"Eleven-thousand credits...I spent that on a bar tab one night..."

Prudence stood in front of the white door. Room 4102 would be the last home she ever had. She stepped closer in, but the door didn't slide open. So she knocked. A few seconds later, it whooshed aside. A short, tan, heavy-set older woman kind of like a sweet potato with a tight dingy brown perm was standing there. "Here. Let me show you" she croaked, waddling out into the hall. She waited for the door to slide shut, but Prudence must have been too close to it. The Gnome-like lady grabbed her by the shoulder and yanked her back. In the process, she seemed to notice her leopard-print hair and melted gold and black makeup for the first time. "Wooow. That's quite a look," she said, and it was clearly not supposed to be a compliment.

"Yeah. You too," said Prudence. She wondered if she was about to have a fight with this woman, right here in the hall, six seconds into their relationship. But the older lady paused for a second, and busted out with such an extended, loud, unpleasantly asthmatic laugh that Prudence made a mental note to never say anything funny to her again.

"So this is how this works. Room 4102, right? Touch the numbers after I say them, but you got to do it quick." Her New York accent was so heavy it was almost a distraction. "One-two-oh-foooah...foooah-one-two-oh...two-foooah-oh-one." The door slid open. "Good. You might wanna FB that." ("FB" was short for "flashback"; touch the "FB" icon on your Sofee and it would preserve the previous fifteen seconds of video and audio from its vantage point.) Prudence did so, then followed the odd woman into the space they would be sharing. "My name is Jordache." There was a pause while Prudence shook off a bizarre, split-second impulse to introduce herself by a completely made-up name. Why? Would this erase her former life? She couldn't come up with a fake one anyway. "You gonna tell me yours? Cuz I'm good either way."

"Pr--it's Prudence," she mumbled.

"Huh? Speak up," Jordache barked.

"Prudence Estrada."

~

Dublin took a wrong turn at some point on the way to his room. He walked past a huge cafetorium, then realized he had gone right past room 4324. He doubled back and found it. It was so close to the cafetorium that if he leaned back a little from his front door he could see some of the long dining tables. The unlocked door slid open and he stepped in uncertainly. "Hello? Anybody home?" Two figures were settled in on the right hand bunk. The black-haired man on the top was sitting up, cross-legged, with his back to Dublin. He was totally absorbed in his Sofce, and didn't so much as turn around.

The man on the bottom had been reclining with his hands behind his head. When he heard the door slide open he rolled out in one quick motion. He was right around Dublin's height; that is to say about five-foot nine. He had a shock of very straight sandy blondish hair jutting from his head, not in a showy way or anything. His face was fairly pleasant but heavily-scarred from the acne that had plagued his teens. From the look of him that would have been about thirty years earlier. "Hey. I'm Daryl."

"Good to meet you. My name is Dublin Dunne. But I'm not Irish!" When he said his name the black-haired man turned around, and poor Dublin about hit the floor. *This is not happening to me again.*

It was the Kalaysian Three-Star!

He grinned wickedly at the new arrival. Dublin heard

him speak for the first time. "Aha! Good! I get roommate request!"

"Request?! We were allowed to make requests?! You requested **me?**"

"Ahh! You good roommate! You no snore!" Without unlocking his eyes from Dublin, the Kalaysian slowly raised his right pointer finger and pressed the middle of the three stars on his forehead. Then, as if this had been the button that turned him into a maniac, he exploded into shrill, staccato machine-gun laughter.

Oh my God. Did he kill a guy for snoring? Is that what that just meant? What if I start snoring?!

Daryl looked back and forth between the two. "I see you've met Ving."

The four sprawling floors that the MCs were confined to were pleasant enough. Clean and functional. It was safe to assume that the hundred story towers above them were much fancier. But it was also safe to assume that when this place opened for business people would be paying more credits for a three-night stay than most of these Goners had made in a lifetime. Building this place was a staggering investment of resources, just **insane**, but it was absolutely one of a kind. There weren't enough gazillionaires in New York, or Hong Kong, or Tokyo, or Dubai, or Moscow to keep La Lune in business, but put them all together, every filthy rich son of a gun on the planet, and there would actually probably be a waiting list for rooms. This place would pay for itself in three years. No doubt the US government had paid for **some** of it already, in credits and MCs...

They walked forever in little packs of red jumpsuits. Their world-weary guides showed them all the points of interest: the conference rooms on the first floor, the cafeteria on the fourth with its bizarre central fountain carved poorly from Moonrock and called Aristophanes' Sacrifice, the gym complex on the second floor, complete with small indoor soccer field and basketball court.

Dublin had a question. "I'm not complaining, but it seems odd that they would have that for us. I mean...we're here to run the clock out. Is this for like...morale or something?"

Daryl stopped in front of a big window that looked out onto the gymnasium. "Well, I believe this is a little side-advantage of the long-term plan. I have to think that when construction is finished here, all of the floors that are taken up now by the MCP will be for hotel employees...I always think I'm going to come down and shoot some hoops, but then by the end of the day I'm just too tired."

A couple of smiles and nods later, it became unspokenly understood amongst the little three-man tour group that yes, this was a basketball court, and yes, maybe it was time to move on. But just as their shoulders started to lean away from the window, two figures popped out right in front of them, walking briskly in nothing but their grav suits from right to left.

Dublin almost ducked. He recognized the swaggering six-foot-four blond guy instantly. It was Jerkboy, with a basketball in his big mitts, walking briskly around the court with a muscular dark-haired man in his early twenties. This fresh-faced man would have been an imposing figure in his own right, at around six-foot-two, if he hadn't been walking shoulder to shoulder with the blonde Adonis. There was an energy between the two that made Dublin feel like...I don't know, it made him feel like he shouldn't be watching. The matching back-of-the-neck-tattoos furthered this impression. Wait-- not exactly matching--the dark-haired man's was a heart icon with the number '89' in it. Dublin vaguely remembered his Grandma playing some Heart 89 boyband songs for him. Jerkboy's tattoo was a club symbol with the number 312 in it. Dublin had never heard of Club 312. At any rate, the two of them didn't seem to notice Daryl, Ving, and Dublin.

It was weird to see Jerkboy interacting with someone in a calm, civil manner. They passed the wide window and continued down the edge of the court with their backs to the three onlookers. Something the dark-haired young man said made them both bust out laughing. Jerkboy slapped him on the back once, twice, but when his hand came down the third time it was with calculated violence. He shoved his companion forward and down, still laughing.

"Did that guy come with your group?" Daryl asked Dublin and Ving. Well, Dublin really, because Ving wasn't going to say anything.

"Yeah," Dublin said, transfixed by what seemed to be the beginnings of a fight. "I don't know what his real name is... we call him Jerkboy. He almost killed a guy back in Houston."

"Hmm. He looks real familiar." Laughing almost good-naturedly, Jerkboy had retreated from the dark-haired boy several steps back in the direction of the onlookers. "He looks like an MC they comatized and sent to Atlanta three weeks ago… I guess not. His nose is different. And his hair is blonder." The man who had been pushed down had gotten to his feet and was stalking back toward the violent blonde beach boy with a big grin on his flushed face. Jerkboy hurled the basketball viciously at him, and it whizzed by his ear with great force. Darkboy seized the advantage of his opponent's forward momentum and took a flying leap. He succeeded in wrapping him up, and the two tumbled to the hardwood in their grav suits, rolling and laughing.

Daryl and Dublin moved on. The Kalaysian hung back for a second, watching the action with undisguised intensity. Dublin shuddered a little at the three-star's apparent thirst for violence. After a couple of moments, he broke free from his trance. He was too cool to race after the two others, but he picked up his pace enough to avoid being left behind.

As they walked, Daryl told them a little about his situation. He was an alcoholic, and suffered from bipolar disorder. He joined the MCP when he felt like he was on the verge of giving in to his violent impulses. If one person suffered terribly or died because of him, then, in his mind, it was too late to redeem himself. He reflected back on a bar fight the week before he had joined up. "If I had *killed* that guy--and I *wanted* to, I really wanted to--then it wouldn't matter how many solar collector towers I installed on the Moon. There's not a number that could have restored balance to the universe."

This is a perfectly normal looking dude, thought Dublin, sinking down into a puffy salmon-colored vinyl chair. *It goes to show you never can tell. Maybe there* **is** *some value in the star-tattoo system...* He risked a fleeting glance at Ving, who, as always, maintained a little separation from Dublin and Daryl, this time by standing and fidgeting a few feet away while they sat.

They were on the fifth floor now, most of which was restricted territory. There was a door that marked the boundary between free-roaming area and forbidden country. Through the glass Dublin could see that it was sleeker and more modern, less Spartan than the functional cement rooms below. People in lab coats went about their mysterious business on the other side of the tiny window. A large man in a dark blue uniform leaned against a wall with his back to the door, eating a pastry and talking down to an attractive younger woman. Causing trouble on his first day on Moonbase 2 was the furthest thing from Dublin's mind, but the pretty lady saw him watching and smiled, looking straight into the poetry of his soul. The hulking security chief followed her eyes and turned. He didn't like poetry. He glared with cold menace at Dublin. He was not happy that this ugly kid had distracted the young lady from whatever story he had been telling. Dublin breezed away instantly, intimidated by the officer and intoxicated by the woman's smile. *What did it mean?*

Daryl had brought them to a common area on the fifth floor that he said had the best view in all of the unrestricted area. And it was breathtaking, looking out from a height of a hundred and fifty feet or so over the gorgeous crater. The complete lack of air to soften the visual edges of everything made the whole landscape look unreal. It was unbelievably crisp and sharp, as if every rock and ridge and tower had been carefully cut out and pasted there. It didn't feel real yet that he was on the Moon. This was very much like an enormous viewing wall. Dublin stopped himself from imagining he was on some grand vacation. He knew it would be all too real, and all too soon.

He couldn't stop himself from touching the large fern in

a pot next to his dangling right hand. Yes, it was real. "So," he said stupidly "this plant is real." He felt like a moron as soon as he said it, and blushed accordingly. Good thing no girls heard him, though there were a couple of other little tour groups ooohing and aaahing over the view.

"Oh yeah, it is," said Daryl. "I wish we had time to go to the greenhouses. It's kind of a hike from here, and I don't want you guys to get all the way out there and have to turn right around if you get summoned."

Dublin stuck his finger down in the dirt, and nudged it around. He said something smart to make up for his brilliant "so this plant is real" observation. "Do they bring soil from Earth, or do they take Moon dirt and do something to counteract the nitrogen deficiency?"

"It's lunar soil. Every time we install one solar collector, we displace about eighty cubic yards of it. It's not great for growing on its own, but they enrich it with human feces to give it nitrogen, and it does alright. Dublin pulled his finger out of the dirt, and tried to figure out what to do with it.

"Is there a..."

"A restroom?" said Daryl smiling. "We passed one back that way, on the left. Well, on the **right** as you head back."

The bathroom was deserted. As Dublin washed his hands at the sink, he stared at his own face in the mirror, lost in thought. He was thinking that even though the view out over the crater had been probably the most astounding view of the natural world that he had ever had, or ever **would** have, he had been distracted the whole time, trying to visualize the lady in the lab coat. He would have traded all the beautiful views in the world for ten more seconds of her smiling at

283

him through the glass, without the security officer there. He felt that in the two seconds her eyes had met his, she had understood his sadness, and had felt wonderfully, deliciously sorry for him. Maybe she would have held him if the door hadn't been there. Maybe she was okay with his face.

He snapped back to reality. His face was right there in the mirror. Nobody was "okay" with it. *This is what she saw through the glass. Why...are...you...so...ugly...Dublin?* He was transported all the way back to fourth grade. "Ug-ly Dub-lin!" (clap-clap, clap-clap-clap) "Ug-ly Dub-lin" (clap-clap, clap-clap-clap)... He couldn't stop the tears. He watched them streaming down his monster face while the warm water was still streaming over his hands. Like it sometimes happened, his self-pity gave way to mounting rage. He wished his fourth grade classmates could see him now. He wished they were all assembled right there, between the trashcan and the door, to see what they had done. "Are you happy?" He was actually croaking the words aloud, spit flying out through gritted teeth. "I hope you're all happy, everyone one of you! Cuz I'm committing suicide on the Moon!" His own words had a great impact on him. He was struck suddenly by this absurd turn of events. He was committing suicide on the Moon. He was laughing like a maniac. Somewhere very deep down in his brain, he was secretly pleased with this little one-man performance. It just needed a dramatic finish, so he wheeled back to the mirror; tears, laughs and spit tumbling out everywhere, and bellowed forth with complete abandon...

"I'M COMMITTING SUICIDE ON THE MOON!!!!"

A familiar noise caught his attention. He turned the water off and listened. Oh yeah, it was his own Sofee. "Dublin

Dunne to Conference Room Eight."

Prudence was just leaving the greenhouses with Jordache and Judy, her other new roommate. Judy was an African-American woman in her mid-thirties. She had been here for three months and, though she wasn't shy by any means, she was a little less brash and exhausting than Jordache.

Prudence didn't really want to go see the greenhouses, but she didn't really want to go see anything, and they couldn't stay in their room. Jordache didn't require a whole lot of feedback to keep a tour going, so they just sort of followed her. The greenhouses were pretty impressive. Two of them were up and running, each about the size of a football field with fruits and veggies growing happily. A third was under construction. Jordache could have shown Prudence every pear and radish, but the smell was a little intense. Jordache thought maybe the little girl wasn't as tough as her hair and makeup indicated, and said as much. Prudence stood back near the entrance/exit, with pink shaded eyes and whited-out face showing no reaction. Her jet-black hair with one glowing pink stripe fell to her shoulders, which shrugged. They were at the end of a long tunnel, so when Prudence got the message to report to Conference Room Four in fifteen minutes she really had to haul it. "Hauling it" was no specialty of hers, so she mentally cursed the old lady and headed back.

When she got back to the first floor of the Moonbase, having outpaced her escort, she absent-mindedly boarded an elevator going up. As soon as the doors opened on the third floor, she remembered that she was supposed to be on the first. She stepped out with the intention of catching the next one descending, but it was chaos in the lobby as hundreds of Goners were also trying to get down to the conference rooms. Skin crawling from the unpleasant jostling, she allowed herself to drift to the side of the mob, and found herself next to a door, one of the old-school kind with hinges. Cracking it open, she saw a stairwell. There were people on it, but maybe like twenty, which compared favorably with the two hundred behind her. She slipped through the door. There were MCs coming down rapidly from the fourth floor, so she got moving. She made it quickly from the third to the second, but then there was a holdup.

A couple of steps down from the landing, a scene was unfolding that would have been transfixing in its stupidity if she didn't have...**four minutes** to get a conference room that was four minutes away. A blonde-haired dude was at the head of the pack. The dark-haired moron behind him, supporting himself with his arms on the two railings, had given him a flying kick in the back. But the blonde guy--oh crap, it was Jerkboy--had braced himself just in time on the left hand rail. When the dark-haired man tried a second kick, Jerkboy wheeled and grabbed his legs. He dragged him down the industrial concrete and metal stairs, laughing as the instigator's shoulders and head bounced disturbingly. Everybody likes to rough up their friends a little, but this was in another league altogether, and the rest of the pack hung back horrified, even though the way was now clear. Prudence bulled her way through the trembling wimps and down the stairs. Out of the corner of her left eye in passing she saw the dark-haired boy take a dab of fresh blood from the back of his head and slap Jerkboy's cheek playfully with it. She didn't see or care what happened after that.

When they lined the newbies up on the wall of Conference Room Four, Prudence kept waiting for someone to realize they had made a mistake. Eighty-two 'veterans' of whatever they were about to be doing sat and applauded the fifty-three newcomers. All of them were huge. Big, strong, lumbering men and women, all five-ten and up.

And then there was Prudence. All four-foot-eleven, one hundred pounds of her. The lineup looked like a row of teeth with one 'broke off'. But nobody said anything. Whatever. They would find out soon enough that she couldn't lift whatever these guys were lifting. Maybe they would just take her out back and shoot her.

"Congratulations to our new arrivals!" a man, in a red jumpsuit like the rest of them, said into a microphone. "Boy are we glad to see you!" There was a slight bit of tired laughter from here and there amongst the seated vets. "And welcome to the Lower Pits!"

Well that sounds about right.

When Kaywin walked into Conference Room Eight, he knew something special was afoot. He had been down the length of the vast hall, and had seen hundreds of Goners pouring into most of the other rooms. There was an austere dignity to the small crowd in this room. He was happy to see Dublin among the seven new recruits lined up against the white plastic wall. Dublin hadn't gotten the memo about being austere and dignified, and he waved wholeheartedly at Kaywin, and grinned from ear to ear in relief.

Kaywin was quietly gestured toward the wall. This room was too big for the thirty-five men and women in red jump-suits who sat, watching the lineup on the wall in awkward silence. He took in the scene as he approached. The first thing he noticed was the taller of the two ascetics looming over the line of newbies in his filthy raiments. Then he saw the Kalaysian three-star next to him. *Man, poor Dublin can't shake this guy!* Out of the periphery of his vision, amongst the seated, he next noticed a handful of civilians, some in jeans and underdogs, some in skirts and boots. When Kaywin reached the wall, the line of newbies swelled from seven to eight. There was about thirty seconds of increasingly uncomfortable silence. Kaywin didn't realize that there was a man with a microphone, until the man with the microphone spoke into the microphone. "We're almost ready here. Waiting on two more..." Kaywin noticed with interest that the speaker was an older man in plainclothes, jeans, pristine white underdogs, and a navy blue "Berkeley" sweatshirt. "You guys were all on time; thank you..." Five seconds later the door, which seemed so far away, whooshed open. Two tall, good-looking but ruffled men entered, laughing, a dark-haired one and a blonde one. Jerkboy.

"Gentlemen, up against the wall, if you please." The two took their time sauntering up to the four men and four women already waiting there. "Alright! Ladies and gentlemen, your new pilots!" As the small crowd applauded politely, Kaywin and Dublin leaned out just far enough to make eye contact with each other. They were both thinking roughly the same thing: *Clowns to the left of me, jokers to the right; here I am, stuck in the middle with you...*

~

So by noon, they all knew (sort of) what they would be doing, and who they would be doing it with. There wasn't much of a grace period; they would all be hard at work tomorrow. So the rest of Tuesday, April 9th, 2126 was spent learning things like how to put on your pit-suit, how to put on your flying suit, what to do if the oxygen flow seemed inadequate, what to do if the temperature control seemed out of whack, what things would get you killed instantly, when it was acceptable to stop working and report to medical, communicating helmet to helmet, what time to use the bathroom before leaving the Moonbase... It caused a murmur amongst the newcomers, as it always did, when they were told that they would be required to take a 'waste inhibitor' every morning. This led to the same question and answer in every one of the ten conference rooms: "What exactly is a 'waste inhibitor'?"

"It's a little yellow pill that prevents you from having to use the bathroom for approximately twelve hours."

"Eww."

There was a lot of information to take in, no matter what unit you had been assigned to. Jobs that wouldn't have required any explanation on Earth became complicated under Lunar conditions. You couldn't just say "take this shovel and start digging a trench from here to that tower." If a new MC stepped on the shovel wrong and ripped their suit they would suffocate in seconds. Freezing to death or suffocating were ever-present dangers. If your thermal control malfunctioned you would die within ten seconds of realizing it. The shadows of Hermite Crater were the coldest areas in the solar system. Even the surface of Pluto, three and a half **billion** miles from the Sun, was balmy in comparison, at minus three hundred and eighty-two degrees. The darker pockets of Hermite got down to minus four hundred and thirteen degrees. If you avoided asphyxiation or freezing, the radiation from the naked sunlight, unfiltered by air, would get you eventually. The outer suits blocked much of this, but not all. Underneath them, their gravity-suits (composed largely of fabric-covered lead filaments) offered a second layer of protection. But, really, this was just prolonging the inevitable...

By six o'clock Prudence's head was swimming and her spirits were flagging. Fortunately, they were released at that point for supper and free time.

She was surprised to learn that they could sit where they liked in the cafeteria, and even more surprised to feel like... maybe...she wouldn't mind sitting with Kaywin and Dublin. They were in higher spirits than she was, as they exchanged stories over their Salisbury steak and peas and mashed potatoes. How could they **not** be? They were pilots, and she was in the pits. The **Lower** pits.

The illusion of spaciousness and undercrowding went up in smoke when the run-down work crews begin piling into the cafeteria; all the men and women who hadn't been held back for the day as tour guides for the newcomers. There were people everywhere. Rough people. People who had been worked so hard that they had to cattle-prod their own spirits into loud, cursing boisterousness to keep from falling down...other people who had been here a few months longer, and were nothing more than mumbling, tottering wrecks.

Prudence felt an urgency to reclaim some space. As soon as the last scrap was gone from her plate, she followed the example of the other early finishers and returned her tray to the counter behind the table where she and the boys had been sitting. She would never in a million years express it, but Kaywin and Dublin sensed that she was feeling down, even further than what was normal for her. Without communicating it, they both wished to stay with her until she rounded the corner towards feeling better.

They wolfed down their last scraps and kept pace with the briskly retreating girl, following her bouncing black and pink hair out of the cafeteria. They passed an interesting scene as both of the ascetics were trying to give away half of their meals to the returning workers, without talking. The taller one had the appropriate words grease-penciled across his broad forehead: **please finish**; the other hadn't completely erased his previous words. It might have been a one or two word question he had asked during the training session; at any rate, the people he was trying to hand off his food to were confused by the phrase **ox please finish** on his forehead.

They didn't get to see the resolution, but it was a safe bet that both ascetics found hungry people to finish their suppers. "Oh my God, I forgot to tell you!" exuberated Dublin. "I thought those two were getting into a fight one morning back in Houston. I walked into the bathroom, and the shorter one was on his knees in front of the taller one...in the filthy bathroom across the hall from my broom-closet, mind you, not the clean one. So the taller one slaps him once, across the face, super hard, and I was like whaaat? Then they switch; the tall one goes to his knees, and the short one slaps the crap out of him!"

"Hmmm," said Kaywin. "I like to wake up with a cup of coffee myself. I guess that sounds about right for those two; more atonement for whatever they've done…"

Prudence slowed down when she realized that Kaywin and Dublin were trying to catch up with her. "Prudence!" Dublin called out. She turned. "What are you going to do?" he asked as they jogged to a halt. She shrugged. "We could shoot some hoops?" She raised her eyebrows, indicating clearly that she had never "shot a hoop" in her life and that wasn't going to change tonight. "Or not; I mean, we could do whatever." The three fell into a walking pace together. "Have you seen the view from the common area on the fifth floor?" Dublin persisted. Prudence finally spoke.

"I think I would rather **not** stare down into the Lower pits tonight."

"Ohhhh…gotcha."

Kaywin chimed in. "You guys ever played cribbage?" Neither of them had ever even heard of it. "It's a card game. Wicked fun. There's a board involved too, but it's mainly for just keeping score."

Prudence shrugged. "Why not." And it goes without saying that if she was in, Dublin was in.

They went to Prudence's room, on the same floor as the cafeteria, but kind of a hike. When they got there they arranged themselves on the floor by Prudence's bunk. They had been pleasantly surprised earlier to learn that some outbound Sofee communication was possible on the Moonbase via an enclosed and monitored mini-web. With a little help from the always-eager Dublin, Kaywin found and sent them the link to his favorite cribbage site, 'Wilfred's Crib'. "If you guys like it, I can bring the real thing tomorrow night."

"You brought an actual cribbage board, and cards?" Prudence was surprised. They had been allowed so few personal possessions, that it seemed to her a strange thing to bring a silly game.

Kaywin smiled as he shuffled the virtual deck of cards. "It was kind of like bringing my whole family with me," he said.

"Ugh," Prudence responded. "No thanks!"

The two kids--Kaywin was going to have to stop thinking of them as 'kids'--caught on quickly and seemed to enjoy it. Prudence's room would have been a good spot if it hadn't been for Jordache. She kept butting into their conversation loudly from the tiny bathroom, where she spent literally the entire two and a half hours of free time doing some elaborate treatment on her hair. Shockingly, she did this every night, only to sleep on it, and then cram it into a Moon helmet the following morning. She had peeked out of the bathroom when they first arrived.

"Oh my Gawd. You're like a little Linsom Felize, with the automatic hayah. Must be nice!"

It was decided they would try cribbage on a real board tomorrow night, in Kaywin's room. The three stayed up playing and talking, quietly, so as not to draw Jordache into their conversation (it didn't work) until free time ended at nine PM.

Prudence lay wide-awake for two hours, staring at the ceiling and dreading the morning.

When Kaywin lay down he had his customary one-sided conversation with Victoria and Nadine. He told them about his new friends for the first time, and about playing cribbage tonight. Nadine played sometimes, but it hadn't been a big part of her growing up. Victoria had been quite good at it, as she had been at almost everything. *Had been...had been...had been...* He sounded the two syllables out in his brain over and over again like a melody for five minutes before falling asleep.

He had the nightmare again, and woke up hollering hysterically. The giant Samoan was leaning over him in the darkness. "Hey! Hey Buddy! It's alright man! It's just a dream!"

"Ohhh, crap; I'm sorry. I woke you guys up."

In the morning, when their alarms went off, Jason swung his gray legs onto the cold floor, and stared at Kaywin. "It's not going to be like that every night, is it?"

Dublin, in room 4324, slept better than he had in awhile. Having a third person in the room with him and Ving, and having actual **beds**, put his mind at ease somewhat about the over-accomplished killer.

Which lasted for exactly one night.

When their alarms went off in the morning at six AM, only two of them woke up. On the top bunk, right over Dublin's head, Daryl lay cold and dead.

12

Sometimes I Think About

The simultaneous ringing of the three Sofees in room 4324 had triggered the overhead lights to come on. The walls went from gray phantoms to white, stark reality instantly. Seconds later, Ving and Dublin rolling out of their respective bunks and planting their feet on the cold floor had caused their alarms to cut off: one, two...

Daryl's alarm kept right on going. Dublin yawned and turned toward where he lay in the top bunk, while Ving stretched and went straight to his freshly cleaned alternate full-grav suit hanging on the wall. He backed his lean but muscular frame against the empty pair of hooks next to the new suit, and, struggling to imitate the technique that Daryl had demonstrated for them the previous evening, he finally succeeded in shedding his dirty one hundred and twenty-five pound suit onto the catches. This done, he slid over and wedged himself successfully into the clean suit, and was ready for his day.

Dublin, the whole time, was staring open-mouthed at Daryl. Their mentor lay flat on his back with his eyes wide open and his face frozen in a mask of horror that would now last forever. "No, no, no, no, no, no, no!" Dublin muttered, having gone from dead asleep to fully adrenalized in like five seconds. He leaned into the creepy airspace over the seeming corpse. He slowly but bravely reached out and touched the shoulder, giving it a shake. It was cold, and the man attached to it was profoundly unresponsive. "I think he's dead! Daryl's dead!"

Ving was as nonplussed as if Dublin had reported that Daryl had stubbed his toe. "Yah, he no look so good." And just like that, he was into the tiny bathroom, brushing his teeth. Dublin was beside himself, trying to figure out what to do. Fortunately his Sofee, detecting the sudden spike in his heart rate, intervened.

"Do you require assistance, Dublin?" the soothing female voice asked him breathily.

"Yes!" he pretty much yelled at his wrist. "Who do I call? We've got a dead body here!"

"Protocol indicates that it would be appropriate to contact Level Four Security. Would you like me to connect you?" The sultriness of the voice seemed incredibly out of place. This was not one of the scenarios he had envisioned when he had set it.

"Yes!"

Seconds later a man was on the line. "Level Four Security, this is Dwayne. Something wrong in 4324?"

"Yes! This is Dublin Dunne [he left out the "but I'm not Irish" part] in 4324--like you just said; sorry; ahhhhhh, weeeee have a dead body in here...it's Daryl; I can't remember his last name. He's dead."

The voice on the line took a few seconds to finish chewing something. "Dublin. You're that goofy kid with the big hair. Just calm down. We'll be there in a minute."

"I don't even--I--hello? Hello?" Dwayne had hung up. Then Dublin panicked and did something stupid. He reached over and turned off Daryl's alarm, getting his fingerprints all over the dead man's Sofee. "Oh my God; **IDIOT!**"

First thought: *They're going to pin this on me! It's always the killer who calls for help! And now my prints are on his Sofee!*

Second thought: *No, Ving is my witness. He knows that Daryl was dead already!*

Third thought: *EXCEPT that Ving probably killed him, and now he can pin it on me to exonerate himself!*

By the time security arrived a minute and a half later, poor Dublin was just about hyperventilating. When the door swooshed open he finally tore his eyes from the corpse, and saw a face entering his room that was scarcely any more comforting. For a moment he thought this whole thing was an elaborate prank. Here came Jerkboy into his room, along with a second guy who must have been "Dwayne." Ving had just finished brushing, and stood with both arms on the bathroom door frame, watching them enter.

They wore the same standard-issue red jumpsuit as everyone else, but they had wide, bright yellow armbands on their left shoulders, indicating security clearance. You wouldn't think that a man could swagger arrogantly while carrying an extendable stretcher into a room to pick up a dead body, but Jerkboy had found a way to do it. Dublin opened his stupid mouth before he could stop himself. "I thought you were a pilot!"

Jerkboy stopped mid-swag and looked down into Dublin's eyes. "I'm a lot of things sweetheart. I'm whatever I want to be. You got a problem with it? Cuz I can go back and get another stretcher!"

Dublin didn't take well to bullies, and had surprised them more than once with his strength and his willingness to defend himself, but he was caught off-guard by the stress of the situation, and by the sheer force of Jerkboy's jerkiness. His cheeks reddened and he stepped aside.

Jerkboy laid eyes for the first time on Daryl's dead body, and burst out laughing. This mirthless explosion was mostly intended to let everyone in the room know how tough he was. As he reached for Daryl's feet, and Dwayne reached for his cold underarms, Dublin felt the need to explain something. "I got my fingerprints on his Sofee when I turned his alarm off. But he was dead already, I swear it."

For some reason this struck Jerkboy as funny. Grinning broadly and unpleasantly as he and Dwayne hoisted the body onto the stretcher, he said to Dublin, "You might be the stupidest person I've ever met. I know you're the ugliest, but I think you might be the stupidest, too. I can't even **believe** you made co-pilot. Not in **my** cruiser; I'll tell you that much." And he laughed again.

Dublin struggled desperately to compose a comeback, like "Oh yeah? Well, have you read *War and Peace*?" or "Oh yeah? Well Prince Andrei begs to differ!" but he couldn't come up with one that didn't sound stupid. Eight seconds later the door swooshed shut and they were gone. There was a long pause. Dublin would later reflect that he had been so absorbed in his anger at Jerkboy at this moment that he had turned his back completely on his one remaining roommate, the man who appeared to have killed Daryl in his sleep. He shouted at the blank white panel.

"We can only know that we know nothing! And that is the highest degree of human wisdom!"

"Oh, snap!" said Ving sardonically.

Prudence reminded herself in the morning that she had signed up for this, and that whatever lay ahead was better than what lay behind. As she geared up with Jordache and Judy, and another woman named Qwayla who had shown up from the late-arriving work crews last night, she was tingling with nervousness. She choked it down to stay cool.

Their Hall-Mother, a woman named Lin, had gathered up the cow-patty supplements for everyone in her little domain. She handed them out along with the little yellow pills, the 'waste inhibitors' that had caused giggles and groans in all of the conference rooms the day before.

They all had to be at their respective worksites by 7:00 AM on the nose, which would require a sharp focus and a brisk pace. There were three layers of suiting up to do, and then the logjam at the compression chambers to deal with, as different groups arriving from different floors and halls merged and reemerged in their separate work units.

The Upper Pit Crews had their own compression chambers, however many stories high, coming out of the back top part of the towers. Their work was mainly on top of that broad ridge, installing even **more** solar collectors. Some groups ventured further afield from that upper point, large groups to the South toward Rozhdestvenskiy Crater, which was larger even than Hermite. It was said that they took a sort of crude train to get there. Smaller groups, not always, but sometimes, went out into the mysterious blackness beyond the north pole---the dark side of the moon. This began virtually in the backyard of La Lune, and went on for thousands of miles. These people didn't come back at the end of the day.

They dressed at the pre-compression lockers. Prudence, as instructed by her Sofee (and Jordache, for good measure) had put on her half-grav back in her room. This was almost a joy to wear. It was heavy enough to keep her stable, but light enough to make her feel physically super-empowered. Once they got to pre-compression, however, they were required to put on an intensely thermal bodysuit over the half-grav. This had Prudence sweating almost immediately. Then came their 'Lunar Acclimatized Surface Survival Suits', which everyone referred to as 'Lassies', complete with domed glass helmets like in the movies. These added another layer of sophisticated heat retention, and Prudence started to feel like she might pass out.

They didn't **look** like family as they suited up. Many different cultural backgrounds and skin tones were represented: Caucasian, African-American, Hispanic, Asian; there was even the enormous Polynesian dude who must have been the roommate that Kaywin had described. Prudence especially stood out. She was by far the tiniest in the locker room, and her hair was by far the most rainbowey. But despite their physical differences, and despite the fact that these people had given up on life, and despite the fact that they were, many of them, radiation-sick, weak, and worn to the nub, they still retained enough empathy to help the newbies with their helmets, and their boots, and their communication systems, and their climate systems. One faulty seal would mean a day-one death, which in this strange new reality was regarded as the unluckiest of tragedies.

The last third of Lower Pit Crew 3 was ready with seconds to spare when the doors to the compression chamber opened. They stepped inside, all forty-five of them, into the rectangular space that was no larger than a good-sized living room. Other than the doors that sealed shut behind them with a suctioney sound, and the doors dead ahead that were waiting to open, the walls were seamless, uninterrupted white plastic. On the ceiling overhead were four identical openings, each about the circumference of a trash can--not the little one in your kitchen, but the big one you wheel to the curb on Wednesdays. Two of them were sealed tightly; the lids of the other two, now that the chamber was sealed, swung open and sucked all of the air out of the room. When these two snapped shut again, they knew it was almost time.

Prudence didn't **hear** it, but she felt the slight vibration up through her boots as the wall in front of them slid open. She was propelled forward by the crowd, and seconds later she had passed over the painted red line they had been forbidden to cross a moment ago, and had taken her first step on the actual surface of the Moon.

She had about a half of a second to analyze the sensations, which were all muted by the layers of gear. The ground felt soft and powdery for a couple of inches, with vague firmness below it. Within seconds, despite the sunlight, she could feel her temperature dropping. The thermal layers that she was cursing five minutes ago were already saving her life. In a matter of moments, she went from burning up and sweating, to comfortable, to the coldest she had ever been in her life. Her lumbering comrades in LPC3 started jogging ahead of her, and around her, toward a well-worn footpath that went down a little hill to the right. Behind her the eleven gleaming silver-pastel towers seemed to rise forever. The solar collectors were behind them, obscured from view, but they imparted a golden halo to the Grand Hotel's distant summit. There was no time for sightseeing, however. Her ear implants sounded off loudly and suddenly, startling her so completely that she had reason to be thankful for the waste inhibitor: "Prudence Estrada! You coming or not?" It was the LPC3 Chief, Dorna Lee. Prudence took off down the path, last in line behind the jogging big bodies. "I **said** are you coming or **not**?"

"I'm coming."

"Okay. I need an immediate verbal response to **all** communications. You don't want to die out here on your first day."

"Understood."

The jogging pace helped her warm up to a survivable temperature. She followed the others until they came to the bottom of the hill. They were in sort of a pit within the giant pit that was Hermite Crater itself. Even though they had come out of the Moonbase pretty much at its center point, between the two massive hangars, and had traveled sideways for close to half a mile, they still had not gotten beyond the edge of the massive complex. They were at a spot below the second tower from the left, as they looked up like ants at the colossal structure. Here was the exposed ancient crater wall, which supported the hangars, the MCP quarters, and the biggest hotel in the known universe. It was rugged in the extreme. At the base of the ridge wall, a line of holes had been drilled, or blasted, each about the same size as the vents back in the compression chamber. They were spaced perhaps thirty feet apart, starting about three hundred feet to Prudence's right and stretching off into the distance to her left, following the curve of the crater rim.

Dorna Lee put herself in front of them. "Newbies on this side." She indicated to her left, back in the direction they had come from. "Vets on this side." She indicated to her right. When the old guard had been separated from the new, a quick head count showed her eighty-two of the former and fifty-three of the latter. They all had to listen to her counting under her breath the whole time, whilst they jumped up and down, or did squats, or ran in place to keep warm. "Okay." She looked at her Sofee through the clear glass window on the left wrist of her Lassie. "I want my usual lateral advancers to head out. I want you to take...Sephal Tatupu, Dinge Barrow, Sarah Clark (she listed eight others, none of whom were Prudence Estrada) with you. Lateral shaft warmers, I want you to take Perrell Washington, Nicotine Millbourne (etc.)...." Still no Prudence. "Debris team, if you can't finish this pile today, with all of this help, I don't know what to do with you. You take the rest of the newbies. Prudence, help with the debris team until we're ready."

Prudence started out after the debris team, then remembered her previous instructions, and said, "Yes Ma'am." In her mind though, she was thinking, *Until we're ready? Until we're ready for* **what**? Whatever it was, whatever it meant, she didn't much care for being singled out. Especially without any explanation. She wanted to ask, but she wasn't sure she had her helmet communications totally figured out. She didn't want everybody else in LPC3 to hear her ask a potentially stupid question. While she hesitated, Dorna Lee just pointed with her laser rifle in the direction of the retreating debris team, and Prudence set out after them.

About eight hundred feet from their unit chief they came to a large mound of debris that had been blasted from the ridge wall during some phase of construction on La Lune. Wheelbarrows and shovels, pretty similar to those used on Earth for hundreds of years, awaited them there, just lying around. Prudence guessed that they didn't have to worry about thieves out here.

If there had been any water content whatsoever in this stuff it would have been frozen together like a giant scoop of ice cream, when the freezer is too cold and you can't get it out of the carton. But the pockets of ice around here--one of the main reasons (along with the near-permanent sunlight to provide power) that the North Pole had been selected for Moonbase 2--were concentrated and isolated. Prudence followed the lead of her mates and picked up a shovel. She attacked the mound like they were attacking it, at a lively clip calculated to keep the blood circulating. Soon the three large wheelbarrows were full. Two people had to man each of them over the bumpy terrain. They took turns, relieving each other when they were about to pass out. When her turn came, she found herself paired ridiculously with some guy who was fifteen inches taller than her, and probably two-and-a-half times her weight. It was a struggle for both of them to keep the wheelbarrow from tipping over in her direction.

Prudence battled with the club-like handle, and while she did she cursed under her breath the idiot back in Houston who had made whatever clerical error had landed her here, with these giants. She should have been piloting, or spying. She thought she had killed it on the spy tests. Why did they bother testing them at all, if they were just going to pull their names out of a hat?

She lasted about a hundred feet before she had to tap out. She could see the dude on the other handle smiling at her as she collapsed for a few seconds into a little gray powdery Moon-bank. She wanted to wipe that smile off of his face. But she knew it wasn't his fault.

They wheeled the heavy debris a full half-mile and dumped it without ceremony into the end of a mini-ravine. It was kind of cool to watch the dust from it roil upward into a little cloud, then fall back down in slow-motion, with the action completely undisturbed by any breeze. Sort of mesmerizing. But they had to get back. Prudence took a long turn with the empty wheelbarrow as compensation for her inadequacy with the full one.

They made this brutal trek four times. Each trip took up pretty much a full hour. By the end of the fourth round, Prudence felt like she was wearing a double-gravity suit instead of a half-grav. The rest of her day-one companions were struggling too, however, many--maybe even **most**--worse than she was.

When they got back from that fourth trip with the empty wheelbarrows, Dorna Lee told them to lay down their tools, and gathered them unto her.

"Alright!" she said. "This is exciting! Let's test out our

new Mole!" Prudence and the rest of the newbies looked around awkwardly, trying to be subtle in case they were the only one who didn't know what a 'Mole' was. Then Prudence felt someone nudge her forward. *What the...*Two, three people were nudging her now, gently, but *what the heck?*

"Well, Prudence, you don't strike me as the shy type," said Dorna Lee. Prudence succumbed to the growing realization that **she** was the Mole. She stepped up to her unit chief with an awful feeling in the pit of her stomach. Awful-awful, not 'wicked cool'-awful.

"Excellent," said Dorna Lee. "Are you nervous?"

"Uh, no, I'm fine; I just don't know what's happening right now..." Even through the glare on her commander's helmet Prudence could see that she was taken aback.

"Jordache!" She was speaking to Prudence's roommate who had been sent around the rim of the crater with the lateral shaft warming crew, whatever that was. She copied Prudence on the communication. "Jordache Johnson! Did you or did you not tell Prudence Estrada that she was going to be our Mole, and have her watch the training video?" There was a long pause, then they heard the unmistakable New York accent in reply:

"Oh crap. I fahgat entiyaly."

"Well that's just **great.**" She ended the conversation. Prudence heard the chief give a deep sigh of exasperation as she weighed their options at this point. "Alright. Come here Prudence. You remember the tunnel test back in Houston?" Prudence's blood ran instantly cold, and she gulped.

"Yes Ma'am."

"Same thing here. You're just connecting the seven wires

of the solar collector to the seven wires of the relay; just clipping them together, like you did back in Houston. They're all color-coded; you're clipping green to green, yellow to yellow, et cetera. Watch out for orange and red. What has happened before, twice, with our old girl, is that she connected red to orange, then had to go back in to fix it. These helmet lights aren't the best at illuminating color contrast, so be diligent. The one thing that will be different from the test is that when all the connections are made, you will have to apply a thermal cuff." She was reaching down into a large pouch at her feet. Mid-panic attack, it struck Prudence as weird to watch a woman crouch down in a spacesuit, untying a little string sash on a silver bag on the Moon. She produced from it a large flexible shiny cuff, a sort of puffy, fabric-like tube. "You'll be in communication with myself, and the lateral advance team. They tell me that the relay wires should be advanced into perfect position for you to connect them with the collector wires. But between you and me they are also not the smartest bunch." She could see the terror in the young girl's eyes, and was trying to put her at ease. *She's trying to settle me down so I don't mess this up.* "So if the relay wires, coming in from your left, are too far along, or not far enough, tell us. Put them through the cuff **first**, or you'll wind up having to disconnect them, put the cuff on, and reconnect. By then, you'd be..." Dorna Lee was about to say 'frozen to death' but decided against this wording, however accurate it may have been. "... really really cold, and very uncomfortable. When the connections are complete, you will slide the cuff into place--not evenly over the connections; you want two-thirds of it over the lateral relay lines and one-third of it over the collector lines; I'll explain why later, but it's important. When the cuff is positioned correctly" (Prudence was struggling not to just take off running at this point, hoping that Dorna Lee would gun her down) "you will pull this tab off, with a sharp quick motion, and it will compress over the connections. I know that sounds like a lot. I'm sorry you didn't get the video." She put her hand kindly on Prudence's tiny childlike shoulder. "Hey. You can do this. I will be watching your helmet feed on my Sofee. I'll be seeing what you're seeing. Take your time and stay calm. We are starting right here in Hole Twelve. Lay down on your belly. No, right here. We're going to tie the rope around your ankles to slow your descent, and to pull you back out." Prudence took a quick glance at La Lune soaring up into space above her; the greatest and most modern of human achievements, and felt bitterly the irony of her primitive rope lifeline. She looked back down at the mouth of the tiny hole, a foot in front of her helmet. It was dark, black as ink, like it could have sucked all the light out of the universe. Her headlight showed her a steep downward pitch, like a playground slide, and then nothing. "Okay, brave girl. Put your arms out in front of you, like Superwoman. If you go in with your arms at your side, you won't have room to get them out in front of you. Alright. I'm going to put the cuff in your hands. Grip it good and tight so it doesn't get trapped under you. Ready? Everybody ready? We are about to have a Mole in the hole; we need everybody focused on hole number twelve right now!" Acknowledgments came in from teams far and near.

"Wait!" said Prudence.

"Yes? What is it? Better to ask it now, whatever it is."

"What happened to the last Mole?"

The commander paused, and sighed. "You're pretty brave, right?"

"Sure."

"Nerves of steel, and whatnot?"

"Sure."

"Alright; she's still in Hole Eleven. But we've got a better rope now."

"Oh my God; did you freak out?" Dublin's eyes were wide as he leaned over the cafeteria table and hung on every word of Prudence's account.

"Naw. I mean; I knew she was dead, or I wouldn't have been there, doing that godawful job." Her teeth chattered as she spoke, and she still looked a little blue under the fiery redness of her hair. "The worst part is the cold. It is so unbelievably cold down in those tunnels, and it's like pressed right up on you. They made me run around between each hole so I wouldn't die."

"Please tell me they let you take a blazing hot shower after you got in!" said Kaywin paternally. Prudence looked so small, huddled up in a little ball on the bench next to him.

"Regular kind-of-warm shower, which still felt great, but I just got the usual four minutes."

"I can get you my blanket!" said Dublin enthusiastically.

"No. I don't want your blanket." She was too tired and cold to even patch insults on to the ends of her sentences.

"My room is literally right there! I can be back in like twenty seconds!"

"Dub! I mean, **Dublin**; I don't want your dirty blanket!

What am I gonna do; wrap up in it like the crazy religious guys?"

Her little slip-up--calling him "Dub" instead of "Dublin"--had not gone unnoticed. The boy blushed, but blundered on. "Just wear it over your shoulders. Who cares? I can even stand behind you so nobody sees."

"Oh, that's much less embarrassing. No, I'm good, thanks. She unhuddled just enough to lift a fork-full of rice toward her mouth, because she was starving too, but her hand was shaking so badly that she dropped it with a clatter. It hit the bench first, which sent it spinning, and rice flew everywhere.

Dublin was done negotiating. "Watch my food," he said, and got up. He set off jogging toward his room, his black afro bobbing with every lope.

Prudence followed him with her eyes for a couple of seconds, incredulous. She felt insulted by his obstinance. "I'm not wearing his stupid blanket," she said, turning back and addressing this to Kaywin, who had been sitting right next to her.

But he was gone too, just like that. It was her turn to blush, in anger and embarrassment. She didn't care, of course, not at all, really...it was his life. It had only been a matter of time until these guys got the message: *No thank you to the Three-Musketeer-thing! I didn't ask you two to be my friends!* The old one had finally gotten it. She would have to be more direct with the young one. She looked over her shoulder and saw Kaywin two tables away across the crowded cafeteria. He was approaching the taller ascetic. As packed as the dining hall was, the odor of this unshowered man and his fellow penitent created a little buffer around them where no one wanted to sit. Who wanted that stench in their nostrils while they were trying to enjoy their one meal of the day? Kaywin did, apparently, because while she watched he said something to the ascetic and sat down right next to him, shoulder to shoulder. *Am I worse than that smell? Yes. I'm worse.*

She wondered what she had said that had finally worked. Did he think that she was being too dramatic or whiney about her first day on the job? Maybe **he** should try being lowered into a tight icy shaft by his ankles. And why was she wasting time worrying about **his** opinion?

She tried to reach the fork that had ricocheted to the floor at her feet, lamenting every lost grain of rice, but it was torture to stretch her arms out. They had been locked out in front of her all day. She contracted quickly back into the feeble circle of her own failing warmth.

Prudence flinched weakly as something heavenly warm suddenly engulfed her. She had been in the middle of a long blink, and wondered for half a second if this was happy death. Any such illusion was shattered when she heard a phony British accent behind her saying, "My Lady." Ugh. **Precisely** why she had said no to the blanket in the first place.

But it was sooo warm. As much as she wanted to, she couldn't bring herself to shrug it off, even when the entire cafeteria noticed what Dublin had done and erupted in mocking catcalls and wolf-whistles. Dublin's red blotches expanded over his whole face in an instant, but he continued to stand there, looming with monstrous awkwardness behind her. "Do you want me to stand--"

"No! Sorry, no. Thanks for the blanket." Dublin had to navigate around the end of the long table, with everyone looking and laughing at him, to finally resume his seat opposite Prudence. His face had fallen in that short time, as he caught the jist of the public sentiment. The jeering and the laughter had carried on a little longer than it might have if a *good-looking* guy had put a blanket over Prudence. They were laughing at the contrast between the ugly boy and the strikingly pretty girl. Their interest was held as they whispered amongst themselves, "That's not possible, right? **That** guy? And **that** girl? No way!"

The plastic bench shook under Prudence, and Kaywin was suddenly back in the seat next to her. "Here," he said, scraping pot roast and rice onto her plate. "You need extra calories. Your body has burned up too many trying to stay warm."

So **that's** why he had gone over to the ascetic. To beg for food for her. What was Prudence going to do with these two weirdos? This was not how men were supposed to act. She couldn't figure out what they wanted...but she was warm enough now to handle the clean fork that Dublin got for her, and she had a lot of food to put on it.

A few seconds later, as usual, Dublin tried to sabotage his own good deed by turning into a raging idiot. "Is the blanket helping, Pru?"

Prudence froze with her fifth heaping spoonful of pot roast and rice halfway up to her open mouth. "Ex**cuse** me?"

Dublin gulped. "Is the blanket helping?"

"Yeah, I heard **that** part. But did you just call me 'Pru'?"

Dublin tried to play dumb. "I don't know. What did you hear?" She continued to glare at him across the table. "Alright; yeah, I did. But you called me 'Dub'!"

"That was an accident!" She **sounded** angry, but there was the slightest smile on her face, and she shoved the spoonful of hot food into it.

"I don't mind. Friends have called me 'Dub' before." *Is this what flirting feels like?*

This kid's flirting with disaster, thought Prudence. "That's fascinating," she responded sarcastically, instantly taking feeble steps to rebuild her crumbling wall. "Tell me more about your imaginary friends, **DUB**." This snarking jibe had the opposite of the intended effect, as he blushed again and smiled. Or maybe she intended the opposite of what she thought she did.

"So do you mind being called 'Pru'?" Kaywin chimed in.

She took her time finishing her bite. Her furrowed brow indicated that she was thinking about it. "Well...seeing as how 'Prudence' is like the stupidest name ever, I don't guess 'Pru' can be any worse."

"Do you want to practice our new names, Pru?" asked Dublin.

"No, Dub, I do not."

Dublin turned to Kaywin. "Can we call you Kay?"

Kaywin sat back, chewing, "Hmm. I have a long history of telling people **not** to call me Kay."

"We could change history!" said Dublin, weird as always.

"I guess it doesn't matter that much to me. Except that 'Kay'; like K-A-Y sounds like a woman's name. You could call me 'K'; like, just the **letter** K..." Every once in awhile he liked to throw a little weirdness back at Dub.

They talked over the entire meal, and back to Kaywin's room. The boys told Pru all about their first day. It was markedly different from hers. Neither of them had had a brush with death yet, although they got a picture of how it might happen, and when.

They had learned a lot the day before back in Conference Room Eight, or CR8. (People here liked to shorten everything like that, to make it sound like they had important official knowledge and experience.) Beyond this introductory training session, their conference rooms would continue to serve as a meeting ground for their respective units. A good deal of time the previous afternoon in the pilots' room had been spent explaining a complicated grid on the viewing wall. One of the new pilots had noticed her name on it, and wanted to know what this meant. "Ah!" said the man in the navy blue sweatshirt. "We were getting there! This is a chart of who is assigned to what cruiser, under which engineer, and in what capacity. It is subject to change, and it does in fact change quite a bit, depending on fatalities, or on the different strengths of different pilots; their compatibility with the different thrust assemblies installed in the different cruisers...but let me back up a little. I suppose I should tell you what's going on here. I'm rambling on and on about the details, and I haven't told you what we are actually working toward." Despite this slight self-deprecation you could tell that this guy was comfortable in front of a crowd. He was too excited about his subject matter to be nervous about what people might think of him. He came across like a good, approachable Professor. "I am Professor Lindsay of the University of California at Berkeley. I am head of the Space Propulsion Engineering Department there." (Well, there you have it.) "There is a lot going on here at Moonbase 2. You have noticed this, I am sure. Most of it I am neither qualified nor authorized to speak about. **Our** area of focus, everyone in this room...we are missing a few of our engineers who are monitoring time-sensitive experiments...our focus is the practical application of theoretical principles of spaceflight acceleration." A few heads turned as Jerkboy yawned flamboyantly. " Every year we challenge our graduate students to build on existing acceleration systems; improve them, or--," he shrugged, "--to ignore them utterly, to try something completely different...something brand new. Every year the students with what we deem to be the twenty most promising proposals are invited to spend a year here at the Moonbase, to put their ideas into action. That's where the heroes of the Meaningful Conclusion Program come into play. You guys--and women--help us test daring new acceleration systems without exhaustive pre-trials. You save us years. Absolutely, you save us years. And someday soon, maybe **this** year, one of these fine minds will come up with an innovation that doubles, triples, or even just obliterates existing speed records for manned spaceflight. Which at the moment--can I help you?"

A repetitive thudding sound had begun to weave its way between his words. It was Jerkboy, banging his head down over and over on his table to express the depth of his boredom. He looked up when Professor Lindsay addressed him. Standing up dramatically, he cleared his throat, as if something very important was about to come out of it. His almost-as-obnoxious friend had to put his fist over his own mouth, fighting to stifle his laughter. He regarded the reckless Jerkboy in giddy transports of affection.

Dublin's active mind liked to match the real-life people around him with their literary doubles, and right now this breathless admirer struck him as kind of *Juliet* to Jerkboy's *Romeo*. Except for the dark hair.

Bruniette, thought Dublin. *I'm going to call that guy Bruniette.*

Jerkboy spoke loudly, feigning deference but commanding the room. "Uh, yes, Professor; can we skip ahead to the interesting part?"

"I assume you are referring to the race." Professor Lindsay turned from the rude boy and his gray eyes swept over all of the assembled MC's. "The culmination of all the trials and retrials and tweaking and rebooting, and the improvements of pilots and propulsion systems alike all leads up to the Valentine's Day Race. Ready or not, on February fourteenth, 2127 all cruisers will attempt maximum acceleration. This is always an exciting day, but a heart-breaking one as well. We always lose a lot of good men and women that day, in the name of scientific progress."

After that, Lindsay got back to the chart, which listed every cruiser, one through twenty, and their engineers and crews. Kaywin and Dublin scanned it. All of the cruisers had weird names, like racehorses. Kaywin recognized a lot of them as very old musical references: *The Pearly Queen, Sunshine Superman, The Famous Flame....* 'JB' was first pilot in Cruiser One, nicknamed *Purple Haze*. Someone named Reginald Ludlow was his co-pilot. Kaywin was surprised to see himself as first pilot in Cruiser Eleven, *Tomorrow Never Knows*. He knew this to be a Beatles song and took this as a good sign.

Dublin was way at the bottom, in a special box marked 'alternates'. But he was happy just to be in the pilots' room.

~

They had spent their first full day partly in CR8 and partly in the hangar where all the cruisers were parked. These old, solid refurbished little spacecraft were things of beauty. With soft rounded edges and bright colors they reminded Kaywin of an amusement park ride he remembered from many many years ago. *Tomorrow Never Knows* was a wonderful cobalt blue snub-nosed little thing, with thin yellow lines that made triangles on it like those that encircled an old-school marching drum. Kaywin shook hands with the designer of its propulsion system, a woman named Jennifer. He and his co-pilot, Rita, trained in and around it all afternoon, but neither they nor the craft were quite ready for flight.

Dublin, as an alternate, had some freedom to explore, but spent most of his day learning the basics on a craft called *A Whiter Shade of Pale* with the other alternates. This little cruiser was more cream-colored than mega-pale, but maybe it had just yellowed over the years.

"So you didn't fly at all today?" Prudence asked. She was still huddled in Dublin's blanket. The three of them sat on the floor in Kaywin's room with the cribbage board between them. She didn't make any effort to hide her jealousy at what sounded like a vacation for the boys.

"I know it sounds cushy, but I do have to get up at five every morning and clean four big restrooms," Dub lamented. He looked directly at Kaywin as he said it. "Remind me again what you have to do for extra work?"

"I'm a number one. I get off scot-free." But he was unapologetic. "There's a lot of studying involved. A **lot**. These guys are trying to go faster than any human's ever gone. One of the engineers might have a design of historical importance, and I could blow the whole thing by, say, not understanding the effect my own forward momentum might have on propellant dispensation, or not being ready for the tricks my eyes might play on me at speeds above a hundred-thousand miles per hour..."

This all still sounded very easy to Prudence. "Poor baby," she said in mocking tones. "Does your brain hurt?"

Kaywin shuffled the deck and started dealing. "A little bit, actually. Thank you for asking."

And so they fell into a little pattern. Every night they ate supper together. Kaywin talked three guys at the end of their long table into trading seats with them so that Prudence could catch the warm air coming out of the kitchen each evening. After eating, they hung out for the first four nights in Kaywin's room, until a vibe that Kaywin's enormous roommate Sephal was putting out made Prudence uneasy. So they switched to Dublin's room, where he dwelt uneasily with the Kalaysian Three-Star and no one else. Kaywin and Prudence thought it might be a little weird in there, but the reality was that Ving kept entirely to himself. While they chatted, played cribbage, watched movies or listened to music, he sat upright in his top bunk (on the right hand side of the room as you came in), always working away on his Sofee. His English was so atrocious that they spoke pretty freely right behind him without fear of being understood. He never even turned to look at them.

Two weeks in, an event occurred over the evening meal

that left a bad taste in their mouths, even beyond the simulated fishcakes. When they were almost all seated, an unpleasantly familiar voice assaulted them unexpectedly from the powerful speakers.

"Listen up!"

Kaywin, Dublin and Prudence exchanged alarmed glances. What on Earth was *Jerkboy* doing in the central circle of the cafeteria with a microphone in his hand? There he was, swaggering maliciously around Aristophanes' Sacrifice and sizing up the ragged crowd with tangible disdain. The microphone and the navy blue security uniform were ominous indications of a rise in status for the dangerous youth. They blinked, hoping the world would be normal again when they opened their eyes. But the image persisted.

"I **SAID LISTEN UP!**" The assemblage hushed. Jerkboy stalked slowly and menacingly around the ridiculous fountain, savoring the fear and obedience that a little simple yelling had garnered him. He looked hyped up and stressed, but not at all about speaking in front of twenty-four hundred people. He didn't give a crap about them. Only something from deep within his own mind was worth the worrying-time. Whatever it was, he took his time pondering it. The mic was in his right hand, and he tapped it against his open left palm while he ruminated, walking one time around the water-feature entirely. Finally, he was ready.

"As most of you know by now, Security Chief Macumber choked to death this morning on a raisin brioche." He was sort of trying to imitate someone who cared. But he lost his handle on it, and the word 'brioche' came out like something between a snort and a laugh. "I don't know if you've ever had one of those things, but they are really dry. Anyways, second officer Dwayne and myself have graciously offered to assume his duties until such time as Houston can train a suitable replacement. This offer was accepted by President Beauregard at 11:34 this morning. Here's a screenshot of our correspondence from earlier today, if anyone doesn't believe me." Dwayne, who usually just projected gooniness with his beefy bully build and his black hair in a strangely undersized bowl cut, looked tonight like he was in way over his head. Drops of sweat rolled down his cheeks, and his scant moustache struggled to catch them all. He'd been staring at the fountain as Jerkboy spoke, trying very hard to avoid eye contact with every one of the gathered thousands. But now he tapped his Sofee, and the viewing screens across the cafeteria all switched from live action lunar landscapes to the text of the supposed interaction between JB and APMCP Beauregard.

"That would take like five seconds to forge," Dublin whispered to Kaywin and Prudence. They had learned a lot of surprising things in two weeks, including the fact that the MCP, at least here at the Moonbase, did handle its own security. Security Chief, First Officer, Second Officer, the fifty or so thugs working underneath them, all of them were Goners. The spirits of the men and women they were charged to police had all been broken like wild animals anyway. Furthermore, they were expendable. If a fight broke out and a couple of MC's were killed, so what? It wasn't worth the cost of hiring outside security. Still, did President Beauregard, way back in Houston, know that JB was the loosest cannon on this battleship?

"Now, a situation has arisen this very day that will allow me to demonstrate some of our policies much better than words could explain them. Pit Crew One. You had a couple of walk-offs today, right? Did you notice? Forrest Glance and Roger Fitzwilliams? Yeah, they decided they were done. They forgot all that stuff they had signed. I'm gonna show you the little conversation they had; it's pretty cute." He nodded sternly at Dwayne, who tapped his Sofee again. The screens changed. They were watching clips of helmet footage from earlier in the day; they were seeing what the two escapees had seen. "Dim the lights" whispered JB in eager, ominous anticipation. "Turn them down completely. I like to watch my movies in the dark." The cafeteria went black except for the thirty large screens. They were inside the helmet of one of these men, shoveling moon debris into a wheelbarrow. He coughed wretchedly, and seemed to fall to his knees. The other one was talking to him, trying to comfort him. The crowd watching the recap could see the second man's face, and the concern on it, even through the glare of his helmet-glass. Kaywin recognized him, but didn't know his name.

"Stay down for a minute. I'll stand guard."

"No. I'm done with this." Still on his knees, he picked up his shovel and flung it. It went six times further than it would have on Earth, seeming to take a long time to come down. Then it hit the rocky ground noiselessly. "I'm going to die on the other side of that ridge. I'm going to lay down where I can see the Earth, and there won't be a gun in my face." (Prudence had heard that the Pit Crew One Chief liked to brandish his laser rifle at people who weren't working fast enough for his liking.)

The first man hesitated. They could hear his heavy breathing.

"This is my favorite part," said Jerkboy, mesmerized.

"I'll go with you. I'd rather die out there with you than (unintelligible crying)."

Jerkboy imitated the man's sob, then pretended to wipe tears from his eyes. "That part gets me every time."

They watched the two men hide behind a large rock until the coast was clear, then make a break for it. From the angle they were taking, they were hidden from the rest of PC1. "The next hour is pretty boring," said Jerkboy. "The only good part is where they swear their undying love for each other. Let's get over that ridge." Now they were in the helmet of the second man. He helped the coughing man down over the lip of the crater, and they both collapsed onto the pillowy dust of its backside. The full Earth hung low and beautiful on the horizon. The two refugees were winded, but they laughed a little at the sight of their long lost Motherland.

"Now here's where **I** first became aware of the situation," said Jerkboy. There was a strange macabre giddiness in

322

his tone. "Out there beyond the rim, out of the shadows, the temperature right now is like two-hundred and thirty degrees. I became concerned for the amount of energy that was being used to cool Mr. Glance's suit. I was worried there wouldn't be enough leftover for you guys tomorrow. All of you guys have kept your promises to the program. Forrest Glance did **not**; so it was an easy decision to turn off his climate control."

They heard the man gasping for air and watched his face redden and fall slack as he began to cook inside of his own Moonsuit. His companion was freaking out, perhaps understanding for the first time that his own life-support systems could be shut off remotely from the Security Room back at the Moonbase. He was looking this way and that, panicking. He finally knelt, embracing his dead friend, apparently trying to pick him up, but even in the half-grav he was too heavy. He gave up and started back toward the base, whimpering. Jerkboy imitated him into the microphone, stopping and laughing occasionally. The assembled MCs watched in horror. "Let's see if he makes it back." They fast-forwarded through every step of Roger Fitzwilliam's return journey, until he got to the point where he and Forrest had decided to go AWOL.

The soaring towers of La Lune had been visible the entire way, but now, rounding a rocky outcrop, he could see the lower levels. He could see the two hangar doors, and the little compression chambers, dwarfed between them. They were open! Pit Crew One was inside, he saw in that fleeting second. Then the doors shut, and he was alone on the surface of the Moon. He paused in horror, then broke into a run. "This was thirty minutes ago." Jerkboy fiddled with his own Sofee as he narrated. "And let's...gooo...live."

They were back inside Roger's helmet. He was still whimpering incoherently and beating his fists against the compression room doors, over and over again, but, like in a nightmare where you try to scream and nothing comes out, they made no sound. "I have an angle I want to show you," said Jerkboy, "which, if we were making a movie about Roger's death, would be perfect, because it gives you a real sense of scale and context." They suddenly were all watching Roger from the back. They were zoomed in tight from a security camera out in the work zone. They slowly faded backwards. Roger dwindled down in size as more and more of the gigantic hotel filled the screens, until he looked like a little silver ant trying to get into a fifty-five gallon barrel. He was screaming for help now. *Please! Please! Please!* "Dwayne. Dwayne." Jerkboy was almost whispering to his assistant, but the mic was still right at his mouth, so everyone could hear. "Put a little reverb on his voice." Dwayne made an adjustment, and suddenly, jaggedly, it sounded like the stranded man was begging for mercy from the blackness of a cave.

Dublin was trying to enjoy his fishcakes, but the grotesque performance made it hard. Kaywin ate successfully, but slowly. Prudence looked up between every few mouthfuls, but didn't let the scene slow her down. She knew it was calculated to intimidate them, and she wasn't going to betray the first sign of squeamishness.

Now Roger gave up. They were back inside his helmet as he began to smash it against the rocks between the two compression chambers. Scratches formed on the high-tech glass, but not so much as a crack. "I don't know about you guys, but I'm bored. Let's say goodnight to Roger." He made a hand-motion to Dwayne. "On the count of three. Help me out. One. Two. Three. Goodnight, Roger!" A few weak voices, the ones closest to the fountain, and most afraid to not cooperate, joined in. Dwayne tapped his Sofee. Roger gasped. The moisture from his breath froze instantly, frosting his viewscreen. Still, the watching twenty-four hundred could sense the motion of his reeling and falling over, freezing and asphyxiating to death in one dumb instant.

The cafeteria was full of second-rate heroes, like you and I, who, if just one or two people had raised their voices or their fists in protests, would have joined in passionately, and ended the reign of Security Chief JB on the day it began. But nobody stood up.

"And **that's** what happens to deserters." Jerkboy dropped the mic. They could hear his unamplified voice a second later: "Dwayne, pick that up."

More and more they came to rely on their time together in Dublin's room. When Kaywin found out how ignorant the two young ones were about old music, he couldn't stop himself from playing it for them. He picked his spots, and tried to never force it down their throats. Dub warmed up to it nicely. Predictably, it was almost impossible to impress Pru. The best review he got out of her was after playing the second of two Who songs for them. "That was better than the last one," she said. Really it was pretty similar to playing old music years ago to his daughter. He told Pru this, when the thought occurred to him one night. They had been hanging out every night in Dublin's room on Moonbase 2 for about a month and a half. As soon as he said it, his face fell a little tiny bit, and a far away look crept into his eyes. Dub should have left him alone, but it wasn't in his nature.

"You've never told us much about your family," he said.

"Well. They're gone. There's not really much more to tell."

"Oh, c'mon; there's a lot more to tell. If there wasn't, you wouldn't miss them so much." They could see the wheels turning in Kaywin's brain as he tried to figure out how far he should go down this rabbit hole. "Do you have some pictures, at least?"

Without answering, Kaywin began to search in his Sofee. He expanded his screen to middling size and turned it to his two young friends sitting cross-legged on the floor in front of him.

"Holy crap, that's your wife?" Dublin exclaimed tactlessly.

"Yeeeahhh...you seem just the slightest bit surprised?

"She married **you?"**

Even Pru had to admit it. "She's pretty."

"Guys, I didn't always look like this. I used to turn a few heads. A couple. Besides, women don't care about looks that much."

Dublin's mouth fell open in shock at Kaywin's little side-note, thrown out there so casually. "I am going to slap you on your fool-mouth!" he cried. "Women don't care about looks?!"

"Not nearly as much as you think." He cast a sidelong glance at Pru. "I'll tell you all about it sometime. I wish I had gotten hold of you before you joined up. I could have given you some advice."

"Advice, huh? Like that old joke about 'being yourself'"?

"No. Good advice. I'll tell you sometime." He turned his Sofee back around and found his favorite photo of his daughter. He couldn't stop himself from sighing, and gazing at it for just a second before showing them. "And that's Victoria. Happy now?"

The picture was from some formal event or other, not long before her death. The camera had caught her with a big smile on her face. She looked beautiful in her red evening gown with white letters that spelled "love" across the front, and long blond curls. She radiated health, happiness, sweetness and self-confidence. Dub gazed at her in wonder. He had never thought about having kids. He was stuck forever on the first step of the process--finding a girl who liked him. But he knew there was something special about it that turned the toughest of men into putty.

Pru looked for a couple of seconds, then turned away. She wasn't proud of the way the picture made her feel. Jealous. Jealous was the word. This girl had friends who loved her and parents who adored her. Well, not anymore.

"She was great at everything. You name it. Soccer, sewing, cooking, basketball, writing, painting, school. And she was so sweet. Just the sweetest thing. I barely even remember her being this big. I still think of her as being three years old. We would dance to 'Chiquitita', and I would carry her. She would laugh because I would always tell her she was so light on her feet. I would say it every time, and she would laugh every time."

"Did you say Chiquitita? Like the gorilla?"

"That's right; I forgot you grew up pretty close to that

thing, didn't you? I don't think there's any relation between the song and the monkey; no…"

"What happened?" Dublin asked, as simply as that. "What happened to your family?" Prudence, though she never would have asked the question herself, leaned forward with her chin on her hands.

Kaywin closed up his Sofee and paused. He looked at the ground. It was only a matter of time before this question came up. He had dodged it with everyone he could, but he liked these kids. He felt like he owed them a little bit more information. He steeled himself and began.

"It was March 17th, 2122. I was working third shift. We had all gone skiing together at Pat's Peak three days earlier, and Nadine had a bad fall and broke her leg." Despite his effort to just recite the outline of his ordeal, he was already talking as if he was under hypnosis, appearing to remember details with great effort. "Her…right leg. She broke it. Her doctor set it and gave her Excelsiadon for the pain. He actually gave her a choice. I can't remember what the other one was…it started with a 'P'…I wish she had chosen that one. We got her prescription filled and went home. We still had the house on Seames Drive back then. Anyway…" he sighed and gathered himself, "Manchester's got a real bad drug problem. I'm not--I'm not going to make a big production out of this. Some junky hacked through the pharmacy records and found all the people who had been prescribed Excelsiadon for the previous two weeks. He broke into one guy's house on the West Side; he wasn't home, so he cleaned him out. Then he…he broke into our house. It was about one-twenty in the morning. He wasn't expecting anyone to be home;

our other car was in the shop, so it **looked** like nobody was home. When my wife woke up and screamed, he stabbed her. She couldn't get away. Vic--my daughter heard the ruckus and ran to help, and the son of a--" He couldn't go on. "Are we done here? Does that answer your question?"

"Did they catch the guy?"

"They caught **a** guy...a guy with an Excelsiadon problem and a violent record, who was seen driving down Seames Drive earlier in the evening."

"Are you saying you don't think it was him?"

"I don't know...there's a couple of things that didn't really add up, but they kind of **made** them add up."

Kaywin's account of the events that had led to him join-ing the MCP led to Dub telling the entire history of **his** sad life, which led to Pru telling them absolutely nothing about her life, prior to meeting them. They weren't **that** close yet, and never would be. However, it did gradually come back to Prudence--what exactly friends were good for. Hardships during the day became a joke with Kaywin and Dublin at night, and the harder the hardships, the bigger and better the joke.

The whole thing was somewhat of a joke to Dub. It was too terrifying to weigh his future without the armor of his humor. His sadness and his happiness were not a contradic-tion. Even in the deepest, darkest depths of his adolescent misery he never lost sight of what an absolute miracle is life. For instance, during a pause in one of their games while Pru was in the bathroom, he picked up a carved wooden cribbage peg, and, studying it closely, reverted to one of his favorite mind-exercises: *What were the odds? What were the odds, when the universe exploded into being fourteen billion years ago, that our solar system would form just as it did? What were the odds that life would begin on the third planet? What were the odds, over hundreds of millions of years, and millions of long-forgotten botanical failures, that maple trees would form? What were the odds that one particular maple tree would be carved into pegs for a strange game invented by a strange semi-intelligent species? And what were the odds that that peg would wind up in a little dorm room on the Moon?* The odds were beyond astronomical. They simply were not believable. It was laughably impossible, and yet here it was.

Dub understood that life was a joke, a good one, the **best ever** in fact, but he also understood that the joke was on him. In true Dublin style, he fancied himself a swordsman, fatally struck, who goes down applauding the skill of his opponent.

But it was getting harder every day to keep his chin up. The schedule was brutal, even for the pilots. Dublin wasn't too proud to scrub bathrooms, but getting up at 5:00 AM seven days a week to do it, and then studying physics concepts that intimidated the crap out of him for eleven hours--it seemed less and less funny. After six weeks, the mood of the whole station was down. Whenever Dublin started to feel sorry for himself, he just had to look at the pit crews and the wire crews stumbling into the cafeteria every night. It started to look like a recurring zombie apocalypse. A couple of the wire ladies sat next to Dublin in his usual spot in the cafeteria. They complained bitterly, and daily: "My time is almost up! I've been here a year and eight months, jogging eleven hours a day; you go eleven point two feet, drive a spike, set the tension, pin the wire; walk eleven point two feet, drive a spike, set the tension, pin the wire...and for what?"

"So, what **do** you think all the wire is for?" asked Dublin one night. He had heard all kinds of theories, rumors, and supposed 'leaked information' about the purpose of this massive job. A few crackpots swore they knew all about it, but as is often the case in life, the more they claimed to know, the more completely they seemed to be off their rocker.

Some thought it was a newer sort of power relay that could be buried later if necessary, the quickest possible network to power basically the entire Earthward face of the Moon. Others were sure it was an early step towards terraforming the dead planetoid, possibly to regulate the surface temperature, freeing up gaseous elements forever trapped in the lunar soil to supply the rudiments of an Earth-like atmosphere. Or maybe the millions of miles of wire were being put in place to **collect** the sun's bountiful energy in a new, ultra-efficient way.

"I got no idea. You know, they **call** it wire, but one of the guys in my crew, he says it ain't even really wire. But he don't know what it is. I hope it's something to do with the whole terraforming thing. That would be cool, to know I'd been a little part of making the Moon into, like, a little Earth. But ain't nobody I know been able to tell me how that would work." She shrugged, and attacked her mashed potatoes with fresh vigor. "It must be important, that's all I know. They's been more of us working on that dang wire than on anything else, at least since I been here."

At least, according to this tired and broken woman, the wire crews seemed to be nearing the end. Everyday brought them closer and closer back to the Moonbase. Stories went around about the earlier days of the wire project, where battalions of MC's would be flown all the way across the Moon's broad face; thousands of miles. There they would have to camp in little pods and make daily sojourns until each little worker colony had advanced something like ten miles forward and five miles wide. Then help would return to advance their pods, maybe bringing reinforcements to replace the fallen if they were lucky.

In this little snow-globe world, where people petered out and died in a year or a year and a half, these short cycles effectively replaced the idea of 'generations' on Earth. Hearing a story from just four years ago meant you were hearing it from someone who had heard it from the generation before, who had heard it from the generation before. It was easy for things to pass into legend overnight. And surrounded as they were by wonders they had never previously imagined, and secrets that eluded conventional explanation, it was easy to accept almost any outlandish story as not only possible, but probable.

"I'm having trouble putting this huge wire project into the context of the 2043 World Lunar Pact...the one from the video. Unless the whole thing is sponsored by a multi-nation coalition." The wire-crew lady blinked at him, chewing elaborately on a pork rib. "You remember the video they showed us on the trip from Earth?"

There was more chewing and blinking. Finally, "Oh...I remember that. Yeah, with the Underdog commercials. Yeah, I don't think that 'World Lunar Pact' is a real thing." Then her crewmate sat down on the bench next to her and they started talking about 'Ernie's fake leg injury' before Dub could ask her what she meant.

~

Red-faced and peeling from daily radiation exposure, blue-faced from the insufferable cold, crazy from confinement, nerves and bodies stretched to their limits, numbed with grief from the loss of friend after friend after friend after friend, the two-thousand or so remaining Goners staggered, limping ghost-like into the cafeteria for an unexpected something or other.

It was May 22nd, 2126, six weeks in for the newest recruits. It was the day after Kaywin had told Dub and Pru the sad details of his former life. It was also a day that history would never forget--try as it might.

The attrition of the brutal labor had thinned their ragged ranks by almost five hundred souls. The mood of the huge room reflected this. The unexpected midday break was viewed with universal suspicion.

Suddenly the entire cafeteria went dark. There was a ten second pause as the crowd murmured in the total blackness. Then a single spotlight came to life in the central fountain area. A familiar, meticulously groomed face with a pencil-thin moustache squinted in its brightness. It was Acting-President Beauregard, lost in the hugeness of his lunch-lady getup, complete with latex gloves and hairnet. "Well! That is bright!" he drawled. "How is everybody? I am so excited to be with y'all on this very special day! What an honor to be here, to thank each and every one of you face to face for the incredible work you have done here. Absolutely incredible. Now. I'm going to show you something that a lot of you have been working on for a long long time. And then, after that, we are going to celebrate with lunch, first, then--" He had to pause for a minute as the crowd of starving Goners, unused to the luxury of a midday meal, burst into cheers. "And then--and then, you will have the whole rest of the day off!" This brought on an outburst of enthusiasm that seemed to startle Beauregard's refined sensibilities a little. When it subsided, he started to circle the fountain slowly in his ridiculous blue outfit. "But first, I want you to remember this day. May 22nd, 2126. People on Earth will remember it, but they won't be able to feel the same sense of pride about it that y'all will." He looked at his Sofee. "We have ten seconds. I want you to look at the television screens. This is the view from Earth. I think we have you watching from Grand Bassam Beach in Ivory Coast, Africa. Let's turn this spotlight off. Quick!"

At this exact moment, a villager deep in the early evening dimness of the Congo Jungle was stepping from the forest rim into a small clearing. He looked up at the skinny crescent Moon, and said something in his native tongue that was intended as tribute to the waning Queen of the Night. He stooped his tired old body down and picked up a double armful of dead branches that would serve as excellent firewood against the chill of the deepening night. He raised back up with a groan, and before he turned homeward, cast one more glance at the sky. Terror contorted his face, and for a moment his voice wouldn't work. Then the scream came out, and flinging the firewood in every direction, he took off at full speed back to his village.

The skinny crescent of the moon had suddenly turned full. And green. And Yellow. It had responded to the old man's prayer in a language he didn't understand.

'DRINK SPRITZ NADA!' it said.

13

Chiquitita

Three bicyclists in Spain tumbled over a cliff, one of them fatally. A nervous man in Belgium, down on one knee in front of his girlfriend on a beautiful warm night outside their favorite cafe, put the ring back in his pocket until tomorrow night and pretended he was tying his shoe. A gondolier in Venice lost his balance and tumbled into the canal. Shock was the reaction of Europe and Africa to this newest and hugest billboard in the history of advertising. North and South America would have to wait a few hours for the spectacle to rotate into view.

After five minutes of 'Drink Spritz Nada!' the moon flashed, over the red and white thumbs-up symbol known around the world, 'available at Uno Mundo.' This was gone in ten seconds, replaced by 'Fly Canadian Airways'. Then 'Lockjaw Chewing Gum' ('available at Uno Mundo'.) More followed, 'Ethical Investments', a preview of the soon-to-come Sofee 48 ('available at Uno Mundo'); the worst was the horror movie ad for 'Face in the Window 13'--a woman yanked back a curtain, and the entire face of the Moon was a menacing human mask that turned red and writhing and demonic. This one was remembered by small children around the world for the rest of their lives, even though it was pulled from the rotation after that first night.

Silence and confusion reigned momentarily in the cafeteria of Moonbase 2. This had not been one of the theories about the wire project. Nobody knew how to react. They had watched friends die for this. It was a huge result that seemed to mean nothing. After a few seconds, there were scattered loud laughs, but they were the kind of laughs that cover up a dangerous resentment.

The timing of the free lunch was no accident, coming as it did on the heels of the big reveal. Neither was dessert. And neither was the free time.

Prudence was nonplussed; she was much more interested in her better-than-usual meal of a genuine pork chop, carrots and quinoa. Kaywin was slightly plussed. Dub was excited at the historical significance of the event, and the science and the politics behind it.

"Are you noticing the smokescreen they're trying to create? Bet you anything Uno Mundo is behind all of this, but we're only seeing them for a little flash at a time. If there's an angry kneejerk public reaction, it will probably be against Spritz Nada, and Canadian Airways."

The woman who sat next to him, the one from the wire crew--they never got her name (and she was dead a week later) was unusually quiet. "Are you shocked?" Dublin asked her. "Are you angry?"

She didn't look up from her food. "Well, I knowed it wasn't no childrens' hospital..."

While they chatted, several of the TV screens around them switched to a live feed of some news conference:

"Senator Brandenberg! How long has this project been in the works, and how have you kept it a secret?"

Brandenberg was at the microphone, glowing like a new mother. "Well, the world has been begging for this for twelve years or more, ever since the science was proposed in 'New World Citizen'...and our employees are just good at keeping secrets. If you pay people enough, and treat them well enough, they will keep a secret!"

"Senator Brandenberg! Is it true that a large percentage of the profits from this advertising will go to feeding the homeless?"

Okay, so it was clear that this was a news conference full of hand-picked and possibly bribed reporters.

"How did you get that information? Yes, it's true, but that was never supposed to be public knowledge."

"Senator! Senator! How many jobs were created at the moment that switch was flipped?"

Brandenberg, in a sharp-looking suit, clean-shaven, with his graying blond ponytail, laughed heartily. "I remember seeing the number. I couldn't tell you. It was in the millions."

"Senator! Senator Brandenberg! Will the full moon be used for advertising, or just when it is waxing or waning?" God, these softball questions...

Another laugh. "What was your name? Steven, I think? No, Steven, we will protect the right of world citizens to their beautiful, natural full moon. We will protect and defend that right."

Watching from her cafeteria bench on the Moon, Prudence groaned into the steam from her carrots. "Ugh. I hate his stupid little scrunchy."

"I hate that whole look, with the three-piece suit and the ponytail," said Dub. "It's duplicitous."

Kaywin turned to Pru. "You know the story behind the blue scrunchy, right?"

"What story?"

Dublin was constantly surprised at the bubble this girl had grown up in. "You really don't know? I thought everybody knew that story. He's only told it like a thousand times!"

Kaywin grimaced at Dub's tactlessness, and jumped in to prevent him from essentially calling Pru stupid one more time. "The blue scrunchy was the one his little sister was wearing when she drowned. He was ten and she was what, six?"

Dub had just shoved an enormous piece of pork chop into his mouth. "Yef. Sixf."

"They were swimming together in the lake on their family farm, and she started to go under. He couldn't get to her in time. Now he uses it to drum up sympathy with voters. He says it was the big turning point for him, when he suddenly realized how precious life was; he never takes a moment of it for granted, and so on. He wears her blue scrunchy as a reminder, a keepsake. You haven't heard this?"

Pru had stopped eating. She was looking straight ahead at the Senator blabbering away on the screen over Dublin's head. In a kind of trance, she shook her head slowly in response to Kaywin's question. "Are you okay?" Dub asked.

"You guys are so innocent" she mumbled mysteriously. "Pretty sure that's not a keepsake. I think it's a trophy."

When they left the cafeteria, the normally clingy Dublin surprised them by announcing that he needed some time alone.

"Are you alright?" asked Kaywin.

"Oh yeah, totally; there's just something I need to work on."

"Is it more poems?" teased Prudence.

Dub looked horrified. "How did you know about my poems? Kaywin!"

"She asked me what I was reading! Then she swore she wouldn't mention it! So we see what a promise from Prudence is worth...I didn't **show** them to her or anything..."

"Uuuuuhhhhg! Now she's gonna want to read them, and once she reads them I'll never get rid of her!" He had heard guys use reverse psychology on girls before. It couldn't hurt to try.

"Pssssh! You **wish**!" And he did; she had no idea how much he wished. She changed the subject right away before this progressed any further. "Kaywin--you can say no if you want--but if you have some time to kill, do you think you could..." Both of the boys were staring at her. She was clearly about to ask for help, or advice or something, and it was so unlike her fiercely independent self that they couldn't help themselves. "...do you think you could maybe--**what**? You guys are freaking me out!"

"Sorry..."

"Sorry, I mean--sorry..."

"Do you think you could show me the basics of piloting? I mean, the very **basic** basics, like how to open the cruiser door and stuff."

Well, this was borderline shocking. Kaywin shook off his

startlement. "Yeah, uh, sure; I'd love to." He tried to play it cool, but his old heart thrilled. It had been years since he had taught anybody anything. He was surprised to feel this sensation. He used to teach Victoria all kinds of things, but during group therapy, when he had to list all of the things he missed about her, he had never thought to mention 'teaching her things'.

They were about to part ways, Dublin to his room right around the corner, and Kaywin and Prudence down to the hangars. Kaywin turned back to Dub. "Does this mean we're not hanging out tonight?"

"Oh yes, we're still hanging out! Actually it's very important that you be there, at the usual time, both of you..."

"For the poetry reading?" Pru jabbed.

"Ha! Worse! Much worse! Alright. See you guys then." He stood rooted to the spot, transfixed by the majestic bobbing rainbow of Pru's hair. As soon as they rounded a corner, he darted to the little janitor's closet opposite the cafeteria, and used his key to sneak inside.

When Prudence sat behind the wheel of *Tomorrow Never Knows* it was love at first sight. The idea of piloting something, being in **control** of something, compelled her deeply.

There were knobs, levers and switches everywhere. The knobs, blue to match the outside of the cruiser (why not?) looked and felt like porcelain, reminding her of the cabinet pulls in her Grandmother's kitchen. Her Grandma had died when Pru was seven, and she hadn't thought about her for so long. She probably couldn't have described the sweet old lady's kitchen until now, when the memory overtook her after a hard nine-year chase.

The best thing about the blue porcelain pulls in her Grandma's kitchen was that little Pru was actually allowed to **pull** them; she could open whatever cabinet she wanted and get out whatever she wanted to eat or drink. She felt safe at 'Gamma's' house, something she couldn't say about any other spot in the world except maybe her secret place in the woods behind her apartment in Geyserville. And she had never wished that her Gamma would die, something she couldn't say about anyone else in her family. Well, except of course her four-month old stepsister Perstephanie.. She stayed with Janelle, though. Prudence had only seen Baby Perstephanie twice. She was adorable, with a mop-top of dark hair, a little button nose, starfish hands and corn-niblet toes.

Some kind of timer went off inside of Pru, reminding her that she would never see these people again, and it was time to move on to less girly things. Happy memories anyway were like one or two souvenir coins...they were pretty to look at, but what was one supposed to do with them if they didn't have a collection?

"This is the lever that releases reactant into the fusion chamber. I've been out eight times and haven't moved this past the minimum setting. It's so hard to control. Jennifer's design is great, but she's limited by having to install it in this old tub."

Prudence was back from daydream-land. "Is it the best one?"

"It's hard to say just yet because we haven't been able to really let it go all out. So far *Purple Haze* has been the best. Jerkboy is a surprisingly good pilot. I would never tell him that to his face, but he's really good." Someone caught his eye through the glass of the windshield, and he pointed at the two approaching figures. "You know who else is really good?"

"Who?"

"The tall ascetic. I'm not sure how he does all the verbal commands without talking, but he's pretty darn good."

"I feel sorry for his co-pilot! Does she have to wear a gas-mask?"

Kaywin laughed. "Trust me. She complains about it every day." At this point, the ascetic, and his student-engineer Larry drew even with the open cockpit door of Kaywin's cruiser.

"What's up, Lafontaine?" said Larry, in a casual tone that clashed with his companion's religious-zealot demeanor. "Do you guys have a right-angle torque hex?"

Kaywin squinted and summoned a mental picture of the tool as described. "Yes. I think so." He climbed past Prudence and down the little ladder. He disappeared with Larry back at the tail end of the blue cruiser. Prudence kept her hands on the wheel and looked down on the gangly ascetic, who was gawking with off-putting blissfulness back up at her.

Prudence had some curiosity about this man and his motives. "Can I ask you a question?" she said. "What did you do? Like, what are you atoning for; what exactly did you *do?*"

The man's smile turned sad. He looked down and fumbled inside the breast of his filthy robes. He took out some kind of ancient-looking wooden pencil thing, with a little string hanging near the tip. Prudence had never seen one, but if her great-great-great-grandmother had been alive she could have identified it as a 'grease-pencil'. With his disgusting robe-sleeve, the ascetic wiped the **3.4780** off of his forehead. Then, with practiced quickness, he wrote **2 bad 2 tell** across his brow.

"But if you don't tell people what you did, aren't you just feeding off their respect and admiration for your holiness, when it sure sounds like you don't **deserve** it?" The man smiled weakly and grimly. It was doubtful that Prudence knew what a real smile even looked like; her pointed barbs seemed to bring out the same mirthless grimace in everyone. He was taken aback. He laughed a short, surprised, ashamed little cough of a laugh, then shut up. He looked away for a second, and when he turned back his dark eyes were brimming with tears. Another forehead wipe.

Best i can do, he wrote.

At this point, Kaywin and Larry returned. "She'll kill me if you don't bring it back," said Kaywin.

"On my word, man. Thanks!" As the two walked off, Kaywin stared after them. He had noticed something for the first time about the ascetic's face. But it was probably nothing. He shook it off.

He had also noticed that the penitent man appeared to be on the verge of tears, and had 'best i can do' scrawled across his forehead. He looked up at Prudence. "What the heck did you do?"

They spent a full three hours together, poking around *Tomorrow Never Knows* and a few of the other cruisers. Prudence got to explore the entire hangar, and their conversation eventually ranged beyond torque ratios and gravitational coefficients. Pru teasingly lamented the daily torture of her own job in the tunnels, compared to the apparently cushy lifestyle of the pilots.

"Well…" mused Kaywin "…you're not wrong…this is obviously far less brutal on a day-to-day basis." He lowered his voice discretely. "But between you and me, it's very well-understood that two or three of these ships are going to blow up the first time their modifiers kick in. And they say the race on Valentine's Day is always a massacre."

"I'd still trade with you in a heartbeat…when I wake up in the morning I feel like my arms are going to snap right off."

"I've heard you're really good at it," Kaywin told her as they walked slowly between the rows of brightly colored cruisers.

"No, I think the last two girls were just really **bad** at it."

"Sephal said the other day you got three relays finished, and started a fourth. He said the shaft-warmers can't keep up with you."

"Just cuz everybody else stinks doesn't mean I'm any good…"

Kaywin laughed. "Is that going to be the title of your autobiography?"

"Ha! That's about right! God, who would read **that** garbage?"

Kaywin smiled his sad half-smile. "I think you could sell two copies or so…but seriously--take a little credit--one of the guys told Sephal that the last girl never finished even **two** relays in a day…"

"Yeah…she's still working on hole eleven." She stepped over a pile of greasy rags, bracing herself on the orange and yellow belly of *Sunshine Superman.*

"Jeez, are they going to just leave her there forever?"

"I wish. Naw, whenever I get caught up on connecting the relays I have to double back and pull her out." Kaywin winced for the dead girl he had never even met, but also for Prudence herself...he had a mental flash of someone pulling **her** dead body out of an icy hole, maybe just weeks or days from now.

"You can have my pudding that night," Prudence added casually. Kaywin stopped. The mental rigors of the last six weeks had defogged him somewhat, but he was still dazed enough from his tragedy of four years ago to think, just for a second, that she had read his thoughts, that she meant the night **she** died. She studied the concern on his rugged face with open disdain. "Cuz pulling dead bodies out of holes is probably not great for the appetite...Holy crap, what happened to this one?"

They had come to the back of the massive hangar. Tucked into the corner was a formerly white cruiser, with the back-end completely burned out. Charry streaks extended all the way up to the nose. "That's *White Rabbit,*" said Kaywin. "She's on a little vacation right now until they get her up and running. She lost her pilot and co-pilot on her first time out." Pru's eyes were wide under her gay-pride bangs. "She was wicked fast though..."

The dingy vessel had indeed shown promise. Her engineer was supposed to be some kind of genius, but he was a spoiled brat who had thrown a tantrum when he'd first laid eyes on the ship he'd been assigned. After tinkering with it for a week, he gave up. Then two men had died just trying to shake the rust off it. He stopped even showing up for free practice, until Lindsay and MacFray forced him--the Commander wasn't paying for some whiny kid to spend a year-long vacation at the Moonbase without even trying. He had repaired *White Rabbit* just enough to get it back off the ground, but Professor Lindsay was not convinced that it was safe enough. Since then he had sat in a folding chair, never taking off his sunglasses and 'leafing' through science journals on his Sofee.

The ship was an understood death trap. Its strobe-rate couldn't even be approximated to the second decimal because of the vessel's own vibrations. "There's a Valentine's Day betting pool down here," said Kaywin as they lingered under the scorch-marks. "The bravest investors give it five seconds at enhanced speed before it blows..."

When they got to room 4324 that evening, it was 7:01. Dublin whooshed the door aside after the second knock. Kaywin's third knock wound up tapping the younger man on the lips. "You're late," he said, and hurried them in. Kaywin looked at the lipstick-stain on his knuckles and puzzled mightily.

As always, the Kalaysian three-star sat in his top bunk on the right-hand side of the room, tapping away feverishly at his Sofee, completely lost in it and oblivious to the shenanigans of the three friends.

Dublin was being unusually distracted and gruff. He had gotten a hairnet from the cafeteria, but it was woefully inadequate for the containment of his voluminous afro. He was wearing a plush pink bathrobe that he'd gotten from God-knows-where. Once into the brightness of his room, with the door shut behind them, they could see clearly that yes, indeed, he was wearing makeup, and lots of it. A quick glance was enough to tell that he had taken a lot of time with it, and still done a terrible job. The ends of the wispy straggles of his shadowy moustache were painted red.

"Is it too late to leave?" asked Prudence, only half-joking.

"Yes," answered Dublin as he guided her to her usual seat on his bottom mattress. He had, a couple of weeks ago, dragged the entire left-hand bunk bed toward the door, so it was more diagonal to Ving's bunk than straight across from it. He had done this the day he had discovered a seven inch-long sharpened piece of steel under the Kalaysian's pillow. He was a half a second closer to the door now, and on the rare occasions that Ving wasn't in the room, he practiced rolling backwards out of the bed and getting the door open. He had improved his time from 3.1 seconds down to a mere 1.6. As an added precaution, he now kept a length of lead pipe under his own pillow. Kaywin and Pru thought he was ridiculous.

Kaywin went to take his normal seat as well, but Dublin grabbed his arm. "I need you over here." He walked the older man over to a spot pretty much right against the cold metal frame of Ving's bunk. "I mean, **please.** Can you stand right...here? No--wait--take a half step to your left. Now don't move."

And just like that the strange ugly boy in drag darted into the tiny bathroom, which was on the right-hand side immediately as you entered the Spartan room, and shut the door. He popped it back open and stuck his head out. "Nobody move. The show will begin as scheduled, at 7:09." Again the door shut.

"Not 7:05...not 7:15...it starts promptly at 7:09. Weirdo…" said Pru. She looked behind her and wondered if she could form Dublin's pillow and blanket into a mock-up of herself, and then slip out unnoticed. No. It was already 7:07. She resigned herself to the situation.

"Well, he needs time to--," Kaywin never finished the thought. The lights had gone out completely. For a second, he thought there might have been a power failure, and his blood ran cold. Any such failure here would mean freezing to death, or asphyxiation, within hours. But then from the heart of the blackness, a Spanish guitar began playing. A glowing yellow light about the size and shape of a pencil appeared on the cinderblock wall straight opposite the seated Prudence. It sputtered for a second or two like an old-timey sparkler on the Fourth of July. Being the only light in the room, it transfixed their gaze. The flamboyant undulations of the guitar seemed to portend something bullfightish. Suddenly, the light unfurled downward into a holographic banner, fluttering in a gentle, imaginary breeze. *"Tonight Only!"* it read. Kaywin and Prudence watched, bemused, as one by one similar banners began to unroll in a circle surrounding them:

"Tonight Only! No Yesterday!"
"Tonight Only! No Tomorrow!"
"Tonight Only! No Earth!"
"Tonight Only! No Moon!"
"Tonight Only! No Fru's Dad!" (Fru?)
"Tonight Only! No Lost Loved Ones!"
"Tonight Only! No Girls Who Borrow Your Winter Hat On a Cold Day and Take the Time to Stitch 'Why Are You So Ugly Dublin?' Inside It!"

"Tonight Only! No Kalaysian Three-Star Waiting to Stab All of Us!"

This last one rippled downward at Kaywin's right shoulder, completing the circle where Ving wouldn't be able to see it if he ever did turn around.

This was all amusing enough, until the Spanish guitar stopped, and a tune began that Kaywin had sworn he would never listen to again.

It was 'Chiquitita.'

At the first dramatic plucking of the guitar, a bizarre image faded into view in the perfect center of the dim room. It was caped in black, with its face hidden in the crook of its left arm, its right arm raised upward and outward expressively. A black bolero trimmed in gold crowned the figure's slightly downturned head. Matching gold braids crisscrossed the legs of the comically undersized matador breeches. The posed holographic figure in black peeked up over the crook of his arm for a second and spoke quickly. "I know that banner says 'Fru' instead of 'Pru', but this program is so weird that it was actually way easier to record this disclaimer than it would have been to go back and fix it."

Suddenly the pre-recorded Dublin was too impassioned by the song's instrumental introduction to hold still any longer, and launched himself into wide sideways sweeps and spins.

The only light in the small gray room emanated from this sparkling matador--this astounding, dancing electric Dublin-ghost--the fluttering banners, and Pru's rainbow hair. Its movements to the medium tempo of the haunting ballad were lumbering and brusque, and yet so utterly carefree, so devoid of the worry of judgment, that Kaywin and Prudence couldn't have looked away if the Moonbase had blown up around them. They were both prepared to blush bright red and avert their eyes at this supremely awkward and sentimental gesture of Dublin's, but a funny thing happened to both of them. When the matador swooped left for a second, their eyes met. They were reading each others' faces, as people often do in unexpected situations, to see if the reaction of their own instincts was appropriate, or to see if the eyes of the other were broadcasting a better way to feel about it. Their eyes registered the same. This bizarre gesture of Dublin's was done with such good intent, sweetness, and total abandon that the man-past-caring and the girl-who-never-stood-a-chance both showed open bemusement in their faces. The unsightly boy had, like them, so little time left in the world, yet he had clearly spent several of those precious hours choreographing (literally) this spectacle.

Pru's eyebrows were raised so high in surprise that they disappeared completely behind her rainbow bangs. Only the corners of her heavily lip-sticked mouth, which were raised slightly *up* instead of their usual slightly down, betrayed her true emotion.

A woman's voice rang out clear and strong, as she took her time with the beautiful melody:

> *Chiquitita, tell me what's wrong...*
> *You're enchained by your own sorrow...*
> *In your eyes, there is no hope*
> *For tomorrow...*

Then something new seemed to catch Pru's attention, from around the corner where Kaywin couldn't see. Her eyes widened almost to the point of horror, and Kaywin prepared to launch himself between the young lady and whatever threat was emerging from the bathroom.

Wow. Just wow.

Six, ten, fifty emotions assaulted Kaywin all at once as the real Dublin, walking on tiptoe slowly, as if in a dream, nimbled hypnotically onto the open dance floor.

He was done up like Kaywin's poor dead daughter.

It was a crude mock-up, to be sure, but there was no mistaking it. It was clearly based on the one picture he had shared with Dublin.

> *How I hate to see you like this...*
> *There is no way you can deny it*

The lyrics and the haunting tune were all coming back to him, though he hadn't dared to listen to the song, their special song together, for probably ten years. He experienced a flash of fury at Dublin's stupid crassness. What kind of idiot fashions a red dress out of a tablecloth, writes the word 'love' across the chest with white paint, makes a wig out of a mop-head, complete with pig-tails tied up with red ribbon, all in simulation of his alleged friend's dead daughter.

The sweetest kind of idiot.

The dialogue inside of Kaywin's head was rapid-fire, out of necessity--he was sure it would be ruinous to their fledgling friendship to punch Dublin square in the face, so he needed to find some kind of restraint inside of himself, and quickly. Victoria--I mean Dublin--was coming right at him, her hands holding out something droopy and black to him.

I-I-I-I can see
That you are oh so sad, so quiet ...she mouthed

"Is this guy for real?"	*Yes.*
"Has he lost his mind?"	*A long time ago, if he ever had it.*
"Does he have any idea how of-fensive this is?"	*No...maybe*
"How many hours did he spend on this joke?"	*Six and a half...and it's not a joke.*
"This is way too soon for me to dive into this kind of memory."	*When would it **NOT** be too soon?*

"You have a point there. But I do way better on my own with this kind of emotion. I barely know these kids."

Kids? These are the last friends you will ever have.

"These are the-- "

Look at the countdown on your wrist.

"These are the last friends I will ever have."

"These are the last friends I will ever have."

Kaywin's eyes refocused on the monstrosity of nature six feet in front of him, this Dublinita. Though his lumbering body was moving with slow, measured drag steps, like the bride of Frankenstein coming down the aisle, his arms, and especially his face, were alive with incredible drama, mouthing the words of the song, and channeling the meaning of the words out through his upper body in wildly over-the-top hilarious gesticulations. It looked like his black eyebrows might come flying off at any second. The equally ridiculous matador had been describing elaborate pirouetting leaps and circles around 'her' as she advanced. Now the bullfighter had paused right next to Kaywin--he registered this out of the corner of his left eye--and was removing his black cloak as if to place it on Kaywin's shoulders. *So this is why I had to stand right here.* He exhaled, and the fury, already diminished, left him completely. He smiled slightly. Dublin, recognizing from this smile that he wasn't going to get punched in the face, smiled too, right as the holographic matador fizzled out. Dub tossed the real black cloak at Kaywin, who caught it, but shook his head. *No way, dude.*

Dublin in his red dress was unfazed. Unexpectedly, he tapped his Sofee, and held up his countdown. He held it aloft centrally and danced around it, then pointed at Kaywin's wrist and held out his hands.

Kaywin's hands were already tying the cloak on as his brain repeated, *"These are the last friends I will ever have."* Dublin-ita grabbed his hands, pulled him in, and they were dancing.

> *Chiquitita tell me the truth…*
> *I'm a shoulder you can cry on…*
> *Yo-o-o-o-ur best friend,*
> *I'm the one you can rely on…*

So this was unbelievably awkward at first, two men, both terrible dancers, trying to dance in approximated gravity suits on the Moon. Whose hand was supposed to be on whose waist--Kaywin's hand--no, Dublin's hand, no Kaywin's, on Dublin's waist. Then where was Dublin's hand…Kaywin's shoulder--no, Kaywin's waist; no, that's not right; back to Kaywin's shoulder; all while laughing uncontrollably. In seconds, they had found some kind of rhythm, halting, because Dublin was still committed to hamming it up to the cheesiness of the lyrics:

> *You were always sure of yourself…*
> *Now I see you've broken a feather…*

Dub had to break free for the next line, which, as it was about to lead into the joyous explosion of the chorus, he recognized as comically critical to his performance. He dropped to his knees, one eyebrow hunkered down, the other raised ridiculously. The lips of his mouth, wide-open, as well as the fingers of his outstretched hand, all trembled with violent, operatic emotion.

> *I-I-I-I-I hope*
> *We can..patch it up together…*

The music almost stopped for a beat and a half; Dublin's head dropped with it; then both exploded upward into the ecstatic abandonment of the chorus. Now they were spinning, wheeling, laughing, singing and dipping all at once. **'Tonight Only'**, **'Tonight Only'**, **'Tonight Only'** kept flashing in Kaywin's retinas as they spun, and, mid pirouette, he realized that it was working. Even if it was for **'Tonight Only'**, he had dropped the pain of all the days and nights **before** tonight, as well as all the dread and apprehension of the dwindling days and nights to come. **Tonight Only. Brilliant.**

> *Sing a new song, Chiquitita…*
> *Try once more, like you did before*
> *Sing a new song, Chiquitita…*

As the raucous polka of the chorus settled back into the slower tempo of the verses, the young man and the older man found themselves completely by chance standing arm-in-arm directly in front of Prudence.

She was a tougher nut to crack. She was still sitting on Dublin's lower bunk, knees together, hands together, pretty face still locked in mock-derision. Both boys noticed however that her beautiful eyes were softer, and her mouth was closer to smiling than either of them had ever seen it. Unrehearsed, and right on time, they each reached their free hand toward her. Again her eyebrows raised, she crossed her arms, and she shook her head in slow motion. The boys smiled bigger, and again without planning it they both tapped the morbid and surreal numbers counting down on their 47's. They reached again toward the little lost lady, and that's when a true miracle happened.

She grasped their hands, got up, banged her head on the crossbar, laughed it off, and began to dance with them.

So the walls came tumbling down...
And your love's blown out a candle...

They went around in a circle, four steps right, four steps back left, four steps right, four back left. Dublin couldn't believe what he had accomplished and it was all over his face. He was beaming, with his little girl wig all askew. Stupid tears of joy, just a couple, spilled out of Kaywin's eyes and rolled unchecked down his bristly cheeks. He didn't wipe them away, because he didn't care, for one, and also he didn't dare unclasp the hands he was clasping.

All is gone
And it seems too hard to handle

Chiquitita tell me the truth...
There is no way you can deny it...
I-I-I-I-I see

That you are oh so sad, so quiet…

Then again, the uplift into the exultant chorus. They gave up on the back and forth now, and skipped like schoolgirls in one direction, laughing, their centrifugal force pushing them outward and requiring firmer hand-grasps to maintain their structural integrity.

The song seemed to reach its conclusion, which was good, because the three of them were near collapsing, but then it rebounded into a silly staccato piano fadeout. They had unclasped sweaty hands, and suddenly Prudence thought that she would make them pay for dragging her into this, and she broke into a ludicrous rapid-fire high step in time to the music, her knees almost touching her chest on every lift. Kaywin and Dub lost their minds laughing, Dublin having just enough breath to say 'FB' to his Sofee. He was smart enough to know that the happiest moment of his miserable life was happening right now, and he wanted to capture something of it. When Pru was done, Dub had one final trick in store. He backed up toward the bathroom and got a running start. Kaywin saw him coming at the last moment and barely had time to catch the solid young man/woman. He staggered back against the Kalaysian's bunk, hollering, "Not light! Not light on your feet!" before they both crashed to the ground and laughed until they cried.

Kaywin went to sleep with a placid smile on his face that night, but it didn't last. He had the dream, the horrible, horrible dream yet again.

It was all so real, every detail. It wasn't their house, but he knew that in the dream, it was their house. It was his night to get up with the baby. Victoria was a terrible sleeper, getting up three or four, or five times every night, without exception. And every time she had to be walked back to sleep, or she would scream and scream, and keep them both awake. So they took turns, so at least one of them could get some kind of sleep every other night. It was barely surviving, but it was the only system they had come up with to not lose their ever-loving minds.

He was exhausted, beyond exhausted, as he padded back and forth along the upstairs hallway in his stockinged feet. He felt like he was patrolling up and down, with the baby nestled on his shoulder, on the lookout for whatever was terrifying her. He sang song after song after song to her; none of them working particularly well. He settled into 'Have I the Right' by the Honeycombs, just because he liked the sound of his own voice singing that one. After forty-five numbing minutes, he could feel Victoria's tiny body relaxing and her breathing growing regular. She was so warm and soft and wonderful up against his shoulder and his neck that he, too, began to relax.

He woke up in a blind terror as he pitched headfirst down the stairs, crushing his tiny baby beneath him. She was dead instantly, broken utterly, and it was his fault. He snatched her up, horror and self-loathing consuming him. He ran with her to the bedroom he shared with Nadine. She was already awake, not so much from the noise as from the massive disturbance in her maternal instinct. She saw what had happened and reacted with strange calmness, sitting up in bed and turning on the lamp. "Oh. She was supposed to have a soccer game Saturday. We'll have to e-mail the coach." This didn't make sense. Then Nadine reached into the bedside table and pulled something out. It was a gun. This, too, didn't make sense; when did they get a *gun?* Before Kaywin could speak the question the gun was against his wife's temple and he was shouting "No! Nadine! Shoot **ME!**"

Then the gun went off, and he woke up screaming. It used to be Ro-Ro standing over him when this would happen, now it was a succession of strangers in a strange land, Les back in Manchester; Lantaff or Steven in Houston, now Sephal and Jason here on the godforsaken Moon.

He apologized to Jason, who grunted as he returned to his bunk. Kaywin lay there for a while, looking at the numbers counting down on his mortal wrist. Just a while ago, when he was laughing with his friends, the numbers were moving too fast. Now they were moving too slow.

Prudence lay awake for a little while, thinking: Grandma's kitchen with the blue porcelain pulls. Baby Perstephanie with her corn niblet toes. Laughing and dancing with...with friends. How many souvenir coins **does** it take to make a collection?

Dublin Dunne didn't fall asleep for three hours. He wasn't counting, but he watched the fifteen second clip of Prudence laughing and high-stepping more than eighty-five times before drifting off to sleep with a goofy grin on his unfortunate face.

∼

Houston, Texas US of A
June 10, 2126…11:12 AM

The summer of 2126 was a memorably hot one. This did not prevent Ms. Octavia Hopkins from continuing to park her blue bullet car every day in spot 0004, and peacefully demonstrating for changes in the MCP.

She stood there on Tuesday, June 10th in sleeveless black funeral attire (donated by a local designer who had seen her story on the news) in the partial shade, under a giant hat, fanning herself.

A scraping sort of clicky sound from far away caught her attention, and she turned to pinpoint its source.

The parking lot was huge, and sloped down a little, then back up, as it approached the MCPNH campus, creating a miniature valley through which a little stream flowed. This was the same stream that had busted through a makeshift dam and caused a commotion at the last mass-funeral ceremony in April.

Far away through the heat that rippled off the blazing asphalt, Octavia saw a lone figure approaching slowly. He was overdressed for the weather in a heat-absorbing black outfit. Even at this distance she could tell that the fancy suit was too small, as if the man had had a massive growth spurt over the course of his journey from the campus.

Vincent Beauregard had a sense of drama about him, and a sense of respect, and dignity and ceremony. ***Common*** sense was unfortunately ***not*** part of this little collection.

He finally had the legal documents prepped to oust the proud Ms. Hopkins from the parking lot owned by the unreachable Mr. Nebraska. It was a 'Third Party Eviction on Grounds of Philosophical Infringement' (or something like that). He could have served these to Ms. Hopkins with a single touch of his Sofee, from the safe distance of his office, and been done with it. But he actually respected the woman nearly as an equal, and thought it would be dramatic and dignified to walk out to her in person and deliver the notice.

Simmons, in Legal, had warned him that it was 97 degrees out, and that the half-mile walk was partially uphill. But Beauregard was no lily-flower. He was determined to play the hero. Things had started out alright. True, his tiny, about-to-burst pants limited the length of his stride to about midway between a C3PO shuffle and a normal human step, but he spurred himself onward down the grassy hill by singing 'I Shall Overcome' to himself.

Things got dicey when he started up the mild incline beyond the stream. He had to stop repeatedly to catch his breath and dab at his forehead with a lace handkerchief. He got about two-thirds of the way to Octavia Hopkins before stopping under a skinny tree, one of four scattered across the huge lot. It had been a brave march, but it was also brave to acknowledge one's limits. He called back to the main building for a car. "Make sure it is ice-cold inside pleeeeaase" he drawled effeminately. The grey bullet arrived two minutes later. It was so cold inside that Beauregard could see his gasping breath. It carried him the last, heroic 800 feet and deposited him in front of the curious Octavia Hopkins.

Getting out and making a show of straightening his black suit---which had been too tight to shift *out* of place during his walk, and would have been too tight to shift ***back into*** place if it had---he extended a freshly sanitized hand to the waiting woman. She took it and shook it, staring Vincent Beauregard in the face the whole time.

"Sofee," said the exhausted executive "please transfer the third party eviction documents to Ms. Hopkins' Sofee."

Octavia's wrist dinged, and she scanned the 'papers' that were supposed to shut down her protest for good. She nodded in understanding of what she was reading. Then she said to her wrist "Sofee, please send Mr. Beauregard the State of Texas Right of Refusal to Vacate Premises Specific to Third Party Eviction on Grounds of Philosophical Infringement, signed on June 3rd, 2126 by Texas Governor Lewis Brady."

Beauregard reddened beyond the pinkness brought on by his physical exertion. He read the documents that she had finalized a week earlier, and laughed bitterly to see the signature of his friend, the Governor, at he bottom. This was the day that he realized that this was not going to be a mere skirmish, but an all-out war. "Well-played" he said, and got back into the grey bullet. "Car! Take me back to headquarters. And slam this door!"

14

Girl

The next morning Pru woke up with a strange feeling. There had been an idea dancing around in her subconscious since all the way back in Houston, and now she was ready; she was done wasting time. She felt determination, purpose, and focus for the first time since...ever. It didn't feel half bad.

She rolled out of bed and turned off her alarm with the fully formed thought in her mind: *If that goofball Dublin can do it, so can I. If Jerkboy can do it, so can I. Someone else can connect these blasted relays. I'm getting into the pilot program.*

She knew it could happen; this group of engineers had lost a couple of pilots already, and they were barely getting warmed up. That meant that two alternates had already moved up into co-pilot positions, and Dublin was now third in line for advancement. They were going to need more alternates from somewhere.

Six grueling weeks had gone by. Six more would pass before the next class of MCs would roll into town. There was a window of opportunity there, and Prudence intended to jump through it. It wasn't even the easy work that appealed to her so much (though it would be nice to not almost freeze to death every day) as it was the thought of being trusted with something that important. And the freedom, and the control. She had watched from the pits a couple of times when some of the cruisers took off and accelerated in whatever direction they felt like. It looked like powerful and elegant fun. She had heard about 'fun' before. She hadn't forgotten for a second that she was here to die, but for the first time in her life, for whatever reason, she was starting to think that the hardships of her short life had earned her something more. She thought maybe the world owed her a little fun.

She had her usual five minutes in the shared bathroom to put on her face for the day. Something like a sense of...frivolity...came over her, and she tried something brand new. She looked in the mirror and closed her eyes. Reaching up under the left side of her hair she fiddled at the controls blindly. She could feel the length approaching her thin shoulders, and knew that was about the limit of what she could fit inside her helmet. So she let off of that button. She held the other one down for four more seconds and stopped. This would be her hair for the day, whatever it looked like.

Oh gross... she thought, and almost redid it, but she had made a promise to herself to stick with the random results. Her hair hung down in curls, glowing green. However it wasn't a bright green, but a pulsing, drab olive. Random thin brown lines simulated forest debris. She sighed, opening her makeup kit. *Radioactive kidnapping victim it is...* She had to do some mixing and layering, but she did walk out of the bathroom four minutes later satisfied. She went with dirty scratched cheeks and eyes that looked red from crying. *Not too bad,* she thought. *I'll just have to have an answer ready cuz people are going to ask what happened to me all day long.*

"God, Girlfriend; what happened to you?" said Jordache before the bathroom door had even finished sliding open.

"I had a bad dream."

It was a little easier going down to the pits with this fresh determination, and with the mindset that nothing could stop her from moving toward her goal.

She worked harder than she ever had before, completing four holes in a single day. None of the unlucky petites who had been thrust into this wretched duty before her had ever completed even **two** in a day. The shaft-warmers were almost getting frustrated with her as they tried to keep up.

She figured that when it came to the question of transferring out, she had to start by asking **somebody, sometime**, so when she was pulled from the fourth hole like a fish out of a frozen Minnesota Lake, and the little cluster of fellow PC3s who had gathered to watch began clapping their silver oven mitts together silently, she figured there was no time like the present, and approached Dorna Lee.

"Ms. Lee, can I talk to you for a second?"

"Yes, but **Dorna** Lee is my **first** name." She switched to public frequency for a second. "Guys, let's bring it in for the day! Lateral Advancer Team, please respond! Lateral Advance--"

"Acknowledged; Lateral Advancers headed your way!"

"So, anyway, Ms. Dorna, I was--"

"Ms. Dorna Lee--one name, three syllables, 'Dorna Lee'."

"Sorry. So, what do I do if I want to transfer to piloting?"

Dorna Lee, who had her attention focused on the ridge, waiting for the Shaft-Warmers and Lateral Advancers to limp into view over its crest, turned suddenly toward Prudence. The entire Moonbase reflected off the glass of her helmet. "Well, you could start by maybe not being so good at **this!**" She looked genuinely caught off guard, but there was also a motherly concern in her tone and on her worn face. "Look, I gotta be honest with you kid; transfers do happen, but it's **who** the Program needs, **when** they need them, and **where** they need them. Otherwise we'd have two thousand pilots, and no Moonbase. Prudence looked down the short distance from her helmet to the lunar soil, and kicked at it unhappily. "We got way behind on these relays when Dottie got stuck. We were behind even before that, really." She sighed. "I absolutely refuse to make you any promises, because I have no control over the situation. But if you can go at the pace you did today, we could be caught up in six weeks, by the time the new class arrives. I can get them to maybe call Houston and have them look out for another Mole, but this is a lot of 'ifs', you understand?" Most of LPC3 had now assembled, requiring her attention. "Prudence!" she said, turning back after having walked a few steps away. "Don't forget; you signed away **everything** when you signed up, okay? No promises!"

Pru nodded, all of the information sinking in, the good and the bad. The little area was filling up with LPC3s. Many of them she knew by name now. She was the youngest of them by far, and the littlest by even farther. They piled up in front of Dorna Lee for roll call, while Prudence dallied a few steps behind her. She had a plan but she had to time it just right. If she got called out for lollygagging, her split second chance would be lost...and, now!

She ducked past Dorna Lee and stopped, facing the entire crew of one hundred and eighteen remaining Goners. "Alright, listen up!" God, her voice sounded so puny coming back into her own helmet. No time to stop. "Shaft-warmers! Lateral Advancers! I need you guys to step up, okay!" They all stared at her in dumb shock. Behind her Dorna Lee had opened her mouth to shut this down, but then she got a feel for where Prudence was going, and let her continue. "I almost died down there today waiting for that third wire assembly. I'm not going out like that chick in Hole Eleven, okay! And listen--what we did today--four relays--" (There were some unexpected hoots and hollers at this point) "let's get used to that! Cuz we're gonna do four every day from now on!"

"So I heard you went ape-dookie on Pit Crew 3 today," smiled Kaywin as Pru stepped into line behind him. An ice-cream scoop of mashed potatoes plopped down on the tray next to his meatloaf. "Thanks Doris."

"What? How did you hear about this?! This was like thirty minutes ago!"

"I usually run into Sephal and Jason in the hall. They said you made quite a scene."

"Oh, God; were they laughing at me?"

"No, quite the opposite in fact. Sephal said it was pretty wicked." Pru blushed slightly but invisibly beneath her smudged toxic-island-castaway makeup. Dublin bounded breathlessly into line behind her.

"Hey Kaywin! Hey Pru--oh my God, what happened to you?"

"I forgot to wear my lead suit today. Full-on solar radiation exposure. Does it suit me?"

"Aaah, makeup. Got it."

Kaywin leaned around Prudence, waiting for his Brussels sprouts. "What's up Dub? Did you hear what Pru did this afternoon?"

Pru gave them both the full story, somewhat glossing over her record-setting achievement. Dublin was awestruck at both the record and the speech. But of course everything Prudence did made his heart beat a little faster.

Once they were seated Kaywin and Dub both hit her with questions. How long had she been interested in piloting? Why hadn't she said something before? What could they do to help? "I think I could take you out with me maybe one night next week" said Kaywin. "Or you know who's really good, and has two free practice slots next week? The tall ascetic."

"How's he gonna teach me anything without speaking?"

"Well, really, there's a lot of course-work you need to get through first anyway," chimed in Dublin. "I could help you with the calculus." This was insulting and disgusting at the same time, because his mouth was packed full of meatloaf as he said it.

"What makes you think I need help with calculus?"

"Do you not?"

"I don't know, but you don't have to just **assume** I do... and please finish that bite before answering."

"Sorry."

The meatloaf was ponderously chewy for some reason, and Kaywin was having to work hard at it as well, but that's not what he was concentrating so intensely about. "I'm wondering who you need to speak to. There's Commander Mac-

Fray of course--"

"If he really exists," Dublin tossed in.

"Right, because we've barely ever caught a glimpse of him...you'd want to talk to Professor Lindsay of course...it couldn't hurt to talk to..." he turned around in his seat, scanning the area to the left of the cafeteria exit "**that** guy, at the Berkeley table, at the end nearest us."

"Which one?" There were a lot of people still milling around and blocking the view.

"The youngish one, with the dark hair. Clean cut. He's the engineer who lost his pilot this week. But he's also Lindsay's right hand man. When you're actually out on the floor, you would think this guy was running the show."

"I still don't see the one you're talking about."

"There! The one who's laughing right now, at the end!"

"Ohhh! You should have just said 'the hot one'." They turned back to their steaming cafeteria trays. Dublin had stopped eating, which was unusual, and was looking at nothing in particular to his extreme left, almost behind him, with a dark cloud across his face.

"**What?**" said Pru to him, pointedly and aggressively, because she kind of already knew what he was thinking and she didn't like it one bit.

Dublin turned his shaggy head back in her direction, but didn't make eye contact, looking down at his Brussels sprouts instead and nudging them around with his fork in their little buttery depression. "Nothing. I'm cool. I'm good." There was a pause, and it was a long, awkward one. "I could have maybe done without hearing how 'hot' Fitz Renaldo is."

It was Pru's turn to cloud over. She had battled long and

hard against the tunnels for eleven hours, then mustered up the courage to rally the entire pit crew. She didn't need any new and unexpected obstacles today, thank you very much. She took a second to compose her thoughts, to **not** say what she **wanted** to say: *I made a big mistake joining in your stupid dance party last night.* Exhaling, she began, with as much tact as she was capable of. "Dublin, please **please** tell me you know that there is nothing going on between you and me…"

Dublin had gone his typical, blotchy, poison-ivy-on-his-face red. His tone was unpleasant and alarming. "I know, I know. I have heard it a hundred freaking times." He spoke the next words in a mocking, high-pitched whine: "You're like a brother to me; it would be weird to think of you that way; I would hate to spoil the relationship we have now. There's someone out there for you; you're such a sweet, smart, funny guy; it's not **me** of course, but somewhere there's a blind girl just waiting--"

"Okay, if you want it like that, you're too ugly for me. I don't find you at all physically attractive. Congratulations. You cracked the code. Is that better? Do you feel better now?"

The blotches on Dub's face had all filled in and connected in a flash, as soon as the word 'ugly' came out. He paused about three seconds, composing himself just enough to be sure that when he opened his mouth, words would come out and not an embarrassing sob. "Actually, yes. I've always known it, and it pisses me off when girls make up all that other crap. I can't be mad when they **don't** say it, and then be mad when they **do** say it. So, actually, yes; it's not great, but it's a little bit better." He looked up and was surprised to see Prudence standing up, and about to leave with her still-half-full supper tray. What right did **she** have to storm off? He was the victim here, right? Her cheeks were red enough to show through the brown streaking makeup, and her eyes were a little tiny bit shinier than usual.

"You're an **idiot!**" she said, verbally clubbing him like a baby seal.

With the old familiar knot in his gut, Dublin watched the newest love of his life turn and walk briskly across the cafeteria. Goners weren't allowed at the Berkeley table (or were they? It just never happened...) but Prudence found an empty seat at the end of the table next to it, and sat down four feet from 'hot' Fitz. Dumbfounded and horrified, Dublin saw, even from a distance, her demeanor flip as quickly and seamlessly as the color of her hair. She was laughing and smiling, with a nervous, giddy energy that he had observed many a time from females when they were talking to good-looking guys. He knew it well, having seen it turn off like a light a thousand times when they turned to face him.

She wasn't more than a hundred feet from him, but it seemed to Dublin that the distance was beyond miles, beyond measuring, as if they weren't even existing in the same historical era. His mouth was still hanging open. "Are you kidding me? She just called me ugly, and an idiot, right to my ugly face, and **she** is mad at **me**? Have I completely lost my mind?"

"Uh, I kind of get it," said Kaywin.

"What is there to get?! It's complete feminine insanity!"

"No, no, no; that's a cop-out. It's too easy to say that. I was married for twenty-one years, and raised a daughter. Usually if you really think about it, you can connect the dots and figure out what's up, why they are upset."

Dublin made a show of screwing up his face in thought and putting a hand under his chin, so it wouldn't hit the table if something super heavy occurred to him. After about two seconds, he was done. "Can you help a brother out here, cuz I'm drawing a blank."

"Okay," Kaywin began "this is all speculation here, but here goes: By even thinking for a minute that Prudence would have romantic thoughts, not just about you, but about **anybody**, really minimizes what she has gone through, and why she is here. I don't think she is capable of trusting another human being--certainly not another man, anymore." Dublin lowered his gaze from Kaywin's face. He pushed his tray forward and looked down at the shiny table, nodding slowly and thoughtfully. Kaywin continued. "On top of that, I think the friendship that you and I have built with her, as meager as it may be, and even though we all three know it will be over in no more than (he looked at his wrist) sixteen-thousand, one-hundred and ninety hours and twenty seconds…(he smiled wryly)…I think this friendship might be her first. Or at least her first in a long, long time, her first as a grown-up…or almost grown-up…God, you guys are so young; too young for this. What is going on in our world?"

Dublin's face had sunk lower and lower, as Kaywin tried to impart gentle wisdom unto him. Now his pimply forehead rested on the cool table. "I'm a little bit sick," he said, "I am a little tiny bit **sick** of people acting like **my** problems are a joke, like I shouldn't be here, and furthermore, like I am the **only** person who shouldn't be here. I know there are a lot of guys without girlfriends out there, and I know that some of

them are just fine, but I have **no idea how**! Yeah for them!"
He stood up suddenly, pushing his chair back from the table
with a loud screeching Velociraptor sound. This, combined
with the angry tone and rising volume of his voice, was starting to attract attention. He could see Jerkboy rising vaguely
in the distance like a lion scenting his prey. But Dublin had
started, and he was gonna finish.

Kaywin had never seen him angry, not even a little, really. It didn't seem to suit him. "I know she's been through a
lot. I know you've been through a lot. I know that everyone
here--," he swept his right arm across the whole of the cafeteria, twisting his body to achieve it "--has been through a
lot, obviously!" His alto voice had begun to tremble with the
strain of holding back tears. "But damn it--**I HAVE TOO!**"
He stormed off.

Kaywin sat with darkened face, elbows on table, hands
clasped in front of him, head inclined slightly downward, as
though he was about to bless the meal. Dublin got about
twenty feet away, then realized he'd forgotten his half-eaten
tray of meatloaf and sides. The entire company of derelict

souls had paused in their eating, except one, and had their three-thousand nine-hundred and ninety-three eyes (I feel like I should explain the odd number; one of the builders was back from the infirmary, having lost an eye, but not his life, on Sunday) fixed on the scene. "Hey Creaturehead! Trouble in paradise?" shouted Jerkboy across the hushed crowd, like any good head of security would do. Dublin kind of/sort of heard him, but he didn't care. Unfortunately, the poor boy had let his guard down when he thought he was exiting the public view, so that now, as he did the right thing and returned to clean up his tray, tears were streaming down his face. Not pretty in his finest moment, he was light years from it now. His chin was pressed all the way down into his chest as he attempted to shield himself from the world.

Doggedly and eternally submissive, his anger had already subsided into repentance and shame. "I'm sorry," he choked out to Kaywin as he fumbled for his tray. He hustled back to the repurposer to scrape it clean. The taller, sandy-haired ascetic intercepted the tray from his hand and gave him a single gentle pat on the shoulder. Dub hauled it out of the cafeteria and down the hall toward his mercifully close bunk. Supper went back to normal, with a little bit of laughter, but less than you might have expected.

The one pair of eyes that had never even looked up were Pru's.

When Kaywin made his way down to the hangar a short time later for his free-practice time, he saw a little something out of the ordinary going on.

Typically, at this time of night, you would find about

twelve to twenty stragglers; engineers still engineering, pilots gearing up for their turn at free-practice, like Kaywin was about to do; alternates staying late to soak up everything they could to get ahead… Tonight however there were more people. Maybe thirty, thirty-five or so, and they were all clustered up.

At the center of the cluster was Commander MacFray, whom Kaywin had referenced at supper before all heck broke loose. He was the elusive man in charge of MCP Lunar Operations, and had only shown his face one other time in six weeks. The discouragingly ubiquitous Jerkboy was with him, apparently in his capacity as Security Chief. And then there was a face that Kaywin hadn't seen in twenty years, and really had no reason to think he would ever see again. It was Rick Dombroski, his roommate and best friend in the Air Corp right from day one. They were peas in a pod. They had had one of those special friendships where you recognize someone instantly as a bird of your own feather, as clearly as if you were both brightly-plumaged parrots in a throng of gray pigeons.

Kaywin had left the Corp for civilian life, and to marry his sweetheart Nadine and start a family, but Rick had gone on to make a career of it. And a good one it had been. Here he was in his Brigadier General Uniform, stars and stripes everywhere, pins and medals jangling as he shook hands left and right. He was a tall, handsome man with close-cropped graying blonde hair. His clean-shaven face was ruddy and weathered. Steady. Grounded. Trustworthy. Without putting out a stern vibe, he had command of the room.

The small crowd had clustered in a little pool of light

from a powerful lamp a hundred feet over their heads, among the metal gridwork of the ceiling. They idled somewhat nervously on the grease-stained concrete between *Tomorrow Never Knows* and *Mr. Mojo Risin'*. It appeared that Jerkboy had been trying to take charge of the mini-tour. It also appeared that neither MacFray nor Dombroski were impressed with his overeagerness and bravado.

Kaywin was borderline elated to see him. In a more formal setting he would have shown a little more restraint, but as it was he had no problem busting into the little circle. "Brigadier General Rick Dombroski as I live and breathe!" He had a strong hand extended to the officer, who slapped it aside and pulled Kaywin in for a hug.

"Kaywin Lafontaine! Kaywin! I got a phone call a couple of months ago from Manchester, telling me you had joined up. I had no idea you'd be here! I thought they'd put you straight through to Atlanta!" Despite the little jest, Kaywin had sensed something wrong in the embrace, in his voice, and in his old friend's face. An unbelievable strain was there that someone less familiar with Rick might not have recognized. He was concerned immediately, but just a fleeting connection of their eyes told him to be cool.

"Ha! I wish! I'd be warm at least!"

"Sure, warm with a fever of a hundred and seven!" Dombroski was referring to the Scourge, a plague-like virus rumored to have been created by the government. If whispers were to be believed, it rotted people alive with a violent, agonizing slowness, the kind that would coax a confession from an innocent heart. Infected Goners supposedly begged for death; but seriously, how would anyone outside of the Atlanta MCP know this? The fleeting image of 'the Rocket' in his purple jumpsuit flashed through Kaywin's brain, but he re-centered instantly in the moment as Dombroski changed his tone. "Listen. So, so sorry to hear about Nadine and Victoria. Absolutely unspeakable." Kaywin just nodded. "So what are you doing here? Scrubbing dishes? Folding laundry?"

"Naw, I'm piloting. I've come full circle. God, I feel like it's twenty-one oh-two again! I was actually getting ready to take this baby out for practice." He pointed at *Tomorrow Never Knows* and began pulling his gloves on.

"Great! I'd love to join you!"

"Aaaaaah...okay; what's the protocol here? Rita, do you mind sitting out?"

"No sir," she half-laughed. Their relationship was com-plicated, but just from her side. She thought Kaywin was handsome and mysterious, and found his faithfulness to the memory of his wife (ironically) deeply attractive. His ability to embrace an old friend with unabashed tenderness in front of an audience only strengthened her opinion of him as 'a catch'. He, for his part, thought she was a good copilot.

Jerkboy's opinion of Kaywin was very much the opposite of Rita's, even before the wimpy, burned-out family man had butted into the conversation he was having with the Brigadier General. Theatrically-open disdain, combined with the look of having smelled something terrible, was all over his face. Kaywin just caught this out of the corner of his eye. *Bruni-ette's gonna take a beating tonight!* he thought.

"Always the gentleman!" said Dombroski. "Thank you Rita, Commander MacFray. Perhaps you could arrange for a makeup practice for Rita this week."

"Of course, Brigadier General."

The small crowd, sensing that the open meet and greet was over, began to disperse. Dombroski turned coldly to the arrogant blonde security chief. "I hope your boys haven't taken my suit already."

"I'll get it for you sir," said Jerkboy, in a much less chipper tone.

"Ah! Thank you, JB."

Ten minutes later, they had taxied into the cruiser compression chamber. This little mini-hangar allowed them to waste a fraction of the oxygen they would have by opening the main hangar doors. "I hope you won't judge me too harshly," said Kaywin, helmet-to-helmet. "These are a lot different from the SR11's we used to fly."

Takeoff was easier than it had been back in their glory days, with the luxury of a fifty-mile runway and the minimal gravity of the moon compared to the Earth. It was when they got off the ground that the handling got tricky, compared to the SR11 at least. "I'm working on the handling right now with Jennifer. It's sluggish; it makes me feel like a rookie. Once we get some elevation you want me to turn over controls to you? Maybe you could give us some pointers?"

Suddenly, a silver-gloved hand patted Kaywin's shoulder and a crumpled piece of paper (paper?) fell into his lap. Keeping his eyes mainly ahead of him as they got some distance from the Moon, and from the other three practicing cruisers, he un-crumpled the paper discretely. It was a packing label or something, and Dombroski had scribbled over it in red marker: *If there is a communications dead spot go to it. If no, turn off all but helmet to helmet.*

Kaywin felt electrified. He had sensed the weight of the world on his old friend's back, and now felt that he was about to be called upon to share it. He did as he was told, turning to starboard and flying over the solar collectors. Their enormous electrical field tended to block communications with the Moonbase, but he turned off their radio too, just in case. "How 'bout both?" he said. He inhaled deeply and stretched, as if the burden he was about to be given was a physical one.

He would remember the moments that followed for as long as he lived.

Brigadier General Dombroski exhaled. Amplified in Kaywin's ears, he could hear a little tremble in the wordless sound, which alarmed him a little because he had never met a braver man than Rick.

"Kaywin, you're about two minutes at this speed from a security field that you won't be able to cross. You'll have to fly around in circles for a while as I talk. I have a whole lot to tell you, and not a lot of time."

"I'm stationed on the Moon as well" Dombroski continued. "I've been here for six months, on the dark side, about four hundred miles dead ahead."

"I didn't know we had anything on the dark side," Kaywin ventured.

"Very few people do. Before I say more, I want you to understand that if you speak a word of this to anyone, I will likely be murdered within hours. It's coming anyway. Not just for me, but for all of us." Kaywin pulled up as the rim of darkness hove into view. He wheeled *Tomorrow Never Knows* around, and settled into what amounted to a huge figure-eight, keeping them away from the barrier on one side and out of Moonbase communication range on the other.

"What's coming?"

"A terrible judgment on the human race. Doomsday. Armageddon."

Kaywin choked down his nerves. "Okay... Okay...are you going to say this whole thing like a prophecy though? Give me something I can work with here; give me some facts…"

"What I am about to tell you is known by exactly eighteen men and women in the entire world, myself included." He sighed weightily. "You wouldn't believe the arrogance, and the stupidity. The worst of them, unfortunately, is calling all the shots. I'm talking about Brandenberg."

"Brandenberg? Rich Brandenberg, the Senator?"

"That's the guy. The Senator, the Entrepreneur, the Presidential Candidate, the second richest man on Earth... and now on the Moon…it was **his** orbiting research lab that discovered the threat. They're the only ones with a telescope powerful enough, and positioned correctly to spot it."

"Rick! For the love of God can we skip to what 'the threat' is?"

"It's a Rogue Interstellar Planet. It will obliterate the Earth--vaporize it--on March seventeenth, 2130. At 8:24 PM Eastern Standard time. It is 1.17 times the size of Earth, with a mass almost doubling it. The hit will be almost direct, less than three degrees off dead center."

Kaywin mouthed the words quietly, "Rogue Interstellar Planet...Is that a joke? R.I.P.?"

"I don't name these things."

Kaywin was letting this sink in. His first selfish thought was that it didn't even matter. This was almost four years away; he would be long dead by then. But his nephews suddenly popped into his head. Then his sister. Then the couple in the apartment across the hall from him back in Manchester who had brought home their newborn first child only a week before he left. Then he thought of all the lives in the world, and all the goodness that remained, despite the evil that had befallen him and his brethren here in the program. He thought of all human history, art and progress being atomized.

His next question, he hoped, would bring an answer to guarantee the safety of all these things. "So what's on the dark side of the Moon? Some kind of defense system?"

"A pistol. A pea-shooter. It's the largest gun ever constructed, and it's a joke. Based on the opinions of two of Brandenberg's 'experts', they think they can blast this thing out of the sky with a hundred-petawatt photon laser assembly. I've got my own expert, a **real** one. He says it will be like...how did he say it...trying to knock down a mountain with a paper airplane. That was the analogy he used. I think the other one was 'like a person on Earth trying to destroy Mars with a flashlight beam'."

"Does this expert of yours have a better idea? Please say yes?"

"Yes, but it's still a longshot, and if it's going to work we need to start **now.** He says we can use the same firing assembly, with minor modifications, and hit the mass off-center with magnetic pulses, at rhythmic intervals, that will create the slightest wobble in its course. The wobble will increase on its own, so that a tiny vibration, started this month, would mean that the Rogue Planet would miss our system completely. But the longer we wait, the bigger the wobble we would need to create. His calculations put next June fourteenth as the last day we could save the Earth, with existing technology."

"Why doesn't he speak up! Why don't **you** come out with this?"

"Kaywin, we are virtually prisoners there. We expressed our opinion on the matter early on, and were shut down by the head scientist, who has almost complete operational authority. The work proceeds only as he directs it. If I speak out against the laser approach one more time, I will be removed from the project."

"Well, that's good, right? Then you can make all this public!"

"I don't mean removed back to Earth. I mean confined to quarters at the assembly as Dr. Whitner is now. He opened his mouth a second time and now he hasn't been allowed out of his cell in two months. I'm not afraid of a little alone time, but if I get locked up, my last card is played, and there will be no one to advocate for common sense, and action!"

"But, if you're under suspicion, how did you get **here**?"

"Look down. Do you see the thin line leading from the back end of the solar collector field, all the way into the rim of the dark side?"

"...no."

"Straight down...dead center."

"Okay. Yeah, got it."

"That's a railway line. It goes fifty miles from Moonbase 2 to a small landing strip. From there it's another three hundred and fifty to the Gun. I'm the only one at the assembly who can fly worth a darn; there's a kid named Bradley who thinks he can. Anyway, every two weeks I fly to that strip and pick up the supplies the Moonbase boys have left the day before. There's no contact; there's no danger in sending me."

"No contact...but you could leave a message in the moon-dust for them, maybe?"

"I did. When I came back two weeks later all the topsoil had been blasted away for a quarter mile around. Your boys here are working with my idiots back at the gun. No doubt."

"What's to keep you from flying right on by, straight home to Earth, or at least into transmission range, and blow-ing the lid off this whole thing?"

"Two things. One is the barrier we are flirting with right now. The other is fuel. Every two weeks they send me just enough fuel to go seven-hundred miles… three-fifty back to the assembly, then three-fifty back out in two weeks."

"Alright, so that being said, how did you get all the way to the Moonbase tonight?"

"I accidentally on purpose crash-landed in your back-yard. I made some adjustments to the cruiser to maximize fuel efficiency six weeks ago, so the last three trips I've been able to accumulate a few extra drops; just enough to get me forty-eight of those last fifty miles. I sabotaged the altitude compensation valve to make it look like an accident. I had no choice but to come knocking at Moonbase 2."

"And they **heard** you?"

"I didn't actually **knock.** I tried to call in to MacFray, but the interference was too much. I cut one of the relays on the upper plateau and the response time was impressive. I was hoping it wasn't life support."

"Good thing you didn't undo a relay in the Lower Pits...I know a girl who would have cut you down, no questions asked!"

A wan smile cracked through the stress lines on the Brigadier General's face. "Sounds like that girl you met in the Philippines. The one who thought you called her over, then went nuts when you said you didn't!"

"Oh Lord, I haven't thought about that in ten years! I've got just enough of a fat roll now that it covers the scar, so I don't see it! No, this girl makes her look like an angel." He felt a twinge of guilt for representing Prudence so one-dimensionally. But his head was swimming with information, and so far none of it seemed particularly useful. He still didn't know what he was supposed to do about all this...

"So, Brigadier General--"

"Really? Call me Rick, you putz."

"So, Rick--back to the matter at hand--what am I supposed to do? How can I help? I don't have a lot of tools or connections here. You probably know all about the setup here; we can get information in from Earth, but absolutely nothing gets out."

"Information gets out somehow, from somewhere on the Moonbase. How many cans of green beans to send; how many gallons of gas...Even if it's just from MacFray. I don't necessarily trust him, BTW. He's not going to help us. Whatever you do is going to be behind his back. If you can get a message out, that's great. Work on that. I'm going to leave you with a couple of contacts on Earth who can be trusted."

"What **I** need to do" Dombroski continued "is to fire that gun. Which I fully intend to do. They won't test-fire it because of the enormous expense, and because they're so darn sure it will work, and they won't know that it **doesn't** work until they fire it. My best opportunity--my only one, actually--will be this coming Tuesday between 0130 and 0200 hours. To answer your question, what I really need **you** to do is to be watching the sky over that quadrant during that time frame. If you see a green flash--it should last almost three-quarters of a second, enough for you to be sure you saw it--then I've done it. Now, all that wins for us is an undeniable demonstration to these fools that one-hundred pettawatts won't get the job done; one-**thousand** pettawatts wouldn't even do it, not even close. It will also get the attention of astronomers on Earth, who, if they analyze the flash will discover it to be man-made, and if they track its direction with their most powerful telescopes, will discover the RIP....we'll make this public knowledge, just like that."

"So here's the deal. Whether I succeed or not, after 0200 hours Tuesday morning I am done for. If they let me live, that's great; but Whitner got solitary for just speaking up twice. When I go rogue and try to fire that thing, I fully expect to be shot."

"I'm worried about my family, Kaywin. Either way, whatever happens. I don't know if they are under surveillance, if someone is going to try to hit me where it hurts...my wife. The girls. You of all people understand that. Look, I understand that you are as shut in as I am, but if you somehow get a chance to get a message to them, whether it's second-hand, third-hand, eleventh-hand, whatever; I know you will do it. I would like them to know what happened to me." Dombroski sighed. "How's the air in here? Have you tried it without a helmet?"

"Not yet but I've heard it's alright." Kaywin could hear

the Brigadier General taking off his helmet behind him.

"Sofee, transfer files Carthage One, Carthage Two, and Carthage Three to Kaywin Lafontaine's Sofee. Those are schematics for the gun assembly, and detailed firing procedures. Sofee, transfer contact info for Dr. Wallace, Dr. Boyd, and Senator McHale. Sofee, transfer contact info for Anita Dombroski, Julie Dombroski, and Carey Dombroski as well. Sofee, make sure you disguise **all** of this, maybe as Beatles songs, we know how Kaywin loves his Beatles; and give it a transfer date somewhere back in January." He lowered his wrist and leaned forward. He knocked on Kaywin's helmet. "Take it off!" he yelled. Kaywin did as instructed. Dombroski undid his suit just enough to reach down and produce an object from inside his Air Corps vest. He handed it to Kaywin. "I don't care where you hide this. It's a backup. It's my old Sofee 45. That's just in case they bust you; maybe you let a friend know where it's hidden, somewhere on the base, if you have a friend that you would trust with your life."

"I have two."

"Good. I still have a few thousand family photos on there that I could never transfer to my 46 or 47."

"They made it super-tricky; I know what you're talking about. One of my friends is good at that stuff, too."

"Good. If you ever need this, look at the Alabama pictures. Alabama one through ninety-five. Those are the files, the same ones I just transferred to your 47. The password for my 45 is the name of that guy in our unit who used to faint every time he saw blood."

"Rico?"

"Good memory. Alright. Are you with me brother? I

know this is a lot to take in. Just remember: If you don't see a green flash--if I fail--I need you to fire that #?@! gun." He pointed at the brilliant blue marble of the Earth, rounding into view, vibrant and resplendent, his arm reaching over Kaywin's shoulder, next to his right ear. "Or those twenty billion people, everyone one of them, are all Goners."

15

Missionary Mary

"Oh, is **that** all…" With his fly-suit half unzipped and his bulky helmet wedged between his left ribcage and the wall of the tiny cockpit, he was shoving the little Sofee 45 randomly down into his underlayers. Kaywin couldn't help it. He smiled, despite the incredible gravity of the situation, then busted out laughing. Dombroski, seated directly behind him, looked as if the shadow of his former self was stirred to life by the warm familiar sound. He smiled a broad smile, but the emotion was too much and he too exploded into laughter. Tears streamed down the cheeks of the hardened military men.

When he caught his breath, and began to put his helmet back on, the Brigadier General observed wistfully, "I'm used to commanding whole squadrons, not passing notes to old burned-out friends in secret. No offense."

"None taken. You think I don't know I'm burned out?" They flew on in silence for a few seconds as they both collected more oxygen, and thought about their conversation. Both wondered what the future would hold, for themselves and humanity.

"How long have Brandenberg's men known about this RIP?"

"Four years almost. That's the reason for the buildup on Mars, I'm sure. No doubt it's the reason for the speed trials, here. They need the technology to go much faster, and they need it very soon. Even after they get it, they'll have to modify it for larger transport vessels, then start Martian Colonization on a mass level."

"God, why don't they come out with this? Don't we need every genius on Earth working on this?"

"They're biding their time with it, hoping to gain something. They're playing it like a game." The two men rode in silence for a spell. "When do we have to be back?"

"Six minutes. How 'bout I take us over the wire field to make this look a little less suspicious?"

"Solid idea. Let's see what the Moon is selling tonight." They wheeled around and headed back at a screaming clip over the solar collector field. Kaywin was careful to turn communications back on before he cleared it; if he waited until they hit transmission-friendly space there would be a suspiciously clean end to the radio silence.

He pressed *Tomorrow Never Knows* to its pre-nuclear limit and gave it some altitude. "Tomorrow we go nuclear!" He had to shout; maxing out the old-school engines like this made for a noisy ride. "This is as fast as she can go until then!"

They ascended gloriously. For the two old pilots, used to circling the much-larger Earth, the smaller globe of the Moon passing below gave them the illusion of astounding speed. In under a minute they began to take in the edge of the wire field. They could make out the individual filaments, glowing white, and a patch of blue to the far South. "What's it say? I can't make it out."

Dombroski tapped at his wrist in quest of the answer. "It says 'La Lune...opening May 2128'. So they are advertising the hotel, finally." Kaywin mused on the sublime redundancy of the words "La Lune" emblazoned across the face of the Moon.

"Alright. Time to bring it in. This was fun! What an unexpected pleasure!" They both knew they were on a public frequency. There could be nothing but small talk from here on out.

As soon as they taxied out of the compression chamber and back into the bay, they knew that something was up. As they rolled delicately back into formation on the hangar floor, they could see that Jerkboy had gathered up eight or ten of his security thugs. There were four cruisers idling back in, but the belligerent youth stood with his arms folded across his barrel chest, and his eyes locked on *Tomorrow Never Knows*. "That kid shows a lot of promise," Dombroski deadpanned for the benefit of anybody listening.

Kaywin played along, right in step with his old comrade. "Yeah...I've got a lot of respect for JB."

The two graying men stooped low to exit the cruiser. There was no telling what MacFray and Jerkboy knew about the situation. It was entirely possible that they would slap handcuffs on the Brigadier General, and that he would never be seen again. Kaywin too was at risk. If they understood that Dombroski was a threat, then it would be easy to slap charges of 'consorting with the enemy' on Kaywin. Without planning it, both conspirators knew that the best course of action was to engage naturally and laughingly with each other, blocking out the tense, menacing energy of the enormous room. Dombroski reassumed his commanding aspect, just in case any swaggering MCs got the stupid notion to lock him up.

"Your cruiser is ready Brigadier General," said Jerkboy, interrupting the carefree banter of the old burnouts. He made no effort whatsoever to mask his suspicion of the situation. "But Commander MacFray wanted me to make it clear that you are more than welcome to spend the night."

"Well that's a charming invitation, Security Chief, but I need to get Perez his insulin. And the men haven't had dessert in a week. But please do walk with us." He knew this was going to happen anyway, and wanted to express his innocent comfort with that. So they walked in super-awkward formation across the bay to Dombroski's repaired army-green cruiser, the Brigadier General and Kaywin Lafontaine strolling leisurely at their head, followed by Jerkboy with his hands clasped behind him, followed by Jerkboy's little gang of thugs; some of them almost drooling for action.

When Dombroski was situated at the wheel of his little vessel, dusty steel supply crates looming over his shoulders, Kaywin was seized with a strange thought, and an urgency to express it. "Brigadier General," he said, then paused to consider his wording. "That young lady I mentioned, the one I said was meaner than that Filipino Girl...she's not so mean. That wasn't fair of me to say. She's had it tough."

Dombroski laughed as he began to warm the engines. "Understood. We're all too mean. And we've all had it tough." He reached uncomfortably for one last handshake. "Good luck to you soldier."

"Good luck to you, Brigadier General."

Where to hide this Sofee 45...*when* to hide it, for that matter...how closely was he being watched? There were long stretches of unoccupied hallway, especially on level three. Some of the guys had stolen a basketball and set up a make-shift bowling alley in one of them. But this would be suspiciously out of Kaywin's way. He needed a quick, temporary hiding spot, then something more secure and long term after that.

He ducked into the common area closest to his room on the third floor. It was luckily abandoned just now. He plopped down in the cushiest chair, next to the biggest fern. While staring wistfully out the window, he forced the little Sofee down deep into the loose soil, then smoothed it over. He continued to gaze for a few minutes, as naturally as he could manage it, then got up and went to his room for the night, exhausted. It hadn't been the most relaxing evening. He was dying to unload the heavy news about the RIP, and the shady cover-up surrounding it, but he remembered the terrible fight between Pru and Dub, and worried that he might have to carry the burden alone for a couple of days. Oh God--what if it was worse than that? What if they never made up? He lay down with this dark thought capping off a ridiculously dark evening.

He told Nadine and Victoria all about it, around an imaginary dinner table, then went to sleep.

The next day was hardly any more of a cakewalk. They were going to take turns giving their cruisers the slightest taste of supplemental drive. A lot of these were nuclear, including *Tomorrow Never Knows*, but some were plasma drives, and a couple were really new and untried. Kaywin didn't have time to study them; he and Rita and Jennifer were consumed utterly with their own vessel, and making sure it didn't blow up the first time it got a taste of fusion.

It was hard for Kaywin not to imagine Jennifer as a daughter-figure. She was so clean-cut, smart, respectful...He could go on, but it was dangerous because the further he got down the list of adjectives the closer he got to describing Victoria...responsible, funny, beautiful, driven--obviously: she was twenty-two years old and making complicated miniscule adjustments to a nuclear fusion drive of her own design.

"Don't worry," she said to her visibly nervous pilot and copilot. "It's my understanding that we usually lose a couple of people on the first day of enhanced-drive practice, but I don't think it will be you two. This drive is good on power, but it's really strong on stability. Just stay alert, and trust the console more than your own eyes, which is hard, I know, but it's the biggest mistake you could make. The sensors will adjust faster than your visual cortex. Trust me guys!" She shook their shoulders. "Cheer up!"

They did trust her and they were right to do so. The burn out of *Paint it Black* right before their turn could have freaked them out, but they let it focus them like never before instead.

When they got up to speed, and Kaywin barely tapped the hyperdrive, it was like nothing he had experienced before. All noise in the cabin disappeared, except Rita and Jennifer's voices. Even though they were piped directly into his ear implants, they still sounded tiny and far away. The stars vibrated until they filled the windows like Van Gogh's *Starry Night*. He was cemented to the back of his bucket seat with more G's than he had ever experienced, and his legs on the floorboard and his arms on the wheel felt like they were stretched ten feet out in front of him. He felt woozy, but remembered to look at the console and not the Van Gogh painting. He was able to keep it true, for the full ten seconds, until he heard Jennifer's urgent voice from a hundred miles away, telling him to "come down off hyper, gently as possible!" And he did.

They were greeted like heroes back at the hangar. Jennifer's face was streaked with tears of joy. When all was said and done, *Tomorrow Never Knows* came in with the fourth fastest time. Jerkboy and Bruniette came in first, of course, in *Purple Haze*, although Jennifer said she was pretty sure they had pushed a little further into hyperdrive than they were supposed to on day one. They celebrated with a shove that turned into a trip that turned into a scuffle that turned into a wrestling match that laid waste to half the hangar. When they were done, they laughed their way past *Tomorrow Never Knows*, and Kaywin heard Jerkboy, blood trickling down from his temple, speak into his Sofee, "Dwayne! Come clean this up!"

Kaywin was torn about what to do. He took to heart Dombroski's warning about not telling anybody anything about the impending end of the world, already one day closer than it had been yesterday. But at the same time he had a terrible fear. He would get up in the wee hours Tuesday morning, and sneak into the common area down the hall to watch for the green flash that would mean Rick had succeeded in firing the hundred petawatt photon laser assembly. He would watch. He would watch diligently.

But what if he blinked?

Also, if the Brigadier General failed, was Kaywin really going to do this alone? There was a lot of missing, necessary information he would need if he was going to bust out of here, like no one had ever done, break into a fortified base and initiate a firing sequence, probably under duress. He would need information; codes, tools, guns, smokescreens and allies. He would need friends.

He thought he would tell Pru and Dub. But it couldn't be in the public eye, at supper. And who knows if he could get them back on friendly terms before Tuesday. He resolved to wait, to watch, and to try to iron out their differences ASAP.

Dublin was glum at the dinner table. He hadn't gotten to experience the sensation of enhanced drive like Kaywin had. Just before they had adjourned for supper, a team had returned with *Paint it Black* in tow, and they had all watched as the charred remains of its pilot and copilot were removed. This tragedy put Dublin next in line for copilot, but didn't do much for his appetite.

Worse, Prudence appeared to have left their little trio forever. She was back in the same seat as last night. She was far, far away and talking to the 'hot' young engineer with more energy and laughter than Dublin had seen from her in their forty-nine suppers together. Not that he was counting. "Can we trade seats?" he asked Kaywin, as soon as his butt hit the seat.

"No," said Kaywin. "Just don't look."

"Don't look? How does **that** work?" He kept glancing

over at Pru. She had obviously stopped by her room after her shift to touch up her hair and makeup. Tonight she had knee-buckling short red hair done up in little waves with gently pointed peaks, and her face was made up almost traditionally. Maybe a little heavy on the light green eye shadow. "Look at her! She's changed her look to appeal to the college type!"

"She changes her look every day. It's nothing. Let's change the subject."

"Okay. You still haven't given me any feedback on my poems."

"Let's change the subject again. Just kidding! I'm just kidding!" Kaywin wiped his mouth. "I haven't finished all eight-hundred yet. I'm about halfway through. They're good. Some of them are really, really good. It gave me a little more insight into why you are here. Man, I wish I had met you sooner. I think I could have helped you out."

"I'm flattered and all, but you're almost three times my age, and....you're a dude?" His raised pitch, and eyebrows, and his twisted-up face made it clear that he was being silly. Kaywin rewarded his willingness to be facetious in the midst of adversity with a small laugh.

"**Not** what I meant. What I mean is, some of the journal entries could have been mine when I was sixteen. All the extremities of language-- '**nobody** could **ever** love me'; I am **absolutely** the **only** one who is feeling what I am feeling--"

" 'Or I would have heard them screaming', " Dublin finished.

" 'Staring down the **darkest** abyss **any** man has ever stared down--'," continued Kaywin.

" 'Wearing further down than I thought I could wear down' "

Kaywin stopped. "Are you going to do this the whole time? Finish every example?"

"Well, you have to say the full rhyme, or it just sounds pathetic!"

"Moving on. These are not healthy perspectives, and trust me, I know they feel like they are true--don't freak out like last night--but they are not; they're not entirely accurate."

Dublin's cheek reddened and his mouth set in a grim line. He was hurt. "I'm sorry man. I don't know if I'm believing that you struggled with the ladies, ever."

"Nadine's the only girlfriend I ever had. And I met her when I was twenty-two. This I swear. So, yeah, I had some rough times."

"Okay, so I'm hearing two different things from you: you say you were just like me when you were sixteen, but then you act like it's all good--it's no big deal. I don't think you understand like you think you understand. It's like this. We, as a race"-- Kaywin sensed that he wouldn't be required to speak for a couple of minutes, and finally dug into his meal with gusto -- "we as a race have only one purpose in life that is real and inarguable: to reproduce, to carry on the species. Maybe somewhere down the line, in fifteen thousand years, we will have something more luminous figured out, but right now it's just **keeping the species alive**. To this end, there are certain physical traits that each gender finds generally attractive in the other--that's nobody's fault, that's just for the betterment of the species; but **I do not have those traits**! I'm not good-looking; not even a little; I'm not a jerk, I'm not rich--**I am a complete genetic zero**; I am a **non-entity** in the eyes of all womankind. I remember back in 'Birds n' Bees

101' there were supposed to be choices we would be making. I'm not making any choices! Except who to be rejected by. We should do a social experiment, when we get the chance. You and I could make the same joke to the same woman in the same circumstances. She would straight up laugh at yours, and act like I was an idiot--"

"Well, women can sense desperation. They would laugh at my joke because they wouldn't feel threatened by the energy I was putting out. Not because of my rampant good-looks."

"So how do I act like I'm not desperate? I mean, I'm completely and utterly **beyond** desperate..." Dub looked around the cafeteria at the human wasteland. "...obviously!"

"There!" Kaywin had found a foothold on Mount Doom. "You just said something promising, without even knowing it. It's too late now, of course," he indicated their surroundings and shrugged "but you said you are **beyond** desperate--that's where kids like us have to get before things get better! **Beyond** desperate! That's good! That's a good place! That's where you really, really stop caring what every girl you meet thinks about you. Then, and only then, do they notice you! I know, I know, it's a terrible irony. You referenced evolution, with desirable physical traits and stuff. Well 'not caring' is a prime, prime example of a **personality** trait that trumps pretty much all physical traits in the eyes of women. Have you ever seen a beautiful woman in love with a jerk?"

"Constantly."

"Have you ever seen a beautiful girl in love with a jerk who wasn't even good-looking?"

"Yes. You showed me your wedding pictures."

"Ha ha. Alright. Here's the wisdom I'm going to hit you with that I wish I could have given to you before you signed your life away: It's not the **jerkiness** that women find attractive."

"Oh yes it is, I can--"

"No no no no no--Dublin--I **promise** you--it's the **confidence**. I know this doesn't seem possible. We don't even realize it until we are in our twenties, because **we** don't give a flip if a **girl** is confident or not. I mean, it might affect the quality of a long-term relationship, but in that first-impression-stage, when our brains are deciding whether a girl is attractive or not, we are actually much more appearance-oriented than females."

"If I hadn't made a scene walking out of here last night, I would get up right now and walk away." This line of reason was an utter slap in Dub's face. Despite his assertions, Kaywin had clearly never been ostracized because of his looks the way Dub had, and always would be.

"Wait. Let me tell you what worked for me."

"You sound like you're about to try and sell me something."

Kaywin ignored him. "I was eighteen. Still no girlfriend, ever. I gave up. I gave up completely. I started to concentrate on my own life, on the things I could control, instead of the constant parade of pretty women waiting to hurt me. I joined the Air Corps"--

"There it is."

"And concentrated on following orders. Then I made great friends, a lot of them. I went out with my friends and had fun. My skin cleared up, I got a better haircut--wink-

wink--I slimmed up and muscled out a little--did you hear the part about the haircut? --I was just out with my buds, having a good time. I didn't even look at the women. For the first time in my life I looked confident. I still didn't look at the ladies, or the spell would have been broken. Finally, the prettiest one ever started dropping me hints, and I said, 'sure!' Nadine loved me so much that I got more and more confident. Now, I could date anyone in this room if I wanted."

Dublin almost spat out his hotdog. "Wow! Pump the brakes, Romeo! You might stand a chance with a few of them. Like Rita."

"Rita and I have a professional, working relationship!" Dublin had never seen Kaywin blush before.

"Yeah, you might not be as perceptive with the ladies as you think you are..."

"What, is it my night to storm out of the cafeteria? Is that what's going on here? Look, I am so beyond ever dating again."

"Where would you even **go** on a date here?"

"I don't know, I hear the Lower pits are lovely this time of year..."

"Mmmm, yes; have you seen the **lower** Lower pits? Breathtaking!"

"I hear they're putting in a pit below the lower Lower pit. It's going to have a coffee bar, and a grotto..."

They had a good laugh together. Neither one of them saw the subtle movement of Pru's eyes from afar, stealing a glance at the two of them every so often.

Fitz was even better-looking close up than he was from a distance, and he was smart, and a little bit funny in a normal sort of way… he seemed to think that he could pull some strings and get Prudence out of the pits and into the piloting program, provided she had come as close academically as she thought she had. She was still angry at Dublin, but she missed her warm spot by the kitchen, and the boys sure did seem to be having a good time without her.

"Did they call you 'the Ugly Kaywin' in school? Did I tell you they used to call me 'the Ugly Dublin'?

"No. You didn't tell me, but I pieced it together from ten or twelve of your poems…the Ugly Duckling. It was a popular video game when I was little. Hey, Dublin?"

"Yeah?"

"You remember how that story **ends**, right?

For the third day in a row, Prudence had pushed the LPC3 to its limits. They were really rounding into form; she didn't have another situation where she got to the bottom of a tunnel and had to wait because the wire array wasn't far enough along. When they hit the pits yesterday morning, after her outburst the previous evening, she had expected grumbling at best, and maybe sabotage at worst. But the only backlash from her tirade seemed to be, oddly enough, the increased respect of her peers.

She found herself ill-equipped to deal with that. She had a few snarky comebacks prepared for the slackards and the malcontents, and was almost disappointed when she didn't get to use them.

Her team was becoming a well-oiled machine. They were making up ground quickly. One new solar collector was erected every day, and its wire array deployed the half-mile from the Upper pits to the Lower. They were still a whopping hundred and fourteen relays behind. If Pru's math was correct--and it was--they would catch up completely by July third. Her replacement from the next batch of MCs should arrive around July ninth. There was no reason, or there **shouldn't** be, that she couldn't do one relay per morning from July third to July ninth, then split her day, spending the afternoons with the pilots. Come July ninth she could train her replacement for a couple of days, and then be done with tunnels. She would be free to work toward a fiery death in the skies. There were a lot of 'ifs' in her formula, but she tried not to think about that.

As soon as they were off-duty, she tried to reach Kaywin on his Sofee. He didn't respond. This could mean a couple of things: He, like everybody else, had only a few minutes after work to change clothes and hustle up to the cafeteria before the lines got too long. Maybe he didn't have time to answer. Or maybe like Dublin, he thought she was a stupid little girl who belonged to them, like a dog. Either way, she needed his help. She was going to have to approach them at supper.

She had set her hair to dirty blonde today, with no flashes, streaks, or pulsing underglow. It was chin-length but very full, curving down to frame her perfect face. The sheer volume of it shielded her a little on either side from public view as she made her way in a direct line from the cafeteria counter to her old seat with the boys.

Dublin's heart was in his throat. He straight up *yearned* for Prudence to stay right there, for things to go back to normal. But Kaywin had coached him on how to handle this moment. "Apologize, and *mean* it, but don't beg. If you are desperate for her to hang out with us, it's going to remind her that you have feelings for her, and push her away. And by no means are you to use poetry."

"But I've got like a four-line thing that sums it all up beautifully--"

"No poetry!"

Prudence sat sideways, avoiding Dublin completely. Her posture indicated that she was there for a few seconds, and only on business. Her eye shadow and her lips were golden rose, and she had used the same shade to make a subtle jagged "x" on each of her adorable little mini-muffin sunset-hued cheeks. Dub felt his resolve slipping. *I dare* **anybody** he thought, looking down at his pizza; *I dare* **anybody** *not to fall in love with her.*

"I need your help," Prudence said to Kaywin.

"I'd be glad to help you," he responded. "Make yourself comfortable." He started eating, just like everything was normal, and she reluctantly swung her legs around under the table and settled in.

"I need flying lessons."

"I can do that. I have free practice Thursday night."

"Don't you have it Tuesday night too?"

"Well, yes, but I had to bump Rita Friday night. She'll kill me if I leave her behind again. We've started to tap into hyperdrive; she's supposed to get her first crack at it Tuesday."

"Well, crap. I can't wait till Thursday."

"Why not?"

"I have it planned out. You guys are six weeks ahead of me. I need to catch up. Will you save that Thursday spot for me, and I'll find someone else for Tuesday?" She looked over her shoulder, around the crowded cafeteria, as if someone might be holding up a sign that read, 'COMPLETELY IN-EXPERIENCED CO-PILOT NEEDED FOR DANGER-OUS FLIGHT TUESDAY NIGHT'.

Up to this moment, she had ignored Dublin complete-ly. What he said at this moment he said suddenly. He didn't know how it happened. The words, as they came out of his mouth, were as much a surprise to him as they were to Kay-win and Prudence.

"Must be nice to be a pretty girl." She wheeled her head around, her hair whipping outward, and stared at him. "You can say whatever you want, and guys will come back. Or if they don't come back, other guys will be around, and you can say whatever you want to them, because the world will never run out of guys. And they'll keep--"

"Must be nice to be an ugly guy." (Did he think she was going down without a fight?) "Sleep all night with both eyes shut. Walk down the street without being harassed. Nobody touching you. Nobody staring. Nobody slobbering. Be made a pilot because you look smart. Read *War and Peace* then tell four hundred people you read *War and Peace*. If you think--"

"**STOP IT!**" Kaywin hissed with unexpected fury through gritted teeth. His heart rate had been climbing this whole time as he felt their little fellowship teetering. He need-ed them to put this nonsense aside so he could take them into confidence about the impending disaster. God, what if he died out here, and Dombroski failed, and nobody even knew?

The two sixteen-year olds stared at him wide-eyed. They'd

been friendly with this even-tempered man for a couple of months, and hadn't seen the first glimpse of anger.

"I **need** you guys! Both of you! You have no idea!" Rage did not come naturally to him. Fortunately three seconds of it had been enough to purge the atmosphere like a bolt of lightning. He carried on in a calmer, gradually lowering tone. "Now, if you guys would each actually absorb a little tiny bit of what the other was saying, this could really be enlightening for both of you. Prudence--if I tell you how intellectual you are, and Dublin--if I tell you how pretty you are, do you think we could all be friends again?" There was a pause, one of the stranger pauses in the short history of the Moon. Dublin broke it.

"My mother told me not to consort with liars. I mean, about him calling me pretty, not about you being intellectual." He had looked up from his untouched pizza slice, and was talking to Prudence. "I believe that humor, however sarcastic and biting, is a sign of advanced intellect. Pru, you are really smart." He seemed suddenly to awaken from the long day-dream of his own concerns. "You know that, I hope. You are really exceptionally intelligent."

This caught Prudence off-guard, clearly, and she squirmed, turning from their view to collect herself. "I feel pressure to call you pretty now. I'm not going to do that. But--but--your eyelashes are quite lush. And you're stronger than you look. You've got really big arm muscles."

She turned back instantly away from him, as far as she could. This meant that Kaywin alone had to absorb the mor-bid spectacle of Dub batting his eyelashes and flexing his muscles.

Kaywin was struck suddenly by the relief he felt. What-ever he was called upon to do in the coming months, he knew he would not be alone. Above and beyond that, it felt good to be the one **giving** advice and help and wisdom. It had not been healthy, he realized, to have been pitied by others for so long, to be pitied by **himself** for so long. He smiled to him-self. He could hear the conversation resuming without him, and a sense of normalcy and comfort returning. He tuned back in and they all finally started eating.

"You know," said Dublin "with those 'x's on your cheeks, if you make an 'o' with your mouth, you look like a game of tic-tac-toe..." Prudence did so, forming an "o" with her lips despite her mouth being full of pizza. Dub seized the oppor-tunity and picked up something off his plate.

"If you put that onion ring on my nose, I will punch you in the face."

When they got clear of the cafeteria, halfway to Dublin's door, Kaywin pulled up short. He spoke just above a whisper to the other two. "So, I have something very, very heavy to drop on you guys, but it is critically important that we not be overheard. Not even by Ving."

It was hard to find a quiet spot from seven o'clock to eight-thirty or so; the halls and common areas tended to swarm with Goners socializing away the troubles of their days. "We could go to my room," said Pru. "Jordache and Judy have basketball on Sunday nights."

Once there, still speaking in cautious low tones, Kaywin told them every word of his interaction with Dombroski. He looked at them in the understandable silence that followed.

"Now you're **both** making 'o's with your mouths."

"And pretty soon there'll be 'x's over our eyes...we are really living this tic-tac-toe metaphor..." said Dublin.

"Except nobody wins..." mused Prudence. They lapsed back into anxious reflection.

"My mom...my cousins...Brian...all my friends at the Deux-Trois..."

"My baby sister..."

Kaywin and Dublin both snapped out of their trances at this quiet mumble from Pru. "You have a baby sister?" Dub asked.

"Yeah...my little step-sister...Baby Perstephanie..."

"Your dad's? With his girlfriend?"

Pru nodded.

The same unspeakable thought flashed through the minds of Kaywin and Dublin. But, being unspeakable, neither spoke it. Kaywin, who had had a couple of days to process the magnitude of the classified information, was ready to move beyond staring with his mouth wide-open, into the planning phase. But Dublin beat him to it.

"So what do we do about this?"

"We watch for the green flash, between one-thirty and two-thirty AM tomorrow night...Tuesday morning, technically," said Kaywin. "If there's no flash, then..."

"Then it's up to us to save the world," said Prudence.

Kaywin's face clouded a little at her use of the word 'us'. "I don't necessarily **need** to drag you guys into this. I needed someone to know, in case something happens to me. Just like if something happens to me, you guys will need to tell someone else."

"Someone? I'll tell everyone!" enthused Dublin. "Why don't we tell everyone right now?"

"I think only bad things can happen if we do that," said Kaywin.

"Such as?"

"Such as killing the three of us, for starters, which--," he shrugged, "--whatever; but they could kill all of us, every MC here, if people started making trouble. Or they could ship the three of us to Atlanta, infect us with the Scourge, and stream video of us rotting alive into the cafeteria daily as a warning to any dissenters. They could take the completely opposite tact, and hush people up with the assurance that the Rogue Planet was taken care of, that there was nothing to worry about. Any assurances they wanted. They could send us fake news reports from Earth if they wanted to drive the point home. They've done an amazing job of keeping information from leaking out of Moonbase 2--I mean, look at what they've built here, without the first rumor getting back to Earth. They have all the power here; they control all of the tools, all of the people, and all of the information."

"Fine, I won't stand up at supper and announce it to everybody."

"Our best chance would be our **first** chance," Kaywin continued. "We would need to make a clean, well-planned, decisive first move before they found out that anybody here knew about the RIP."

"As soon as **they** know that **we** know, we are dead, or shut off even more completely than we are now...or both," summarized Pru.

"So what kind of well-planned, decisive move are we

talking?" Dublin asked.

"Well, the obvious one is to make a break for it in our cruisers, land at the gun assembly, gain entrance somehow, and fire the gun," said Kaywin. All three of them spoke barely above a whisper, just in case the room was bugged.

"God, the security codes, though!" responded Dub. "We would need the code to bypass the barrier between us and the dark side, **or** the code to bypass the barrier at the end of the flyzone on the Earth side; **then** the code to get into the gun assembly--"

"Got that one," said Kaywin, referring to the files Dombroski had shared with him.

"Then the launch codes for the actual laser cannon."

"Got it...I **think.** I have something that **looks** like a launch sequence, but it's not marked as such."

This news excited Dublin. "So it's just the code for one of the barriers we need, then."

Pru had heard enough of this over-simplification. "You know they'll just **shoot** us as soon as we get in, right?"

"We scrounge up some guns and blast our way through."

Pru rolled her eyes. "You guys just loooove to blow stuff up, don't you." The boys looked at each and nodded.

"Yeah, we do."

"Yeah, it's pretty cool."

"How many times have you watched those stupid Wisconsin Johnson movies? You know in real life bad guys have better aim, right? We can't just 'blast our way through'... How'd that work for Napoleon, in Russia?" Dublin felt an electric shock go through his body at Pru's reference to the 'war' in *War and Peace.* "He got outsmarted, right?"

"Right," was all the flustered boy could mutter.

"So how about we try something completely different?"

"We're listening," said Kaywin.

"How about we hijack their freaking wire-field, and instead of a Moon-sized ad for Uno Mundo, we use it for a message to all twenty billion people on Earth. I know Brandenberg's got everything, all the money, all the power, but he can't hush up everybody. That's beyond covering up. They would rip him to shreds if he tried to drag his feet in stopping this rogue planet thing..." The boys exchanged looks.

"Brilliant," said Dublin. "I didn't even think about that.

"Problem is, they would rip **each other** to shreds as well..." Kaywin paused and looked up, musing, his eyes fixed on a random cinder block in the far wall. "God, the scene there would be on Earth when people realized what was happening!"

Pru hadn't weighed this into her equation. "True. Twenty billion people all finding out at once that they had three years left to live. It'd be like that Gashole Event times a billion."

Dublin furrowed his brow. "Are you trying to say 'Gesster Event'?"

"Whatever it was where that politician got hit by the meteorite, and people said it was the Hand of God, and everyone lost their minds and banned dancing, and candy and all that for like five years..."

Kaywin snapped out of his reverie. "We don't know if the wire-field is even operated from the Moonbase. It could be controlled remotely from the Earth. But I can't see any reason not to pursue both angles. Hopefully Dombroski is successful and fires that thing; then Brandenberg's science

411

team will **have** to acknowledge that they have been on the wrong track. Hopefully, this is all moot. For now let's keep our eyes and ears open. Most of all, let's play it cool, alright?" Nods and mumbled "yeahs" ratified this loose agreement. Then a pause. Then Dublin had a musing that he couldn't hold in.

"What if this **is** the Hand of God?"

Pru was quick with an answer. "If it's the Hand of God, we won't be able to stop it. If it's not, we will."

Kaywin smiled. You had to like the girl's confidence. "Meanwhile, let's get you some flying lessons."

He laid the groundwork for Pru during the day Monday, when he crossed paths with the tall ascetic in the hangar. "Hey...I have a favor to ask of you. It's no biggie if you can't, or if you just don't want to, or whatever." The tall man just stared at him, smiling. It was useless to wait for a prompt from him to continue, so Kaywin just barreled on. "You know my friend Prudence? Short? Rainbow-colored hair, sometimes? All kinds of colors, all the time, like Linsom Felize?" The ascetic nodded; he probably was not a pop-music fan, but even people living in caves (which was a real thing in recent years--the living-in-caves movement) knew Linsom Felize.

"Well--I'm going to get her to ask you herself, but I wanted you to know that she is **going** to ask you about taking her along with you on some of your free-practices. You've got two this week, and I can only give her one cuz Rita is kind of gung-ho about not missing any time..."

The grungy man was eagerly wiping the residual black grease marks off his forehead. Conveying 'yes' in his face and mannerisms, he wrote no prob chlorina never free practice.

"Oh...excellent!" Well, that made sense; Chlorina (his co-pilot) complained constantly about the smell of the un-showered zealot, so it wasn't surprising that she would shun free-practice, or seek out someone other than her assigned partner. "Great! Do you want to maybe sit with us at supper tonight?" Kaywin knew from observation that both ascetics were careful to not establish permanent seats in the cafeteria, denying themselves even the minor comfort of feeling like they belonged in one particular spot.

Still smiling grotesquely, the lengthy man gave a little curtsy in his robe, which Kaywin took for a 'yes'.

Dublin so far had not had occasion to interact much with the tall ascetic. The man's true height became more and more apparent as he shuffled closer to the table Dub shared with Kaywin and Pru. He was six-foot-six, or close to it, but very thin--almost dangerously so. Prudence had her back to him, and was shoveling food in her mouth as fast as she could. The cafeteria was filling up rapidly, but there was a buffer of space between Pru, Kaywin and Dub at the long table's end, and the rest of the crowd. There had been an explosion the Thursday before that had marked the end of the road for five former wire-crew members, including the three who had filled that penultimate space.

Kaywin saw the greasy monk coming and remembered that he had invited him to sit with them. He also remembered that he had failed to give his friends a heads-up that they would be having a dinner guest, of sorts. He and Dub exchanged a quick glance. Dublin had a thought that he would have been too ashamed to speak aloud...*that freak is about to sit with us*... He blushed and looked down at his oatmeal in penitence. A lifetime of being excluded, and he was **that** ready to exclude someone? Shame...

Prudence caught the subtle change in Dublin's demeanor and furrowed her brow ever so slightly, in direct proportion to her curiosity. Before she could ask him what was wrong with his stupid face, she was lifted upward a little off of the bench by the weight of the relative giant sitting down next to her.

"You smell," she said, by way of greeting. The other two tensed, bracing for the impact of the newcomer's reaction. He had, after all, enough spirit left in his huge frame to slap the snot out of his fellow ascetic every morning, if Dublin was to be believed. Probably this was nothing more than a reflex of Pru's. Being startled, it was very important to her to quickly shine a light on something other than her own vulnerability.

The ascetic turned his great head, long and skinny like his body, and smiled at Prudence. Straight teeth showed, overall too yellow for the movies, but with two lower teeth, side-by-side, **really** burned brown, probably by some repeated, unhealthy habit. They corresponded with a dark spot on his lip. It was easy to connect these dots in the short two seconds of his smile.

Some of the details of the ascetic's face, which had been troublesome to make out from a distance, now came into focus. But they gave more questions than answers. He was Caucasian, but with an almost reddish skin tone. It looked like he had a little darkness to his complexion naturally, and then had spent a great portion of his life out of doors, maybe even living on the streets. He looked a little burnt. His hair was short and sandy, matching the slight bristle of his cheeks and jaw. These cheeks were a little bit sunken, like he was sucking on a straw, though of course he wasn't. The browns of his eyes were brown, but the whites were a little yellow and a little red. Whatever had burned his lip and his teeth had also destroyed his eyes forever. He had to have been clean of any pollutants for some time now, but his face, and apparently his soul, would never recover from the ravage. Seventy-seven hour work-weeks on half-rations weren't helping with any of this. Perhaps more than any of the 1800 derelict souls stuffing food into their mouths behind him, this man's countdown was written all over his face. And it was faster than the one on his wrist.

Prudence shamelessly gawked upward at the ghastly grinning mask. "God, dude, I think your modeling career is **over**." She hadn't been satisfied, apparently, with the ascetic's bland response to her first insult. She came up empty again, provoking only a soundless laugh.

But she wasn't going to rest until she got the abuse back. Subconsciously, she knew she was even lower than this wreck of a man. It was difficult for her to ask a favor without this being acknowledged. She actually put down her fork, straddling the bench and turning to face the gentle giant, as though **she** was the one being insulted. Her delivery this time was so sarcastic and mean that, not for the first time, and not for the last, Kaywin and Dublin were embarrassed to be sitting with her.

"Are there **just no words** for the way you feel right now?" she queried meanly.

His smile faded a little and he too put down his fork. He reached into his greasy robe, causing Dublin to flinch. He pulled out his primitive writing utensil and began to write on his forehead.

Meanwhile, Kaywin stared at the man, transfixed. The height difference between Pru and the ascetic was so great that he could see right over her zebra-striped bob and into the other's mysterious face...

A strange, unwelcome idea sparked to life in Kaywin's exhausted mind. The ravages of the ascetic's face were laid out before him like a treasure map; the clues of his former drug addiction were like little footprints going across it...but where was the 'X'?

From across the table, Dublin studied the scene as if the characters were all new to him. The sad shell of the ex-military man seemed hypnotized. The tiny, insulting gorgeous punk girl watched as the grimy twenty-second-century giant monk wrote on his forehead with a grease pencil. It reminded him of some of the Bob Dylan songs Kaywin had played for them. But his ultimate conclusion was: *These people are wrecked beyond repair. These people are destroyed. I'm not living a Tolstoy novel. This is Dostoyevsky all the way...*

Lessons. Start 2night? wrote the ascetic.

"Oh...sure...I was going to ask about that," said Pru. "Thanks?" Men who didn't behave like men still confused her. The ascetic smiled and got up to leave. "Uh, wait. I feel like maybe I should know your name." He sat back down and wiped his forehead 'clean' with his blackened sleeve. Then he wrote, '---'

"That's a minus symbol."

He shrugged. "Can I ask you a question?" interjected Kaywin unexpectedly. "Where are you from?"

For the first time, the ascetic's face betrayed something other than absolute openness. He appeared to have to think for a second. He was a little slower wiping his forehead. **Philly,** he wrote, then smiled and nodded. Then he was gone, leaving the band of three behind.

"Boy!" observed Dublin. "The Attabuoys have fried that guy completely!"

Prudence de-straddled the bench, turning back toward Dub and sitting normally. She stared at him like he was a total idiot. She was proud of never having willingly and knowingly taken a drug in her life. But she knew, better than most, *which* drugs did *what* to people, and what marks were left behind.

"Attabuoys!" she spat at Dub. "Wow. You really **are** a country boy. That clown's a Novahol-fiend. Novahol, or Excelsiadon."

Forty-five minutes later, Prudence wondered what she had gotten herself into. She was flat on her back as *Black Magic Woman* powered almost straight upward. The click, click, click of the altometer marking off every hundred feet reminded her of the beginning of a roller coaster ride; climbing, climbing, climbing, every second more tense than the last.

They achieved a certain altitude and leveled off. Her monitor showed that they had elevated 8.35 kilometers above the lunar surface, into the training cone. This was not a physical structure; there was nothing out the windows that offered any idea of it. It was better described as an energy field. It disabled the engines of any ship that approached it too closely. Controllers on the Moonbase itself would then have to bring in the helpless cruiser remotely or issue a recon vessel to tow it. So if a cruiser brushed the sides of the cone, a blazing thrill ride on the way out turned into a drowsy return at a tedious clip.

The 'narrow' point of this training cone, some hundred miles across, encompassed Moonbase 2 and most of the Lunar North Polar region. From there it widened outward into space, allowing cruisers to experiment with ridiculous accelerations, with some margin for error, to a distance of four-thousand miles. If the full Moon were a face that smiled on the Earth, the test-flight cone would be like a small, out-flaring hat that was somewhat in danger of falling off the back of its head. It was desirable that, as ships rocketed outward, they would, as much as possible, escape the gravitational influence of both the Moon and the Earth. This way, engineers could more accurately assess their potential speeds in gravity-free 'deep' space.

Waxing philosophical was not a particular hobby of Pru's. But when *Black Magic Woman* ascended above Hermite Crater Rim, and she saw the Earth in all its blue glory for the first time in a couple of months, it was not possible to pretend anymore that her life hadn't changed. California was dead ahead in the sky, for just a few seconds before they turned about to put it behind them. She had been there, cooped up in a tiny bedroom in a tiny town only eight weeks ago. It seemed like a lifetime away, so how could it not be far enough? Her skin crawled with the memory. She had zero regrets about leaving. Anything, including death, was better. The unholy stench of the large man two feet in front of her was like a noseful of lilacs in the light of her former life.

The ascetic was as quiet as she expected he would be. She would have to learn by watching.

They wheeled away from the Earth and and further into the invisible cone. The conventional engines were brought to full power. Pru was now traveling faster than she had ever gone. She could really feel the speed more in the small cruiser than she had in the bulky, slower transport. The silent ascetic pulled a lever roughly, and Pru could feel a change in the belly of the beast. The back of her neck tingled as if the ghosts of her natural hair were trying to stand up. She saw her own worried face reflected in the cruiser window, and tried to get a grip.

"Anything I should be doing right now to prepare for this?"

The ascetic turned around, propping his left arm over the back of the seat. Grinning broadly, he prepared to write across the smudgy red desert of his forehead.

"Shouldn't you be looking where you're going? Pru protested anxiously. He reached over with his grease pencil hand, tapping the monitor in front of her with the long nail of his right pinky. He **was** watching, just upside down and backwards. He began to write:

'H' 'O'...the grease pencil was worn down and he paused to pull at the paper sheath.

"Boy, you had better keep on writing!" said Pru as her seat began to vibrate.

'H' 'O' 'L' 'D' 'O' 'N'!

And they were off.

There was a moment, it might have been less than a second, where Pru blacked out. Her first feeling, on reawakening, was exhilaration. Everything was strangely quiet. Even more curious was the view out of the side windows. The sky looked like it had been painted by that Dutch guy, the nutjob who had cut off his ear and mailed it to some lady. Every star had vibrated itself into a heavenly golden spiral. Together in their countlessness, they filled up the darkness. She had the sensation of mind-shearing speed. Her body was plastered back against her seat. She couldn't have leaned forward if she had tried. But instead of feeling helpless, she felt immensely, thrillingly powerful. She saw the giant in front of her making adjustments, but it was all in peaceful slow motion. The snail's pace effect of his movements made him look ponderously huge, like a thousand-foot tall monster stepping over and through highways and apartment buildings.

Most gloriously of all, she had the sensation of real distance piling up between herself and her former life. Maybe it was the enhanced levels of oxygen being pumped into her helmet that was making her feel...**happy**. Or maybe it was the enhanced levels of not-being-used-by-the-world.

For a mere sixty seconds, they sizzled across their corner of the cosmos, like the finishing flourish of a founding father's quill across some kind of sky-wide declaration of independence. Just that quickly they covered half of the four-thousand miles before ground control slowed and buffered them, turning them homeward with a nudge. There was enough information on her monitor for Pru to do some quick math. She was breathing heavily when she spoke.

"Did we just go a hundred and twenty-thousand miles per hour?"

The ascetic just grinned and nodded. He wiped his forehead and wrote again.

Next month-third year!

It was late when they returned to the hangar. Only a few stragglers remained, a couple of the engineers who seemed to never eat or sleep or do anything other than tinker, and the crews of two other cruisers who had returned from free-practice minutes before them.

Prudence let her guard down for a moment with the ascetic... 'Minus', or whatever his name was. It wasn't that she felt any more safe or comfortable with him than she did with Kaywin and Dub; she just felt like she could keep the mute giant at arm's length emotionally, that a little gushing wouldn't be taken as an overture of affection for him. "That was the most amazing, awfullest thing I have ever done." She even **almost** added "thanks."

The reeking penitent smiled his usual smile, which got kind of old when you spent a little time with him. It had been a busy evening with the grease pencil for him, but he spelled out one last message. **Wicked! Want to fly Thurs.?**

"Yes. Definitely." She mused for a second as they walked toward the changing rooms. "**Wicked**? What are you, from New Hampshah, like Kaywin? Manchestah?" She thought it was funny, but the smile drooped from the ascetic's face. He disappeared into the men's' locker room without a forehead-scribble. Whatever.

"I like your sneaking-around hairdo, Fru," Dublin whispered to the tiny shadow looming into the dimly lit common area on level five.

Pru's hair was black and shoulder-length, with bangs down to her pupils, and was amazingly devoid of *sheen*. Her face was shielded from view, not that anyone was watching at one-twenty in the morning. "Thanks. Yours is terrible."

Kaywin was already glued to the giant window. He didn't turn as the other two tiptoed up on either side of him. "I told Dub already." He pointed to a spot where the crater rim curved away in the distance to their left. "You see the little point in the ridge there? Where it looks like a worn-down cat-ear?"

"Yes."

"Okaaaaay, now follow it right," he was slowly pivoting

the finger, "until you get to the little cleft."

"Okay. Got it."

"That's the part of the sky we should be studying the hardest. I'm keeping my focus dead-center. Dublin, can you concentrate on the right side and a little beyond it, just in case?"

"Yes."

"Fru-Fru, can you keep watch on the left portion?" Kaywin was all business tonight; he threw in the Fru-Fru thing to let them know that **friendly**-Kaywin was still alive and well, and would be back with them tomorrow.

"Not if you keep calling me that."

"Alright. I'm going to tell you guys something you already know. Do not look away. If you have to blink, make it quick." He wanted to see this green flash. Then he wanted to breathe a sigh of relief and go back to bed. In the morning, he wanted to wake up, eat his cow patty, and work hard all day to make *Tomorrow Never Knows* the fastest ship in the known universe. He wanted to follow this routine for a few months, break the speed record on Valentines Day, then die in his sleep that night of natural causes. He would dearly love to do all this without the fate of the entire Earth resting on his tired shoulders. He had been standing there in the cold dark common area for thirty minutes already. He did breathe a miniature sigh of relief that his friends were there to help him. "I wish our video function wasn't blocked. I would really like to record this, to be sure."

"We can't record the whole thing, but if we **think** we see something we can use the flashback function to preserve the previous fifteen seconds," said Dublin, careful not to tear his attention from the sky above the ridge.

"What? How does that work?"

"Like this." Dub raised his Sofee to his mouth, still looking straight ahead like he was hypnotized. "FB."

Kaywin could hear tiny voices from Dub's wrist, "*I wish our video function wasn't blocked. I would really like to record this, to be sure.*" The video, if they had been looking at it, would have shown them only Kaywin's right butt-cheek, toward which it had been pointing at the time.

"That's great! That's perfect! Let's do that; if we see anything, do the FB thing!"

Anyone watching the three from behind would have seen them raise their left wrists in unison and rest them on the lip of the giant window, pointing outward. A few seconds of silence followed. Then Prudence whispered, "How come we can use FB but not regular video?"

Dub answered from the other side. "FB is new to the 47's. It uses a completely different storage file. Security here hasn't caught up." And he was correct. Security doesn't usually catch up with technology until someone breaches it, and the need for correction becomes obvious.

More silence followed. This time Kaywin broke it with a whisper. "How did you record your matador dance-thing?"

"That was a file photo of myself that I pretty much animated. That was more of a cartoon than a video of a live performance." These were the last words spoken for several minutes. The little band of three stood there, unflinching, for almost an hour, well before and well after the one-thirty to two AM time frame that Dombroski had specified. At 2:14 AM, Kaywin Lafontaine's forehead bumped into the thick glass in a moment of overwhelming weakness and despair. The other two read his mind. He thought about pulling them in with his arms, to feel less alone in the impossible task that lay ahead. Then he remembered Pru slapping away his hand like two days ago when he had put it on her shoulder to get her attention about something. Damaged goods, all of them. So he used his words.

"Well guys," he spoke quietly to the floor at his feet, "looks like it's on us."

Dublin turned toward the other two in the semi-darkness. His jaw was set. They couldn't *see* it trembling, but they could hear it in his voice. "That's alright. We can do it."

"Let's save the world."

16

I Can't Stand It

This whole hero thing was almost over before it began. Dublin watched in horror the next morning as Kaywin was led out of Conference Room 8 by Jerkboy and Bruniette. *What do they know?* **How** *do they know it?*

Kaywin was outwardly composed but inwardly shaking as he and his two burly escorts rode in the oversized lift from the first to the fifth level. He struggled to mentally prepare himself for whatever was about to happen, but he could only guess what that might be. He weighed the possibilities as the elevator elevated.

Bruniette, behind him, kept poking Jerkboy in front of him with his rifle, until Jerkboy, quick as lightning, jabbed the butt of his own rifle with great force into his provoker's gut.

This little exchange told Kaywin something. JB was limiting the horseplay. Normally he and his bud would be rolling around on the floor by now, slamming each others' heads into the wall. He was practicing his 'respectable' face, his 'I-can-be-trusted-with-this-chief-of-security-position' face. This indicated, in Kaywin's mind, that they were about to visit Commander MacFray himself. So this was big. He gulped, and imagined himself to be completely innocent of any espionage. He was a lonely man who had come here to die. *Kill*

427

me now, if you want.

They disembarked on the fifth level and headed briskly down the corridor toward the forbidden zone. Trying to not appear interested, Kaywin saw Jerkboy enter a code on the security lock. The MCP had cut corners wherever possible. That's why in Houston they had stayed in old college dorms; that's why they had ridden in dangerously outdated transport vessels to the Moonbase, and that's why the touchscreen here wasn't even set up for palm-print recognition. He tried desperately to recognize the sequence that Jerkboy was entering, without turning his head the slightest bit in that direction. But it was like eleven digits, and he entered them super-fast.

The door, airtight like all of them on the Moonbase (so that a crack or a bullet-hole somewhere in the enormous complex wouldn't suffocate all of them) slid open. The small infirmary was on the right as they pushed through. This was for MCs who were too injured for the downstairs nurse to handle, but not so injured that they had to be shot (anything that took longer than a week to recover from, and you were probably done for).

One of the doctors just inside the open door of the infirmary was eating a donut. Jerkboy threatened her on his way by, "If those donuts are all gone when I get back I'm going to kill somebody." Coming from someone else this may have been funny. Not from him.

Just after that, on the left, was the Security Chief's Office. It said so right on the door. This time Kaywin tried a little strategy. Instead of trying to memorize the entire code, he concentrated on retaining the first four digits. Four-Three-One-Two. It wasn't much, but it was something.

Sure enough, when the door slid open Commander Mac-Fray's face, with its red-lidded eyes and thin lips, came into view. He was leaning his tall but slight body against JB's desk with his arms crossed. He unfolded himself into the upright position as his security goons entered with their person of interest in tow.

"Sit down." He gestured to a solitary chair four feet in front of him. It was a comfortable, high-backed chair, upholstered with green velour and set solidly on mahogany legs carved in the likeness of lion's paws. It matched the strange, austere dignity of the room. It looked like they had passed through some kind of wormhole from Moonbase 2 into the study of a nineteenth-century country estate. Dark wood shelves with real books lined two of the walls. The high ceiling was pocked with rising tiers of little domes--almost as if a perfect cluster of grapes had been turned upside-down and pressed upward to leave an impression--softly lit and awash in painted detail. Thin, graceful wooden arches crisscrossed them. The room was very much out of place with the stark modern cleanliness of the rest of the Moonbase. It must have been the quirky request of the megalomaniac behind the entire complex--this had to be Brandenberg's office on the occasions he chose to visit his Grand Hotel on the Moon. Odd that a man so devoid of class should seek to surround himself with it...and Kaywin wondered too if the Senator knew that a wild animal was prowling his study in the guise of 'Security Chief'.

Two things let the prisoner know that he had not been magically transported to the Pre-Civil War countryside. The entire wall behind the huge oaken desk was thick glass looking out over Hermite Crater. A strange view, framed as it was in the trappings of antiquity. The other thing was the nearly wall-sized viewscreen on the left. In the one second it took to sit down, Kaywin glanced at it casually and saw two icons that made his heart race, above and beyond the tension of the coming interrogation:

'Low orb bound' said one.

'High orb bound' said the one below it.

Low orbit boundaries and high orbit boundaries? Maybe? Could these contain the codes to bypass the flight boundaries? Before he could daydream much further, Commander MacFray continued.

"Let's make this brief, Mr. Lafontaine. I don't put a lot of time in my schedule for nonsense. So tell me why you set your alarm for one-oh-five this morning."

That wasn't the question Kaywin was expecting. Was that all they knew? That he had set an alarm? Did they know that Dombroski had attempted to fire the gun assembly very shortly after that? Did they infer a connection, especially after the two had spent a free-practice cruiser session together a few days earlier? Did they have access to Kaywin's Sofee? Or were they **assuming** he had set an alarm, based on hidden cameras recording his late-night stroll...If they had access to his Sofee, was it **complete** access? If so, it was only a matter of time before they found the gun assembly blueprints and firing codes, disguised as Beatles songs and Alabama vacation photos.

They might know everything.

They might know nothing. *Let's give them nothing to work with.*

"Well...it's a little embarrassing...it's for my roommates' sake as much as mine. See, since my wife and daughter were killed four years ago--"

At this point, Jerkboy yawned exaggeratedly.

His rude, stupid antics didn't usually get under Kaywin's skin, because he knew that was exactly what the disturbed youth wanted, but this time the crass insensitivity caught him with his guard down. For a split second, he thought it might be just as good to go down fighting. Why not punch this arrogant jock right in his sneering pretty-boy face, one time, really good, and then get shot? Kaywin actually stood up, and fairly quickly, with the thought of doing this. But the look on Jerkboy's face--a look of surging gleeful surprise at the possibility of a fight, like a kid rounding a corner on Christmas morning to see a pile of presents that dwarfed his wildest imaginings--stopped him in his tracks. *This is just what he wants. I will be throwing everything away if I hit him. Possibly throwing away all of humanity...*

He re-routed himself and pretended that he had only been getting up to lean against the back of the chair. Jerkboy's grin widened even further. He knew the old man had just chickened out.

"Since they were killed," resumed Kaywin "I keep having this nightmare, where I'm walking the baby to sleep, and we fall down the stairs--I guess there's no need to describe it--but anyway, it's horrifying, and I wake up screaming--"

"Like a little girl?" Jerkboy asked.

"--yes. Like a little girl." Kaywin had recovered his composure. "Sephal doesn't get too cranked up over it, but I can tell that Jason--you know Jason Vindaloo--is getting pretty sick of it. Which, I don't blame him. Anyway, I don't have the dream **every** night, but when I do it's usually right around two-thirty. I can't tell you how many times"--he was picking up steam now, hoping the onslaught of his words would demonstrate to them that he wasn't having to weigh them carefully before spitting them out, that he had nothing to hide-- "I can't tell you how many times I've woken up screaming, and my Sofee says '2:32 AM'." Jerkboy was back to leaning against the bookshelves a few feet away, cleaning under his left-hand fingernails, using his right-hand fingernails to do so. Kaywin continued, "I thought maybe I should try something new. So I set my alarm for 1:05, to break up my sleep cycles, to see if maybe it would stop me from having the nightmare..." He sat back down in the green chair. Commander MacFray just stared down at him silently, like a pastor regarding the cold corpse of a congregation member between hymns. Kaywin played stupid. "Should I not be doing that?"

"Should-I-not-be-doing-that?" JB parroted in a mocking, high-pitched whine.

"You were awake for quite some time. It was past 2:30 AM when you returned to your bed." MacFray's face was unreadable as he said this.

"I went for a walk. I was enjoying my own thoughts. I don't have too much time left to live, and our days are very busy, of course."

"Where did you go?"

"The common area just down the hall from here. It's got the best view. Again, should I not be doing this?"

"We don't have a stated policy against it. Let's call it a **preference.** I would **prefer** for you to never do that again."

There was cold menace in his voice. "Are we clear on this?"

"Yes sir."

"Alright. Go back to work. All of you."

It was a super-awkward walk back past the infirmary, through the security door, and past the common area. Jerk-boy strode angrily, with a lot of frustrated, suspicious ideas tumbling around in his thick skull. Everything he *ever* did or said was angry, of course, but usually there was a level of self-amusement to it...a sadistic pride in the bootprints that he left on the face of life. There was none of that now as the three of them walked in silence. The situation had clearly not been resolved to his satisfaction. Had the Commander of Moon-base 2 MCP Activities not been there, Kaywin had no doubt that the questioning would have been less delicate.

When they got on the elevator to descend back to level one, it was deserted. Everybody was already hard at work at their various duties around the Moonbase. A cold chill ran down Kaywin's spine as Bruniette positioned himself rather closely behind him, despite the plentiful space in the lift built for thirty-plus people. As soon as the doors slid shut, Jerk-boy hit a button, pausing the elevator. Kaywin felt his arms pinned suddenly behind him. He had no intention of fighting back, so he just braced himself.

JB's massive right fist rocked the left side of his face. He felt his lip split, and a tooth loosen, as the blood gushed around it. "Did you have a good time with Dombroski the other night?" He followed this with two slams to Kaywin's gut. Bruniette released the older man as he doubled over, gasping for breath and spitting blood. His left molar twinkled and bounced in slow motion across the cold floor of the lift.

He said nothing and did nothing, though his pride compelled him strongly to get up and give these two a fight.

He had a good long blink, and when he opened his eyes, Jerkboy was crouched down inches from his face. Kaywin could smell the coffee and breakfast pastry on his hot breath. "I don't know what you're up to Lafontaine. But I **will** know. And when I find out, I'm gonna hurt you real bad, until you beg for the Scourge."

Kaywin raised up to his hands and knees to catch his breath, a string of bloody drool still connecting him to the floor. Jerkboy's 'good' spirits had returned, and when the elevator doors opened on Level One, he shoved Bruniette forcefully into the corridor, where an older woman tripped over him. This amused JB to no end. The doors closed on his rasping laughter, leaving Kaywin alone.

With the arm of his red jumpsuit, he mopped the blood and the tooth toward him. The lost molar made him think of his daughter. He wondered if the tooth fairy came to the Moon. He thought that Victoria, wherever she was, might get a kick out of it if Daddy put the tooth under his pillow tonight. He put it in his pocket and stood up. With his other sleeve, he dabbed at his messed up mouth. He pushed the button to open the lift doors and started back to work.

Blood on his left sleeve, swinging out in front of him; blood on his right sleeve, swinging out in front of him. *Well, there you have it. They are officially on to us.*

Dublin was furious when he saw his beaten-up friend return to the conference room. But at the same time, he was relieved that Kaywin hadn't been detained, or killed.

They listened to Kaywin's almost whispered account over supper that night, as he tried to chew with the right side of his mouth only. He glossed over the beating and focused his account on the intriguing file names he'd caught a glance at on JB's viewing wall. It was good information--now what to do with it? Pru cooperated with his unspoken wish to not obsess on the elevator episode (it took more than a busted lip and a lost tooth to impress her anyway) but Dublin kept steering the conversation back to the beating, rehashing it with youthful angst. He promised revenge. Kaywin talked him down repeatedly. He eventually let it slip that he was going to put the tooth under his pillow. Dublin thought it was hilarious. Prudence had never heard of such a thing.

Kaywin got a good laugh the next morning, making his face hurt.

The tooth was gone from under his pillow. In its place, wrapped in a napkin, was half of a biscuit.

"**Half** a biscuit?" cried Dublin, as he and Kaywin approached CR8 a little while later. "That dang Sephal! The tooth fairy was supposed to bring you a **whole** biscuit!"

It was a good thing they had each other. The weeks following the little inquisition in Jerkboy's office were a repeating pattern of relentless labor, cruiser practice at higher and higher speeds, and, on the nights when they didn't have access to free practice, the habitual meetings in Dub's room.

Ving was usually there, pecking away at his Sofee screen like a Kalaysian chicken, deep in his own little world. Monday and Wednesday nights it was his turn to practice, and they could speak a **little** more freely. They really didn't know how much they were being watched, or listened to. The little dorm rooms that they called home would eventually house the civilian labor force that would keep 'La Lune' running; it didn't **seem** like there would be much use for built-in hidden cameras or microphones. But their mission was too important to take chances. They spoke mostly in code. Trying to bust out of the fly zone and reach the gun assembly was trying 'to get tickets to the Valentine's Dance'.

They gave it this name because they had decided early on that the speed trials on Valentine's Day would likely be their last chance to make a run at their target. Obviously they hoped to fire the assembly much sooner than this, as soon as possible. The more time they could leave for the legitimate scientists of Earth to tackle the issue of the Rogue Planet, the better.

The 'Low Orb Bound' and 'High Orb Bound' icons that Kaywin had noted on Jerkboy's viewing wall seemed like their best starting point. But how to get to that starting point? So far, they had the first four digits of a ten or eleven digit code, the one for JB's office. As for the other lock, the outer security area lock, they had nothing.

Dublin considered himself something of an expert at bypassing protections with his Sofee, a mildly successful amateur hacker… But it seemed very likely that their Sofee activity was at least *available* for Jerkboy and MacFray's viewing pleasure. In fact, it was more probable than not at this point that they were actively monitoring it.

"One slip-up and we're toast," was how Pru summarized the situation.

They were deep into the program now, and its ravages

were written all over them like crude paintings over the cave walls of their personal despair.

Neither Prudence, nor Dublin, nor the much older Kaywin had ever been involved in a car accident. Twenty-second century highway technology made it almost impossible for vehicles to contact each other. But every time they experienced nuclear acceleration in their cruisers--especially *Tomorrow Never Knows*--their bodies underwent a similar trauma. Every muscle in their thinning frames clenched, muscles they never knew they even **had** before. This instinctive, spasmodic bracing for impact was hard to control. The best pilots were the ones who had mastered it mentally. Jerkboy, Ving, and a couple of others all walked away from a practice flight like it was nothing. The others crawled from their cramped cockpits like an eighty year-old man out of a well. It wore them down like nothing they had ever experienced.

Pru was the hardest to behold. She was pushing herself beyond her limits. At first, she was like a tiny pony out in the lunar pits, pulling the entire crew behind her. But they had risen to the challenge of her aggressive pace, barreling through four relay connections per day consistently. But unlike Prudence, these pit crew Goners spent **their** evenings relaxing and refreshing themselves, or collapsing into their bunks early. Prudence spent them studying the piloting manuals, practicing in the cruisers, or scheming weakly with the boys. Occasionally there was an old episode of *Atlantica* or *Planet of the Guinea Pigs* that Dublin swore she just **had** to watch (she always regretted it) or a song that Kaywin would talk her into listening to ("Turn it off! I'm not listening to a song called 'Dear Prudence'!") but mainly she seemed intent on killing herself with work.

It was harder to make time for saving the world than any of them had expected. They were all three willing, but what a struggle it was turning out to be. They were all overwhelmed by the workload, and underwhelmed by their lack of heroic instincts and their inability to plot under pressure. It was an alarming torpor they found themselves in.

"I can't do it," said a frustrated Dublin one night. "There is no discreet way to 'purchase tickets' for the 'Valentine's Dance'. If we could just somehow get into the 'ticket office' I think I could bypass the protections and make a purchase on the two tickets you saw." He had been making bolder and bolder attempts, with no success; but apparently with no repercussions either, if you don't count some very strange, lingering looks from Jerkboy. Either no one in Security had noticed the activity on his 47, or they were laughing (over their breakfast pastries) at the feebleness of his attempts.

"I could set my alarm for 1:05 AM again. That got me into the 'ticket office' last time." Kaywin was stretched out on his back on Dub's bottom bunk with his right arm draped over his aching eyes. Tiredness dripped from the tenor and tone of his mumbling voice. Here he was, still alive. His wife and daughter were not. This whole thing was more than he had bargained for. He couldn't help thinking about the easier ways out he could have taken.

His exhaustion was bad enough. Now a *new distraction* had begun to chip away at his sanity as well, like a slowly dripping faucet...

He studied the ascetic. He watched his mannerisms, his patterns, his comings and goings, as if there would be clues hidden in these things that he could decipher about the man's cryptic past. More and more he began to suspect and despise him. He saw him in a new light. What if he wasn't holy and repentant? What if he was an addict, and a coward, and a fake? Was he wasting away in remorse for something terrible he had done? Or was he gloating, laughing as he stole two more years of life, two more than the justice system might have allowed him? Was he a man of God?

Or was he a murderer?

June 14, 2126

"Psssst! Dub!"

"Oh my God Pru! You scared the crap out of me! What are you doing up? It's like five o'clock in the morning!"

"I need you to hide something for me."

Dublin had just opened up the janitor's closet in his cleaning quadrant, the one on Level Four right outside the cafeteria. He could see Pru's tiny silhouette against the slightly lesser dimness of the corridor behind her. She was carrying something dark and bulky. "What is it?"

"Just hide it. Quick. I have to get back to bed. Hide it good. People are going to be looking for it."

Fifty minutes later her alarm went off, along with Jordache and Judy's. Jordache made her usual I-can't-believe-it's-time-to-get-up sound, a low, wet, husky growling rumble that sounded like a vicious dog choking on its own blood. Prudence and Judy winced at each other, like they always did. Then Prudence stretched, yawned, and headed into the tiny bathroom. She stepped back out a half a second later without having used it. She seemed to have noticed something on the wall between the bathroom door and their front room door, or rather, something **missing.**

"Where's my half-grav? They didn't bring me my half-grav!"

A scene ensued. The head of laundry had to get involved. He was a burly man named Robert who hated doing laundry, and couldn't have thought of a worse way to live out his final days. But he was no match for Dorna Lee, who was fired up at the prospect of her entire crew being delayed because of a stupid mistake by one of Robert's MCs. The room was searched. Other rooms were searched. The crew of three assigned to deliver the clean grav-suits on their hall was questioned. Time was ticking away, and Dorna Lee was running out of patience.

"Just get her a new one!"

"Stella says she delivered it."

"Just **get** her a new one!"

"I'm not spending my morning filling out a report for a missing half-grav that Stella says she delivered!"

"Then don't fill out a report! Look, we have got twenty-five minutes to get to the compression chamber! I'm not sending Prudence out to die in a full-grav suit; now **get her a new one!**"

Robert got her a new one.

Late June was the end of the road for a couple hundred more Goners.

A power failure in a small section of Level One during the middle of the night caused the heat to falter. There was an immediate, sharp drop in temperature. Battery-powered alarms were in place for just such an emergency, but they failed in three of the rooms. Eight MCs froze to death in their sleep.

A worse problem piggybacked on top of this one. The sudden violent temperature drop had caused some of the construction materials on Level One to contract, resulting in a breach to the air-seal the following evening. The artificial atmosphere was like "see ya," rushing out through the small crack in seconds. The emergency systems worked in this case. The corridor hatches were sealed instantly and automatically; the problem was that one hundred and ninety MCs had been enjoying their evening free time in it. They gasped out their last over chessboards and reruns.

Between these freak accidents and the more 'natural' (or at least usual) rate of attrition, the ranks of Goners at the Moonbase were thinning rapidly. It was eerie, by early July, to cast one's eyes around the cafeteria. Except for the two ascetics, and a handful of freaks who had yet to make friends (even in a roomful of other freaks) people tended to sit where they had always sat. So it looked like hundreds of poor souls had just been plucked up out of their seats randomly and dumped in some trash heap somewhere.

This was the condition of the little MC colony on July 8th, 2126, when reinforcements rolled into Hangar One and spilled, slipped and tumbled out of the enormous transports. They tripped and bounced into the same strange little world that Kaywin, Dublin and Prudence had by now grown used to.

Jason Vindaloo was supposed to be the one to hang back and greet the new arrival in room 3347, but he had suffered an apparent heart attack three days earlier. He'd been moved quickly upstairs to the infirmary, and neither Kaywin, nor Sephal, nor any of their acquaintances caught wind of his whereabouts ever again.

It fell to Kaywin to make the newcomer feel welcome. It was strange and wonderful to relax on his bunk while he waited. Finally, at 10:02 (about fifteen minutes later than he expected) there was a knock on the door. He wooshed it open.

There stood his new roommate, Alphonso. Kaywin was surprised at the man's age and condition. He appeared to be in his late seventies, at least. He was tallish and rail-thin, and tottered unsteadily. Some of this imbalance was to be expected of course, as he acclimated to the reduced gravity. But Kaywin felt that some of it was age-related. Maybe he would stabilize once they got him into his full-grav.

What alarmed Kaywin even more was the fact that Alphonso had required the kind assistance of two women to even **find** room 3347. They stood there now supporting the old man by his elbows. The same concern that Kaywin felt was written across their faces. He reached his hand out to shake Alphonso's. The newcomer responded a couple of seconds later, robotically.

There was a familiar glassy look to the man's dark eyes. They were tragically vacant, like Kaywin's grandfather's had become in his final years. *What is going on here? This can't be right! This man has Alzheimer's Disease!* Alphonso spoke.

"Are we in Lawrence or Fall River? They've changed some things around, huh?"

Prudence waited for her new roomie with something that

was nearly happiness. This woman, she had found out only yesterday, was going to be the new Mole!

When Dorna Lee had told her in the cafeteria last night, Pru had nodded, and smiled her half-smile. Then, much to her own surprise she had had to excuse herself to the bathroom for a minute. Sitting there in a stall, she felt hot tears of relief streaming down her little cheeks and wreaking havoc on the Yin and Yang symbols she had painstakingly drawn.

The mole job was in a much more do-able state than it had been three months earlier, when Pru had been shoved into it. On July 6th, she had connected the last of the delinquent relays.

She'd gotten a little piece of cake for dessert that night, in recognition of her awesome achievement. Dorna Lee had grabbed the microphone from the hand of Aristophane, or whoever it was, and made a brief announcement, praising her. There was a little round of applause. A lot of the MCs looked a bit surprised. *That little punk girl? Did what?*

Prudence had kept her head down, staring deeply into the pores of her yellow cake-slice, imagining each of them to be a cold, dark hole on the Moon. She found a blank space in her mind and just counted the holes. Finally the applause was over. Thank God. She had no idea what to do with this feeling.

Now, sitting on her bunk and waiting for the new chick, she was confident that whoever it was, she could **surely** handle one relay per day. If not, that was Houston's problem. Finally, a knock. The door slid open, and she greeted her replacement.

Elsie was taller than Prudence, though still short. She was

in her late thirties, and super-thin and mousey. She appeared to be vapid...frail...she moved with a sort of medicated, deliberate slowness. Thinning light-brown hair fluttered dreamily as she entered the stark dorm room. Her voice was high, very soft, and a little afraid, like she was trying to get through life without ever once offending anybody. Prudence couldn't help picturing the first conversation between this wisp of a woman and the brash New-Yorker, Jordache. She had doubts instantly about this woman's stamina, her intelligence, and, most worrisome of all, her gumption.

But hey. She would fit in a hole.

Pru enjoyed a full week immersed in the pilot program, eight days actually, before she got pulled aside in the corridor outside Hangar Two right after changing out of her flight-suit one evening.

And what a week it had been. The pilots were practicing very basic maneuvers at low-enhanced speeds, which sounds easy, but was clearly not. Even Jerkboy struggled to alter his flight pattern by five degrees without spinning out of control. When the co-pilot of 'Yellow Submarine' died of head trauma after one of these exercises, Kaywin had a difficult, cryptic conversation with Rita. She agreed, tearfully, to transfer to 'Yellow Submarine' so Kaywin could train Prudence full-time. Pru had taken full advantage, actually taking the controls of *Tomorrow Never Knows* for like twenty seconds during a straight-line flight. Dublin was finally getting some legit co-pilot time, though a permanent spot had not yet opened up. This was deadly fast work, but it was so much better than the tunnels.

As soon as Prudence saw Dorna Lee's face in the corridor after that eighth day, her heart sank. She knew right away what was about to happen. She felt so low and so defeated that she might as well have been back in her room in Geyserville.

"Can I talk to you Prudence?"

"No." She said it, but couldn't exactly run away or anything. So she stood and listened.

"Elsie got herself electrocuted today. I'm so sorry, Prudence. There's just nobody else here, on the entire Moonbase who can do this job right now. We can try again in October..."

Pru stared down at the shapes of her tiny black boots on the grey carpet. Then she saw someone on her left emerging from the door she had just come out of. In a shocking breach of protocol, she reached out, lightning fast, and grabbed his arm with all the force of her dark surging emotions. She grabbed him like a parent about to lose her mind on a misbehaving three-year old. "Fitz! We need you here."

"Ow?" said Fitz Renaldo, grabbing the arm she had just released.

"The stupid new mole is dead already." Now she squared up to address Fitz and Dorna Lee equally and forcefully. Her voice trembled with emotion. "Here's the deal. I will do your one [word I can't repeat] relay per day, to keep up with the solar collectors. Since everyone on this [same word] Moonbase is too fat or too stupid. But I finish by 10 AM and I come back inside to the pilots. Everyday. Or there's no deal at all."

"Prudence, they're not going to agree to an extra opening and closing of the compression chamber every--," Dorna Lee started to say.

"Then there's no deal."

Fitz jumped in. "Prudence, I'm sorry to see you have to go back, but I don't think there's any 'dealing' about it--,"

"There is so. There is either a deal, or I kill myself, like I should have a long time ago. You think you can stop me but you can't. There are five ways I could do it. I promise you." She crossed her arms and cocked her hip out. Her glare was unflinching, frightening, and imperious. Fitz looked at Dorna Lee. Dorna Lee looked at Fitz. Fitz spoke, each word a semi-note higher than the last, indicating his concession to the greater strength of her spirit. "I guess we'll see what we can do."

Weeks passed in dragging helplessness, and then months. "We're getting nowhere," said Dublin. "It's freaking **October** and we don't have the flyzone boundary codes. We don't even have the security hall codes. Is human history about to end because we're too tired to care?"

"Not exactly **nowhere**," answered Kaywin. "We can steer a cruiser now at enhanced speeds. That's important."

"Yeah," said Prudence, echoing Dub's hangdog tone. "We can steer it into a wall."

"We need an idea to get us into security," Dublin said, without offering one.

"Kaywin's old. Maybe he could have a heart attack," said Prudence.

"They would test him down here and know he was faking it," Dublin replied. "But he could break a leg or something."

They all looked at each other. They all wondered tiredly why they hadn't thought of this in July, or August, or September. And they suddenly had the starting point they had been desperate for.

October's reinforcements brought no replacement for Prudence. That's alright. She wasn't really expecting one.

The new batch of MC's was huge, and brought a lot of questions.

For starters, there were several more lost-looking senior citizens, like Kaywin's roommate Alphonso.

There were a great number of immigrants, non-English speakers. If you looked at their dazed faces passing by you could almost **see** them thinking in another language.

And then there was Malcolm, a young man with all the physical and facial indicators of a person with Down Syndrome. His features were a little on the flat side, and his eyes had the distinctive upward slant. He was somewhat short and somewhat heavy. He also looked unusually happy for someone entering Suicide City.

Did all of these people know what they were doing when they signed up for the MCP?

Did all of them even **sign up**?

The sheer volume of the latest class of Goners indicated more to Kaywin, Dublin and Prudence than it did to their fellows, who labored on in ignorance of the Rogue Interstellar Planet. This was a desperate build-up by Brandenberg and his cronies. No doubt the same thing was happening on Mars, possibly in even greater numbers. The **rich** people of Earth, at least, would have sanctuary when disaster struck.

Did Brandenberg **know** that his gun was inadequate? Did he know it perfectly well, and was simply content to let the Earth be destroyed?

"Surely not," whispered Kaywin at the supper table. The cacophony of new voices in the cafeteria covered up their conversation. Even the thirty televisions were drowned out. They could speak almost freely.

"So why wait? If he thinks his gun will destroy the RIP, why not destroy it today? Why not yesterday? Why not four years ago when they discovered it?" asked Dublin. He was talking to Kaywin and Prudence, but looking over their heads at one of the screens, which was not his custom. His brow furrowed. He put down his fork. Prudence and Kaywin turned around to see what he was staring at.

On the television, Rich Brandenberg in his Dizastra 3000 glided slowly through a throng of screaming, burning Hawaiian Islanders. His lips were moving but the cafeteria was too noisy for them to hear what he was saying. It didn't matter. They'd seen this one a hundred times. Dublin, mesmerized, intoned Brandenberg's lines:

"Hey, Ohana, is this the way to the beach?" He removed his helmet just to take off the greasy blue scrunchy, reshape his pony-tail, and put it back on. Something big and flaming fell out of the sky, killing a man behind him instantly. The camera panned back as he took the hint and put his helmet back on. It became obvious now that he was on a surfboard, riding a lava flow slowly down a jungly mountainside. His board was burning away under his feet but he didn't care. *His board was burning away under his feet but he didn't care!*

There was a huge, very realistic explosion behind him, audible even over the throng in the Moonbase 2 cafeteria. The hundreds of Polynesian extras went up in flames. "Ooooh! Something *nasty's* coming!"

Dublin shook himself out of his trance. "They just showed a Dizastra 3000 commercial, followed by a JulesVernia commercial, followed by a Mars Colony commercial, followed by a Dizastra 3000 commercial...He **wants** this RIP thing to get close! He wants to bleed every last credit out of this that he can! He wants a worldwide panic!"

Kaywin and Pru turned back around toward Dub. Their eyes were wide. Kaywin mumbled something, but they were all so locked in to each other that they could hear it, plain as day.

"And then he thinks he's going to swoop in at the last minute with his big gun, and save the world..."

"And win the Presidency," whispered Dub.

Pru counted one-two-three on her fingers. "The Earth. The Moon. And Mars. All his." Disgust clouded her face. "When's the next flight to Jupiter?"

Dublin had no less than three new roommates. He, like Kaywin and Pru, was fired up by the insidiousness of Brandenberg's plan, and ready to renew their efforts to prematurely fire his stupid gun. But now they had no place to convene. Suicidal people swarmed the Moonbase; even the formerly quiet common areas were mobbed. In their highly excited state, our three heroes found the unstable cackling of the newcomers jarring and unsettling.

Dublin fidgeted his hands around in his pockets and found something that gave him an idea. "Follow me," he said.

Five minutes later, they were entrenched in their new headquarters. The janitor's closet wasn't the Ritz-Carlton, but it would do.

"You need to lose your key tonight," Prudence said to Dub. "And get a replacement tomorrow."

"Why?"

"Because! You are one fatality away from a permanent co-pilot gig! Which means…"

Kaywin finished her sentence. "Ooooooh, which means you won't have janitor duties anymore!"

Their brains seemed sharpened by the epiphany they had had. Neurons were firing that hadn't fired in months; ideas were flying, and for a short time it seemed as if they might actually be able to pull off the impossible.

One evening a couple of weeks later, Kaywin was stepping out of 3347 to head to supper. Alphonso, still alive, exited the room just ahead of him, and seemed to be surprised to see a familiar face passing in the hall. "Hey! You!"

The ascetic turned and doubled back. He said nothing, of course, but his open features demonstrated a willingness to listen.

"Why didn't you paint the trim?"

The ascetic drew a question mark on his forehead.

"Why didn't you paint the trim?"

Kaywin intervened. Through the super-gentle tone of his voice he tried to convey to the ascetic that Alphonso was not necessarily in his right mind. "Alphonso, buddy, I think you might have the wrong guy…"

"Don't tell me I've got the wrong guy! Five-thousand credits is a lot of money, especially after I bought the paint! You were supposed to come back and do the trim! My apartment building, 108 Cedar Street, in Manchester!

Panic flitted across the ascetic's face. And it wasn't about a paint job. He looked for a second like he might take off running.

"Alphonso," said Kaywin. "I'll find out about the trim. You go on to supper before the chicken's all gone." Then they were alone in the hall, the man on the edge of doing something terrible, and the nervously grinning zealot. Seconds passed. Kaywin thought his heart might explode.

"You from Manchester?" he said finally.

Once, the ascetic wrote. Kaywin nodded.

"You an addict? An Excelsiadon addict?"

The tall, filthy burned-out man knew he was in grave trouble. Nonetheless, he indicated to the once on his forehead again.

"Why are you here? Why did you join up?"

He got to the point. "Did you kill someone?"

The ascetic looked downward and breathed. He made the sign of the cross, then started to wipe his forehead. Kaywin felt a sweltering hot disgust at the symbolic gesture; he was not a religious man himself, but his Mother was a devout Catholic. This was an insult to her, and to everyone everywhere who had **refrained** from evil in the name of something bigger than themselves. If this man had murdered--if this was the man who had ruined him--and he was casually wiping it away with four flicks of the wrist...Kaywin didn't know what he might do. The man was writing again.

Beyond Judgemen-- Kaywin slapped him in the face and the grease pencil went flying. It was a feeling-out slap. He wasn't violent by nature. He was testing the ascetic's reaction, and his own willingness to do this.

"Did you kill my wife and daughter?"

The ascetic crouched and retrieved his grease pencil, still somehow trying to maintain his despicable, hypocritical air of holiness. He stood back up straight, and finished what he had started, forming the final little cross: **Beyond Judgement.**

The grease pencil flew twenty feet down the hall as Kaywin broke the man's jaw with a ferocious haymaker. People were rounding a corner in that direction. There was about to be a scene, and justice might be thwarted forever. Kaywin reached back and entered his room code. The door slid open. He held his left arm out, inviting the ascetic inside. The tall wretch knew well what he deserved, and entered willingly.

Once inside, he turned to face Kaywin behind him and fell to his knees. With no words exchanged, Kaywin understood that this was no supplication for mercy. It was an acceptance of his sentence. Without really thinking much about it, he closed his hands around the ascetic's throat with strange slowness. Then he squeezed. The warm meat of the condemned man's neck felt so odd on his own fingers. He watched the face redden, and the eyes bulge. It was horrible and disgusting. *I'm supposed to* **want** *this, right? This demon ruined me, and struck my two angels from the face of the Earth. I should be relishing this. It should feel wonderful to watch his hideous face turn blue...*

Oh my God, what am I doing? He felt an invisible hand on each of his shoulders, pulling him back. He knew that one was Victoria's and the other Nadine's. *Oh my God. What must they be thinking of me?*

His hands flew apart like oppositely charged magnets. "It's not helping!" he sobbed. "It's not helping!"

The ascetic rolled spasmodically on the floor, laboring to refill his agonized lungs with sweet oxygen. "Get up!" Kaywin screamed at him. "Get up!" He kicked him hard on the back of his thigh, which seemed contrary to his very recent act of mercy. With a colossal effort, and shaking violently, the miserable wretch got himself to his knees again. Kaywin towered over him, also shaking, but with electric rage; at the ascetic, at Brandenberg, at Jerkboy, at Pru's father, at all the girls who wouldn't even get a cup of coffee with Dub, at the economics that were about to damn the world, and the politics that were helping, at the complete and utter dementia he had descended into since March 17, 2122... His fists clenched and unclenched like powerful robot hands fed by a sputtering loose wire. His teeth clenched beyond clenching, and hot tears streamed down his distorted face, frozen at the very extremity of despair. His eyes searched frantically for something that would keep his mind from flying apart, and they found a spot on the ceiling directly above him that seemed to do the trick. He held this astonishing pose for eleven seconds without exhaling. The ascetic had recovered just enough to remark the oddness of the scene, and to wonder how it was that he himself was alive, while Kaywin seemed to be choking under invisible hands. Then, as quickly as three dominoes falling, the stricken man exhaled with a lurch, tore his gaze from the ceiling tile, and thudded to his knees violently, arriving face to face with the demon who defied revenge by begging for it.

"Alright," gasped Kaywin. "So we see how **that** went. I can't...I can't do it. I want to, and I think you want me to, but I can't...my girls... my girls don't want me to. My girls don't want me to kill you." They knelt there, panting like dogs and avoiding eye contact for a couple of minutes. Kaywin sort of came to after that; he started to feel like his old self who wouldn't hurt a fly.

He sensed that the ascetic was waiting for permission to get up and leave. "You can go." The broken-jawed, red-faced bleeding penitent staggered to his feet, looking ashamed. "Hey," said Kaywin, still on his knees. "I don't think he'll ask, but if does, what do I tell Alphonso about the trim?"

The ascetic felt around in his robe, then remembered that his grease pencil had gone flying down the hall. He stepped out in search of it. The door shut automatically behind him. Thirty seconds later there was a knock. Kaywin hit the button and it opened, from right to left. The trembling wreck had come back in his filthy robe, with the answer on his forehead.

Sorry

17

Dance This Mess Around

"Are you ready?" asked Kaywin. "It has to be a break. They're not going to send you up to the infirmary for a sprain, or a deep bruise…"

Dublin was at the top of the ladder that led up to the cockpit of *Tomorrow Never Knows*. He was only ten feet off the ground, but with the weight of his full-grav and the unforgiving concrete of the floor below, he figured it would be enough of a fall to break his leg.

Kaywin had wanted to go first, but Dublin had reminded him that he was under suspicion. "We're **all** under suspicion," had been Kaywin's response.

"Yeah, but you're the only one who's actually been taken in for questioning. I get the first shot at injuring myself. Besides, if I get in I have the best chance of hacking into the boundary code files."

Kaywin had to concede. It seemed wrong to let a perfectly good young man break himself, but it helped to remember that Dub was on the scrapheap like the rest of them.

Dub cleared his mind, the way he used to do before jumping off the old railroad trestle into Lake Hartwell. He backed out of the cockpit and deliberately misstepped. Kaywin just saw him disappear downward.

Dublin's leg caught awkwardly between the top two rungs. This altered his trajectory so that he took the fall more on his upper right arm, and then on his head. He blacked out, just for a couple of seconds.

When he woke up, he was still lying just as he had landed. He could hear McNinney, the engineer on *Maybelline*, tinkering away not more than fifteen feet from him. The deal was that Kaywin was supposed to play stupid and let someone else realize that Dublin had fallen. Otherwise suspicions might be aroused. So Dub lay there blinking up at the lights for a solid ten seconds, feeling the tingling numbness all through his body and mentally trying to diagnose himself. *Broken arm? Hopefully... Broken shoulder? That'll do...Fractured skull?...Sure feels like it...*

Finally McNinney, who had seen the whole fall, realized that nobody else was going to check on this idiot. "You alright?" Dublin could hear him ratcheting something as he asked.

"Yeah," Dub croaked instinctively. "I mean...maybe...I think so?...I think I need to go to the nurse. My shoulder hurts pretty bad."

There was a pause, and more ratcheting. "Alright," said McNinney. Backup in the cockpit of *Tomorrow Never Knows*, Kaywin sighed in exasperation at the engineer's bedside manner. He stuck his head out of the cruiser.

"Oh my God. Are you okay?" He said it just loud enough to attract attention to the scene, but not so loud that it looked like a setup.

"Uhhh, maybe **not**." Dub started to sit up, then lay back

down again. His left hand clutched at his right shoulder. A few people wandered closer, every one of them hoping somebody else would take charge. Eventually someone felt guilty enough to help the ugly kid up and walk him to the nurse's station in the corridor behind the hangar. It was Rita.

As the shock wore off, Dub became more and more convinced that he had successfully broken his shoulder. But the nurse, after a brief exploration of the area, told him it was just a bruise. Dublin protested, until she finally agreed to x-ray it.

Not broken. Dublin went back to work upset that he had failed, but with the memory of the nurse's cool hands on his bare shoulder to balance the disappointment.

Kaywin saw him come back into the bay and cursed under his breath. They had agreed to take turns. They had gentlemanly (or condescendingly; **you** pick) insisted on Pru going last. Hopefully it wouldn't be necessary. For the moment it fell on Kaywin. He would have to come up with something good.

He had been looking out for ideas all day. He didn't know if he had the guts to cut himself on the metal saw. He could expose himself to the nuclear reactor in the belly of the cruiser, but the risk there was that he might not live to tell about it. *So it falls on me...*he thought.

--That's it! It 'falls' on me!

He knew how he was going to do this. It would have to wait until tomorrow morning, but he knew exactly how he was going to do this.

Every cruiser was a little different, otherwise this wouldn't be a competition, it would just be a job at a factory. In the case of *Tomorrow Never Knows* the coolant coil had to removed after every enhanced-propulsion flight. They had to clean it perfectly and completely replace the coolant. Otherwise there was a real risk of blowing up on the next flight. This was not practical of course; a better cooling system would have to be developed if and when Jennifer's design was adapted for larger ships; but the goal here and now was to break the speed record for manned spaceflight. They would worry about the pain-in-the-butt maintenance stuff afterwards.

The coolant coil on their ship would have been forty-eight hundred pounds on Earth, give or take. So even at the discounted Lunar Gravity it weighed in at a nice, bone-crushing eight hundred pounds. There were two spares that had been removed from defunct cruisers; otherwise he wouldn't have risked damaging this one.

It was usually Kaywin's job to gently drop the coil mechanically onto a dolly and roll it to the 'Lift and Wash'. At this little community-use station it would then be attached to a hoist. It had to be elevated as it was cleaned so that every little nook could be accessed, and so that it wasn't sitting in its own runoff. There were three buttons on the wall behind the station: the one with the arrow pointing up, which raised the coil gently, the one with the arrow pointing down, which lowered it gently, and the one with the image of hands releasing a bird, which released it completely. Done in sequence this was all perfectly safe. Some idiot one time thought the bird being released meant 'up', and almost broke his buddy's hand. They had all been told this story. Maybe that's why the idea was ready-to-go in the back of Kaywin's mind.

"So I get to be your idiot?" cried Dublin when Kaywin proposed the plan in the janitor's closet that night.

"Or I can be the idiot, and you can be the one with the broken arm..."

"No, it's cool; I'll be the idiot."

Just by coincidence the next morning, Dublin Dunne happened to be walking by as Kaywin Lafontaine was getting ready to scrub his cruiser coil. "Hey man," said Kaywin, and the boy stopped in his tracks. Kaywin's gloved left hand rested for a minute on the lip of the chemical sink; the half-ton chunk of metal slowly swaying above it. "I didn't raise this thing up enough; I got the top and sides but I can't get the bottom. Can you--AAAAAAAGGGHHHH!!!!"

A highly nervous Dublin had pressed the button too early. This made for a convincing-looking accident; problem was that Kaywin's hand was a little too far back. The early release, combined with the swaying of the coil, had only succeeded in mangling Kaywin's left middle finger.

It hurt like the devil, especially with the chemical wash seeping into it. And, oh yes, it was broken, very much so, but at the end of the day it was one finger. It wasn't getting him into the infirmary.

Kaywin wasn't mad, and Dublin knew it. But when the finger was all cleaned, splinted and swaddled up he did hold it up good and straight for Dub to see.

Prudence didn't seem at all surprised or worried that her turn had come to maim herself for the future of humanity.

"I got it" was all she would say on the matter. She was

rocking back and forth on her empty upside-down five-gallon detergent bucket in the janitor's closet. They had the cards and the cribbage board set up in case someone busted in, but they weren't playing. "Let's go over the approach to the Valentine's Dance one more time" Pru said. "I've got Plan A down, but I don't think you guys are taking Plan B seriously enough. I think it's highly unlikely that all three of us make it to the Dance alive. I think Plan B should really be Plan A."

The other two weren't finished talking about how she was going to injure herself. "I could get one of those pneumatic--"

"I got it."

"I'm glad you're so confident," said Kaywin "just be aware that four--"

"I **got** it."

"Wanna hear a song?"

"I want to figure out how we get from Airlock One at the Dance Hall all the way to the punch bowl."

"It's a good song."

"Is it 'Dear Prudence'?"

Long pause. "Maybe."

"Not going to happen." They eventually got themselves on the same page. Huddled around Dombroski's old Sofee 45 they scarfed up the blueprints and codes of every 'Alabama Vacation photo' and rehashed for the hundredth time the details of where they would land near the gun assembly, where Airlock One was located beneath the massive weapon, the code for entering it, blah blah blah while they tried to stay awake. Late in their meeting, Pru remembered a bit of news.

"Did you guys hear about the tall ascetic?" Kaywin instantly hung his head in shame. They had been watching for days as the wretch with the broken jaw had struggled to eat his suppers. Wanda in the cafeteria would liquefy his meals for him, but if she was busy, or off-duty, he was out of luck. Now his malnourishment had reached a critical point. "He passed out at the wheel of *Black Magic Woman*.. He's been demoted to copilot of---wait for it---wait for it---the *White Rabbit!*"

"Wow!" said Dublin. "Ving and the ascetic ***together?*** Those conversations are going to epic!" Kaywin didn't like it. Everyone was here to die, but he felt directly responsible now for getting the ascetic demoted to death-mobile duty. He felt like he had robbed the man, potentially, of several months of life. Then he remembered what the ascetic had taken from ***him*** and he knew that he would sleep just fine that night.

Now the parting hour was at hand.

"Prudence," said Kaywin as they all stood up. "Are you going to try to hurt yourself tomorrow?"

"Nunya," she said, as in "nunya bidness."

"It sounds ridiculous, but be careful."

"Oh my God. Thanks for reminding me. Dublin--I need your spare key."

"What key?"

"The key to this closet, moron!" He handed it over without questioning her. When he placed it in her palm, their fingers touched for half a moment. He hung his head in his usual shame at the baseness of his thoughts. He prayed that she would still be alive in the world tomorrow.

It was 1:24 AM the next morning. Moonbase 2 was asleep

and her halls were very dim and deserted. From around a corner, five feet off the ground, a head popped out and scanned the approach to the janitor's closet.

Once she had gained the sanctuary of the closet, Prudence got on her belly and reached up under the lowest of the metal utility shelves on the left hand side. Her little hand came back with something that was mostly corroded and rusty, but sharpened and silvery at the tip.

She studied the railroad spike almost nostalgically for a minute. She had prepared it seven months ago back in Houston, in case her father had come to the stupid funeral thing. If he had tried to get her out of there somehow, she was totally prepared to kill him. Luckily, he had figured out that she couldn't earn any more drug-money for him, so he didn't show up. She'd gotten the spike through every bag-search and metal detector since. How could she **not** be a little attached to it?

She had kept it with her whenever possible; when **not** possible it had stayed stuffed into a small slit in her mattress. Until last week. Thanksgiving night to be exact. Something apparently small and very important had gone missing from the hangar. Everyone with access was a suspect. Rumor spread that Security was conducting room searches and body searches; she had just enough warning to get 'Rusty' stashed in the janitor's closet.

She could have retrieved the makeshift weapon five hours earlier when she'd been scheming in here with Kaywin and Dublin; but if one of them ever lost their mind and made a move on her, she didn't want them to know what her defensive strategy might be. She felt a twinge of guilt for thinking this way. But it was just a twinge, and it went away as soon as the thought did.

She paused before coming out of the closet. With the spike in her right hand, she spoke down at her left wrist. "Sofee. Change my Flashback prompt from 'FB' to "Oh my God, make it stop hurting!""

"Mole in the Hole!" shouted Dorna Lee at 7:51 the next morning. Two men lowered Prudence into the minus-three-hundred degree temperatures of tunnel number 447. None of them had noticed the tiny rip in the outer seal and thermal layers of her left Moon-boot. Pru had been feeling the cold already even on the upper crater plateau, even though it was relatively bathed in slanting solar rays. She had struggled not to limp noticeably on the walk down to the Lower pits. Now she was worried that she might have made the cut in the protective fabric too big. The pain was like being stabbed with an icicle; but the icicle wouldn't break, it just kept on stabbing.

She worked frantically on the relay, partly to distract herself from the pain, and partly because she didn't want to fall behind again.

Her plan was to work until the pain was intolerable--and then count to sixty. She had to quit working before the connection was half done because her hands were shaking so badly. She struggled to control her breathing while she waited. The moment came when the pain in her lower leg was the worst physical agony she had ever experienced. She started counting.

When she got to thirty-three she could no longer hold the tears back. She could feel the hot wetness messing up the small skull symbol on her left cheek, and the medium-sized one on her right. She tried to ignore the pain (forty-two seconds), she tried pretending the sensation of absolute cold was actually the sensation of intense heat (forty-nine seconds), she tried focusing in on the pain, and **relishing** it (fifty-eight, fifty-nine, SIXTY!) "DORNA LEE I'VE GOT A PROBLEM HERE GET ME OUT OF HERE QUICK I HAVE A PROBLEM DORNA LEE **DO YOU COPY?!**"

Dorna Lee had some kind of emergency kit with her: she slapped a temporary patch over the compromised fabric, barking orders and making threats the whole time. She didn't want to lose the best Mole in the history of the Moon, but beyond that she had a real affection for the little punk girl.

Pru was struggling to not lose consciousness. If she passed out, this whole stunt was useless. They got her into the compression chamber, then into the Level One locker rooms where two nurses awaited with a gurney.

As the affected area of her foot and lower leg were exposed to the warmer temperatures of the interior of the Moonbase, the agony became more than she had bargained for. They were in the lift, headed to Level Five, when rainbow lights began flashing behind her eyelids and the room began to spin. Not now, with the critical moment nearly at hand! She tried to prop up on her elbows to keep from blacking out. This sent extra blood flow to her lower body, and her left foot throbbed so violently that her stoic demeanor cracked a little and she cried out. But she stayed propped up.

Finally they got out of the lift and hustled down the hall toward the doors to the security area. The two nurses were rolling her headfirst. Pru dropped back into a fully reclined position, as if overcome. She put the back of her left hand over her left eye. She could hear the eleven numbers being punched in. The doors opened, and they started to roll her through. When Prudence cried out, she didn't have to fake it the way she had rehearsed it in her head. It came out only too naturally:

"Oh my God, make it stop hurting!"

The colored splotches of light began to obscure her vision again, and with the first half of her mission in the bag, she allowed herself to slip into painless blackness.

Prudence woke up alone in the middle of the night. She had passed out from the pain many many hours earlier, and they had given her something to keep her under for a while. This had just worn off. She panicked for a few seconds. She couldn't feel her left leg at all. Frantically she put her hands down under the cool sheets. Okay. Her leg was still there.

That business being sorted out, she moved on immediately to the second portion of her plan. "Sofee," she whispered. The darkened display lightened halfway. "Let's be super-quiet. Remember Jerkboy?"

"I don't have any record of a person named 'Jerkboy'."

"He's the man who attacked me in the woods in Houston on April First of this year. His real name is JB."

"I know JB."

"Yes. You tried to do a silent synch with his 47 a couple of times, and failed."

"I am sorry."

"It's alright. You still have that Sofee imprint on file, right?"

"Yes."

"Good. Anyway, what I need from you is to wake me up silently the next time Jerkboy approaches those security doors."

"At what proximity shall I awaken you?"

"Not critical. Let's say thirty feet. Now--do you know where the Security Chief Office doors are?"

"Yes."

"Give me a second silent alert when he is keying in his code for those doors. Now. I'm going to hold you up high so you can see out these windows. Tell me when you have a visual lock on the Security Chief Office keypad."

"Got it."

"Perfect. Now, let's change your Flashback prompt one more time. Change it to '(yaaaaawn); how long have I been asleep?' "

It cost Prudence three of her toes, but she accomplished in twenty hours what none of them had been able to do in five months. The FB of the second code was dim and distant, and somewhat obscured by Jerkboy's hand, but they were able to hone in on it and correctly extrapolate the two digits that were in question.

"So when do I do this?" asked Dublin. "When do I break in and get us some boundary codes?"

"You? What do you mean **you**?" fired Prudence. She jabbed at his injured shoulder with one of her little crutches. The three of them were sitting in the janitor's closet on their upside-down buckets. Her tone was aggressive, but for the most part their first 'Valentine's Dance Committee' meeting in a week had been enthusiastic, almost **happy**. They were flush with their first real taste of success.

"Well--it doesn't make sense for **all** of us to break in. It would be kind of a stupid risk...And of the three of us I think I stand the best chance of getting into those files. No offense."

"None taken," said Kaywin, exactly at the same moment Pru said, "You're an idiot."

"No, you're right," Kaywin conceded, though he too was not happy about it. He felt like he had dragged these two kids into something dangerous, and now they were doing all of the work. "One thing to consider. Dub, if you get busted, the crap is going to hit the fan. If you're able to get one of the codes, and get it from your Sofee to one of ours, maybe we can take our shot at the gun assembly without you, even if they're hauling you away. But we need for Pru to recover enough to get her clearance back. If there are two of us we double our chances. Pru, what did Dr. Ellis tell you this morning?"

Prudence scowled under her layered hair, lavender glimpses glowing from under a light peach curtain. "She said one week. December Nineteenth."

"I thought you said she had a crush on you?" Dublin said.

"She **does**, moron--that's why she won't rush me back!"

Kaywin nodded. A momentary silence turned into half a minute. The reality was sinking in. "There's your answer. We could go on December Nineteenth."

"We don't have free practice on the nineteenth," Pru reminded him.

"Let's say December Twentieth, then."

He studied each of their young faces in turn. They were washed-out rainbows of unhealth. Greyer and thinner every day from malnutrition, pinker from radiation...Pru even had a little yellow jaundice going on as well, a cumulative effect of the waste-inhibitors the pit-crews were required to take every morning.

A nervous electricity passed between them. It reminded Kaywin of the strange moment that night back in Houston when they had first fallen into each others' company. But this time there was no mystery about it. The fateful date had been spoken aloud. December 20, 2126. Pretty much at the same moment they had all three imagined the date as their last. Either spelled out in a formal e-mail from the President of the United States to their families, or etched in the cold granite of their tombstones. Not decades away, not children and grandchildren away, not two years or even one year away, but next week. December 20, 2126.

Anyone paying special attention--like Professor Lindsay, and Fitz--would have noticed the sudden urgency that Kaywin and Dublin brought to the free practice drills over the next few days. They attempted faster, sharper corners. They hit straight-line speeds that turned some heads in the hangar. Jennifer expressed concern for the structural integrity of *Tomorrow Never Knows*. "That was awfully close to half-speed, Kaywin. Don't blow up my ship...I know you think I'm kidding, but until we get the strobe-rate perfect to the fourth decimal point, it **will** explode somewhere between sixty-one and sixty-four percent enhanced speed." Kaywin grinned wordlessly as he climbed down the ladder to the hangar floor. His temporary co-pilot, a newer alternate who was filling in while Pru's foot healed, put the exclamation point on Jennifer's warning by falling to his hands and knees and throwing up. "There. See what you did? You clean it up. That's all you." She walked away.

The only cruiser that promised disaster more than *TNK* was *White Rabbit*. This ship looked twenty years older and dirtier than the rest. ("At what point do they start calling it *Black Rabbit?* Dublin had joked back in November.) Any pilot or copilot who complained about their cruiser or expressed concern for their safety was reminded that "at least you're not in the *White Rabbit*." Ving's superior abilities kept it from crashing outright, but it was still laughable to watch it limping around in the skies overhead, leaving a slowly dissipating plume of pink exhaust behind it.

There had been a day back in August when a handful of misguided pilots, after a rocky test-flight, had stupidly thrown around the idea of going on strike, as if they hadn't signed away their rights to safe air-travel. Jerkboy caught wind of this and strong-armed Lindsay and Fitz into mandating that every pilot and co-pilot take a little lap around the Moonbase in the trash-heap that was *White Rabbit*. This two-day exercise blanched some faces, emptied some stomachs, whitened some hairs and made men out of boys. But it stopped the complaining.

Dublin was going to attempt to break into the Security Office just before midnight on the nineteenth. If he got a boundary code, or both boundary codes, they would use them to bust out from the confines of the practice cone on the twentieth. Their final free practice leading up to this was on the eighteenth. Dub was still co-piloting, but his pilot, Chlorina, usually let him take the reins of their cruiser, *Mr. Mojo Risin'*, during free time, with an ever-changing lineup of alternates to assist him. There was no holding the boys back tonight. Jennifer couldn't watch. She shielded her eyes from the monitors as Kaywin (accidentally) broke the manned spaceflight speed record, at a hundred and forty-one thousand miles per hour. This edged out JB's record of a week earlier, and drew much more attention than he had bargained for. In the hangar afterwards, whilst shaking hands and getting aggressively zealous 'pats' on the back, Kaywin saw Jerkboy glaring from across the bay, with his usual menace, but also with his brow furrowed in thought.

"This is too easy," thought Dublin as he crept through the dimness of Level Five, expecting to be pounced upon at any moment. His fingers trembled on the keypad, but he got it right. The doors into the forbidden zone sounded like thunder to him as they opened. He cringed in the dark before continuing on. He saw patients in the infirmary from a construction accident earlier in the day. He edged toward the left-hand wall in case any of the mangled MCs were awake and watching.

Having arrived at the Security Chief Office Doors, Dublin had one of those 'awakening' moments. You know those little flashes that come out of nowhere, when you feel like you've just awakened from a long dream to find yourself in the strangest circumstances: *I was just having my diaper changed on the beach; am I really about to step out on stage to play saxophone in a retro-surf band?* That sort of moment.

It was all so surreal. He remembered kissing his bust of Tolstoy goodbye, and now this? Breaking and entering in an attempt to save the world?

He pressed the numbers, but he must have messed one up. He had begun to wonder, halfway through, if maybe Jerkboy was inside. He shook off the dreadful idea and made another stab at it. The lock clicked open. He looked left and right down the lonely, shadowy corridor, then he ducked inside.

He had to navigate around some basic protections, but this was easy stuff, the kind of thing he was used to doing to watch Wisconsin Johnson movies a day earlier than the rest of the world.

The '*Low Orb*' file and the '*High Orb*' file both appeared to be exactly what they had supposed them to be. He transferred both to his Sofee, backed out of them, and covered his digital tracks. He opened the door as slowly as it would go. He about had a heart attack. A nurse had just walked past the door, at the same pace that it was opening, one step ahead of noticing it out of her periphery. It was the one he'd seen

through the glass on his first day, who had seemed to understand and pity him, without words. He almost couldn't stop
himself from speaking to her, but thankfully, after opening
his mouth, he ran out of things to say, and then it was too
late. She entered the infirmary and was gone, and he would
probably die tomorrow anyway.

"Some 'Last Supper'," complained Pru a little incautious-
ly. She sat down with her two friends, who had already started
on their Swedish tofuballs.

"It's not as bad as it looks," said Dublin.

"So did you find out who you're taking to the dance tonight?" she asked Dub, meaning *who's your copilot going to be for
this suicide mission?*

"It's Ed Burroughs."

"Too bad for him," said Kaywin. "But he won't put up
a fight." In the context of their ongoing Valentine's Dance
analogy this sounded terrible. But they had precious little
time for laughing. Kaywin lowered his tone and leaned in.
The other two followed his lead. "So let's go with Plan A. Pru
and I will be slotted first in *Tomorrow Never Knows*. We take off
like we're going for the record again, but we ease off early
and coast. You and poor Ed will be slotted third. Wait your
turn unless you hear the Moonbase chattering at me and Fru-
Fru. If they start asking tough questions, just take off in *Mr.
Mojo Risin'* as fast as you can, and bring it hard to starboard.
By the time you get there we will hopefully have disabled
the field on that side, and, fingers crossed, we will already be
across the line ourselves. Questions?"

"I have a comment," whispered Dub. "Thanks for being

my friends."

The other two nodded as if acknowledging important information.

"I'm going to miss you two," said Kaywin.

Prudence felt pressure to emote. She wrinkled up her white face with painted-on railroad track scars. "You guys are alright."

It all went just as planned, except...

The codes didn't work.

"Tomorrow-Never-Knoooows, what happened out there?" asked Fitz, strolling up with all kinds of questions about the bizarre practice he had just witnessed.

"I don't know; we just lost power..."

"What were those numbers you were calling out there, buddy?"

"That was a booster sequence I've been working on." A decent lie.

"Mr. Mojo Risin', what the heck do you call **that** little maneuver?"

"Which one? The one where I was talking to Ed and took off when it wasn't my turn? Or the one where I pitched it about too hard and lost control?"

"Either one buddy. You pick. Not good, you guys, not good..." Fitz walked away, shaking his head.

When Kaywin, Dublin and Prudence climbed slowly out of their cruisers in defeated silence, they could see a cluster of three men behind the glass of the little hangar office.

It was never good when Commander MacFray got involved. But there he was, locked in a heated, secret conversation with Professor Lindsay and JB. The insufferable young man was red in the face and miming violently. Dublin swore that he had pointed at them. There were indications of feeble protest from the older two, before they began to nod in at least partial agreement.

Whatever the argument was, Jerkboy was winning.

The shocking announcement came first thing the following morning. Conference Room Eight went dead silent in its aftermath. It was Professor Lindsay who had delivered it, as softly as such a thing can be delivered:

"For a variety of reasons, none of which I am able to disclose at this time, the annual speed trials--" there was a rising electric hum from the speakers. Lindsay took two steps backwards, as instructed. "The annual speed trials have been moved up. They will not take place on Valentine's Day as usual, but rather..." he hesitated with uncomfortable, apologetic sadness. "But rather, three days from now, on December twenty-fourth."

The buzz spread like wildfire. It was bad news for everyone in the piloting program, nothing less than an early death sentence for many of them. Certainly Ving and the ascetic in *White Rabbit*, almost certainly Kaywin and Pru in *Tomorrow Never Knows*, and they would absolutely be joined in death by several others. It was not unlike an annual game of Russian roulette to begin with, but even more so now that they only had three days to make final adjustments.

It was only too easy for Kaywin, Dublin and Prudence to slip back into their natural state of hopelessness. It was ridiculous, looking back, to think that they could have saved the world against these impossible odds. They sat dejected and almost dead silent over supper that night, poking at their food. "I'll scan those files. **Again.** Maybe I missed something," mumbled Dublin. A full minute passed before any of them spoke again.

"We'll need to pick some trustworthy people to at least tell what we know. Maybe someone can sneak a message out in an empty crate or something. I don't know," said Kaywin.

"We can't even hang out tonight. Or tomorrow night. Or at all," said Prudence. "We need to spend every waking moment in the hangar, trying to figure out how to not blow up."

This statement of fact hit Dublin hard. He dropped his fork onto his plate with a frustrated clatter. He sat back and looked off across the cafeteria, at nothing in particular. His eyes just craved something that he would miss less than the faces of his two best friends.

He saw Malcolm, the young man with Down Syndrome, walking across the cafeteria with his tray. He was smiling his huge smile and shuffling awkwardly. Dublin knew it wasn't right, but just for tonight he envied Malcolm. He seemed thrilled with his simple existence, 24/7. Shame on whoever had fooled him into joining the MCP. He knew better than to stare at the young man, but Malcolm hadn't noticed. He was laughing as he got closer, and exchanging greetings with seated friends to his left and to his right.

He was about to pull even with Kaywin, Dub and Pru when Dublin saw Jerkboy and Bruniette approach him going in the opposite direction. Malcolm was looking to his right and laughing.

Jerkboy stuck his leg out and tripped Malcolm.

Only a few people saw it, but unfortunately Dublin was one of them. There was no decision, no weighing of consequences. He saw a despicable act and he flew up to avenge it. Jerkboy hadn't even finished laughing when Dublin exploded into him from the side. Jerkboy's tray went flying in the one-sixth gravity, and the population of the entire cafeteria, inflated by the heavy classes of July and October up to nearly five-thousand people, was instantly aware that something special was happening. On worn-out legs, they all rose from their seats as one to bear witness.

It took a half a second for Dublin to realize what he had long suspected: he was just as strong as this gym-rat imbecile. And he was the **real** kind of strong, outdoors from dawn to dusk, running through the mud, uprooting small trees with his bare hands, moving boulders from where he didn't want them to where he **did** want them, **that** kind of strong. Not the steroid-taking, barbell-pumping kind of strong that expands the flesh without expanding the man. He had climbed, struggled and battled through a wild world that didn't give a damn about him. His fists rained down on Jerkboy's face with terrible fury and strength. *They had it wrong. I knew it, my whole life. The girls had it wrong. I knew I was stronger than all the bullies. Take that, natural selection! This is your champion?* **I** *am your champion!*

Suddenly, he was in a chokehold. Bruniette, to the disappointment of the crowd, had snuck up behind Dublin and snatched him up off of his friend. Jerkboy staggered to his feet. Blood dripped off his face. He was still laughing, to show the riveted crowd (which might as well have been a small town) that he was still the master of the situation. It was like a germophobe's nightmare; every gasping cackle that racked his muscular frame sent medium-velocity blood splatter everywhere. Bruniette, even from his advantageous position, struggled to control the raging beast that only two minutes earlier had been that ugly kid, Dublin Dunne. Dublin was lifting his own legs off the ground and kicking at Jerkboy, then leaning way forward and lifting Bruniette off the ground. Before he could quite get him spilled over the top however, one of the other security thugs added his own weight to the fray. Once he was adequately restrained, Jerkboy punched him square in the face, twice, very hard. The crowd groaned in sympathy. "Leave him alone!" Someone shouted from a safe distance. Now Dublin's nose and mouth gushed blood. It was going to be rough night for the janitors. Dublin answered by spitting a mouthful of blood at Jerkboy. Jerkboy pulled out his pistol and held it against Dub's head. Voices that had been too afraid to speak up could no longer hold back. "No, no, no" "Come on now!" "Be cool" "Don't do it!" sounded from all around the messed-up huddle. Jerkboy tuned them out by hugging right up on the helpless boy. He had things to tell him that he didn't care for the rest of the Moonbase to hear. He put his mouth all the way up to Dublin's right ear, and re-positioned the large white pistol up to his left.

"If I do it like this, I can get both of us at once…" he whispered sickly. "That's actually very tempting. I said it to sound tough, but as I'm thinking about it it's actually very tempting. But I'm not quite finished here." He re-positioned the gun again, pointing it up through Dublin's jaw and into his brain. "I'm stalling for time here. You can probably tell. I'm trying to decide if I still need you or not." He actually started counting, his hot breath tickling Dublin's ear. "Fourteen pilots, fifteen--your little girlfriend's back, right?"

"She's not my--," Dublin began. Then he remembered that he might be about to die anyway. "Yeah, she's back. She's my beautiful girlfriend, and she's back."

The crowd held its breath. Prudence was surprised to realize that she was holding hers, too. She was standing on her seat so she could see. She was close enough to jump right onto the sweaty, bloody clump of manhood if she wanted... Kaywin was holding her back by the fabric of her jumpsuit, wordlessly reminding her that there was more than just Dublin's life at stake here.

"Thirty-eight, thirty-nine...huh. I think I need your stupid ugly face." He took one big sweeping step back. " I just need to fix one thing." He clubbed Dublin viciously with the pistol twice, then, while he was too blinded to see it coming, he buried his massive fist deep in his gut. The security goons released him and he hit the floor. Up came the few bites of food he'd eaten before this whole thing started, picking up some more blood along the way.

Jerkboy was finished. He and his thugs scattered like cockroaches. The spots abandoned by security were taken up by friends and Good Samaritans, with Kaywin and Prudence at the lead.

When it was clear that the storm had blown over, people began to pat Dub on the back and congratulate him, like he had done something. Someone brought him a cup of water, always the cure in these situations. "Crap!" said Dub, remembering something. "I totally knocked my tray over, didn't I."

"We'll find you something, Bud," said Kaywin. After about two more minutes, he and Prudence got Dublin to his feet. Then they steered him back toward his seat.

"I might as well go straight to the--what's this?"

On the table where he and Prudence and Kaywin had been sitting every night for eight months was a stack of fifty-something biscuits. And they were still coming, being passed from every direction, from two seats down, and from clear across the cafeteria. "I'm thinking doggy bag," slurred Dub. "Doggy bag, then nurse."

There just wasn't much that could be done in three days to make these cruisers safe at maximum enhanced speed. Frustration and defeatism ran rampant throughout the hangar. If you saw a smile during this time, it was a sarcastic, doomed one. Arguments broke out between pilots and co-pilots, pilots and engineers, between different cruiser teams wanting to use the same part, or tool... All struggled under this (justified) fatalistic droop in spirit. Overnight the mood had gone from "*Let's go faster than any human has ever gone before!*" to "*Let's get this over with.*"

No official reason was ever given for the reckless schedule change but Kaywin, Dublin and Prudence were unanimous in believing it was their fault. Security must have been on to them the whole time. Their feeble little stunt during practice time must have been the last bit of proof they needed. And it was probably true that the handful of ships that would survive the speed trials were just as ready now as they would have been on Valentine's Day. The flipside of that coin was that the ones who **hadn't** figured it out by now weren't going to figure it out in a month and a half. Who knew what else was happening behind the scenes? Maybe this class of engineers and pilots was a disappointing one. Maybe there was a better class chomping at the bit for their turn. Why not flush out the riff-raff in December, and bring in the wunderkinds in January. With the puppet-master of the whole Meaningful Conclusion Program, Rich Brandenberg, knowing what he knew about the Rogue Interstellar Planet, knowing the urgency of speeding up the commute from Earth to Mars, was it really any wonder? A month and a half shaved off the lives of this handful of Goners might save the lives of many millions. It was still a hard hand to be dealt. It was like the whole Rose incident back in Houston, except this time there would be fifteen, twenty, maybe even thirty sacrificial lambs...

TNK was doomed. It had set a record, but its problems with enhanced accelerations over sixty-one percent were **not** solved, would not **be** solved in so short a time, and were a death sentence. *White Rabbit* was doomed. *Pearly Queen*, *Tarkus*, and several others stood no chance. *Mr. Mojo Risin'*, co-piloted by Dublin, was among the few that people were betting on. *Purple Haze* was the understood champ. Good for Jerkboy. Good for Bruniette. Dublin, seated in the cockpit of *Mr. Mojo* and trying to eat a stale biscuit without his loosened tooth falling out, could see the two bullies laughing across the bay. He turned back and looked in the other direction, where Kaywin was helping Prudence and her half-foot down from the ladder of *Tomorrow Never Knows*.

He couldn't help feeling like all the justice had disappeared from the world.

~

It was in this state of mind that Dublin Dunne returned to his dorm room on the night of December twenty-third, a few minutes after nine. He entered his room code with spiritless, dragging fingers. The door whooshed open just as perkily as ever, and Dublin, tired eyes to the ground, watched his stupid, useless feet stepping in. Maybe for the last time ever.

His head jerked up instantly. Something was up. The lights were on. It was 9:09 PM. Why were the lights on? Why was Ving pacing nervously, face all glistening with sweat, making the three blue star-tattoos on his forehead look fresh and new and painful?

And where were his roommates? The sane ones?

Ving was frighteningly excited to see him. Dublin had never seen him in any kind of agitated state. Obviously, it must have happened at least three times before… Still, it was weird… He was so used to seeing the Kalaysian moseying with his hands in his pockets down at the hangar, or crouched in his top bunk, back turned, typing away… It didn't make sense to his eyes, like seeing his grandmother doing chin-ups, or Uncle Kevin playing a violin…

As soon as Ving saw Dublin he did a scary, tiptoeing silent charge and grabbed the younger man's wrist. He pulled him into the center of the bare room, where seven months earlier Dublin had made a fool of himself dancing in a matador outfit for his friends.

For eight or more seconds Ving just grinned broadly and stared into the wide, frightened eyes of the shaggy-headed youth. "Dublin!" he finally whispered. "I get it!"

Pause. More pause. "**What?!**"

"You memory good? This no go in Sofee." Dub just shook his head in utter confusion. "Take deep breath. Concentrate." He looked absolutely out of his head. He should have taken his own advice. He suddenly grabbed the back of Dub's head and pulled him in. He whispered something in the boy's ear. To watch Dublin's eyes at this moment was to see confusion piled on confusion. Ving made him repeat back what he had said.

"Good. You tell no one. Only two people." Then he turned and reached under his pillow.

Dublin had been on guard for this moment since the get-go. But he had expected it in the middle of the night; he had practiced for a sneak attack. So when Ving produced the jagged shard of unfinished slag metal from his bedding, in broad lamplight, Dub, for a millisecond, was at a loss. But he recovered quickly and dove for his lower bunk and the length of pipe hidden there under his pillow. He scrambled and got it, bracing for the shocking, pinching bite of steel into his back, and hoping it would miss his spinal column, and his vitals...

When he whipped back around, brandishing his steel pipe, he thought that maybe he had descended into a madness so total that he would never again recover.

There stood the Kalaysian, still grinning, convulsing repulsively, the shard of waste-metal buried deeply in his chest. The blood hadn't even started yet--wait--there it was, swelling up around his hands, still clutching at the exposed couple of inches of weapon. Ving skipped the part where he might have fallen to his knees, instead crashing straight downward on his right side. Almost unconsciously, Dublin noted the shattered pieces of the man's Sofee; he had destroyed it ear-lier and now collapsed among the pink plastic shards.

At this point, when Dublin couldn't have told you what his middle name was, or what two plus two equaled, the doors to 4324 slashed open again and Jerkboy charged in. He pulled up short at the grotesque crime scene.

"Control, take Dublin Dunne **off of the grid, now!**"

"I didn't do it! He must have--"

"I know you didn't do it you stupid idiot!" JB looked down at the dead man in the rapidly expanding pool of blood, and he began to laugh.

Dub's two surviving roommates, who had been warned away from their own dorm room, and had fetched security, now crowded around the entrance, their faces melted in hor-ror.

"The best part--wait--I gotta double-check--" Jerkboy's laughter was rolling over the entire scene, washing away any and all human emotion. "Yup!" he exulted after consulting something on his Sofee, something that made his day. "The best part of this is--," he had to collect his breath, "the best part of it is…"

"You get to race tomorrow in *White Rabbit*."

18

The Little Drummer Boy

There was a ringing in Dublin's ears, from emotional, physical and mental overload. He had never been so confused in his short life. He just stood there looking and feeling like a complete idiot.

JB was shouting orders to security guards who kept popping up out of nowhere. Then he was shouting orders to others over his Sofee. In very short order, a stretcher was produced, and Jerkboy, with a flip and a hand-swoop of his golden hair, leaned over and grabbed Ving's arms, which were already beginning to stiffen around the object he had plunged into his chest. One of the security goons snatched up the dead man's legs, and without any ceremony, like they were picking up a sack of dirty laundry, they deposited the still-warm corpse on the stretcher and began to carry him out.

When Jerkboy had backward-shuffled up even with Dublin, near the door, he stopped in his tracks. His chiseled features registered absolute disgust as he surveyed this 'Dublin Dunne', his polar opposite, this whimpering, simpering Mama's Boy who had surprise-attacked him in the cafeteria three nights earlier. The scowling Security Chief apparently just wanted to stand there for a second and *feel* the measure of his own superiority over this life-long loser. But it turned out that he had something to say as well.

"I know more than you think I know, Creaturehead," he hissed at Dublin. His face was inches from the bewildered boy's. Dub studied in mute confusion the handsome face, the cut lip he himself had given him, the bruised cheek he had given him, and the crazy wild eyes that genetics had given him. "I'm only keeping you alive so I can watch you burn tomorrow. That's my Christmas present to me. If you try **anything** tonight I **will** know." His voice got even lower, and more sinister, and he leaned in until his nose was almost touching Dublin's. "I've got rooms and closets and corners on this Moonbase that nobody knows about. Give me a reason and I will take you there and make you suffer like you've never suffered before. Then I'll get your girlfriend. Then I'll get your boyfriend. You understand me?"

Dublin didn't understand **anything** right now, but felt vaguely the importance of getting this clown out of here before Ving's message began to fade from his memory. He kept repeating the Kalaysian Three-Star's final words over and over in his head. He diverted just enough focus away from this task to acknowledge the posturing thug looming over him with a slight nod.

Jerkboy grinned widely, apparently unbothered by the split on his lip. His voice was no longer a secretive whisper. "Good." He repositioned the stretcher in his big hands. "You're a janitor right?" He nodded to the pool of blood streaked all over the back end of the dorm room floor. "Clean that up."

Finally he got moving again. He and his yellow-banded comrade maneuvered Ving's remains into the hallway. Dub's eyes were fixed in that direction, but he was deep, **deep** in thought. Everything happening around him was like raindrops rolling off his windshield. Bruniette appeared, coming down the hall, right as JB and his friend had cleared the doorframe with the stretcher and were about to reset their course toward the elevator. Taking advantage of the fact that Jerkboy's hands were occupied supporting his half of the stretcher, Bruniette slapped what appeared to be a slice of salami right on his buddy's face. The latter, almost without hesitating, let the handles drop. The last thing Dub saw before his room doors whizzed shut was JB taking off after Bruniette. The doors whizzed back open a second later and Dublin's two surviving roommates kind of snuck back in.

The peculiar phrase that Ving had been so adamant for Dub to remember was just repeating over and over again in his head. Ecksitwalf naandi naanfaad eseffen...Ecksitwalf naandi naanfaad eseffen... What **was** it? It made no sense... The room around him was returning to normal, if you didn't count Wayne throwing a towel in the middle of the bloody mess and trying to mop it all up with his foot. Dublin was still standing in the same spot near the door a few minutes after that as his roommates climbed into their bunks for the night. He eventually, very mechanically, did the same.

He lay awake for hours. The nonsense words went around and around in his head like bats around a belfry. What did they mean? Why would Ving spout this line of gibberish at him like it was so important, and then kill himself?

"Sofee," he whispered in the darkness. He paused. Ving

had said, "This no go on Sofee"; **that** much he had understood...but Dub would be dead in twelve hours. If "Ecksitwtwalf naandi naanfaat eseffen" was helpful information, he would need to pass it on to someone...

"Yes, Dublin?"

"Quieter."

"Is this good?" It mirrored the volume of his whisper exactly.

"Perfect." He sighed. Here goes. "Can you translate something from Kalaysian to English for me?"

"Certainly."

"Ecksitwalf naandi naanfaat eseffen."

"This is not Kalaysian. Nor is it any language that my makers are aware of."

"Crap."

"That one I know."

"Very funny."

"Are you sure you are pronouncing it correctly? It sounds like..." She gave him an alternate inflection, and Dublin just about leaped up out of the bed. His mind raced, his heart raced, his flagging spirits surged, and in the wreckage of his young life all around him he suddenly recognized hope.

Throwing all caution to the wind, he tried to text Kaywin and Prudence, but he was blocked. He remembered JB telling Control to "remove Dublin Dunne from the grid." *Shoot. Which roommate is least likely to kill me if I wake them up?* He decided on Wayne, in the bunk right over his. He had the tougher exterior, with all his tattoos and piercings, but the more laid-back personality.

"Wayne!" Dublin hissed in the darkness. "Wayne! Wake up!"

"What? What's wrong?"

"I need a huge favor, man. Huge. Can you send a text for me? I'm blocked."

Wayne sat up. "Sure." Dub showed him the message he had tried to send, and Wayne attempted to send it from his 47.

No luck. They were all blocked.

This can't wait. This is too important. Dub decided to try a different spot, maybe down the hall a little ways. If that didn't work, he would walk all the way to Pru's room, or to Kaywin's room, and deliver the news in person.

He opened the door and stepped out quietly. Two rifles, one from his left and one from his right, clacked together over his chest.

"You'd best just turn around and go back to bed, son," said the older guard. "And don't bother sending any of your buddies out either. No one leaves till 0800."

Dublin, for once in his life, was out of ideas. He ambled distractedly back to his bunk and thought about trying to sleep. Instead he wound up researching the *White Rabbit* and trying to come up with a strategy to keep it in one piece. The best minds of his generation couldn't help him solve the riddle of pushing the nuclear drive to its maximum with an imperfectly tuned strobe rate, and surviving to brag about it. He struggled against his destiny for an hour and a half before he fell asleep.

Dublin's alarm went off in his ears. He lifted his great shaggy head up from his drooled-on pillow. The first thing that popped into his brain was a lyric from one of those crazy old songs that Kaywin had played for him and Pru:

'This will be the day that I die.'

He had been so preoccupied the night before with cryptic messages and nuclear strobe-rates that he had forgotten to panic. And now here it was. His last day alive.

He blinked and gazed around him at the sheer wonder of it all. What a privilege, what an honor it had been to be alive. The dingy brown paint on the bedrail was a miracle. The hair on his hands was a miracle. The feathers in his pillow came from a beautiful bird back on Earth, with a graceful long, snowy white neck and a cute orange beak. A waddling, swimming, flying miracle.

Visions of this goose carried his waking mind back to early elementary school when the kids all called him the 'Ugly Dublin'. For the first time in his life, he shook the memory away, instead of wallowing in it. He didn't have the time left for it. He stood up. He was no Ugly Dublin today. Today, his last day alive, he was going to make a difference. Today he was going to do everything in his power to save those mean kids, who didn't know any better, to save Ms. Cobb, who had taught them better, to rescue everybody from a doom they didn't even know was coming. Today, he was a swan.

His roommates had been roused by their own Sofees. They sat up and watched him with wordless respect. It was a curiosity to see how a man behaved on a day that he knew would be his last. Dublin did a single pirouette for his own amusement and headed into the bathroom.

There was his face in the mirror. It wasn't so bad today. Something about the Lunar climate had cleared up his acne at least. And the pinking from the radiation suited him a little better than his former pale blotchiness. Malnutrition had sunken his cheeks somewhat. He wasn't hating it, at least not compared to what he was used to seeing in the mirror.

He began to brush his teeth. *The last time I will brush my teeth.* He thought of how his mother had taught him to brush, and followed these guidelines as if she was standing there watching him. He finished and put his brush down, and rinsed. He turned and hugged the air where he had imagined his Mom to be. "Thanks Mom," he said out loud.

He relinquished the bathroom to Derrix, his other roommate. He and Wayne and the rest of Moonbase 2 all had the day off to watch the speed-trials. Dublin changed into his clean full-grav. He pulled himself up straight. "You guys ready?" he asked his roommates who had fallen in behind him.

"More like are **you** ready?" said Derrix.

"As ready as I'm going to be." He felt two hands pat him on the back.

"Good luck, Dublin."

"Yeah, good luck, man."

He hit the button to open the door, and the guard who had fallen asleep with his back against it tumbled into the room. He leaped up and donkey-kicked blindly, then seemed to get his bearings. He straightened his jumpsuit and acted like nothing out of the ordinary had happened. Then he gestured with his rifle for Dublin to go on out ahead of him.

The hall was deserted, but then they turned the corner and the cafeteria came into view. There was a lot of activity in it; Dublin recognized a lot of pilots and copilots milling around. They were enjoying a full breakfast with coffee, and eggs, and Canadian bacon. That must be the meat product that Bruniette had slapped in Jerkboy's face last night, Canadian bacon. There was the quiet hum of early morning conversation in the huge room, but it almost came to a complete stop when the ugly boy with the armed escort rounded the corner. To Dublin's amazement, after he had exchanged eye contact with the small crowd, a few of them began clapping about something, then it was several of them, and then most. Someone in their midst shouted "Go, Dublin!" and he realized that the show of respect was for him.

"You want anything?" The older guard asked him, gesturing toward the cafeteria. Even his demeanor had softened. "You can't go in but I can send someone to grab something for you."

Dublin shook his head. He had zero appetite, and he had a lump in his throat that he wasn't sure a pancake could even get around. "You sure? We gotta wait here anyway..."

"I'm good," he said. "Thanks."

Prudence had a similar awareness, the second that she woke up, that this would be her last day alive. She told herself that she was relieved. She should have done this by herself years ago.

She woke up in great pain. The bleeding had made her head stick to the pillow.

Right before bed last night she had steeled herself in the mirror for the coming judgment day. *You will never touch me again,* she had said in her mind to the long line of evil phantoms that had never stopped haunting her, even here on the Moon. *Never again.* She didn't want to die looking the way they had made her look. She was sick of this stupid wig, and the stupid makeup. She was angry that she had been robbed of her life, and jealous of her former classmates and friends who had graduated a few months ago and were moving on to do whatever the hell they wanted. Oh well. They didn't know it, but in about three years they would all be Goners, too.

She had leaned forward on the sink and gazed deeply into her own eyes, beginning to brim with tears of self-pity. She couldn't stand that weak little girl either. She hated the punk girl and she hated the weak little one. *Well, I guess that's why I'm here*, she thought.

At this point she had grabbed the back of her sixty-thousand credit adjustable wig--one of only four in the world--and ripped it right off of her bald head.

She had tried to do it in one clean tug, but it had taken several, each more violent than the last. Finally, she separated it from herself completely. She hurled it forcefully into the tiny trashcan and looked back into the mirror. Her head was covered in blood. She kept toweling it away and it kept coming back in two long lines They started up high on her head, one just right of her right eye and one just left of her left eye; then back down from the crown almost to what would have been the dainty nape of her neck, had she been in any way, shape or form *dainty*.

It took an hour of gentle pressure from the nearly saturated towel before the bleeding had stopped enough for her to lay down. Once there, in the darkness, with her roommates already asleep, she turned her emotions off like a switch, and she didn't expect that she would ever again turn them on. She had tried giving a crap about herself and other people for a couple of months, and it had gotten her exactly where she had always known it would. To death's door, with the world just as screwed up as ever behind her.

It was more comfortable, more usual for her this way. This was just like being back home in Geyserville. This way, at least, everything was somebody else's fault. Her eyes turned cold and she was ready for the last twelve hours of her life. *That's better. Now let's get this over with* were the terms and tone of her mental surrender.

The most random, stupid, useless images paraded through the fresh vacuum of her consciousness. The expensive silver dress that Mr. McConnell had bought her. The color of a school bus. The purple fur of her favorite childhood TV character. The one fork in their silverware drawer back home that didn't match the others. A field trip to the redwood forest. The blue porcelain knobs in her Grandma's kitchen. The last one before she fell asleep was the stupid name that someone had wasted time painting on the cruiser that was about to be her coffin:

Tomorrow Never Knows…

Kaywin, many years earlier in his military career, had a couple of times faced the slim *possibility* of death. Standing here in the cafeteria, waiting, fidgeting, he had no choice but to embrace its probability…even *inevitability*…

This waiting seemed cruel and unnecessary.

Eventually he calmed himself with the memory of a conversation he had had with Dublin back in the summer. They had been talking about death, in particular about how to not freak out about it every time they looked at the time ticking down on their Sofees. Dublin had a lot of original thoughts on a lot of things. Kaywin tried to remember what his friend had said, and adapt it to himself:

Yes, today I die. But I've been there before. I began life in my mother's womb sometime back in…(he did the math)*…in March of 2079. Wherever I was the month before that, in February of 2079, or January of 2079, or 2017, or 1865 when the Civil War ended and Lincoln was shot, or 476 when Rome fell, or 10,000 BC when hunters conspired against the wooly mammoths, or fourteen billion years ago when the Big Bang exploded; wherever I was* **then** *is where I'm going back to* **now**. *These last 47 years have been the* **strange** *part, the anomaly…I'm going back* **home**. *I don't remember it, at least not on a conscious level. It must have been very comfortable and peaceful. I will be there forevermore. I just need to relax. Don't even* **need** *to, really; the ending is the same.*

We'll make a good show of it. Pru and me will do what we signed up to do. We will push that cruiser to one hundred percent enhanced acceleration, we will set the new speed record, and when we blow up it will be so instantaneous that we won't ever know it happened.

Then I hope I get to see them again. He imagined Nadine's radiant, beautiful, wise and happy face very close to his. She would be laughing about the whole thing, now that they were back together. He imagined Victoria's weight as she ran and launched herself at him, trusting him to catch her, never doubting that he would. *I wouldn't mind if Dub and Pru were there too…*

While he soothed himself with these bemusements, the non-CF8 stragglers in the cafeteria were ushered out in little groups. Kaywin hardly noticed it was happening. He just looked up and all the happy-go-lucky people with donuts were gone.

He heard the charged, muffled thump-thump of some-one removing the microphone from Aristophanes' stony grasp behind him. He turned and saw Professor Lindsay, looking much less chipper than usual. He wasn't even wear-ing anything 'Berkeley', as if trying to distance himself and his beloved University from the irresponsibly premature pro-ceedings here. Kaywin began to wonder how it was that they were **this** close to beginning, and there was as of yet no sign of Prudence or Dublin. It was easy to scan the sixty or so people remaining in the enormous cafeteria and see that they were not there.

"Alright," Lindsay said, and his tone was as uncharacter-istically defeated as his demeanor. "Let's get on with this. As some of you may know already, we lost Ving Soo last night. Dublin Dunne will pilot *White Rabbit.*

Oh my God. Dublin. Kaywin had heard about the Ving sui-cide, but none of them knew who was going to draw the short straw that was *White Rabbit.* He blushed a little bit in anger at the pointed injustice of it.

"This slides co-pilot Helena Daks of *Tarkus* into *Mr. Mojo Risin'*, and Foster Robbins from the alternates into the co-pilot chair of *Tarkus.* I hope you have all logged enough flight hours to feel comfortable in these new assignments. If not, I'm sorry. My hands are tied at this point, and we will all have to do the best we can with the circumstances we find ourselves in."

"You have been briefed on the format. The seventeen remaining cruisers will all exit the hangar together. You will taxi out onto the runway according to your assigned number, but **backwards**; number 17 will taxi out first, followed by 16, followed by 15, et cetera. You will take off and maintain minimum speed. *Purple Haze* is number 17, so JB will lead a looping timekill formation. As each cruiser takes off they will fall into formation. When all 17 cruisers are in flight, and engines are warm and loose, *Purple Haze* again will lead you into a widespread **linear** formation, again at minimum speed, and from there the fun begins." He said the word 'fun' but you could tell he didn't mean it. "After that, it's 1 through 17. Cruiser 1 will get a thirty second countdown. At the end of the countdown, you will accelerate ahead of the formation, bringing your conventional engines to full speed within one minute, and then…" He hung his head in shame at what he was required to say next, because he knew it was a death sentence for many of these people, and he knew that it could have been avoided. "And then we need to see enhanced acceleration, from zero to one-hundred percent, in the ensuing twenty seconds."

"Your fellow MCs are grateful for the day off; they will enjoy the drama of today's speed trials from right here in the cafeteria. Extra cameras have been placed within the practice cone, to augment the video angles from the cruisers themselves. If you feel a little extra courage out there today, that's your comrades watching you and cheering for you."

He paused. He looked down at the pink, green and brown-mottled cafeteria floor for a few seconds to collect himself for his closing sentiments. He looked back up, and stoically attempted to make eye contact with each of the 34 pilots and copilots fidgeting in front of him.

Where in the world is Dub? Where is Fru-Fru? Kaywin daydreamed that they had somehow weaseled out of this. Now Lindsay was speaking again.

"It is my fondest wish that when we sit down to dinner tonight in this cafeteria, there will be 17 intact cruisers in the hangar, and 34 intact pilots and copilots enjoying Christmas ham, and pudding, and whatever else they are serving tonight."

"But this would take a miracle. So--," He choked up a little. "So be strong. Do your best. We salute your service to the Meaningful Conclusion Program, and Godspeed to all of you." He turned and tried to put the mic back in Aristophanes' hand, but he fumbled it, and Aristophanes made no adjustments to help him, so it tumbled into the water fountain. Hands covered ears as a painfully loud, terribly electric crackling and hissing assaulted the senses of the nerve-strained audience. Then a few laughs relieved the tension, and they were organized into a long, single-file line, with a confident Jerkboy at the head. They stood silent for eleven seconds. Then they started their slow walk toward whatever the future held for them.

As if the anxiety wasn't thick enough, the powers-that-be had arranged for the cruiser crews to march the length of each floor in succession. So instead of just taking the lift from the fourth to the first floor, and getting on with it, they had to go from the cafeteria to the lifts at the **far** end of the fourth floor, then down to the third floor, then walk back the whole length of the third floor to the lifts right below the cafeteria. They were compelled to weave their way back and forth and downward like this, turning a three-minute death-march into a twenty-minute test of will.

The good part was that their entire path was lined on either side with cheering, clapping, saluting and hollering fellow Goners. The show of support at first was moving to Kaywin, then it got a little horrifying as he realized how many thousands of faces he was passing, how many thousands of good people had signed their lives over to the Program, just here on the Moon! That wasn't even counting the many more thousands back on Earth mining precious metals to make the rich richer, or the thousands giving up their lives on Mars to build cozy homes for Brandenberg and his cronies.

He began to feel as down and helpless as a man can feel. They had failed in their mission to fire the gun assembly. Earth was likely doomed. Kaywin had told everything he knew to Sephal, including where he'd hidden Dombroski's Sofee 45 yesterday, with the blueprints and codes on it, but what could Sephal do? Probably not more than he and Dublin and Prudence had done.

When they had first rounded the corner coming out of the cafeteria, he had seen Dublin a little distance down the side hallway, flanked by two security guards. The young man had started to shout something when he saw Kaywin, but one of the guards instantly clapped his hand over his mouth. Turning to look back a few seconds later, Kaywin saw that Dublin had been strong-armed into the back of the line. He could hear a little extra surge of enthusiasm for the boy, who had gained a measure of celebrity for decking Jerkboy. The shouts of "Dub-lin, Dub-lin, Dub-lin!" formed constantly just behind Kaywin's left and right shoulders as the crowd caught its first glimpses of the young superhero at the back of the line, requiring two six-foot security guards to prevent him from laying waste to the entire Moonbase.

A couple of times, Kaywin peeked backwards. Dub was forty feet behind him, and seemed desperate to convey something to him. But every time a sound came out of his mouth, he was muzzled aggressively with a beefy hand.

When Jerkboy had led the line most of the way down the Level Four main corridor, he stopped suddenly. He barked something into his Sofee. On Kaywin's left the door to room 4102 whisked open. A security guard inside it pushed out a tiny mangled bald girl. She stumbled passively into Kaywin. The little face was so empty of spirit that Kaywin didn't even recognize her for a second.

"Prudence! Oh my God!"

The face turned up to him. No makeup adorned it. Two gruesome lines of clotted blood tracked backwards from crown to nape. The hollow eyes registered no emotion. She seemed to not recognize him either.

"What's up?" she said robotically. Kaywin had the almost irresistible compulsion to hug her and protect her, but he and Dublin at various times had both made the innocent mistake of touching her when she wasn't expecting it, and both had nearly been kicked.

The line began moving again. Kaywin tried awkwardly, with words, to resuscitate Prudence emotionally. "Pru!" he whispered to her as she walked along in front of him. She seemed to waft almost ghost-like. "Pru! Are you okay?"

No answer.

"Pru! I need you here with me, okay? I don't want us both to die alone in that cruiser, three feet away from each other."

No answer.

When they got to the lifts at the end of Level Four, they all, at Jerkboy's direction, piled into Lift B--*except* for Dublin and his private goon-squad, who stepped into Lift A.

The thirty-odd Goners in Lift B disembarked first onto Level Three. Right as Prudence and Kaywin were filing past Lift A, its doors opened. Dublin was framed in its doorway. He formed a peace sign with his right hand, casually so as not to alarm his escorts, and silently mouthed something.

Kaywin absorbed this for a second, but couldn't make sense of it. "What was *that*?" he asked Pru. She turned to him without slowing.

"Two," she said quietly, and disinterestedly. "He wants us to tune our cruiser radio to the channel we were going to use in Plan B. Channel 56."

They were missing *something* here...why was Dublin under such tight security? Did they think that he had killed Ving? And why did he want them to tune their radio to this obscure frequency? Probably to say goodbye...*probably*...

Kaywin started to wonder these things out loud. "You don't think--"

"Don't be stupid. They've got him under guard as part of

Jerkboy's payback. Dublin looked like a hero when he beat the crap out of him the other day. Now he's making him look like a coward, like he was trying to run away from the speed trials. Dublin wants to open a channel between us so he can make sure *we* know he's not a coward. Which we know. Then he's going to tell you that you're like the dad he lost when he blew his brains out. Then he's going to tell me that he loves me."

This all made sense, and was delivered curtly to discourage any response. Kaywin shut up for a couple of floors.

When they reached Level One, and began the nearly half-mile final stretch of their journey, Kaywin began to feel the tingling sensation throughout his body that he had felt in the first minutes after signing himself up for the MCP, that strange, ironically blissful super-awareness of being alive. It was a trick of his physical system, just to make sure that he didn't give up living too lightly.

They were approaching the public restrooms just outside the hangar. A narrow shelf girded the corridor wall on their right for twenty feet leading up to the bathroom, and twenty feet beyond it, somewhere for people to put their flight gloves, or their extra clothes, or whatever, while they used the toilets. There were more security personnel here than regular Goners, maybe in the suspicion that there would be some last second runaways. But the guards here were mainly lounging and laughing. Two of them right before the restroom were huddled up, not even watching the pilots. Kaywin was feeling alive, and a little rebellious, and he also wanted to do something to spark Prudence. He reached right behind one of the huddled guards and took his travel mug full of coffee. Then he drank all of it and threw the mug down where it bounced away across the thin carpet.

This had the desired effect. Prudence, just in front of Kaywin, saw the motion out of her right eye. She half-turned and half-smirked. Then she one-upped him. Well, maybe **thirty** or **forty**-upped him:

There **had** been **three** guards just beyond the restrooms. Seconds earlier guard 1 had been in the middle of telling what he thought was a really good racist joke to guard 2. Guard 3 had clearly said to guard 1, "Hey man, watch my rifle while I take a whizz." Guard 1 had waved him off like a fly, determined not to mess up on the timing that was critical to the joke being hilarious. Guard 3 took this wave as an acknowledgment that yes, of course he would keep an eye on his rifle.

As casually as if she was dragging her fingertips along a cool cave wall, Prudence Estrada reached out and grabbed the rifle.

Kaywin about fell over. When he had sort of realized what Pru was about to do, he had swayed to the right a little to block her little arm from view. Now he turned to survey the crowd behind him. *No big deal...nothing to see here...just checking out the view behind me...hey, what's up, Dub, way at the back... yeah, peace sign right back at you...* He slowly reined in the scope of his vision, finally focusing for a split second on the pilot's face two feet behind him.

The man was smiling. He had seen everything. He laughed when Kaywin's eyes met his. "Go for it, man."

Kaywin whipped back around to offer some advice to Pru on hiding the rifle. It was already gone. She must have had second thoughts and tossed it aside.

Now they were entering the hangar. Kaywin could sense the crowd behind them turning and rushing up to the cafeteria to get good seats for the action. A bit morbid, maybe, but why not.

Guards closed in a little on Kaywin and Prudence at this point. There was suddenly all this open space to work with. They didn't want either of them making a dash for Dublin.

They were ushered apart and into their respective locker rooms. Dublin had been bullied into the men's room they had just passed, and someone had gone to get his flight gear.

They are really determined that we are some kind of threat, thought Kaywin. His brain was desperate to peacefully resign itself over to 'meaningful conclusion', but suspicion kept poking at it. *Channel 56...we'll see...*

When he came out of the locker room a few minutes later there was a mild scene starting up in front of him, and another one behind him. Dublin, in his flight suit a hundred feet across the bay, had said something angrily to the lazy engineer of the *White Rabbit*. He had caught the man reattaching a panel on the charred cruiser. Beside him on the floor was the ship's fusion strobe.

The small wire and metal device was about the size of a lunchbox, but without Superman or Chewbacca on it. This object, unimpressive from the outside, had been the focus of the engineer's lackluster energies for a year and a half, and even though it didn't work well at all just **yet**, he had lazy, vague hopes of tweaking it into serviceability at some point, and maybe having a magazine article written about him. This was all well and good for the engineer, but it meant that Dublin and the ascetic wouldn't be able to *regulate* their enhanced speed at all. It would be instantaneous maximum acceleration. Instant death. Any fighting chance they might have had was now stashed under the Berkeley-burnout's folding chair.

Dublin was furious, and wrestling with the younger guard. The engineer was embarrassed, but he was one of those idiots who express their embarrassment by getting angry and defensive. You know, like it's never **their** fault.

The scene unfolding **behind** Kaywin was equally perplexing and disgusting. He turned to see what the hubbub was about.

Out strode Jerkboy from the locker room. Exclamations from the others emerging expressed amusement, surprise and jealousy.

He was wearing a Dizastra 3000.

How he had obtained this special privilege, especially as he was about to race in *Purple Haze*, the **safest** of the 17 ships, was beyond everyone. Strangely, the almost-always swaggering young man didn't seem to be flaunting his suit. He didn't seem to be that proud or happy about it.

Jerkboy walked out with speed and purpose, apparently in response to the Dublin situation, cuz he hustled straight over to the tussling trio. He had something whitish brown in his gloved hand. He pulled the guard's hand off of Dub's mouth and forced the object inside.

Bruniette was five steps behind and erupting in laughter. "Ha ha ha! You just put your dirty sock in that boy's mouth!" At this point the tall ascetic gangled by, and climbed up the ladder into the *White Rabbit*. Jerkboy gestured toward him, but kept his eyes locked on Dublin.

"It's not mine. It's **his**."

Dublin's eyes began to water at the sheer intensity of the flavor index unfolding in his mouth. JB was all business today, no laughing or gloating. He detached his rifle from his side in a graceful swoop and leveled it at the bridge of Dublin's nose.

"You take that sock out of your mouth and I will drop you like a wildebeest. Get into that cruiser!"

Dublin shook his arms free and glared into Jerkboy's icy blue eyes. Kaywin watched the boy weigh his options, then turn and climb up the cruiser ladder into the belly of the lame beast. Then he watched a moribund Prudence drag herself up into *Tomorrow Never Knows*.

At least Dublin's fire isn't out, he thought. At this point the guard behind Kaywin was tired of waiting, and gave him a little shove toward *TNK*. Kaywin took the hint, and boarded the blue and yellow cruiser. Prudence, or the little broken child who **used** to be Prudence, sat dejectedly in the copilot's chair. She wasn't even bothering to cram her wounded head into her helmet. She stared at her silver-booted feet. Kaywin started to sit in the pilot's seat, in the front. Then he had a thought. "You do it," he said to Pru. "Your turn." A slight shimmer passed over the girl. She didn't show any more emotion than that, but somewhere deep in her heart she acknowledged that she was being trusted with something important; with her own life and with Kaywin's.

"Whatever," she said, and got up. When they were done shimmying around each other in the cramped space, and Kaywin went to sit down in the copilot's seat, he saw the rifle on the floor beside it. He thought about asking, but just laughed.

Prudence had her hands locked on the wheel already. She knew what Kaywin was chuckling about. Her head was turned, and her sad, vacant eyes were locked on Jerkboy, still standing next to the *White Rabbit*, barking orders into his Sofee.

"If we make it back today I'm going to shoot that man."

Dublin was puzzling over something. A note had been left for him on the pilot's seat, written in grease pencil on three squares of toilet paper. 'Turn off cooling coil till temp reach critical, plus five second' it said. *Whaaaaat? That would be suicide!* "Hey!" he said to the ascetic, turning around in his seat to face him. "Did you write this?"

He watched the ascetic's glassy yellow eyes follow the disturbingly poop-like writing across the toilet paper. The poor penitent (who looked like he might drop dead today anyway, even if they survived the speed trial) shook his head.

"You think Ving did?" Shrug.

The wrecked friar fumbled for his grease pencil. He erased the words peace to all from his forehead. He replaced them with the single word merit and pointed his bony finger at the bathroom tissue. Then he shrugged again, as if to say, "it's worth a shot."

"Let's try it. I don't get how that would help, but it beats not trying anything. Now listen." Dublin sighed. He had felt for a long time like he was living in a movie. The movie always been a bad tragic comedy, with the emphasis on the "tragic". Now he felt like he was in an action flick, so he delivered his lines accordingly. "First: You don't have any mouthwash, do you? I didn't think so. Secondly: There's some crazy stuff about to go down. I need you to sit tight and follow my lead, alright? You'll have to just trust me." The ascetic stared hard at the boy and nodded slowly. "Okay. I'm putting you in charge of turning off the cooling coil and not turning it back on until five seconds after critical." He shook his head at the madness of it. He turned forward in his seat and then back again for one more comment. "And *not* passing out…"

Round and round they flew until all 17 ships had joined the formation. They made two more loops so that the engines of cruiser number one, *Yellow Submarine* could get warm and loose. She was the last one out of the hangar, and would be the first to show the Moonbase her maximum speed. She was one of the few expected to do well.

Warmups finished, JB in *Purple Haze* led them into the long, linear formation that Professor Lindsay had described. He set the pace going forward, and the other sixteen cruisers matched it.

Tomorrow Never Knows was the eleventh ship in the stretched-out line. Dublin, in slot fifteen, would have a few minutes to cry when his friends blew up, before it was *his* turn to blow up. After that, Jerkboy, in slot 17 would have about two minutes to finish laughing before he pushed *Purple Haze* to maximum enhanced acceleration, breaking every speed record and returning to the Moonbase as a hero.

Dublin this entire time had been frantically trying to raise his friends on Channel 38, the one they had agreed on if they had to go to Plan Two. Or the one he *thought* they had agreed on. He began trying random ones. There was another one they had talked about specifically; he thought it might be Channel 66, but that didn't work either. He paused for a minute in sheer frustration.

He rested his head back against the seat and began to grow very sad. He thought about how totally different, **in-credibly** different this December 24th was from every other one he had experienced. He thought about going to his grandparents' house every Christmas Eve, since before he could remember. The happy relatives, the cousins (who he hardly ever saw the rest of the year), the loud party around the sandwich buffet in the basement, the gorgeous, silent Christmas tree in the living room upstairs. You could sit on the barstools and laugh and eat olives and chips with your cousins, then drift alone upstairs to look at the tree with its fat, frosted bulbs. There was a big window in the living room, and one year it snowed. That was his favorite Christmas Eve. Actually, it was the favorite moment of his entire life, before meeting Prudence.

He snapped back to reality as *Yellow Submarine* flashed out of the formation, way over to his left. Everyone held their breath--but not for long. In about three seconds the narrow streak of light turned into a giant fireball. "Ooooh, my God, seriously?" exclaimed Dublin. This did not bode well for any of them. He was getting more and more fidgety and scattered. He began to fumble again with the radio, trying to find his friends. He couldn't believe he had wasted thirty seconds in a fruitless daydream. He **had** to get through to them. If it came down to it, and time was running out, he decided, he would have to deliver his message to them over channel one, with **everybody** listening. *What if they're flipping channels, trying to find me?* he worried. *We'll never find each other!*

~

Kaywin watched cruiser number two sizzle out of the formation and completely out of visual range in less than a second. This was a good run, one of the only ones of the day, and a fast one, too. This served to steady the heart rates of the other flight crews, just seeing that it could be done. Cruisers three and four undid the good by being completely obliterated.

Cruiser Five was *Mr. Mojo Risin'*, Dub's old ship. Kaywin listened to the countdown for the green, lizard-looking vessel. He slipped into a reverie, staring at the bloody mangled lines on the back of Prudence's head. He didn't know exactly what it had meant to her to tear the wig off, but he understood that it had to represent some kind of separation from her former life, and a desire to die as herself, and not a **cartoon** of herself. Part of him wished that he could have experienced a similar declaration of self here at the eleventh hour. He wouldn't have had the guts.

When Kaywin had this thought, it made him realize something else: He didn't just **like** Prudence Estrada; he **admired** her. He cared deeply for her. He was **proud** of her. He opened his mouth to tell her as much, and then closed it again. It was embarrassing. She didn't want to hear that kind of thing anyway. She would gag on it.

On the other hand, had anyone ever told her these things? Anyone? Ever?

Then *Mr. Mojo Risin'* blew up, the third in a row and the fourth out of five. Its reactor overloaded very shortly into advanced acceleration, meaning it hadn't achieved as much separation from the pack as the other three had. Its fireball filled the sky, and gasps and curse words from even the most stoic of the pilots flooded channel one. Kaywin tapped Prudence on the shoulder. The fact that she almost jumped out of her seat in the wake of *Mr. Mojo's* demise told him a couple of things. One, she was still alive, and still afraid to die. Two, she wasn't wearing her seatbelt. "Prudence! Put on your helmet so I can talk to you!" he bellowed from behind his own thick glass visor. "And put on your seatbelt!" She complied numbly with both of these requests. *Wow. She must really be freaked.* He held up three fingers. Channel three.

"Alright. What do you want?" she said. "Are you there?"

"Yes. I want to tell you a couple of things." There was the silent sound of Pru listening. "I'm proud of you. Very, very proud of you. The first time I met you I thought you were nothing like my daughter. I couldn't have been more wrong. You might be the smartest person I've ever met. Don't tell Dub I said that. You are so strong and determined and wonderful. You risked your life; you gave up half your foot trying to save the world. When you got up and danced with us--" he started to choke up at the memory "--that might have been the bravest thing of all. I think you are hilarious and wonderful. I would have been proud to call you my daughter." *Pearly Queen* metaphorically dashed out of the gates through the windows ahead of them, and made a wonderful run of it. "The other thing is this. If we can't find Dublin before cruiser 8 goes, I'm going to tell everyone everything. I told Sephal, and I love the guy, but if we couldn't do it--if *you* couldn't do it--I don't know how he's going to. We can't leave it like this. Twenty billion people…do you agree? Am I crazy?" Cruiser seven punctuated his speech with a horrific explosion.

They were running out of time, fast. Kaywin could see Pru's tiny shoulders shuddering, and he knew he had made her cry. He opened his mouth to apologize, then…

"Yes, you are crazy!" Dublin's voice! "How I am not the smartest person you've ever met? Just kidding. I wasn't even the smartest person in my graduating class."

"Dub! How long have you been listening!"

"Just like 15 seconds; now quick! Meet me on the Channel **that is the same number as the highway that Bob Dylan revisited!**" There was no time for Kaywin to congratulate Dublin on remembering one of his old music lectures.

Three seconds later they were all on Channel 61. "Listen!" Dublin sounded crazed, bossy and adamant, and rightly so. Outside their windows Cruiser 9 made it pretty far, but burned out nonetheless. "You guys know this is not a secure channel right?"

"Right," answered Prudence.

"I've got a bunch of stuff, so just listen. First--try turning **OFF** your cooling coil, and not turning it on till *five seconds past critical*…"

"What?" Kaywin exclaimed. "Are you crazy? That's--"

"I have no idea if that's good advice or not, but that's what we're gonna try over here; someone left me a note in the cruiser about it; it must have been Ving. We're gonna blow up anyway, right? Next--Kaywin:" There was a sigh and a pause here that none of them had time for. When he resumed there was a catch in his voice. "I just want to say, Kaywin, that--" he was struggling to hold back tears "--it's meant a lot to me these last eight months, you being here with me, I mean, all the good advice I'll never get to use and all...I don't remember my father very well, but I tend to think he was a lot like you. Running out of time here...you guys remember that this is *not* a secure channel, right? Anybody who wants to could be listening right now, understand? So if I tell you something important, you're gonna have to act on it immediately, right? You got it?"

"Yeah, we got it," said Kaywin, not really knowing what Dublin was talking about, but getting the hint that he wasn't going to finish his speech until someone acknowledged the openness of the channel. Outside their window, the sky lit up like a fourth of July fireworks finale as cruiser 10 and her crew were absolutely obliterated. It looked like she had been carrying a million crates of Roman Candles. A countdown began on their displays and in their headsets.

Tomorrow Never Knows was next.

Dublin voice shook with emotions beyond what most of us will ever feel. "Sooo, Prudence, I just wanted to say to you--"

"No, no, no, no!" She knew darn well what he was going to say.

"Let me finish."

"No! Do **NOT** say what you are going to say!"

"Repeat after me: XC129947!"

"XC129947?" Prudence had no--

A robotic female voice from the console interrupted her thought. *"Security protocols removed"* it said, like it was no big deal. Kaywin looked at Prudence. Prudence looked at Kaywin.

Kaywin heard himself *screaming*:

GO GO GO GO GO!!!!

19

Higgle-Dy-Piggle-Dy

All hell broke loose.

Dublin's revelation hit them like a bolt of lightning. Instantaneous *purpose* wiped all fears away. Everything the three of them had planned and practiced flooded back into their brains in a millisecond. The countdown for *Tomorrow Never Knows* had only gotten down to 18 seconds, but Prudence floored it.

The blue and yellow cruiser shot forward like a bullet (except fifty times faster) and nosed to the left as sharply as she dared. Kaywin and Prudence both swooned momentarily, really unavoidable at this extreme acceleration, but were roused by their own adrenaline in under two seconds. They rocketed through the still-expanding, gloriously colorful remains of *Sympathy For the Devil* and toward the dark side of the Moon.

Their course toward the gun assembly had been installed as one of the presets for months. The challenge now was controlling the angle and speed as they followed it--without blowing up.

A red line on Pru's monitor described the elliptical curve of their planned approach. She wrestled with the wheel as the green line of their actual progress danced out of control to the left, then to the right of the red one. The cruiser shuddered horribly. It seemed to be shaking towards something disastrous and inevitable. She and Kaywin both had a similar thought: *So this is what a cruiser feels like right before it explodes...* If they had looked away from their displays, either of them, they might have been fatally mesmerized by the fantastic scene out of the wraparound windows. The countless stars again filled the sky with gorgeously spiraling, Van Gogh-like radiance, but at this speed a strange visual effect deluded the eye even further. They seemed to alternate, 10,000 stars shutting off as a new 10,000 lit up, all phasing by like Christmas lights slowly circumnavigating a tree. The mysterious dark side of the Moon itself was only discernible as a large inky gap in this mind-blowing display looming out of their left-hand windows. It was nauseating to think about guiding a ship blindly at this speed toward a tiny landing strip on the huge black surface, but that's exactly what they were attempting.

Kaywin's knuckles whitened on the auxiliary wheel, ready to take over if Prudence's lesser body-weight became insufficient to influence their course. With one eye, he followed the green and red lines, thinking that maybe he should have taken the lead on this final flight. But he didn't know for sure that he would have done any better. His other eye was fixed on the core temperature, which in the few seconds since their dashing out of the formation had gone from acceptable to near-critical. He had decided to follow Dublin's untried, second-hand advice, and let the temp go to critical and beyond.

It was with horror that both of them, concentrating for their lives, were distracted by the streak of someone passing them on their right. This cruiser followed a similar curve to-

ward a similar spot, and at the same breakneck speed. It overtook them because it was staying so much truer to the course.
With uncanny expertise the purple vessel wasn't wasting time
slipping to leftward and rightward like *TNK*. Kaywin, not
daring to rip his eyes from the temperature gauge, asked the
ship's computer. "*Tomorrow Never Knows*! What cruiser just
passed us?"

"*Purple Haze*," came the answer. Jerkboy. Boy, his finger
must have been on the trigger the whole time, expecting this
rebel run of theirs. And he too must have had this course laid
in, just in case…

Prudence, stretched to her psychological limit, made a little noise, a little cry of despair. "Don't worry! You just drive!"
Kaywin had to yell at the top of his lungs over the rickety
thunder of their vessel's complaining. Pru steadied a little,
hitting the imaginary red line more and more as they angled
aggressively toward the Moon.

Jerkboy was ahead of them but they were gaining slowly.
Suddenly and unexpectedly, his threatening voice was in their
ears. It shook with the turbulence, and seemed to creep into
their heads almost in slow-motion. They both had the impulse to slap at their ears as if there were a little insect crawling inside.

"Little girl," it said, almost in a sing-song. "I'm going to
kill you!"

Something new screamed past them toward *Purple Haze*.
For a second they were blinded by its plume of pink exhaust.
It was the *White Rabbit*.

"Dublin!" They both shouted.

"Easy Dub!" continued Kaywin. "You're going to ram
them!"

"Heck yeah, we're going to ram them!" Dublin shouted back.

Dublin had no faith that *White Rabbit* was going to hold together any longer than it already had. He liked the way it flew better than the others he had piloted. It would have been nice to try it when he had some control over the speed.

He had understood from the moment that Ving had killed himself that this would be the day of his reckoning. Even with his prodigious imagination, he just couldn't visualize a scenario where he would survive this.

He had been a nervous wreck all night and all morning. But the moment that his BFFs took off on their rogue trajectory toward the gun assembly, that all changed. He'd gotten the code to them, first of all, and that was (almost literally) the weight of the world off of him. Now his one and only purpose was to do everything in his power to help them fire that stupid gun, prove that it was NOT going to be adequate to destroy the RIP, and call the attention of all the *legitimate* scientists of Earth to the monstrous, unchecked threat.

All the nervousness and fear left him. All of it. He felt pure focus and purpose. He trusted his copilot to turn the cooling coil back on at critical-plus-five-point-zero. There was no way this would actually stop them from blowing up, but he hoped it would buy them enough time.

When they blew, he meant to take Jerkboy with them. In this moment of sublime clarity, he wasn't even *mad* at the man. God knows what **his** childhood had been like, what **his** trials had been, for him to have turned out like he did. But he too must die today.

Even though Dublin had been the one to basically fire

the starting gun by proclaiming the boundary code, he had fumbled at the controls, and wound up trailing his friends and the never-fumbling JB. He had whiffed on the acceleration at first because after he had said 'XC129947' he had tried to say 'and I love you', but his mouth had tripped over itself and produced some two-syllable bit of gibberish. Oh well. It was just as well that he hadn't distracted Prudence with that garbage, especially since he *knew* she didn't love him back.

Pru meanwhile was getting the hang of this, and the green line on her monitor was beginning to merge with the red. This was good timing, as suddenly, at the top of the screen, a little flashing "X" appeared. This was the big gun, the source of all this commotion. A little landing strip blinked next to it, about one/eighth the size of the one she was used to at the Moonbase.

Above the top edge of the monitor, out of the window straight ahead, she realized that the exhaust from *White Rabbit* was turning more and more orange, and less and less pink. *They're about to blow,* she thought. She had to collect herself for a second. "They're about to blow," she said as matter-of-factly as she could fake it to Kaywin. "How far back do we need to be?"

"Shhhh!...so are we...and...now!" Kaywin flipped a switch and the cooling coil hummed to life. "Brace yourself!" Tomorrow Never Knows reached a temperature at which it *should* have blown up, but after quickly cresting it began to fall steadily. "It worked! It doesn't make sense, but it *worked!*"

"So now we have to land this thing," mused Prudence. Ahead of them they saw *White Rabbit's* exhaust turn a deeper orange, and ominous blood-red flashes flared around the plume's perimeter.

"Come on, Dublin," growled Kaywin through his teeth. Suddenly the violent hues evaporated from the cruiser's wake, and its happy pink tones rebounded in force. "Yes! Way to go, Dublin!" Kaywin would never be sure, but he thought he saw Pru's tiny shoulders heave a couple of times, the way somebody's shoulders might do if they were trying to stifle a sob of relief.

White Rabbit's cooling coil had come on in the nick of time, and now she seemed to find a new gear. She was pressing *Purple Haze* hard, threatening to bump her in the butt and throw both cruisers into a spin that would have been fatal. They were entering rapidly into the Moon's gravitational pull; there was no way either ship would be able to right itself in time to avoid a horrific impact with the surface.

"Back off, Creaturehead!" threatened JB. Dublin made no answer. There was no need for talk. "Hey, Brokejaw! You need to take control of that ship!" For the ascetic, of course, there was **never** need for talk. Jerkboy had no choice but to pull *Purple Haze* aside. *White Rabbit* roared on by, followed closely by *Tomorrow Never Knows*. Suddenly, the good guys had the lead. Jerkboy had dipped his ship out, and now he dipped it right back in, deftly maneuvering into position behind *TNK*.

"We're gonna have to slow down soon!" yelled Kaywin. If they dropped down out of enhanced drive too late, they would crash into the Moon. If they dropped down too soon, then Jerkboy and Bruniette would get there first. It was going to be even trickier for Dublin; thanks to his engineer he couldn't ease out of enhanced drive. He would have to go from all to nothing. "Dublin! Switch back to our 'Plan A' channel!"

Dublin switched to 38. "Alright; I'm here!"

"Good! You gotta drop out soon, man!"

"I know, but I need to step aside so you don't ram me!"

The three ships were in very tight formation, and flying very fast. There was going to be a nasty pileup if they didn't work this out. "Same with us, or *Purple Haze* will steamroll us!"

"How about I elevate a hundred feet and you drop down a hundred? We have about eight seconds by the way!"

"Let's do it in five, four, three, two, one!"

White Rabbit went up. *Tomorrow Never Knows* went down. *Purple Haze* took advantage of their wasted movement and drew even. Now they were a stupid-looking little *stack* of ships, in some kind of sandwich-like formation, blistering towards instant death. They were playing 'chicken' with the Moon. They hoped Jerkboy would blink first and drop out of enhanced drive.

But it wasn't happening. "Listen for my cue," said Kaywin in a voice that was intended to sound reassuring. Warning lights were flashing all over Pru's monitor. "Kaaaaywin?" she said. Time was running out. The moment came when they had to concede, or die in a fiery crash without having fired the gun. Still Kaywin hesitated. "Now!"

But *Purple Haze* had dropped out just as Kaywin had opened his mouth. The other two cruisers maintained enhanced drive for just a half-second longer, but at two-hundred and eleven-thousand miles per hour it was enough to gain a valuable lead. If they had turned their ships around to look, *Purple Haze* would not have even been in visual range.

The new problem was braking. *White Rabbit's* fore-thrust-ers, designed to push back against the cruiser's forward mo-mentum, didn't seem to have the "umph" that *TNK's* did. Dublin was slowing, but not enough. He kept his eyes glued to the monitor, straining every nerve to decelerate, and trying to get somewhat parallel with the runway. The view ahead was terrifying, utter black unknown. It was like running blind-folded through a forest just as fast as you could, knowing you would slam into a tree at *some* point, but not knowing exactly when. He shouted to the ascetic, who he hoped was still con-scious behind him: "We only have six miles of runway! When we touch down I need you to apply the emergency brake, and then lock the wheels entirely! They'll be torn to shreds, but we won't need them after this, understand? I'm just going to try to keep her true!" There was no answer of course. Dublin hoped that no news was good news.

He decided he had time for one more comment.

"Prudence? Fru-Fru?" There was a pause. She too was concentrating very hard on all the details of not-crashing-and-dying. Plus, she had an idea of what was coming next.

"What? Just tell me later, okay?"

"I love you. Dublin Dunne, out."

His wheels slammed into the runway. There were a few lights stretching out on either side of the narrow paved lane for its brief extent. It was a pitiful landing strip, with pitiful lighting, and still easier to follow on the monitor. Dublin had the fore-thrusters maxed out, and was straining every nerve to keep the cruiser straight. The ascetic had done as he had been instructed, hitting the emergency brake first, and then locking the wheels entirely. Terrible groans flooded the cabin, like a thousand demons reaching up and trying to drag the two Goners back down with them to the land of the miserable dead. It took about two seconds for every scrap of specially engineered rubber to come flying off the wheels. After that was a horrible sustained scraping whistle, like a broken bagpipe **inside** their heads. Ahead of them more lights loomed, the end of the runway, and, to its left, the base of the enormous gun assembly! There was a padded bank where the landing strip terminated, backed by a low, natural hill. They were going to hit it, and pretty hard. *Steeeady…* Dublin thought. Then *I love you, Mom. I'm sorry.*

Then, *I hope I've done enough.*

Tomorrow Never Knows fared much better when it groped its way down the dim runway thirty seconds later. True, Prudence used all but the last forty feet of it, but it was a controlled and smooth landing, especially for someone so new to the art form.

"Remind me to tell you about Amelia Earhart," said Kaywin, smiling, as they began to frantically unbuckle.

"Why does everyone think I'm stupid?" Prudence protested. "I did a fifteen-page report on Amelia Earhart. I know all about her. Remind **me** to tell **you** about Amelia Earhart!"

Kaywin had no choice but to laugh. Prudence, the **real** Prudence, was coming out to play. Which was good, because they were going to need all of the fire and sass in their arsenal to pull off what they were about to attempt. They ignored the safety checks that *TNK* was pressuring them to make before exiting the vehicle, and just busted out. They knew they had only seconds, maybe a full minute, before *Purple Haze* came screaming in.

They had studied this part of the plan pretty hard; they had the codes memorized; they had the simple layout memorized... But it was different seeing it in person; plus they had *NOT* planned on being pursued--at least not this hotly. "Here comes Prince Charming" deadpanned Kaywin as soon as his booted toes touched the tarmac. Prudence landed next to him, and followed his gaze down the runway. Indeed, a streak of light was dipping out of the starry night toward the far end of the landing strip.

"You gonna wait here for a kiss?" And she was off running toward the dim underbelly of the gun assembly.

A quick glance up at the massive structure told them a lot. It was barely lit, so as not to attract attention. This was not really a necessary precaution; virtually no ships trafficked across the lunar backside. There was just enough light though, for Kaywin and Prudence to realize how enormous this thing was.

It looked pretty much like you might expect a giant gun to look. A fat, squat pentagonal building nearly a mile in diameter was supported by concrete columns, huge and numerous, sunk deep into the lunar bedrock. Funny to call it 'squat' when it rose to a height of more than a thousand feet, but when you're five thousand feet across you're going to be called squat. Crowning the top of this epic foundation was the hugest gun ever forged by humankind. This monstrous marvel, though it was built to fire a hundred-pettiwatt photon laser, was styled very much like a standard heavy artillery piece, the kind you might see mounted on a battleship or a seaside fortress. Just like that but 1000 times bigger. They could just make out a few enormous red letters along its length: 'THE BRANDENB...' It didn't take a genius to fill in the rest. They had named the gun 'THE BRANDEN-BERG'. It was built to swivel, side-to-side and up-and-down, and it stuck out so far from the face of the Moon that it did seem very capable of defending the inner solar system from asteroids or meteors approaching from almost any angle. But right now, if Dombroski's information was good, it remained fixed on the massive Rogue Interstellar Planet. As the Moon orbited the Earth, and the Earth orbited the sun, the giant gun swiveled to remain locked on the distant, but rapidly approaching, threat. There would be two periods per year when it could not hit this target, a ten-day stretch in April and a ten-day stretch in October. Today was December 24th. The lock should be good.

Kaywin looked back down. It would be easy to trip and fall, running across this unknown landscape in a flight suit in the dark. He noticed that Pru, several steps ahead of him, had grabbed the rifle from the floorboard of *TNK*.

They were both getting more and more concerned that they had seen no sign of Dublin, or the *White Rabbit* itself, for that matter. Neither was ready to speak the question aloud just yet. Then, without slowing her run, Kaywin saw Pru turn her head after rounding a little hill. When he reached the same spot five seconds later, he saw the tail end of Dublin's cruiser sticking up. It had hammered into the padding and ploughed up and almost completely over the hillock. Real concern flooded his mind, but he pushed it back. If Dublin was dead, they would mourn him and honor him in their hearts later. Or join him in a few minutes.

"Dublin!" Kaywin hollered into his mike. There was no answer. Unusual static was making helmet-to-helmet communication difficult. When Pru had been right next to him, it was fine, but it seemed like the further apart they got, the worse the interference was. Probably this had to do with the incredible amount of energy stored at the assembly, waiting to explode out across the universe.

The view ahead of them was suddenly illuminated a little more brightly. At first Kaywin thought that they had triggered some motion-activated auxiliary lighting. Then he glanced behind them and saw, to his horror, *Purple Haze* screaming silently down the runway. It was slowing, but not enough. Its forward momentum was finally stopped when it slammed into *Tomorrow Never Knows*, which in turn was sent rolling and careening off the landing strip right towards Kaywin and Prudence!

"Pru look out!" Kaywin dove aside, and much to his relief saw Pru do the same. Their dented ship pitched to a stop after having wiped the lunar surface clear of their footprints. They were back on their feet in a flash and running for their lives.

It was creepy to hear **nothing** from behind them on the airless terrain; they knew that Jerkboy and Bruniette must be getting out of their cruiser in hot pursuit, and maybe even firing at them, but their ears were useless in assessing the encroaching danger.

They reached a door that they knew did not lead yet into the livable section of the assembly base; it opened into the rocky underbelly. Prudence was calmly entering the code as

Kaywin skidded up next to her. An unpleasantly familiar, taunting voice buzzed in their ears, but they couldn't make the words out. Casting his eyes back while Pru tried the handle, he saw that their hunters had not yet surmounted the ridge a hundred feet behind them. If they could just get through this door with time enough to relock it, it would be a mere two hundred foot jaunt to the inner door.

The door opened. Prudence looked at Kaywin. Kaywin looked at Prudence. Their hearts sank into their Moonboots.

The diagram they had memorized was backwards. The inner door was dead ahead--and almost a mile away.

A green laser shot suddenly burned up a hole in the door-frame inches from Kaywin's hand. The abused girl and the man who had lost it all took off running with every ounce of strength they had left.

Green flashes streaked by them and sent up clouds of Moondust. This gave them a meager screen, but it wasn't enough. One hit--**any** hit--would violate the integrity of their life-supporting suits and they would suffocate. Then they would freeze solid, just for good measure. A strange ex-hilaration suffused through Kaywin. He remembered studying flight manual after flight manual back at the Moonbase, for hours and days on end, his stomach empty, his brain sore and overspilling. With death ready to strike him down at any moment, he grinned.

"Now *this* is more like it!" he shouted to Pru.

"Shut up and run!"

"Got it. Bob and weave; bob and weave, Pru!" The untamed terrain was working in their favor; they dodged down hills and bumps galore, and they tried to trend their scamper toward the closest row of concrete columns, on the left. "You're missing half a foot! How are you running so fast?!" Kaywin gasped as he struggled to keep pace.

"I'm wearing my half-grav! And, I'm sixteen!"

It was an odd race, one Kaywin could never have imagined six or seven years ago when he used to race up Seames Drive with Victoria. Before too long they had reached the relative sanctuary of the giant concrete pillars. They staggered, limped and leaped over the choppy landscape to the left of the titanic columns. But when Jerkboy and Bruniette gained this outer edge as well, still a couple of hundred feet behind them, they had a better idea of where Kaywin and Prudence would be popping out, and their laser fire got unnervingly close, At one point Pru could feel chips of concrete raining down on her helmet from a blast just over her right ear. She took this warning seriously and changed tack. "Follow me!" she yelled to her struggling partner. The distance between them had been growing, and along with it, the static in their headsets.

"What?"

"I said *FOLLOW ME!*"

They ducked back into the wide alley to the right of the columns. Pru wheeled around and took a knee. As Kaywin battled toward her, his lungs about to burst, he saw her shoulder the laser rifle and steady it toward a specific point behind him. He stumbled to the side a little bit to give her a clear shot. He could see the green flash and feel the hum of concentrated energy as it seared by him.

This was Pru's first time firing a laser rifle, and she could have done a lot worse. She didn't **hit** Jerkboy, but just as he emerged from behind a giant pillar and reached the top of a little ridge beyond it she obliterated the ground at his feet. He took a violent spill and his rifle went flying.

Pru fired a second shot at the emerging Bruniette, which missed him badly but caused him to pull up momentarily in surprise. It was apparently news to these guys that Prudence was armed and dangerous. She wasted no time in wheeling back around and racing onward. Thanks to her rifle blasts Kaywin had caught up. They were close enough now for clean communication.

"There's a third person after us. When I fired the first time I saw a silhouette back there!"

"Dublin?" wheezed Kaywin hopefully.

"I don't know." Their questions were half-answered a few seconds later when they rounded a corner and safely reached the red metal staircase with the door at the top that led to the interior of the gun assembly. To their great joy and enormous relief, they saw their friend at the top. He was punching numbers on the keypad repeatedly, and there was desperation in his aspect. Prudence and Kaywin clambered up after him. The boy turned when he felt the staircase tremble, and they could see tears and blood on his face.

"I can't remember the code! I can't remember!"

"I got it; I got it, Dub." Kaywin shouldered his way past Dublin and his untimely self-loathing. There was no time for 'hey-what-happened-to-you' but he suspected that the boy had suffered a significant head-injury in the process of crash-landing the erstwhile *White Rabbit*. Prudence let Kaywin work the keypad and turned with rifle ready back toward the corner they just rounded. She fired a random warning shot into the shadows to make JB and his buddy-buddy think twice about pouncing. They were in an exposed position at the top of the lighted stairwell, and despite the lowness of the wattage in their eyes it was very difficult to see back into the darkness. Suddenly a green streak blinked at them, and Kaywin cried out in pain. He clutched at the back of his left leg.

The door opened, and they tumbled inside. Dublin clubbed his arm at a red button on the interior wall and the door whisked shut.

The compression chamber was tiny, but brightly lit. All three of them understood instantly that Kaywin's suit had been compromised. They had seconds to pressurize the chamber or he would asphyxiate. Kaywin had stumbled in and crumpled to the floor in agony. "Dublin, get some air in here! I got the door!" They could feel the vibrations of heavy footsteps ascending the red stairwell beyond. Prudence leveled the laser rifle at the outside door, aiming upwards at a spot that she guessed would be chest high on their relentless pursuers.

Adrenaline surged through Dub. He rallied through his confusion enough to enter a viable sequence on the compression chamber touchscreen. Oxygen flooded the cramped room as Kaywin fumbled desperately at his helmet. Gradually, with the returning air came returning sound; it was like their ears were becoming unstopped after a descent in an airplane. They could suddenly **hear** the metal stairwell just inches outside creaking under the significant weight of the muscular unfriendlies. JB was pounding at the outer door, but it wouldn't accept his sequence because Dublin had been quicker on the draw and had already deftly activated the inner one. It was impossible to open the inner and the outer doors at the same time, or a large portion of the assembly base would be depressurized. The inner door opened and Kaywin lunged through it as he ripped his helmet off, sucking in lungfuls of sweet oxygen. Dublin followed him and Prudence brought up the rear. Right before she stepped out, she thought she heard a third set of moonboots echoing up the exterior stairwell. Station security? The ascetic? Her imagination?

There was no time for congratulating each other on making it this impossibly close to their goal. The thinly carpeted corridor they found themselves in extended a hundred feet to their left and a hundred feet to their right. The approach to the firing room from here was fairly straightforward, and all three of them had it committed to memory. They set off at a brisk limp to the right.

Three hallways branched off at right angles from this corridor; it was like a giant capital 'E', and they were headed for the bottom leg. They made it around the corner as fast as they could and pulled up short.

Oh God. They had all three made the same mistake. They

should have realized from their miscalculation down under the station that the blueprint they had memorized was backwards, a mirror image of the actual gun assembly. This corridor dead-ended at a door marked '39'. They didn't have the stupid code for door 39; they needed door 37.

The hallway they needed was in the complete opposite direction, at the *top* of the capital "E". Prudence reversed course and *started* back around the corner into the main corridor. The compression room door, halfway down, suddenly opened and she leaped backwards into hiding. Dublin started to say something into his headset and the other two shushed him mutely and emphatically. Kaywin indicated for them to open their helmets, so they could communicate without being overheard. Having done so, the young boy and the young girl both cursed silently at their stupidity in choosing the wrong corridor. Kaywin limped forward a little and gave the slightest peek around the corner, bracing himself for the possibility that Jerkboy's face might be *right there* peeking back, that their noses might touch and then he might be shot.

Just as he looked, a very tall, gangly, deathly-thin figure stumbled out of the compression chamber. He had been shoved out as a human guinea pig, to test the water. If Prudence was watching with her finger on the trigger, **he** would be the one to absorb her laser blast. His glass faceplate slid aside into his helmet. It was the ascetic.

This beaten down, starved, choked, broken wreck of a man must have been knocked unconscious for several minutes in the *White Rabbit* landing. He had to be *pushed* into the dangerous hallway not because he clung to any desire to live, but because he was severely concussed, lost in a daydream--a horrible one, to be sure. He was almost completely checked out. Kaywin watched him turning his horrible red face slowly, scanning the hallway. It was easy to imagine the ascetic, in a similar glazed and repulsive state, standing in Kaywin's kitchen after breaking in almost five years ago, in the middle of the night, sniffing the air for the sickly-sweet scent of his precious Excelsiadon and ready to kill for it.

Kaywin saw the ungainly head turn as slowly as an oscillating fan first to the left, in the direction they *should* have gone, and then to the right. Mesmerized, Kaywin was a split-second too late in pulling his head back. He saw the ascetic raise a skeletal arm, with the mottled royal blue and black fabric of his flight suit drooping off of it, and point down the hallway right at their little hiding spot.

"We've got trouble. Big time. They're headed this way."

The band of three looked around them in a panic. The little hallway that they cowered in had only one door leading away at the end of the 30-foot run, door 39. Dublin leaped toward it and frantically entered the code they had memorized for door 37 , the one they were *supposed* to be dealing with at this point. No luck. He pawed frantically at the keypad, hitting pretty much all of the buttons at once like some brat kid on an elevator. When he turned back around, Pru had handed her laser rifle over to Kaywin and was emphatically miming for Dub to come back and...what? Hoist her up?

The interior wall of their momentary prison was not actually a wall per se, but an eight-foot high chain link fence butting up against a nine-and-a-half-foot tall energy cell. Safety zones had to be maintained around this powerful mega-battery--one of a staggering 24,024 just like it, housed in giant circles, 286 per level, 84 levels high. There was a narrow gap between the top of the quietly humming energy cell, and the ceiling above it.

Without their suits on, after months of under-feeding, Kaywin and Dublin **might** have been able to stash themselves into this meager gap to hide from the slowly approaching Jerkboy, Bruniette, and the ascetic. But the time they needed was just not there. They would be sitting ducks; no way would they be able to slither out of sight before JB lit them up with laser-fire. So when Dublin saw what Pru was suggesting, he understood. Their parting moment was at hand.

He ran back on tiptoe to hoist Prudence up. He and Kaywin would stand side-by-side and fight as hard as they could for as long as they could to buy her some getaway time. It would be one gun, on their side, versus two guns and a human shield. It would be up to Pru now to scamper away and fire the mother of all guns.

As Dublin raised Prudence up (she was surprisingly light--he didn't know she was wearing the half-grav) he regretted only that he would never hear her answer to his confession of love. *I mean, I **know** the answer…but maybe I don't? And maybe she would break my heart gently, and I could die knowing that I was closer than I thought…*

But when Prudence got her elbows onto the top edge of the energy cell she didn't clamber on up like Dublin thought she would. She instead removed her little helmet, quickly and deftly, and heaved it sideways with great force. Then she sent something flying after it, something small, and pink and round that she'd been clutching in her right hand.

The helmet rolled and bounced along the top of the 40-foot wide energy cell, making a strange, clunky rumble over the heads of the hunters in the hallway. One of them--probably Jerkboy--shushed the other two. Then came the higher echoey pinging of the little pink ball.

The helmet reached the far edge of the giant brown battery and crashed into the corridor facing the compression chamber, the middle arm of the "E." Next was heard a loud female voice, Pru's voice, crying out in frustration: "IDIOT!!! COULD YOU **BE** ANY LOUDER?!!!"

The 'Say-What?' ball. Awesome. Did she always carry that thing around?

From her little perch on Dub's shoulders, the *actual* Prudence could just see the tops of the three approaching helmets. She saw the tallest one, belonging to the ascetic, bobbing and jerking. She could tell he'd been grabbed and muscled to the front again as they reversed course toward the racket. He was resigned to his fate. The other two had only to position him where they needed him. Pru held out her left hand to her friends below, indicating to them to wait and to be super-quiet for a minute. When she was sure that Jerkboy and company had taken the bait, she whispered to Dublin to let her down slowly.

"They think we've gone down the middle hall. We need to creep by quickly and very, very quietly, okay? They won't be on that trail for long. Let's go!" All this in an urgent whisper. Kaywin, still holding the laser rifle, peeped again around the corner just for surety. He realized that his hands were cramped and sore from just a few seconds of gripping the weapon desperately tightly, expecting someone to jump out and shoot him dead at any moment.

His eyes confirmed what Pru had told them already. The coast was clear. They advanced around the corner and made a pathetic, limping, tiptoeing run toward the middle corridor. When they reached it, Kaywin stopped them with his left arm and peeked around the new corner. Jerkboy, Bruniette and the ascetic were all gathered in front of the door at the far end of the hallway. JB, in his ridiculous segmented silver suit, was pressing a code into its keypad. Their backs were turned fully. For a split second, Kaywin realized that if his aim was true he could take one of them out, *maybe* two, before they could return fire…then he remembered the Dizastra commercial where Brandenberg gets caught in a some kind of robot uprising and gets pounded with laser-fire--and, as always, emerges unscathed. He calculated (correctly) that it would be better to just move on. He waved Dub and Pru across the exposed eight-foot space, hanging back to provide cover if needed. Just as he scurried behind them on the **correct** path to the firing room, he thought he saw the door at the end of the hall **open** in response to the code Jerkboy had entered. *How does he know these codes? Does he know* **more** *than us? Does he really think we went that way or is he taking a shortcut to the firing room?* The answers to these three questions were all the same: **Hurry up! Hurry up!** And **HURRY UP!**

He caught up with his friends and they hustled around the next corner into the hallway they should have entered the first time. Dublin was still woozy from his head injury. "That was **amazing**!" he whispered to Prudence. Where did you get a 'Say-What' ball?"

"I keep a lot of little things handy," she said, locked in on their destination.

"I think she has *special powers!*" Dub slurred to Kaywin.

Kaywin too was concentrating on their mission. "They're not special," he said. "They're girl-powers." He finally took a second to make eye contact with Dublin as they ran along. "Standard-issue. You'll find out someday."

They reached the door at the end of the hallway. Kaywin punched in the code, and to their great relief the door slid open. They passed through it into the largest indoor space ever created by man.

They were standing on a red metal walkway that formed an enormous ring around the building's hollow interior. This was the bottom-most of 84 red circles, rising above them to a dizzying height. In the center of this open space was a thousand-foot tall green steel cylinder, like a giant rocket. Thin cables ran from each of the station's energy cells to this central cylinder, drooping gracefully in the stark fluorescent light to form what could have been some kind of epic string sculpture. Even though they were indoors, on the airless Moon, this jaw-dropping space was breezy on their naked faces, and the slightest fabric rustle or footstep seemed to echo for days. Kicking themselves for pausing to stare, with the fate of their mother-planet at stake, they scurried hurriedly to their left along the obnoxiously clanging walkway. The circle it described was so vast that if you focused your eyes on a small section of the red railing you couldn't even tell that it had any curve to it.

Their directions from Dombroski had so far been good (now that they had reversed everything mentally) and their plan was solid. Thirty paces leftward brought them to a crude elevator; it was more like a large birdcage on a chain, really. No code was needed here, and in seconds they were ascending with nauseating speed past ring after ring of red metal. Very quickly the height became scary, and it was about this time that they saw and heard three figures burst out of a door far below them onto the walkway of Level One.

Some distance had been gained, but all stealth had been lost; their little birdcage-rocket made a terrible groaning racket as it climbed. "Step back!" shouted Kaywin to his companions. There wasn't much 'back' to step to, but they pressed themselves as much as they could against the rear end of the lift. Jade-colored light flooded the cage as a laser blast from below hit near the top of the elevator door. It continued to rise, and the concentrated flow of green energy melted a long oval in the front screen, big enough for a middling-sized man or a small woman to tumble out of to their death. The actual mechanism of the lift had not been compromised, and Kaywin, Dublin and Prudence sped past the final twelve floors to the uppermost--the one on which history would either be made, or wiped clean forever. Below them, Jerkboy, Bruniette and the ascetic scurried in the other direction toward the nearest functioning elevator.

Kaywin, Dub and Pru left a terrible, crackling racket behind them as they disembarked onto the 84th floor. JB's laser blast had severed two of the cables that linked the energy cells to the master cylinder. These fell with great weight, sputtering with such violence that Kaywin felt a little awe, and a little incredulity that this display of force represented the output of only two of the assembly's 24,024 cells; just 1/12,000 of its might. The might that they were minutes from unleashing.

Dublin crashed to the floor as they ran out of the elevator. He was fine; they just helped him up. He was obviously concussed from his crash-landing. "I'm so sleepy," he yawned.

"You have a concussion," explained Kaywin, trying to prop the boy up. "Or two. Stay awake Dub; we're almost done buddy; we need you!"

"I'm good. I'm all better," Dublin answered, staggering sideways into the wall. Kaywin (ignoring the screaming pain of his own laser-seared calf muscle, with the plastic of his suit melted right into the flesh) ducked up under Dublin's left arm, wrapping it around his own neck, and tried to support him. Pru turned and noted this, took back the rifle that Kaywin held out to her, and led onward at an unaltered and very brisk clip. She was quite the sight with her bloodied wig-less head dipping and rising as she hustled on her half-foot. They were motivated to keep up with her, and they almost did.

Prudence gave a quick study to every door they raced past. *Cell Mon 15-18, Cell Mon 19-22, Grease Mount 5*...Meanwhile they had no way of knowing how quickly their pursuit was catching up. Finally, they came to a door that looked like all the rest, but Prudence skidded to a halt in front of it.

'BRNDNBRG MSTR NO ADMIT' it read.

Pru set upon the keypad with great energy, pushing in the code they had all memorized and quizzed each other on for months.

It didn't work.

She tried it again. Nothing. Kaywin tried it, just in case. It was no good. He wiped at his sweaty brow in frustration. "They must have changed it. They must have changed it after Dombroski tried to fire it." Panic crept in and began to undermine their focus...

"What do we do?" gasped Dublin, looking down the curve of the hall in the direction that they could reasonably expect Jerkboy and company to appear at any second. "Can we blast our way in?"

"Stand back," said Pru. She leveled the rifle at the center of the door.

"Wait!" exclaimed Dublin. "You don't have a lot of charge left on that thing...aim **here**; that's where the locking mechanism is housed. It's in every Plasmo Zenith movie. If it doesn't open maybe I can at least reach through and hit the button inside."

Prudence adjusted her aim. "*Grand tradition of the Three Stooges*," she muttered, still appalled, eight months later, at Dublin's obsession with the entire slapstick genre. With these words she commenced to blasting in the area of the lock. The rugged door in that one little spot began to melt and slough away; small gobs of molten metal dripped onto the carpet, catching it on fire at one point. Kaywin stomped it out quickly. Finally the door *started* to open--then stopped. It was only with great, combined effort that they were able to force it open about ten inches. This was enough room for Prudence, who scooted in. It was immediately clear that Kaywin and Dublin weren't getting through with their helmets on. As they struggled to remove them with trembling hands, loud alarms began to sound, startling them and needlessly reminding them that their time was running out. First Dublin, then Kaywin squeezed painfully through the narrow gap.

They found themselves in a surprisingly small room for such an important function. Large monitors crowded the black walls, displaying live camera feeds from all over the station. These were mainly actionless scenes from inside and outside the base, gray and white lunar landscape here, the mind-boggling length of the gun barrel there... They could see the runway on one, with the wrecked cruisers bottled up at the end.

The most disturbing images were of station personnel being roused to action by the alarms and making all haste toward the firing room.

Prudence was seated with her back to the boys, hacking frantically at the computer. To her left was a shockingly cartoonish big red button, under an impenetrable frosted glass cap. The complicated sequence, entered correctly, wouldn't *fire* the Brandenberg itself. It would cause the glass cap to separate into two halves and retract into the blackish gray stone of the tabletop. Then a simple press of the button would unleash the single greatest burst of energy in human history.

Dublin, reading the frustration of Pru's body language, ran up, grabbed her shoulders and gently guided her aside. This was his area of specialty, and, head-swimming or not he would get this right. Just seconds into his attempt however, he heard over his shoulder the sickening sound of running boots, and a great commotion outside the mangled door. Kaywin had picked up the laser rifle off the shiny black floor where Prudence had unceremoniously dropped it; now he threw it back to her and charged toward the narrow opening.

A strange face, the face of a man they didn't know, poked in angrily, shouting angry words. He started to bring his own rifle around to fire it through the gap but Kaywin punched him in the face twice in rapid succession. The man went flying backwards with much greater force than he expected. *These are scientists, not soldiers, sure, but still…* A second later this little mystery was solved as a much more familiar face poked through. Green light flashed toward the handsome features, but Jerkboy pulled away just in time. Not surprisingly, the ascetic was then shoved through the hole in his place.

He collected himself and stood up straight, then charged right at Dublin's exposed back. Pru unleashed her last rifle blast at the giant's legs, and he hit the floor. "I'm so close!" shouted Dublin. "Like five seconds!"

Jerkboy heard this, and with enough brawn to make any man think twice about engaging him in hand-to-hand combat, he violently shouldered the broken door completely off of its track. Kaywin, thinking that the ascetic was accounted for, dove with all of his strength to hold off the relentless, arrogant JB before he could bring his rifle to bear on Prudence or Dublin. As he wrestled with the laughing, spitting Jerkboy, the younger man's brutish strength carried them over the threshold and onto the floor of the firing room. Behind them the ascetic had regained his feet. Prudence, nineteen inches shorter than the zealot, and out of laser power, swung the rifle at his head with everything she had left. The giant caught the barrel in his skeleton hand, inches from his ugly face, and wrested it from her grip. He shoved Prudence aside viciously, as if allowing real anger to flow through him for the first time in years. She lost her footing, and nothing remained between the bad guys and Dublin.

"Got it--," yelled Dublin in curtailed exuberance, just starting to reach for the red button. The rifle was around his throat, crushing his larynx with cruel strength; his arms were pinned uselessly to his side. He was lifted out of his seat by the ascetic and swung around to face the defenders of the gun assembly, who now poured in through the open door with rifles drawn. Prudence started to make a diving leap for the red button, but the heavy, muscly weight of the man they had always called Bruniette came crashing down on her. The game was up. The attempt had failed. Earth was doomed because they were too weak to save it.

It took three men to hold back the struggling Kaywin, driven mad with impotence as Jerkboy stood up and relinquished him to station security. This was like trying to get the baguette to the homeless Parisian girl, times a million. Dublin being choked to death in front of his eyes, Prudence crushed under the weight of some conscienceless brute. These kids had become almost his own children. He flailed and shouted, trying to explain to the scientists that the destruction of humanity would be on their hands. All to no avail.

Jerkboy was talking, saying something cocky and stupid, relishing his final mastery of the slippery situation, but Dublin couldn't hear it. His ears were ringing and the bright splotches of light were bursting behind his eyelids, much like when he had passed out at the Greenville MCP office. Then, for some reason, the pressure on his throat relaxed a little. Fresh air filled his lungs. Strangely, he felt hot tears dripping down his back. He began to think he had lost his mind, maybe a long time ago. Without warning, the ascetic let him drop entirely, and shoved him toward Jerkboy.

The strange giant lifted his right hand and brought it down on the red button.

A voice that none of them had ever heard before came out of his mouth and trembled over the shocked, speechless little crowd.

"Kaywin! I didn't kill your wife and daughter. But I think I know--"

Green fire washed over him, and the ascetic was no more.

20

Dominance and Submission

The strange man, whoever he was, lay dead. Whatever his name had been, whatever his addictions had been, whatever vows, promises, or oaths he had broken, whoever he had hurt, or killed, or whatever, the miserable wretch lay stretched out dead with his cranium partially exploded.

The red button that the ascetic had pushed had set the firing process into motion. There was no 'abort' option; there was no turning back. The same button seemed to have finally pushed the sweaty-faced Jerkboy over the edge. He was absolutely beside himself with rage. An unbroken nineteen-second stream of curse words cascaded at high volume from behind his gritted teeth as he stomped and danced around the room in raw frustration. Nobody else, from Kaywin, Dublin, and Prudence, to station personnel, even his BFF Bruniette, dared to speak or move a muscle, lest they join the dead man in a heap on the floor.

Jerkboy probably could have kept going, but after nineteen seconds something strange happened. Utter silence fell. Everybody all at once noticed that the ambient, constant hum of the 24,024 energy cells had gone quiet. It was eerie. Then there was a single ominous 'clang' that echoed up to them from far below. After that the humming returned, and started to build…and build…and build… It rose in pitch and volume from *magnificent* to *frightening,* to downright *irresponsible*… A sense that they were about to witness history settled over every one of the thirty-six tiny humans in the gargantuan building; all gathered together in one small room and frozen in the most ridiculous poses. Whatever was about to happen had never been witnessed before. The drone gradually achieved an intensity that humbled thirty-five of them with its suggestion of power. Hair bristled on every neck, goose bumps rose on every arm, then, comically, every hair on every head stood straight up. The freshly balded Prudence felt a little left out as she stared around the room until she made eye contact with the one other bald person, a portly middle-aged man who was vaguely grinning. They nodded a distracted little polite nod at each other, as if to say *I, too, have no hair; nothing to be ashamed of…*

Other than the unflappable Jerkboy, every man, woman and child temporarily forgot their role in this little play. No words seemed necessary or even possible. Kaywin, Dublin and Prudence, even Bruniette, looked to the faces of the scientists for some kind of mute indication of what to expect and how to feel about it, but they saw only shock and curiosity reflected back at them, under lions' manes of electrified hair.

There came a moment when the hum became unbearable. Almost in unison all thirty-six of them clutched at their ears. Then suddenly it trailed off and died. Everyone's hair was released from the outward position as if by magic.

Kaywin, still on the cold black floor, had been on the

verge of passing out from exhaustion, and delirious relief. He watched one of the female scientists. As if in a dream, her long brown hair drifted back down to her head with hypnotizing grace. For one awful second, Kaywin feared that the *Brandenberg* had failed to perform, that all of their efforts had been in vain. But then a shockwave of compressed air and electricity trampled over them, deafening them, and he relaxed into happy unconsciousness.

Houston, Texas U S of A
December 24, 2126...5:59 AM

The light blue bullet car eased slowly up the gravel road and came to a stop at the guardhouse. The guard still smiled a little smile every morning at the inspiring and dogged persistence of Octavia Hopkins. It helped, of course, that he didn't have to choose sides on the issue; he just had to punch the clock and comply with the legalities.

The determined woman had become a little famous, but eight months into her daily protest the media attention had died down for the most part. It was only *news* for a couple of days in April, before it became *old news*... On May 2nd a man in Oregon appeared to have been pushed over a cliff by his house robot. This stranger and more sensational story had dominated headlines nationally for a couple of months, and Ms. Hopkins' quest for information on the death of her son, Latrell, was largely forgotten.

Now it was Christmas Eve, and a solitary news vehicle had been dispatched to the scene for one last wrenching of the national heart. It had to wait outside the gates and launch its little drones over the fence to gather footage. The bored newsman sipped a powerful black coffee at his desk inside the meatloaf-shaped truck. He looked forward to being done with this in a couple of hours, then driving to Dallas to spend the holiday with his parents. He didn't know that something was about to happen that would trap him here for days.

As the window of the blue bullet car retracted, the guard complimented Ms. Hopkins on her dark green Christmas dress. With a furtive glance toward the parked news truck, he reached behind him and produced a small, nicely wrapped present. The woman exclaimed pleasantly, with genuine warmth and gratitude. Then she handed the man a home-made fruitcake. This was his favorite, which she remembered from a conversation they had had a couple of weeks earlier. *You shouldn't have! Where did you find the time? I'm not going to share any of this!* etc. was the gist of his response.

As he opened his mouth to speak further, a new pair of headlights rounded the corner and cruised toward the guard-house. "Let me let you through, Ms. Hopkins. Merry Christ-mas." He wanted to get the gates opened and shut in case this newcomer had any ideas about driving on through. As the gates began to close behind the blue bullet car, however, the guard realized that if the approaching green bubble *wanted* to, it would have time to follow Ms. Hopkins right on through. So he got out of the tiny guardhouse and positioned himself in the middle of the road with his hand extended.

In his parked meatloaf truck, the newsman coughed, sending a couple of donut crumbs flying, and he sat up to observe this new development.

"Good Morning!" said the guard as the window of the green bubble slid open. "Can I help you with something?"

Inside the car, dressed in his best suit (though it was clearly not an expensive one) was an old man. "Good morning," he returned. "I'm just here to park next to Octavia Hopkins."

The guard listed the three approvals that the man would need. To his surprise, Mr. Fleming had them all. And they were legit. He had no choice but to let the man through. His conscience, however, required him to check one more thing.

"You don't have any ill-intentions toward Ms. Hopkins, I hope?"

"Oh, no no no…quite the opposite!"

The guard studied the man's honest old face for a second and decided he was telling the truth. "Alright. You behave in there. Merry Christmas."

"Merry Christmas."

Old Mr. Fleming was true to his word. In fact, not wanting to obscure Octavia's 'I-want-to-know-what-happened-to-my-baby' display, he parked his green bubble car on the opposite side of the roadway. Then he got out and surveyed its position, and was satisfied. He stuck his head back in the window and gave some brief instructions to the car. Withdrawing, he hitched up his long grey slacks. He briefly turned and sent a nervous little smile and a wave to the semi-celebrity across the way. Not disguising her curiosity in the least, Octavia Hopkins waved back politely. She would wait a minute, to see what this man was up to, before returning the smile.

The old man had shrunk somewhat with age and sadness, but was still tall and dignified. He reached back into the car for the fedora that matched his suit. He placed it on his almost completely bald head, crossed his long arms, and leaned back against the green bubble as its video displays came to life in the pre-dawn chill.

Ms. Hopkins had to walk back toward the guardhouse a little ways to get a proper view of the newcomer's car. She did so slowly so as not to appear overeager. When she turned and looked, her heart leapt and tears came to her eyes. She was no longer alone out here in the cold. The message board that glided up out of the top of the green bubble, like a shark fin up out of the water, read:

Jennifer Fleming ~ Born 2/23/2048 ~ Diagnosed w/Alzheimer's 7/3/2122 ~ Disappeared 7/7/2126 ~ Died 10/12/2126 ~She should have died in my arms~

~

The best view from the finished sections of Moonbase 2 was not from the common area on Level Five, as Daryl had told Ving and Dublin on their first day there, a lifetime ago. It was from the Security Chief's office a couple hundred feet down from it.

This is where Jerkboy, surrounded by the upper echelon of his cronies, sat on the edge of his desk laughing, with a mostly-empty glass of eggnog in his hand. It was late on Christmas Eve, and he was recounting to them, as best as he could without revealing classified information, the dramatic events of that morning and afternoon. Yes, there was a modest-sized gun being built on the dark side of the Moon to defend the Earth from potential inner-solar system asteroids. Yes, Kaywin Lafontaine, Prudence Estrada, and Dublin Dunne had carried out a terrorist attack on this gun assembly, accidentally firing it in the process. Their motivation remained to be determined. Fortunately, JB had been on to their plot for some time, and had heroically thwarted their attempt to blow up the assembly. Yes, the three terrorists were being kept alive for questioning, and would eventually be sent to Atlanta to be infected with the latest laboratory-enhanced Scourge virus. They would die in horrible agony, and disgrace, as they deserved.

Bruniette corroborated his friend's story, though clearly a lot of it didn't match up to what he himself had witnessed. He knew that he had seen much, much more than he was ever supposed to see. He was therefore content to lay low, and agree with JB's extraordinary account. Secretly, he marveled at the craftsmanship of the story; the mental acuity it took to twist the details into a believable narrative. Questions from their laughing buddies led to answers from JB just bursting at the seams with masterful misdirection. The eggnog flowed, along with the laughs and the back-slapping. It was about as fun as a Christmas party could be for people waiting around to die.

Then a soft tone from JB's Sofee indicated an incoming message.

The party went downhill from there.

"*Happy Birthday!*" the message led off, cheerfully enough. "*Heard about the mess on the Dark Side. Check your countdown.*" The grin sloughed off of Jerkboy's dash-gummedly handsome face. In a split second, he had gone from victorious man to defeated child. With a trembling finger he tapped at his screen. The countdown to his guaranteed death, the sweet release from the crap-heap of his miserable life, had changed. It had gone from just over a thousand hours, back up to *ten thousand*. An entire year had been added. As if everything else hadn't been *unfair* enough, *cruel* enough, he was going to have to choke down another year of this wretched *imitation* of life.

He dismounted from the giant mahogany desk with a forced, exaggerated laugh. He began to usher people out of his office unexpectedly. "Party's over. Everybody out. Eeeeverybody out. Yeah, ha ha ha, party's over. Everybody out. Everybody ***OUT!!!***"

Bruniette was the last out the door, turning back toward his friend with brow furrowed in concern. He was used to JB's mood swings, but this was extreme. "What was that-" the door whooshed shut and he finished his question under his breath, to himself. "What was that message?"

Inside his grand office, JB paced like a wild animal, wringing his hands. He walked away from the wall-sized viewscreen for a third time, and when he turned back, he noticed that the unjustly inflated numbers of his countdown were now scrolling across it, mocking him. Adrenaline flooded through his exhausted system. He lost control.

He picked up the enormous desk and staggered with it toward the viewscreen. With every step his fury grew and he mastered his grip on the awkward weight. With a roar that rattled his evicted buddies in the hallway, he heaved the desk into the viewing wall and shattered it.

The floodgates opened on the young man's rage. He hefted a ponderous wooden chair like it was nothing and started swinging it like a club. And so began the utter destruction of the Security Chief's office.

In the corridor outside, the concerned whispers of JB's stooges halted. Bruniette was worried, really worried for his best friend, and was no longer satisfied to leave him to his own devices. He hammered at the door with his fist, but JB ignored him. Parting the small crowd and getting a running start, he launched himself into the thick white metal repeatedly and desperately. The racket from inside the office had died off suddenly, but this was in no way reassuring to him. Not at all. He redoubled his efforts, and the door began to dent.

Inside the office, which may as well have been bombed, JB climbed over the fallen shelves and the ravaged, ancient books, slowly approaching the overturned desk at rest in a sea of broken glass. He reached through the shards to open the top left drawer. He took out a small white laser pistol. Blood from his fresh cuts rolled down the shiny handle. He saw his own handsome face reflected in it, a face he despised, before a little curtain of blood closed over the ghostly image. He stood back up and clambered his way across the rubble to the grand front window. He looked at the unbelievable terrain for the last time, noting how the imported colors of Earth, red, blue, green, purple, all of them, were gradually filling in the grey landscape. He didn't know what 'beautiful' was, but he wondered if this might be it…

The gun rose up until the cold barrel touched the tingly skin in front of his right ear. He closed his eyes, and exhaled.

Then the gun went spinning out of his hand as the only person who had ever understood him took JB down with a beautiful flying tackle.

Oh no, the dream again.

It was brand new and dreadful to Kaywin every time. Even though he didn't remember *what* was going to happen, he twitched and turned in his sleep, consumed with vague horror.

Back and forth he walked with restless baby Victoria, back and forth in the middle of the night, singing every song he knew, it seemed. He was exhausted, just so unbelievably tired and sleepy that he could barely shuffle his feet along over the dingy carpet. 'Maybelline' didn't work. He sang 'Black Magic Woman'. Irish lullabies that had worked on babies for centuries didn't work on his baby. 'The Wheels on the Bus'. 'Dear Prudence'. 'Sit Down, I Think I Love You'. On and on and on. Nothing.

Finally, after what seemed like hours, she drifted off to sleep during 'Have I the Right'; Kaywin could feel her tiny soft warm weight relax on his shoulder. He wasn't fooled by this little trick of hers. He knew that if he laid her back down in her crib right now, she would explode like a little time bomb into tears, probably waking Nadine up in the process.

So he decided to make a few more slow, feet-dragging passes up and down the hallway at the top of the stairs. He almost nodded off at one point, but he jerked his head back up and just stood there for a second in the dead silence. He made a move toward the nursery, then, for whatever reason, turned around and brought Victoria back to the room he shared with Nadine.

His wife wasn't awake, but when he opened the door (very very quietly, he thought) she rolled over to face him and reached out sleepily for the soft warm baby. He handed her over in slow motion so she wouldn't wake up. When she had been transferred safely and successfully, he tiptoed around to the other side of the bed and climbed in without disturbing his young bride and his daughter. Right before he drifted back to sleep he heard Nadine say, "I love you."

"I love *you*..."

Then five-month old baby Victoria said, "I love you daddy," and he dozed.

When he woke up, for real this time, it took Kaywin some time to get his bearings. He was in the infirmary back at Moonbase 2.

"Sofee," he whispered.

"Yes?" his wrist whispered back at him.

"What time is it? How long have I been asleep?"

"It is 1:33 AM. You have been asleep for eight hours and fourteen minutes. Merry Christmas."

"Merry Christmas. Has Santa come yet?"

"Not yet. Soon. Your blood oxygen levels are still quite low. I suggest that you go back to sleep."

"Okay."

"Dublin? Dublin Dunne, right?"

Dublin rolled over. It was the middle of the night, and a male nurse was leaning over him. He held something in his hands that looked like a limp dead cat. When he adjusted his grip on it, there was the slightest flicker of rainbow fiber optics in the darkness of the infirmary.

It was Prudence's wig.

Dub sat up painfully, beginning to remember where he was and why. "How did you--"

"Shhhhh! One of your janitor friends found this in the trash. He gave it to somebody, who gave it to me.

"Can you just shove it down in my bag? Over there?"

"Right on. Go back to sleep."

When all three of the renegade moon-criminals were awake, they sat up in their cots in the infirmary and surveyed each other. And laughed...

"We look like straight up war-casualties," said Dublin.

"I don't think I've ever been this sore in my life," said Kaywin. "So why do I feel so good?" There was a thoughtful pause under the flickering fluorescence.

"Because we did it," said Prudence, softly and hoarsely.

"Are you coming down with something?" Dublin asked her. He saw that her bald head had been cleaned up. He thought about mentioning the wig, but decided to wait.

"Not yet. But I feel a real bad case of the Scourge coming on." They laughed, less afraid of the future than they had been in some time.

"I can't believe we did that. Can you guys believe we just did that?" Dub seemed different, Kaywin noted as he shook his head in shared disbelief. Psychologically more confident. Even physically he had changed in their short time on the Moon, a time that was coming to an end. His skin was clearer, his voice deeper…he just seemed a little less awkward.

Kind nurses brought them a special Christmas breakfast of ham and eggs and pancakes, in quantities that could not *possibly* have been sanctioned by anybody who knew what they had done. They ate every last bite. When the plates were cleared, the first little fears about what might happen next began to nip at them. None of them cared to ruin the mood for some time, so they talked about their various holiday traditions. Prudence had little to bring to this topic, so it was she who changed it.

"I wonder if they'll question us today," she mused. "It being Christmas and all. Or I wonder if they'll wait till tomorrow."

"I have a problem," said Dub suddenly.

"You don't say!" burst out Pru, grinning. But Dublin was looking down at his hands in such a thoughtful manner that the other two were made aware of his earnestness. He had something serious to drop on them, and he wasn't joking.

"It's a stupid problem. It's a problem I can't fix." He

gulped once before looking each of them in the eyes and finishing his thought.

"I don't want to die anymore. I want to live."

Naturally, shock registered on both of his friends' faces, before Prudence exploded in laughter, so loudly and boisterously that Kaywin and Dublin stared at her--and then had no choice but to join in. They couldn't hold out against this level of ironic mirth. Pru had just enough scarred cynicism left in her to think that this was absolutely the funniest thing she had ever heard in her life. Her laughter was at first pointed and a little forced, like it used to be when she was still trying to scare these two clowns away. Now she wanted them to stick around, and knew that they would, so she laughed in the freedom of the friendship they had forged together. Before long her gasping and giggling was completely real and out of her control. Not for the first time, and not for the last, Kaywin marked the strangeness of the scene, as he too laughed, and laughed, and laughed.

But another conversation was going on in his head. *Alright. So Dublin wants to live. Not possible, not possible at all really… But a lot of things aren't possible, and sometimes they happen. How could we spring Dub free?* Ideas formed, one after the other, and he followed each of them to dead-end after dead-end.

The next mission was forming in Kaywin's head. He knew he couldn't save Dublin; that was just stupid.

But he also knew that he would die trying.

About the Author

Kenyon P. Gagne was born and raised in majestic New Hampshire, and is immediately uncomfortable referring to himself in the third person. I live now in Upstate SC with my wife and two daughters. I recently (did not) celebrate thirty years in the grocery industry; nothing against it, I just always imagined that I would have busted free into a more creative occupation decades ago. I love my family and friends, books and music, and just being alive. *The Goners, Volume One* is my first novel. If you can't tell by the weight of it, it contains most everything I have learned up to this point.

For more about *The Goners, Volume One,*
and for information about Volumes
Two and Three, please check out:
thegonersbykenyongagne.com